PUFFIN BOOKS

Boy
and
Going Solo

Roald Dahl was born in 1916 in Wales of Norwegian parents. He became one of the most successful and well known of all children's writers. When he died in November 1990, *The Times* called him 'one of the most widely read and influential writers of our generation' and wrote in its obituary: 'It was well said of Dahl that he "knew how to steer an unwavering course along the hairline where the grotesque and comic meet and mingle" ... Children loved his stories and made him their favourite ... Some believe that they will be classics of the future.'

Among these classics are *James and the Giant Peach*, *Charlie and the Chocolate Factory*, *The Magic Finger*, *Charlie and the Great Glass Elevator*, *Fantastic Mr Fox*, *The Twits*, *The BFG*, *The Witches*, winner of the 1983 Whitbread Award, and *Matilda*, winner of the 1988 Children's Book Award.

ROALD DAHL

Boy
and
Going Solo

PUFFIN BOOKS

Find out more about Roald Dahl
by visiting the web site at
www.roalddahl.com

PUFFIN BOOKS

Published by the Penguin Group
Penguin Books Ltd, 27 Wrights Lane, London W8 5TZ, England
Penguin Putnam Inc., 375 Hudson Street, New York, New York 10014, USA
Penguin Books Australia Ltd, Ringwood, Victoria, Australia
Penguin Books Canada Ltd, 10 Alcorn Avenue, Toronto, Ontario, Canada M4V 3B2
Penguin Books India (P) Ltd, 11 Community Centre, Panchsheel Park,
New Delhi – 110 017, India
Penguin Books (NZ) Ltd, Cnr Rosedale and Airborne Roads, Albany, Auckland, New Zealand
Penguin Books (South Africa) (Pty) Ltd, 5 Watkins Street, Denver Ext 4,
Johannesburg 2094, South Africa

On the World Wide Web at: www.penguin.com

Penguin Books Ltd, Registered Offices: Harmondsworth, Middlesex, England

Boy first published in Great Britain by Jonathan Cape Ltd 1984
Published in the USA by Farrar, Strauss & Giroux 1984
Published in Puffin Books 1986

Going Solo first published in Great Britain by Jonathan Cape Ltd 1986
Published in the USA by Farrar, Strauss & Giroux 1986
Published in Puffin Books 1988

Boy and *Going Solo* published in one volume in Penguin Books 1992
Published in Puffin Books 1993
This edition published 2001
1

Text copyright © Roald Dahl Nominee Ltd, 1984, 1986
All rights reserved

Made and printed in England by Clays Ltd, St Ives plc

British Library Cataloguing in Publication Data
A CIP catalogue record for this book is available from the British Library

ISBN 0–141–31141–X

Contents

Boy

Contents

An autobiography is a book a person writes about his own life and it is usually full of all sorts of boring details.

This is not an autobiography. I would never write a history of myself. On the other hand, throughout my young days at school and just afterwards a number of things happened to me that I have never forgotten.

None of these things is important, but each of them made such a tremendous impression on me that I have never been able to get them out of my mind. Each of them, even after a lapse of fifty and sometimes sixty years, has remained seared on my memory.

I didn't have to search for any of them. All I had to do was skim them off the top of my consciousness and write them down.

Some are funny. Some are painful. Some are unpleasant. I suppose that is why I have always remembered them so vividly. All are true.

R.D.

Starting-point

Wendy House

Alfhild Ellen and Else me and Astri
Radyr

Papa and Mama

My father, Harald Dahl, was a Norwegian who came from a small town near Oslo, called Sarpsborg. His own father, my grandfather, was a fairly prosperous merchant who owned a store in Sarpsborg and traded in just about everything from cheese to chicken-wire.

I am writing these words in 1984, but this grandfather of mine was born, believe it or not, in 1820, shortly after Wellington had defeated Napoleon at Waterloo. If my grandfather had been alive today he would have been one hundred and sixty-four years old. My father would have been one hundred and twenty-one. Both my father and my grandfather were late starters so far as children were concerned.

When my father was fourteen, which is still more than one hundred years ago, he was up on the roof of the family house replacing some loose tiles when he slipped and fell. He broke his left arm below the elbow. Somebody ran to fetch the doctor, and half an hour later this gentleman made a majestic and drunken arrival in his horse-drawn buggy. He was so drunk that he mistook the fractured elbow for a dislocated shoulder.

'We'll soon put this back into place!' he cried out, and two men were called off the street to help with the pulling. They were instructed to hold my father by the waist while the doctor grabbed him by the wrist of the broken arm and shouted, 'Pull men, pull! Pull as hard as you can!'

The pain must have been excruciating. The victim screamed, and his mother, who was watching the performance in horror, shouted 'Stop!' But by then the pullers had done so much damage that a splinter of bone was sticking out through the skin of the forearm.

This was in 1877 and orthopaedic surgery was not what it is today. So they simply amputated the arm at the elbow, and for the rest of his life my father had to manage with one arm. Fortunately, it was the left arm that he lost and gradually, over the years, he taught himself to do more or less anything he wanted with just the four fingers and thumb of his right hand. He could tie a shoelace as quickly as you or me, and for cutting up the food on his plate, he sharpened the bottom edge of a fork so that it served as both knife and fork all in one. He kept his ingenious instrument in a slim leather case and carried it in his pocket wherever he went. The loss of an arm, he used to say, caused him only one serious inconvenience. He found it impossible to cut the top off a boiled egg.

My father was a year or so older than his brother Oscar, but they were exceptionally close, and soon after they left school, they went for a long walk together to plan their future. They decided that a small town like Sarpsborg in a small country like Norway was no place in which to make a fortune. So what they must do, they agreed, was go away to one of the big countries, either to England or France, where opportunities to make good would be boundless.

Their own father, an amiable giant nearly seven foot tall, lacked the drive and ambition of his sons, and he refused to support this tomfool idea. When he forbade them to go, they ran away from home, and somehow or other the two of them managed to work their way to France on a cargo ship.

From Calais they went to Paris, and in Paris they agreed to separate because each of them wished to be independent of the other. Uncle Oscar, for some reason, headed west for La Rochelle on the Atlantic coast, while my father remained in Paris for the time being.

The story of how these two brothers each started a totally separate business in different countries and how each of them made a fortune is interesting, but there is no time to tell it here except in the briefest manner.

Take my Uncle Oscar first. La Rochelle was then, and still is, a fishing port. By the time he was forty he had become the wealthiest man in town. He owned a fleet of trawlers called 'Pêcheurs d'Atlantique' and a large canning factory to can the sardines his trawlers brought in. He acquired a wife from a good family and a magnificent town house as well as a large château in the country. He became a collector of Louis XV furniture, good pictures and rare books, and all these beautiful things together with the two properties are still in the family. I have not seen the château in the country, but I was in the La Rochelle house a couple of years ago and it really is something. The furniture alone should be in a museum.

While Uncle Oscar was bustling around in La Rochelle, his one-armed brother Harald (my own father) was not sitting on his rump doing nothing. He had met in Paris another young Norwegian called Aadnesen and the two of them now decided to form a partnership and become shipbrokers. A shipbroker is a person who supplies a ship with everything it needs when it comes into port – fuel and food, ropes and paint, soap and towels, hammers and nails, and thousands of other tiddly little items. A shipbroker is a kind of enormous shopkeeper for ships, and by far the most important item he supplies to them is the

fuel on which the ship's engines run. In those days fuel meant only one thing. It meant coal. There were no oil-burning motorships on the high seas at that time. All ships were steamships and these old steamers would take on hundreds and often thousands of tons of coal in one go. To the shipbrokers, coal was black gold.

My father and his new-found friend, Mr Aadnesen, understood all this very well. It made sense they told each other, to set up their shipbroking business in one of the great coaling ports of Europe. Which was it to be? The answer was simple. The greatest coaling port in the world at that time was Cardiff, in South Wales. So off to Cardiff they went, these two ambitious young men, carrying with them little or no luggage. But my father had something more delightful than luggage. He had a wife, a young French girl called Marie whom he had recently married in Paris.

In Cardiff, the shipbroking firm of 'Aadnesen & Dahl' was set up and a single room in Bute Street was rented as an office. From then on, we have what sounds like one of those exaggerated fairy-stories of success, but in reality it was the result of tremendous hard and brainy work by those two friends. Very soon 'Aadnesen & Dahl' had more business than the partners could handle alone. Larger office space was acquired and more staff were engaged. The real money then began rolling in. Within a few years, my father was able to buy a fine house in the village of Llandaff, just outside Cardiff, and there his wife Marie bore him two children, a girl and a boy. But tragically, she died after giving birth to the second child.

When the shock and sorrow of her death had begun to subside a little, my father suddenly realized that his two small children ought at the very least to have a stepmother to care for them. What is more, he felt terribly lonely. It was quite obvious that he must try to find himself another wife. But this was easier said than done for a Norwegian living in South Wales who didn't know very many people. So he decided to take a holiday and travel back to his own country, Norway, and who knows, he might if he was lucky find himself a lovely new bride in his own country.

Over in Norway, during the summer of 1911, while taking a trip in a small coastal steamer in the Oslofjord, he met a young lady called Sofie Magdalene Hesselberg. Being a fellow who knew a good thing when he saw one, he proposed to her within a week and married her soon after that.

Harald Dahl took his Norwegian wife on a honeymoon in Paris, and after that back to the house in Llandaff. The two of them were deeply in love and blissfully happy, and during the next six years she bore him four children, a girl,

me at 8 months

another girl, a boy (me) and a third girl. There were now six children in the family, two by my father's first wife and four by his second. A larger and grander house was needed and the money was there to buy it.

So in 1918, when I was two, we all moved into an imposing country mansion beside the village of Radyr, about eight miles west of Cardiff. I remember it as a mighty house with turrets on its roof and with majestic lawns and terraces all around it. There were many acres of farm and woodland, and a number of cottages for the staff. Very soon, the meadows were full of milking cows and the sties were full of pigs and the chicken-run was full of chickens. There were several massive shire-horses for pulling the ploughs and the hay-wagons, and there was a ploughman and a cowman and a couple of gardeners and all manner of servants in the house itself. Like his brother Oscar in La Rochelle, Harald Dahl had made it in no uncertain manner.

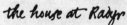

the house at Radyr

But what interests me most of all about these two brothers, Harald and Oscar, is this. Although they came from a simple unsophisticated small-town family, both of them, quite independently of one another, developed a powerful interest in beautiful things. As soon as they could afford it, they began to fill their houses with lovely paintings and fine furniture. In addition to that, my father became an expert gardener and above all a collector of alpine plants. My mother used to tell me how the two of them would go on expeditions up into the mountains of Norway and how he would frighten her to death by climbing one-handed up steep cliff-faces to reach small alpine plants growing high up on some rocky ledge. He was also an accomplished wood-carver, and most of the mirror-frames in the house were his own work. So indeed was the entire mantelpiece around the fireplace in the living-room, a splendid design of fruit and foliage and intertwining branches carved in oak.

He was a tremendous diary-writer. I still have one of his many notebooks from the Great War of 1914–18. Every single day during those five war years he would write several pages of comment and observation about the events of the time. He wrote with a pen and although Norwegian was his mother-tongue, he always wrote his diaries in perfect English.

He harboured a curious theory about how to develop a sense of beauty in the minds of his children. Every time my mother became pregnant, he would wait until the last three months of her pregnancy and then he would announce to her that 'the glorious walks' must begin. These glorious walks consisted of him taking her to places of great beauty in the countryside and walking with her for about an hour each day so that she could absorb the splendour of the surroundings. His theory was that if the eye of a pregnant woman was constantly observing the beauty of nature, this beauty would somehow become transmitted to the mind of the unborn baby within her womb and that baby would grow up to be a lover of beautiful things. This was the treatment that all of his children received before they were born.

a letter from Papa

... The best tonic both for body & brain I should say is plenty of fresh air & exercise. Long deep drafts of sea air before breakfast, in fact before every meal & shipping should beat any chemical concoction.

Kindergarten, 1922–3
(age 6–7)

In 1920, when I was still only three, my mother's eldest child, my own sister Astri, died from appendicitis. She was seven years old when she died, which was also the age of my own eldest daughter, Olivia, when she died from measles forty-two years later.

Astri was far and away my father's favourite. He adored her beyond measure and her sudden death left him literally speechless for days afterwards. He was so overwhelmed with grief that when he himself went down with pneumonia a month or so afterwards, he did not much care whether he lived or died.

If they had had penicillin in those days, neither appendicitis nor pneumonia would have been so much of a threat, but with no penicillin or any other magical antibiotic cures, pneumonia in particular was a very dangerous illness indeed. The pneumonia patient, on about the fourth or fifth day, would invariably reach what was known as 'the crisis'. The temperature soared and the pulse became rapid. The patient had to fight to survive. My father refused to fight. He was thinking, I am quite sure, of his beloved daughter, and he was wanting to join her in heaven. So he died. He was fifty-seven years old.

My mother had now lost a daughter and a husband all in the space of a few weeks. Heaven knows what it must have felt like to be hit with a double catastrophe like this.

Here she was, a young Norwegian in a foreign land, suddenly having to face all alone the very gravest problems and responsibilities. She had five children to look after, three of her own and two by her husband's first wife, and to make matters worse, she herself was expecting another baby in two months' time. A less courageous woman would almost certainly have sold the house and packed her bags and headed straight back to Norway with the children. Over there in her own country she had her mother and father willing and waiting to help her, as well as her two unmarried sisters. But she refused to take the easy way out. Her husband had always stated most emphatically that he wished all his children to be educated in English schools. They were the best in the world, he used to say. Better by far than the Norwegian ones. Better even than the Welsh

Me and Mama
Radyr

ones, despite the fact that he lived in Wales and had his business there. He maintained that there was some kind of magic about English schooling and that the education it provided had caused the inhabitants of a small island to become a great nation and a great Empire and to produce the world's greatest literature. 'No child of mine', he kept saying, 'is going to school anywhere else but in England.' My mother was determined to carry out the wishes of her dead husband.

To accomplish this, she would have to move house from Wales to England, but she wasn't ready for that yet. She must stay here in Wales for a while longer, where she knew people who could help and advise her, especially her husband's great friend and partner, Mr Aadnesen. But even if she wasn't leaving Wales quite yet, it was essential that she move to a smaller and more manageable house. She had enough children to look after without having to bother about a farm as well. So as soon as her fifth child (another daughter) was born, she sold the big house and moved to a smaller one a few miles away in Llandaff. It was called Cumberland Lodge and it was nothing more than a pleasant medium-sized suburban villa. So it was in Llandaff two years later, when I was six years old, that I went to my first school.

Me, six

The school was a kindergarten run by two sisters, Mrs Corfield and Miss Tucker, and it was called Elmtree House. It is astonishing how little one remembers about one's life before the age of seven or eight. I can tell you all sorts of things that happened to me from eight onwards, but only very few before that. I went for a whole year to Elmtree House but I cannot even remember what my classroom looked like. Nor can I picture the faces of Mrs Corfield or Miss Tucker, although I am sure they were sweet and smiling. I do have a blurred memory of sitting on the stairs and trying over and over again to tie one of my shoelaces, but that is all that comes back to me at this distance of the school itself.

On the other hand, I can remember very clearly the journeys I made to and from the school because they were so tremendously exciting. Great excitement is probably the only thing that really interests a six-year-old boy and it sticks in his mind. In my case, the excitement centred around my new tricycle. I rode to school on it every day with my eldest sister riding on hers. No grown-ups came with us, and I can remember oh so vividly how the two of us used to go racing at enormous tricycle speeds down the middle of the road and then, most glorious of all, when we came to a corner, we would lean to one side and take it on two wheels. All this, you must realize, was in the good old days when the sight of a motor-car on the street was an event, and it was quite safe for tiny children to go tricycling and whooping their way to school in the centre of the highway.

So much, then, for my memories of kindergarten sixty-two years ago. It's not much, but it's all there is left.

Llandaff
Cathedral School,
1923–5
(age 7–9)

Else, me, Agfhild

A picnic with Mama

The bicycle
and the sweet-shop

When I was seven, my mother decided I should leave kindergarten and go to a proper boy's school. By good fortune, there existed a well-known Preparatory School for boys about a mile from our house. It was called Llandaff Cathedral School, and it stood right under the shadow of Llandaff cathedral. Like the cathedral, the school is still there and still flourishing.

Llandaff Cathedral

But here again, I can remember very little about the two years I attended Llandaff Cathedral School, between the age of seven and nine. Only two moments remain clearly in my mind. The first lasted not more than five seconds but I will never forget it.

It was my first term and I was walking home alone across the village green after school when suddenly one of the senior twelve-year-old boys came riding full speed down the road on his bicycle about twenty yards away from me. The road was on a hill and the boy was going down the slope, and as he flashed by he started backpedalling very quickly so that the free-wheeling mechanism of his bike made a loud whirring sound. At the same time, he took his hands off the handlebars and folded them casually across his chest. I stopped dead and stared after him. How wonderful he was! How swift and brave and graceful in his long trousers with bicycle-clips around them and his scarlet school cap at a jaunty angle on his head! One day, I told myself, one glorious day I will have a bike like that and I will wear long trousers with bicycle-clips and my school cap will sit jaunty on my head and I will go whizzing down the hill pedalling backwards with no hands on the handlebars!

I promise you that if somebody had caught me by the shoulder at that moment and said to me, 'What is your greatest wish in life, little boy? What is your absolute ambition? To be a doctor? A fine musician? A painter? A writer? Or the Lord Chancellor?' I would have answered without hesitation that my only ambition, my hope, my longing was to have a bike like that and to go whizzing down the hill with no hands on the handlebars. It would be fabulous. It made me tremble just to think about it.

My second and only other memory of Llandaff Cathedral School is extremely bizarre. It happened a little over a year later, when I was just nine. By then I had made some friends and when I walked to school in the mornings I would start out alone but would pick up four other boys of my own age along the way. After school was over, the same four boys and I would set out together across the village green and through the village itself, heading for home. On the way to school and on the way back we always passed the sweet-shop. No we didn't, we never passed it. We always stopped. We lingered outside its rather small window gazing in at the big glass jars full of Bull's-eyes and Old Fashioned Humbugs and Strawberry Bonbons and Glacier Mints and Acid Drops and Pear Drops and Lemon Drops and all the rest of them. Each of us received sixpence a week for pocket-money, and whenever there was any money in our pockets, we would all troop in together to buy a pennyworth of this or that. My own favourites were Sherbet Suckers and Liquorice Bootlaces.

One of the other boys, whose name was Thwaites, told me I should never eat Liquorice Bootlaces. Thwaites's father, who was a doctor, had said that they were made from rats' blood. The father had given his young son a lecture about Liquorice Bootlaces when he had caught him eating one in bed. 'Every ratcatcher in the country', the father had said, 'takes his rats to the Liquorice Bootlace Factory, and the manager pays tuppence for each rat. Many a ratcatcher has become a millionaire by selling his dead rats to the Factory.'

'But how do they turn the rats into liquorice?' the young Thwaites had asked his father.

'They wait until they've got ten thousand rats,' the father had answered, 'then they dump them all into a huge shiny steel cauldron and boil them up for several hours. Two men stir the bubbling cauldron with long poles and in the end they have a thick steaming rat-stew. After that, a cruncher is lowered into the cauldron to crunch the bones, and what's left is a pulpy substance called rat-mash.'

'Yes, but how do they turn that into Liquorice Bootlaces, Daddy?' the young Thwaites had asked, and this question, according to Thwaites, had caused his father to pause and think for a few moments before he answered it. At last he had said, 'The two men who were doing the stirring with the long poles now put on their wellington boots and climb into the cauldron and shovel the hot rat-mash out on to a concrete floor. Then they run a steam-roller over it several times to flatten it out. What is left looks rather like a gigantic black pancake, and all they have to do after that is to wait for it to cool and to harden so they can cut it up into strips to make the Bootlaces. Don't ever eat them,' the father had said. 'If you do, you'll get ratitis.'

'What is ratitis, Daddy?' young Thwaites had asked.

'All the rats that the rat-catchers catch are poisoned with rat-poison,' the father had said. 'It's the rat-poison that gives you ratitis.'

'Yes, but what happens to you when you catch it?' young Thwaites had asked.

'Your teeth become very sharp and pointed,' the father had answered. 'And a short stumpy tail grows out of your back just above your bottom. There is no cure for ratitis. I ought to know. I'm a doctor.'

We all enjoyed Thwaites's story and we made him tell it to us many times on our walks to and from school. But it didn't stop any of us except Thwaites from buying Liquorice Bootlaces. At two for a penny they were the best value in the shop. A Bootlace, in case you haven't had the pleasure of handling one, is not round. It's like a flat black tape about half an inch wide. You buy it rolled up in a coil, and in those days it used to be so long that when you unrolled it and held one end at arm's length above your head, the other end touched the ground.

Sherbet Suckers were also two a penny. Each Sucker consisted of a yellow cardboard tube filled with sherbet powder, and there was a hollow liquorice straw sticking out of it. (Rat's blood again, young Thwaites would warn us, pointing at the liquorice straw.) You sucked the sherbet up through the straw and when it was finished you ate the liquorice. They were delicious, those Sherbet Suckers. The sherbet fizzed in your mouth, and if you knew how to do it, you could make white froth come out of your nostrils and pretend you were throwing a fit.

Gobstoppers, costing a penny each, were enormous hard round balls the size of small tomatoes. One Gobstopper would provide about an hour's worth of non-stop sucking and if you took it out of your mouth and inspected it every five minutes or so, you would find it had changed colour. There was something fascinating about the way it went from pink to blue to green to yellow. We used to wonder how in the world the Gobstopper Factory managed to achieve this magic. 'How *does* it happen?' we would ask each other. 'How *can* they make it keep changing colour?'

'It's your spit that does it,' young Thwaites proclaimed. As the son of a doctor, he considered himself to be an authority on all things that had to do with the body. He could tell us about scabs and when they were ready to be picked off. He knew why a black eye was blue and why blood was red. 'It's your spit that makes a Gobstopper change colour,' he kept insisting. When we asked him to elaborate on this theory, he answered, 'You wouldn't understand it if I did tell you.'

Pear Drops were exciting because they had a dangerous taste. They smelled of nail-varnish and they froze the back of your throat. All of us were warned against eating them, and the result was that we ate them more than ever.

Then there was a hard brown lozenge called the Tonsil Tickler. The Tonsil Tickler tasted and smelled very strongly of chloroform. We had not the slightest doubt that these things were saturated in the dreaded anaesthetic which, as Thwaites had many times pointed out to us, could put you to sleep for hours at a stretch. 'If my father has to saw off somebody's leg,' he said, 'he pours chloroform on to a pad and the person sniffs it and goes to sleep and my father saws his leg off without him even feeling it.'

'But why do they put it into sweets and sell them to us?' we asked him.

You might think a question like this would have baffled Thwaites. But Thwaites was never baffled. 'My father says Tonsil Ticklers were invented for dangerous prisoners in jail,' he said. 'They give them one with each meal and the chloroform makes them sleepy and stops them rioting.'

'Yes,' we said, 'but why sell them to children?'

'It's a plot,' Thwaites said. 'A grown-up plot to keep us quiet.'

The sweet-shop in Llandaff in the year 1923 was the very centre of our lives. To us, it was what a bar is to a drunk, or a church is to a Bishop. Without it, there would have been little to live for. But it had one terrible drawback, this sweet-shop. The woman who owned it was a horror. We hated her and we had good reason for doing so.

Her name was Mrs Pratchett. She was a small skinny old hag with a moustache on her upper lip and a mouth as sour as a green gooseberry. She never smiled. She never welcomed us when we went in, and the only times she spoke were when she said things like, 'I'm watchin' you so keep yer thievin' fingers off them chocolates!' Or 'I don't want you in 'ere just to look around! Either you *forks* out or you *gets* out!'

But by far the most loathsome thing about Mrs Pratchett was the filth that clung around her. Her apron was grey and greasy. Her blouse had bits of breakfast all over it, toast-crumbs and tea stains and splotches of dried egg-yolk. It was her hands, however, that disturbed us most. They were disgusting. They were black with dirt and grime. They looked as though they had been putting lumps of

33

coal on the fire all day long. And do not forget please that it was these very hands and fingers that she plunged into the sweet-jars when we asked for a pennyworth of Treacle Toffee or Wine Gums or Nut Clusters or whatever. There were precious few health laws in those days, and nobody, least of all Mrs Pratchett, ever thought of using a little shovel for getting out the sweets as they do today. The mere sight of her grimy right hand with its black fingernails digging an ounce of Chocolate Fudge out of a jar would have caused a starving tramp to go running from the shop. But not us. Sweets were our life-blood. We would have put up with far worse than that to get them. So we simply stood and watched in sullen silence while this disgusting old woman stirred around inside the jars with her foul fingers.

The other thing we hated Mrs Pratchett for was her meanness. Unless you spent a whole sixpence all in one go, she wouldn't give you a bag. Instead you got your sweets twisted up in a small piece of newspaper which she tore off a pile of old *Daily Mirrors* lying on the counter.

So you can well understand that we had it in for Mrs Pratchett in a big way, but we didn't quite know what to do about it. Many schemes were put forward but none of them was any good. None of them, that is, until suddenly, one memorable afternoon, we found the dead mouse.

The Great Mouse Plot

My four friends and I had come across a loose floor-board at the back of the classroom, and when we prised it up with the blade of a pocket-knife, we discovered a big hollow space underneath. This, we decided, would be our secret hiding place for sweets and other small treasures such as conkers and monkey-nuts and birds' eggs. Every afternoon, when the last lesson was over, the five of us would wait until the classroom had emptied, then we would lift up the floor-board and examine our secret hoard, perhaps adding to it or taking something away.

One day, when we lifted it up, we found a dead mouse lying among our treasures. It was an exciting discovery. Thwaites took it out by its tail and waved it in front of our faces. 'What shall we do with it?' he cried.

'It stinks!' someone shouted. 'Throw it out of the window quick!'

'Hold on a tick,' I said. 'Don't throw it away.'

Thwaites hesitated. They all looked at me.

When writing about oneself, one must strive to be truthful. Truth is more important than modesty. I must tell you, therefore, that it was I and I alone who had the idea for the great and daring Mouse Plot. We all have our moments of brilliance and glory, and this was mine.

'Why don't we', I said, 'slip it into one of Mrs Pratchett's jars of sweets? Then when she puts her dirty hand in to grab a handful, she'll grab a stinky dead mouse instead.'

The other four stared at me in wonder. Then, as the sheer genius of the plot began to sink in, they all started grinning. They slapped me on the back. They cheered me and danced around the classroom. 'We'll do it today!' they cried. 'We'll do it on the way home! *You* had the idea,' they said to me, 'so *you* can be the one to put the mouse in the jar.'

Thwaites handed me the mouse. I put it into my trouser pocket. Then the five of us left the school, crossed the village green and headed for the sweet-shop. We were tremendously jazzed up. We felt like a gang of desperados setting out to rob a train or blow up the sheriff's office.

'Make sure you put it into a jar which is used often,' somebody said.

'I'm putting it in Gobstoppers,' I said. 'The Gobstopper jar is never behind the counter.'

'I've got a penny,' Thwaites said, 'so I'll ask for one Sherbet Sucker and one Bootlace. And while she turns away to get them, you slip the mouse in quickly with the Gobstoppers.'

Thus everything was arranged. We were strutting a little as we entered the shop. We were the victors now and Mrs Pratchett was the victim. She stood behind the counter, and her small malignant pig-eyes watched us suspiciously as we came forward.

'One Sherbet Sucker, please,' Thwaites said to her, holding out his penny.

I kept to the rear of the group, and when I saw Mrs Pratchett turn her head away for a couple of seconds to fish a Sherbet Sucker out of the box, I lifted the heavy glass lid of the Gobstopper jar and dropped the mouse in. Then I replaced the lid as silently as possible. My heart was thumping like mad and my hands had gone all sweaty.

'And one Bootlace, please,' I heard Thwaites saying. When I turned round, I saw Mrs Pratchett holding out the Bootlace in her filthy fingers.

'I don't want all the lot of you troopin' in 'ere if only one of you is buyin',' she screamed at us. 'Now beat it! Go on, get out!'

As soon as we were outside, we broke into a run. 'Did you do it?' they shouted at me.

'Of course I did!' I said.

'Well done you!' they cried. 'What a super show!'

I felt like a hero. I *was* a hero. It was marvellous to be so popular.

Mr Coombes

The flush of triumph over the dead mouse was carried forward to the next morning as we all met again to walk to school.

'Let's go in and see if it's still in the jar,' somebody said as we approached the sweet-shop.

'Don't,' Thwaites said firmly. 'It's too dangerous. Walk past as though nothing has happened.'

As we came level with the shop we saw a cardboard notice hanging on the door.

We stopped and stared. We had never known the sweet-shop to be closed at this time in the morning, even on Sundays.

'What's happened?' we asked each other. 'What's going on?'

We pressed our faces against the window and looked inside. Mrs Pratchett was nowhere to be seen.

'Look!' I cried. 'The Gobstopper jar's gone! It's not on the shelf! There's a gap where it used to be!'

'It's on the floor!' someone said. 'It's smashed to bits and there's Gobstoppers everywhere!'

'There's the mouse!' someone else shouted.

We could see it all, the huge glass jar smashed to smithereens with the dead mouse lying in the wreckage and hundreds of many-coloured Gobstoppers littering the floor.

'She got such a shock when she grabbed hold of the mouse that she dropped everything,' somebody was saying.

'But why didn't she sweep it all up and open the shop?' I asked.

Nobody answered me.

We turned away and walked towards the school. All of a sudden we had begun to feel slightly uncomfortable. There was something not quite right about the shop being closed. Even Thwaites was unable to offer a reasonable explanation. We became silent. There was a faint scent of danger in the air now. Each one of us had caught a whiff of it. Alarm bells were beginning to ring faintly in our ears.

After a while, Thwaites broke the silence. 'She must have got one heck of a shock,' he said. He paused. We all looked at him, wondering what wisdom the great medical authority was going to come out with next.

'After all,' he went on, 'to catch hold of a dead mouse when you're expecting to catch hold of a Gobstopper must be a pretty frightening experience. Don't you agree?'

Nobody answered him.

'Well now,' Thwaites went on, 'when an old person like Mrs Pratchett suddenly gets a very big shock, I suppose you know what happens next?'

'What?' we said. 'What happens?'

'You ask my father,' Thwaites said. 'He'll tell you.'

'You tell us,' we said.

'It gives her a heart attack,' Thwaites announced. 'Her heart stops beating and she's dead in five seconds.'

For a moment or two my own heart stopped beating. Thwaites pointed a finger at me and said darkly, 'I'm afraid you've killed her.'

'*Me*?' I cried. 'Why just *me*?'

'It was *your* idea,' he said. 'And what's more, *you* put the mouse in.'

All of a sudden, I was a murderer.

At exactly that point, we heard the school bell ringing in the distance and we had to gallop the rest of the way so as not to be late for prayers.

Prayers were held in the Assembly Hall. We all perched in rows on wooden benches while the teachers sat up on the platform in armchairs, facing us. The five of us scrambled into our places just as the Headmaster marched in, followed by the rest of the staff.

The Headmaster is the only teacher at Llandaff Cathedral

School that I can remember, and for a reason you will soon discover, I can remember him very clearly indeed. His name was Mr Coombes and I have a picture in my mind of a giant of a man with a face like a ham and a mass of rusty-coloured hair that sprouted in a tangle all over the top of his head. All grown-ups appear as giants to small children. But Headmasters (and policemen) are the biggest giants of all and acquire a marvellously exaggerated stature. It is possible that Mr Coombes was a perfectly normal being, but in my memory he was a giant, a tweed-suited giant who always wore a black gown over his tweeds and a waistcoat under his jacket.

Mr Coombes now proceeded to mumble through the same old prayers we had every day, but this morning, when the last amen had been spoken, he did not turn and lead his group rapidly out of the Hall as usual. He remained standing before us, and it was clear he had an announcement to make.

'The whole school is to go out and line up around the playground immediately,' he said. 'Leave your books behind. And no talking.'

Mr Coombes was looking grim. His hammy pink face had taken on that dangerous scowl which only appeared when he was extremely cross and somebody was for the high-jump. I sat there small and frightened among the rows and rows of other boys, and to me at that moment the Headmaster, with his black gown draped over his shoulders, was like a judge at a murder trial.

'He's after the killer,' Thwaites whispered to me.

I began to shiver.

'I'll bet the police are here already,' Thwaites went on. 'And the Black Maria's waiting outside.'

As we made our way out to the playground, my whole

stomach began to feel as though it was slowly filling up with swirling water. *I am only eight years old*, I told myself. *No little boy of eight has ever murdered anyone. It's not possible.*

Out in the playground on this warm cloudy September morning, the Deputy Headmaster was shouting, 'Line up in forms! Sixth Form over there! Fifth Form next to them! Spread out! Spread out! Get on with it! Stop talking all of you!'

Thwaites and I and my other three friends were in the Second Form, the lowest but one, and we lined up against the red-brick wall of the playground shoulder to shoulder. I can remember that when every boy in the school was in his place, the line stretched right round the four sides of the playground – about one hundred small boys altogether, aged between six and twelve, all of us wearing identical grey shorts and grey blazers and grey stockings and black shoes.

'Stop that *talking*!' shouted the Deputy Head. 'I want absolute silence!'

But why for heaven's sake were we in the playground at all? I wondered. And why were we lined up like this? It had never happened before.

I half-expected to see two policemen come bounding out of the school to grab me by the arms and put handcuffs on my wrists.

A single door led out from the school on to the playground. Suddenly it swung open and through it, like the angel of death, strode Mr Coombes, huge and bulky in his tweed suit and black gown, and beside him, believe it or not, right beside him trotted the tiny figure of Mrs Pratchett herself!

Mrs Pratchett was alive!

The relief was tremendous.

'She's alive!' I whispered to Thwaites standing next to me. 'I didn't kill her!' Thwaites ignored me.

'We'll start over here,' Mr Coombes was saying to Mrs Pratchett. He grasped her by one of her skinny arms and led her over to where the Sixth Form was standing. Then, still keeping hold of her arm, he proceeded to lead her at a brisk walk down the line of boys. It was like someone inspecting the troops.

'What on earth are they doing?' I whispered.

Thwaites didn't answer me. I glanced at him. He had gone rather pale.

'Too big,' I heard Mrs Pratchett saying. 'Much too big. It's none of this lot. Let's 'ave a look at some of them titchy ones.'

Mr Coombes increased his pace. 'We'd better go all the way round,' he said. He seemed in a hurry to get it over with now and I could see Mrs Pratchett's skinny goat's legs trotting to keep up with him. They had already inspected one side of the playground where the Sixth Form and half the Fifth Form were standing. We watched them moving down the second side . . . then the third side.

'Still too big,' I heard Mrs Pratchett croaking. 'Much too big! Smaller than these! Much smaller! Where's them nasty little ones?'

They were coming closer to us now . . . closer and closer.

They were starting on the fourth side . . .

Every boy in our form was watching Mr Coombes and Mrs Pratchett as they came walking down the line towards us.

'Nasty cheeky lot, these little 'uns!' I heard Mrs Pratchett muttering. 'They comes into my shop and they thinks they can do what they damn well likes!'

Mr Coombes made no reply to this.

'They nick things when I ain't lookin',' she went on. 'They put their grubby 'ands all over everything and they've got no manners. I don't mind girls. I never 'ave no trouble with girls, but boys is 'ideous and 'orrible! I don't 'ave to tell *you* that, 'Eadmaster, do I?'

'These are the smaller ones,' Mr Coombes said.

I could see Mrs Pratchett's piggy little eyes staring hard at the face of each boy she passed.

Suddenly she let out a high-pitched yell and pointed a dirty finger straight at Thwaites. 'That's 'im!' she yelled. 'That's one of 'em! I'd know 'im a mile away, the scummy little bounder!'

The entire school turned to look at Thwaites. 'W-what have *I* done?' he stuttered, appealing to Mr Coombes.

'Shut up,' Mr Coombes said.

Mrs Pratchett's eyes flicked over and settled on my own face. I looked down and studied the black asphalt surface of the playground.

''Ere's another of 'em!' I heard her yelling. 'That one there!' She was pointing at me now.

'You're quite sure?' Mr Coombes said.

'Of course I'm sure!' she cried. 'I never forgets a face, least of all when it's as sly as that! 'Ee's one of 'em all right! There was five altogether! Now where's them other three?'

The other three, as I knew very well, were coming up next.

Mrs Pratchett's face was glimmering with venom as her eyes travelled beyond me down the line.

'There they are!' she cried out, stabbing the air with her finger. ''*Im* . . . and '*im* . . . and '*im*! That's the five of 'em all right! We don't need to look no farther than this, 'Eadmaster! They're all 'ere, the nasty dirty little pigs! You've got their names, 'ave you?'

'I've got their names, Mrs Pratchett,' Mr Coombes told her. 'I'm much obliged to you.'

'And I'm much obliged to *you*, 'Eadmaster,' she answered.

As Mr Coombes led her away across the playground, we heard her saying, 'Right in the jar of Gobstoppers it was! A stinkin' dead mouse which I will never forget as long as I live!'

'You have my deepest sympathy,' Mr Coombes was muttering.

'Talk about shocks!' she went on. 'When my fingers caught 'old of that nasty soggy stinkin' dead mouse . . .' Her voice trailed away as Mr Coombes led her quickly through the door into the school building.

Mrs Pratchett's revenge

Our form master came into the classroom with a piece of paper in his hand. 'The following are to report to the Headmaster's study at once,' he said. 'Thwaites . . . Dahl . . .' And then he read out the other three names which I have forgotten.

The five of us stood up and left the room. We didn't speak as we made our way down the long corridor into the Headmaster's private quarters where the dreaded study was situated. Thwaites knocked on the door.

'Enter!'

We sidled in. The room smelled of leather and tobacco. Mr Coombes was standing in the middle of it, dominating everything, a giant of a man if ever there was one, and in his hands he held a long yellow cane which curved round the top like a walking stick.

the cane

'I don't want any lies,' he said. 'I know very well you did it and you were all in it together. Line up over there against the bookcase.'

We lined up, Thwaites in front and I, for some reason, at the very back. I was last in the line.

'You,' Mr Coombes said, pointing the cane at Thwaites,

'Come over here.'

Thwaites went forward very slowly.

'Bend over,' Mr Coombes said.

Thwaites bent over. Our eyes were riveted on him. We were hypnotized by it all. We knew, of course, that boys got the cane now and again, but we had never heard of anyone being made to watch.

'Tighter, boy, tighter!' Mr Coombes snapped out. 'Touch the ground!'

Thwaites touched the carpet with the tips of his fingers.

Mr Coombes stood back and took up a firm stance with his legs well apart. I thought how small Thwaites's bottom looked and how very tight it was. Mr Coombes had his eyes focused squarely upon it. He raised the cane high above his shoulder, and as he brought it down, it made a loud swishing sound, and then there was a crack like a pistol shot as it struck Thwaites's bottom.

Little Thwaites seemed to lift about a foot into the air and he yelled 'Ow-w-w-w-w-w-w-w-w-w!' and straightened up like elastic.

''*Arder!*' shrieked a voice from over in the corner.

Now it was our turn to jump. We looked round and there, sitting in one of Mr Coombes's big leather armchairs, was the tiny loathsome figure of Mrs Pratchett! She was bounding up and down with excitement. 'Lay it into 'im!' she was shrieking. 'Let 'im 'ave it! Teach 'im a lesson!'

'Get down, boy!' Mr Coombes ordered. 'And stay down! You get an extra one every time you straighten up!'

'That's tellin' 'im!' shrieked Mrs Pratchett. 'That's tellin' the little blighter!'

I could hardly believe what I was seeing. It was like some awful pantomime. The violence was bad enough, and being made to watch it was even worse, but with Mrs

47

Pratchett in the audience the whole thing became a nightmare.

Swish-crack! went the cane.

'Ow-w-w-w-w!' yelled Thwaites.

''Arder!' shrieked Mrs Pratchett. 'Stitch 'im up! Make it sting! Tickle 'im up good and proper! Warm 'is backside for 'im! Go on, warm it up, 'Eadmaster!'

Thwaites received four strokes, and by gum, they were four real whoppers.

'Next!' snapped Mr Coombes.

Thwaites came hopping past us on his toes, clutching his bottom with both hands and yelling, 'Ow! Ouch! Ouch! Ouch! Owwwww!'

With tremendous reluctance, the next boy sidled forward to his fate. I stood there wishing I hadn't been last in the line. The watching and waiting were probably even greater torture than the event itself.

Mr Coombes's performance the second time was the same as the first. So was Mrs Pratchett's. She kept up her screeching all the way through, exhorting Mr Coombes to greater and still greater efforts, and the awful thing was that he seemed to be responding to her cries. He was like an athlete who is spurred on by the shouts of the crowd in the stands. Whether this was true or not, I was sure of one thing. He wasn't weakening.

My own turn came at last. My mind was swimming and my eyes had gone all blurry as I went forward to bend over. I can remember wishing my mother would suddenly come bursting into the room shouting, 'Stop! How dare you do that to my son!' But she didn't. All I heard was Mrs Pratchett's dreadful high-pitched voice behind me screeching, 'This one's the cheekiest of the bloomin' lot, 'Eadmaster! Make sure you let 'im 'ave it good and strong!'

Mr Coombes did just that. As the first stroke landed and the pistol-crack sounded, I was thrown forward so violently that if my fingers hadn't been touching the carpet, I think I would have fallen flat on my face. As it was, I was able to catch myself on the palms of my hands and keep my balance. At first I heard only the *crack* and felt absolutely nothing at all, but a fraction of a second later the burning sting that flooded across my buttocks was so terrific that all I could do was gasp. I gave a great gushing gasp that emptied my lungs of every breath of air that was in them.

It felt, I promise you, as though someone had laid a red-hot poker against my flesh and was pressing down on it hard.

The second stroke was worse than the first and this was probably because Mr Coombes was well practised and had a splendid aim. He was able, so it seemed, to land the second one almost exactly across the narrow line where the first one had struck. It is bad enough when the cane lands on fresh skin, but when it comes down on bruised and wounded flesh, the agony is unbelievable.

The third one seemed even worse than the second. Whether or not the wily Mr Coombes had chalked the cane beforehand and had thus made an aiming mark on my grey flannel shorts after the first stroke, I do not know. I am inclined to doubt it because he must have known that this was a practice much frowned upon by Headmasters in general in those days. It was not only regarded as unsporting, it was also an admission that you were not an expert at the job.

By the time the fourth stroke was delivered, my entire backside seemed to be going up in flames.

Far away in the distance, I heard Mr Coombes's voice saying, 'Now get out.'

As I limped across the study clutching my buttocks hard with both hands, a cackling sound came from the armchair over in the corner, and then I heard the vinegary voice of Mrs Pratchett saying, 'I am much obliged to you, 'Eadmaster, very much obliged. I don't think we is goin' to see any more stinkin' mice in my Gobstoppers from now on.'

When I returned to the classroom my eyes were wet with tears and everybody stared at me. My bottom hurt when I sat down at my desk.

That evening after supper my three sisters had their baths before me. Then it was my turn, but as I was about to step into the bathtub, I heard a horrified gasp from my mother behind me.

'What's this?' she gasped. 'What's happened to you?' She was staring at my bottom. I myself had not inspected it up to then, but when I twisted my head around and took a look at one of my buttocks, I saw the scarlet stripes and the deep blue bruising in between.

'Who did this?' my mother cried. 'Tell me at once!'

In the end I had to tell her the whole story, while my three sisters (aged nine, six and four) stood around in their nighties listening goggle-eyed. My mother heard me out in silence. She asked no questions. She just let me talk, and when I had finished, she said to our nurse, 'You get them into bed, Nanny. I'm going out.'

If I had had the slightest idea of what she was going to do next, I would have tried to stop her, but I hadn't. She went straight downstairs and put on her hat. Then she marched out of the house, down the drive and on to the road. I saw her through my bedroom window as she went out of the gates and turned left, and I remember calling out to her to come back, come back, come back. But she took no notice of me. She was walking very quickly, with her head held high and her body erect, and by the look of things I figured that Mr Coombes was in for a hard time.

About an hour later, my mother returned and came upstairs to kiss us all goodnight. 'I wish you hadn't done that,' I said to her. 'It makes me look silly.'

'They don't beat small children like that where I come from,' she said. 'I won't allow it.'

'What did Mr Coombes say to you, Mama?'

'He told me I was a foreigner and I didn't understand how British schools were run,' she said.

'Did he get ratty with you?'

'Very ratty,' she said. 'He told me that if I didn't like his methods I could take you away.'

'What did you say?'

'I said I would, as soon as the school year is finished. I shall find you an *English* school this time,' she said. 'Your father was right. English schools are the best in the world.'

'Does that mean it'll be a boarding school?' I asked.

'It'll have to be,' she said. 'I'm not quite ready to move the whole family to England yet.'

So I stayed on at Llandaff Cathedral School until the end of the summer term.

Going to Norway

The summer holidays! Those magic words! The mere mention of them used to send shivers of joy rippling over my skin.

All my summer holidays, from when I was four years old to when I was seventeen (1920 to 1932), were totally idyllic. This, I am certain, was because we always went to the same idyllic place and that place was Norway.

Except for my ancient half-sister and my not-quite-so-ancient half-brother, the rest of us were all pure Norwegian by blood. We all spoke Norwegian and all our relations

lived over there. So in a way, going to Norway every summer was like going home.

Even the journey was an event. Do not forget that there were no commercial aeroplanes in those times, so it took us four whole days to complete the trip out and another four days to get home again.

We were always an enormous party. There were my three sisters and my ancient half-sister (that's four), and my half-brother and me (that's six), and my mother (that's seven), and Nanny (that's eight), and in addition to these, there were never less than two others who were some sort of anonymous ancient friends of the ancient half-sister (that's ten altogether).

Looking back on it now, I don't know how my mother did it. There were all those train bookings and boat bookings and hotel bookings to be made in advance by letter. She had to make sure that we had enough shorts and shirts and sweaters and gymshoes and bathing costumes (you couldn't even buy a shoelace on the island we were going to), and the packing must have been a nightmare. Six huge trunks were carefully packed, as well as countless suitcases, and when the great departure day arrived, the ten of us, together with our mountains of luggage, would set out on the first and easiest step of the journey, the train to London.

When we arrived in London, we tumbled into three taxis and went clattering across the great city to King's Cross, where we got on to the train for Newcastle, two hundred miles to the north. The trip to Newcastle took about five hours, and when we arrived there, we needed three more taxis to take us from the station to the docks, where our boat would be waiting. The next stop after that would be Oslo, the capital of Norway.

When I was young, the capital of Norway was not called

Oslo. It was called Christiania. But somewhere along the line, the Norwegians decided to do away with that pretty name and call it Oslo instead. As children, we always knew it as Christiania, but if I call it that here we shall only get confused, so I had better stick to Oslo all the way through.

The sea journey from Newcastle to Oslo took two days and a night, and if it was rough, as it often was, all of us got seasick except our dauntless mother. We used to lie in deck-chairs on the promenade deck, within easy reach of the rails, embalmed in rugs, our faces slate-grey and our stomachs churning, refusing the hot soup and ship's biscuits the kindly steward kept offering us. And as for poor Nanny, she began to feel sick the moment she set foot on deck. 'I hate these things!' she used to say. 'I'm sure we'll never get there! Which lifeboat do we go to when it starts to sink?' Then she would retire to her cabin, where she stayed groaning and trembling until the ship was firmly tied up at the quayside in Oslo harbour the next day.

We always stopped off for one night in Oslo so that we could have a grand annual family reunion with Bestemama and Bestepapa, our mother's parents, and with her two maiden sisters (our aunts) who lived in the same house.

When we got off the boat, we all went in a cavalcade of taxis straight to the Grand Hotel, where we would sleep one night, to drop off our luggage. Then, keeping the same taxis, we drove on to the grandparents' house, where an emotional welcome awaited us. All of us were embraced and kissed many times and tears flowed down wrinkled old cheeks and suddenly that quiet gloomy house came alive with many children's voices.

Ever since I first saw her, Bestemama was terrifically ancient. She was a white-haired wrinkly-faced old bird who seemed always to be sitting in her rocking-chair, rocking away and smiling benignly at this vast influx of grandchildren who barged in from miles away to take over her house for a few hours every year.

Bestepapa was the quiet one. He was a small dignified scholar with a white goatee beard, and as far as I could gather, he was an astrologer, a meteorologist and a speaker of ancient Greek. Like Bestemama, he sat most of the time quietly in a chair, saying very little and totally over-whelmed, I imagine, by the raucous rabble who were destroying his neat and polished home. The two things I remember most about Bestepapa were that he wore black boots and that he smoked an extraordinary pipe. The bowl of his pipe was made of meerschaum clay, and it had a flexible stem about three feet long so that the bowl rested on his lap.

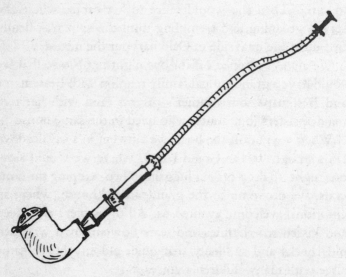

All the grown-ups including Nanny, and all the children, even when the youngest was only a year old, sat down around the big oval dining-room table on the afternoon of our arrival, for the great annual celebration feast with the grandparents, and the food we received never varied. This was a Norwegian household, and for the Norwegians the best food in the world is fish. And when they say fish, they don't mean the sort of thing you and I get from the fishmonger. They mean *fresh fish*, fish that has been caught no more than twenty-four hours before and has never been frozen or chilled on a block of ice. I agree with them that the proper way to prepare fish like this is to poach it, and that is what they do with the finest specimens. And Norwegians, by the way, always eat the skin of the boiled fish, which they say has the best taste of all.

So naturally this great celebration feast started with fish. A massive fish, a flounder as big as a tea-tray and as thick as your arm was brought to the table. It had nearly black skin on top which was covered with brilliant orange spots, and it had, of course, been perfectly poached. Large white hunks of this fish were carved out and put on to our plates, and with it we had hollandaise sauce and boiled new potatoes. Nothing else. And by gosh, it was delicious.

As soon as the remains of the fish had been cleared away, a tremendous craggy mountain of home-made ice-cream would be carried in. Apart from being the creamiest ice-cream in the world, the flavour was unforgettable. There were thousands of little chips of crisp burnt toffee mixed into it (the Norwegians call it *krokan*), and as a result it didn't simply melt in your mouth like ordinary ice-cream. You chewed it and it went *crunch* and the taste was something you dreamed about for days afterwards.

This great feast would be interrupted by a small speech of welcome from my grandfather, and the grown-ups would raise their long-stemmed wine glasses and say 'skaal' many times throughout the meal.

When the guzzling was over, those who were considered old enough were given small glasses of home-made liqueur, a colourless but fiery drink that smelled of mulberries. The glasses were raised again and again, and the 'skaaling' seemed to go on for ever. In Norway, you may select any individual around the table and skaal him or her in a small private ceremony. You first lift your glass high and call out the name. 'Bestemama!' you say. 'Skaal, Bestemama!'

Bestemama and Bestepapa (and Astri)

She will then lift her own glass and hold it up high. At the same time your own eyes meet hers, and you *must* keep looking deep into her eyes as you sip your drink. After you have both done this, you raise your glasses high up again in a sort of silent final salute, and only then does each person look away and set down his glass. It is a serious and solemn ceremony, and as a rule on formal occasions everyone skaals everyone else round the table once. If there are, for example, ten people present and you are one of them, you will skaal your nine companions once each individually, and you yourself will also receive nine separate skaals at different times during the meal – eighteen in all. That's how they work it in polite society over there, at least they used to in the old days, and quite a business it was. By the time I was ten, I would be permitted to take part in these ceremonies, and I always finished up as tipsy as a lord.

The magic island

The next morning, everyone got up early and eager to continue the journey. There was another full day's travelling to be done before we reached our final destination, most of it by boat. So after a rapid breakfast, our cavalcade left the Grand Hotel in three more taxis and headed for Oslo docks. There we went on board a small coastal steamer, and Nanny was heard to say, 'I'm sure it leaks! We shall all be food for the fishes before the day is out!' Then she would disappear below for the rest of the trip.

Fra Havna, Rössesund   Eneret A. Mathisen fotograf Tönsberg

We loved this part of the journey. The splendid little vessel with its single tall funnel would move out into the calm waters of the fjord and proceed at a leisurely pace along the coast, stopping every hour or so at a small wooden jetty where a group of villagers and summer people would be waiting to welcome friends or to collect parcels and mail. Unless you have sailed down the Oslo-fjord like this yourself on a tranquil summer's day, you cannot imagine what it is like. It is impossible to describe the sensation of absolute peace and beauty that surrounds you. The boat weaves in and out between countless tiny islands, some with small brightly painted wooden houses on them, but many with not a house or a tree on the bare rocks. These granite rocks are so smooth that you can lie and sun yourself on them in your bathing-costume without putting a towel underneath. We would see long-legged girls and tall boys basking on the rocks of the islands. There are no sandy beaches on the fjord. The rocks go straight down to the water's edge and the water is immediately deep. As a result, Norwegian children all learn to swim when they are very young because if you can't swim it is difficult to find a place to bathe.

Sometimes when our little vessel slipped between two small islands, the channel was so narrow we could almost touch the rocks on either side. We would pass row-boats and canoes with flaxen-haired children in them, their skins browned by the sun, and we would wave to them and watch their tiny boats rocking violently in the swell that our larger ship left behind.

Late in the afternoon, we would come finally to the end of the journey, the island of Tjöme. This was where our mother always took us. Heaven knows how she found it, but to us it was the greatest place on earth. About two hundred yards from the jetty, along a narrow dusty road, stood a simple wooden hotel painted white. It was run by an elderly couple whose faces I still remember vividly, and every year they welcomed us like old friends. Everything about the hotel was extremely primitive, except the dining-room. The walls, the ceiling and the floor of our bedrooms were made of plain unvarnished pine planks. There was a washbasin and a jug of cold water in each of them. The lavatories were in a rickety wooden outhouse at the back of the hotel and each cubicle contained nothing more than a round hole cut in a piece of wood. You sat on the hole and what you did there dropped into a pit ten feet below. If you looked down the hole, you would often see rats scurrying about in the gloom. All this we took for granted.

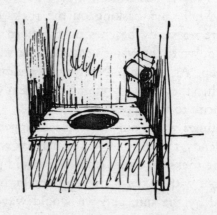

Breakfast was the best meal of the day in our hotel, and it was all laid out on a huge table in the middle of the dining-room from which you helped yourself. There were maybe fifty different dishes to choose from on that table. There were large jugs of milk, which all Norwegian children drink at every meal. There were plates of cold beef, veal, ham and pork. There was cold boiled mackerel submerged in aspic. There were spiced and pickled herring fillets, sardines, smoked eels and cod's roe. There was a large bowl piled high with hot boiled eggs. There were cold omelettes with chopped ham in them, and cold chicken and hot coffee for the grown-ups, and hot crisp rolls baked in the hotel kitchen, which we ate with butter and cranberry jam. There were stewed apricots and five or six different cheeses including of course the ever-present gjetost, that tall brown rather sweet Norwegian goat's cheese which you find on just about every table in the land.

After breakfast, we collected our bathing things and the whole party, all ten of us, would pile into our boat.

Everyone has some sort of a boat in Norway. Nobody sits around in front of the hotel. Nor does anyone sit on the beach because there aren't any beaches to sit on. In the early days, we had only a row-boat, but a very fine one it was. It carried all of us easily, with places for two rowers. My mother took one pair of oars and my fairly ancient half-brother took the other, and off we would go.

My mother and the half-brother (he was somewhere around eighteen then) were expert rowers. They kept in perfect time and the oars went *click-click*, *click-click* in their wooden rowlocks, and the rowers never paused once during the long forty-minute journey. The rest of us sat in the boat trailing our fingers in the clear water and looking for jellyfish. We skimmed across the sound and went whizzing through narrow channels with rocky islands on either side, heading as always for a very secret tiny patch of sand on a distant island that only we knew about. In the early days we needed a place like this where we could paddle and play about because my youngest sister was only one, the next sister was three and I was four. The rocks and the deep water were no good to us.

Every day, for several summers, that tiny secret sand-patch on that tiny secret island was our regular destination. We would stay there for three or four hours, messing about in the water and in the rockpools and getting extraordinarily sunburnt.

me, Alfhild, Else Norway 1924

In later years, when we were all a little older and could swim, the daily routine became different. By then, my mother had acquired a motor-boat, a small and not very seaworthy white wooden vessel which sat far too low in the water and was powered by an unreliable one-cylinder engine. The fairly ancient half-brother was the only one who could make the engine go at all. It was extremely difficult to start, and he always had to unscrew the sparking-plug and pour petrol into the cylinder. Then he swung a flywheel round and round, and with a bit of luck, after a lot of coughing and spluttering, the thing would finally get going.

When we first acquired the motor-boat, my youngest sister was four and I was seven, and by then all of us had learnt to swim. The exciting new boat made it possible for us to go much farther afield, and every day we would travel far out into the fjord, hunting for a different island. There were hundreds of them to choose from. Some were very small, no more than thirty yards long. Others were quite large, maybe half a mile in length. It was wonderful to have such a choice of places, and it was terrific fun to explore each island before we went swimming off the rocks. There were the wooden skeletons of shipwrecked boats on those islands, and big white bones (were they human bones?), and wild raspberries, and mussels clinging to the rocks, and some of the islands had shaggy long-haired goats on them, and even sheep.

Now and again, when we were out in the open water beyond the chain of islands, the sea became very rough, and that was when my mother enjoyed herself most. Nobody, not even the tiny children, bothered with lifebelts in those days. We would cling to the sides of our funny little white motor-boat, driving through mountainous white-capped waves and getting drenched to the skin, while my mother calmly handled the tiller. There were times, I promise you, when the waves were so high that as we slid down into a trough the whole world disappeared from sight. Then up and up the little boat would climb, standing almost vertically on its tail, until we reached the crest of the next wave, and then it was like being on top of a foaming mountain. It requires great skill to handle a small boat in seas like these. The thing can easily capsize or be swamped if the bows do not meet the great combing breakers at just the right angle. But my mother knew exactly how to do it, and we were never afraid. We loved every minute of it, all of us except for our long-suffering Nanny, who would bury her face in her hands and call aloud upon the Lord to save her soul.

In the early evenings we nearly always went out fishing. We collected mussels from the rocks for bait, then we got into either the row-boat or the motor-boat and pushed off to drop anchor later in some likely spot. The water was very deep and often we had to let out two hundred feet of line before we touched bottom. We would sit silent and tense, waiting for a bite, and it always amazed me how even a little nibble at the end of that long line would be transmitted to one's fingers. 'A bite!' someone would shout, jerking the line. 'I've got him! It's a big one! It's a whopper!' And then came the thrill of hauling in the line hand over hand and peering over the side into the clear water to see how big the fish really was as he neared the surface. Cod, whiting, haddock and mackerel, we caught them all and bore them back triumphantly to the hotel kitchen where the cheery fat woman who did the cooking promised to get them ready for our supper.

I tell you, my friends, those were the days.

A visit
to the doctor

I have only one unpleasant memory of the summer holidays in Norway. We were in the grandparents' house in Oslo and my mother said to me, 'We are going to the doctor this afternoon. He wants to look at your nose and mouth.'

I think I was eight at the time. 'What's wrong with my nose and mouth?' I asked.

'Nothing much,' my mother said. 'But I think you've got adenoids.'

'What are *they*?' I asked her.

'Don't worry about it,' she said. 'It's nothing.'

I held my mother's hand as we walked to the doctor's house. It took us about half an hour. There was a kind of dentist's chair in the surgery and I was lifted into it. The doctor had a round mirror strapped to his forehead and he peered up my nose and into my mouth. He then took my mother aside and they held a whispered conversation. I saw my mother looking rather grim, but she nodded.

The doctor now put some water to boil in an aluminium mug over a gas flame, and into the boiling water he placed a long thin shiny steel instrument. I sat there watching the steam coming off the boiling water. I was not in the least apprehensive. I was too young to realize that something out of the ordinary was going to happen.

Then a nurse dressed in white came in. She was carrying a red rubber apron and a curved white enamel bowl. She put the apron over the front of my body and tied it around my neck. It was far too big. Then she held the enamel bowl under my chin. The curve of the bowl fitted perfectly against the curve of my chest.

The doctor was bending over me. In his hand he held that long shiny steel instrument. He held it right in front of my face, and to this day I can still describe it perfectly. It was about the thickness and length of a pencil, and like most pencils it had a lot of sides to it. Toward the end, the metal became much thinner, and at the very end of the thin bit of metal there was a tiny blade set at an angle. The blade wasn't more than a centimetre long, very small, very sharp and very shiny.

'Open your mouth,' the doctor said, speaking Norwegian.

I refused. I thought he was going to do something to my teeth, and everything anyone had ever done to my teeth had been painful.

'It won't take two seconds,' the doctor said. He spoke gently, and I was seduced by his voice. Like an ass, I opened my mouth.

The tiny blade flashed in the bright light and disappeared into my mouth. It went high up into the roof of my mouth, and the hand that held the blade gave four or five very quick little twists and the next moment, out of my mouth into the basin came tumbling a whole mass of flesh and blood.

I was too shocked and outraged to do anything but yelp. I was horrified by the huge red lumps that had fallen out of my mouth into the white basin and my first thought was that the doctor had cut out the whole of the middle of my head.

'Those were your adenoids,' I heard the doctor saying.

I sat there gasping. The roof of my mouth seemed to be on fire. I grabbed my mother's hand and held on to it tight. I couldn't believe that anyone would do this to me.

'Stay where you are,' the doctor said. 'You'll be all right in a minute.'

Blood was still coming out of my mouth and dripping into the basin the nurse was holding. 'Spit it all out,' she said, 'there's a good boy.'

'You'll be able to breathe much better through your nose after this,' the doctor said.

The nurse wiped my lips and washed my face with a wet flannel. Then they lifted me out of the chair and stood me on my feet. I felt a bit groggy.

'We'll get you home,' my mother said, taking my hand. Down the stairs we went and on to the street. We started walking. I said *walking*. No trolley-car or taxi. We walked the full half-hour journey back to my grandparents' house, and when we arrived at last, I can remember as clearly as anything my grandmother saying, 'Let him sit down in that chair and rest for a while. After all, he's had an operation.'

Someone placed a chair for me beside my grandmother's armchair, and I sat down. My grandmother reached over and covered one of my hands in both of hers. 'That won't be the last time you'll go to a doctor in your life,' she said. 'And with a bit of luck, they won't do you too much harm.'

That was in 1924, and taking out a child's adenoids, and often the tonsils as well, without any anaesthetic was common practice in those days. I wonder, though, what you would think if some doctor did that to you today.

St Peter's,

1925–9

(age 9–13)

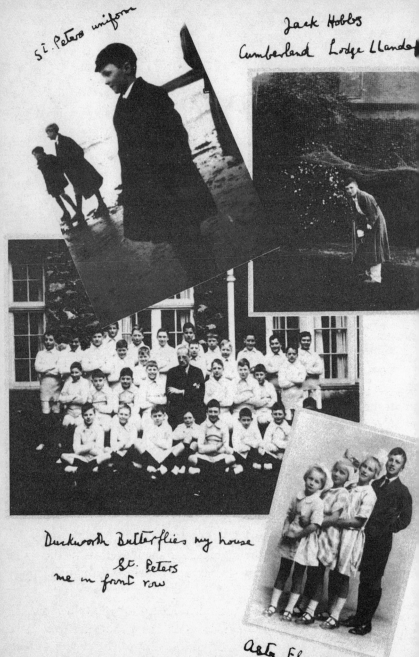

St. Peters uniform

Jack Hobbs
Cumberland Lodge Llandof

Duckworth Butterflies my house
St. Peters
me in front row

Asta Else Alphild me
Cardiff 1927

First day

In September 1925, when I was just nine, I set out on the first great adventure of my life – boarding-school. My mother had chosen for me a Prep School in a part of England which was as near as it could possibly be to our home in South Wales, and it was called St Peter's. The full postal address was St Peter's School, Weston-super-Mare, Somerset.

Weston-super-Mare is a slightly seedy seaside resort with a vast sandy beach, a tremendous long pier, an esplanade running along the sea-front, a clutter of hotels and boarding-houses, and about ten thousand little shops selling buckets and spades and sticks of rock and ice-creams. It lies almost directly across the Bristol Channel from Cardiff, and on a clear day you can stand on the esplanade at Weston and look across the fifteen or so miles of water and see the coast of Wales lying pale and milky on the horizon.

In those days the easiest way to travel from Cardiff to Weston-super-Mare was by boat. Those boats were beautiful. They were paddle-steamers, with gigantic swishing paddle-wheels on their flanks, and the wheels made the most terrific noise as they sloshed and churned through the water.

On the first day of my first term I set out by taxi in the afternoon with my mother to catch the paddle-steamer

75

from Cardiff Docks to Weston-super-Mare. Every piece of clothing I wore was brand new and had my name on it. I wore black shoes, grey woollen stockings with blue turnovers, grey flannel shorts, a grey shirt, a red tie, a grey flannel blazer with the blue school crest on the breast pocket and a grey school cap with the same crest just above the peak. Into the taxi that was taking us to the docks went my brand new trunk and my brand new tuck-box, and both had R. DAHL painted on them in black.

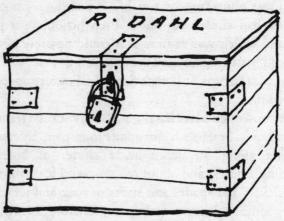

A tuck-box is a small pinewood trunk which is very strongly made, and no boy has ever gone as a boarder to an English Prep School without one. It is his own secret store-house, as secret as a lady's handbag, and there is an unwritten law that no other boy, no teacher, not even the Headmaster himself has the right to pry into the contents of your tuck-box. The owner has the key in his pocket and that is where it stays. At St Peter's, the tuck-boxes were ranged shoulder to shoulder all around the four walls of the changing-room and your own tuck-box stood directly below the peg on which you hung your games clothes. A tuck-box, as the name implies, is a box in which you store your tuck. At Prep School in those days, a parcel of tuck was sent once a week by anxious mothers to their ravenous little sons, and an average tuck-box would probably contain, at almost any time, half a home-made currant cake, a packet of squashed-fly biscuits, a couple of oranges, an apple, a banana, a pot of strawberry jam or Marmite, a bar of chocolate, a bag of Liquorice Allsorts and a tin of Bassett's lemonade powder. An English school in those days was purely a money-making business owned and operated by the Headmaster. It suited him, therefore, to give the boys as little food as possible himself and to encourage the parents in various cunning ways to feed their offspring by parcel-post from home.

'By all means, my dear Mrs Dahl, *do* send your boy some little treats now and again,' he would say. 'Perhaps a few oranges and apples once a week' – fruit was very expensive – 'and a nice currant cake, a *large* currant cake perhaps because small boys have large appetites do they not, ha-ha-ha . . . Yes, yes, as *often* as you like. *More* than once a week if you wish . . . *Of course* he'll be getting plenty of good food here, the best there is, but it never tastes *quite* the same as home cooking, does it? I'm sure you wouldn't want him to be the only one who doesn't get a lovely parcel from home every week.'

As well as tuck, a tuck-box would also contain all manner of treasures such as a magnet, a pocket-knife, a compass, a ball of string, a clockwork racing-car, half a dozen lead soldiers, a box of conjuring-tricks, some tiddly-winks, a Mexican jumping bean, a catapult, some foreign stamps, a couple of stink-bombs, and I remember one boy called Arkle who drilled an airhole in the lid of his tuck-box and kept a pet frog in there which he fed on slugs.

So off we set, my mother and I and my trunk and my tuck-box, and we boarded the paddle-steamer and went swooshing across the Bristol Channel in a shower of spray. I liked that part of it, but I began to grow apprehensive as I disembarked on to the pier at Weston-super-Mare and watched my trunk and tuck-box being loaded into an English taxi which would drive us to St Peter's. I had absolutely no idea what was in store for me. I had never spent a single night away from our large family before.

St Peter's was on a hill above the town. It was a long three-storeyed stone building that looked rather like a private lunatic asylum, and in front of it lay the playing-fields with their three football pitches. One-third of the building was reserved for the Headmaster and his family. The rest of it housed the boys, about one hundred and fifty of them altogether, if I remember rightly.

As we got out of the taxi, I saw the whole driveway abustle with small boys and their parents and their trunks and their tuck-boxes, and a man I took to be the Headmaster was swimming around among them shaking everybody by the hand.

I have already told you that *all* Headmasters are giants, and this one was no exception. He advanced upon my mother and shook her by the hand, then he shook me by the hand and as he did so he gave me the kind of flashing

the Loony Bin!

grin a shark might give to a small fish just before he gobbles it up. One of his front teeth, I noticed, was edged all the way round with gold, and his hair was slicked down with so much hair-cream that it glistened like butter.

'Right,' he said to me. 'Off you go and report to the Matron.' And to my mother he said briskly, 'Goodbye, Mrs Dahl. I shouldn't linger if I were you. We'll look after him.'

My mother got the message. She kissed me on the cheek and said goodbye and climbed right back into the taxi.

The Headmaster moved away to another group and I was left standing there beside my brand new trunk and my brand new tuck-box. I began to cry.

Writing home

At St Peter's, Sunday morning was letter-writing time. At nine o'clock the whole school had to go to their desks and spend one hour writing a letter home to their parents. At ten-fifteen we put on our caps and coats and formed up outside the school in a long crocodile and marched a couple of miles down into Weston-super-Mare for church, and we didn't get back until lunchtime. Church-going never became a habit with me. Letter-writing did.

Here is the very first letter I wrote home from St Peter's.

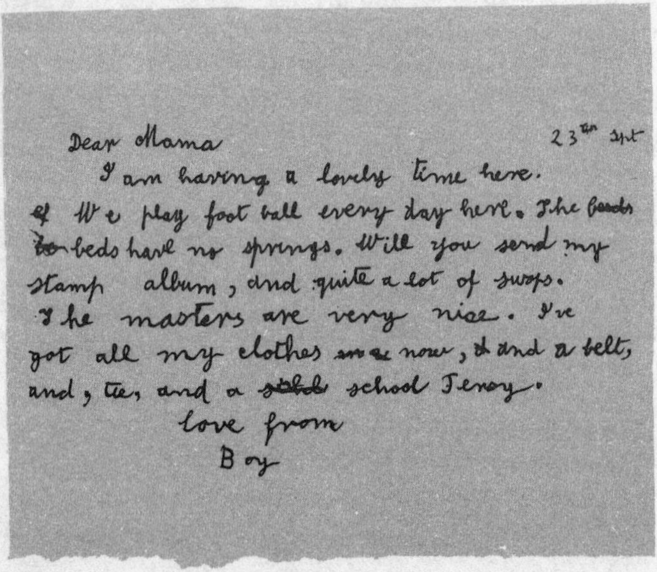

Dear Mama   23ᵗʰ Srt

I am having a lovely time here. We play foot ball every day here. The beds have no springs. Will you send my stamp album, and quite a lot of swops. The masters are very nice. I've got all my clothes now, and a belt, and, ties, and a school Jersey.

love from

Boy

From that very first Sunday at St Peter's until the day my mother died thirty-two years later, I wrote to her once a week, sometimes more often, whenever I was away from home. I wrote to her every week from St Peter's (I had to), and every week from my next school, Repton, and every week from Dar es Salaam in East Africa, where I went on my first job after leaving school, and then every week during the war from Kenya and Iraq and Egypt when I was flying with the RAF.

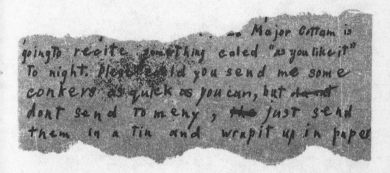

... — Major Cottam is going to recite something coled "as you like it" To night. Please could you send me some conkers as quick as you can, but dont send To meny, the just send them in a Tin and wrapit up in paper

My mother, for her part, kept every one of these letters, binding them carefully in neat bundles with green tape, but this was her own secret. She never told me she was doing it. In 1967, when she knew she was dying, I was in hospital in Oxford having a serious operation on my spine and I was unable to write to her. So she had a telephone specially installed beside her bed in order that she might have one last conversation with me. She didn't tell me she was dying nor did anyone else for that matter because I was in a fairly serious condition myself at the time. She simply asked me how I was and hoped I would get better soon and sent me her love. I had no idea that she would die the next day, but *she* knew all right and she wanted to reach out and speak to me for the last time.

When I recovered and went home, I was given this vast collection of my letters, all so neatly bound with green tape, more than six hundred of them altogether, dating from 1925 to 1945, each one in its original envelope with the old stamps still on them. I am awfully lucky to have something like this to refer to in my old age.

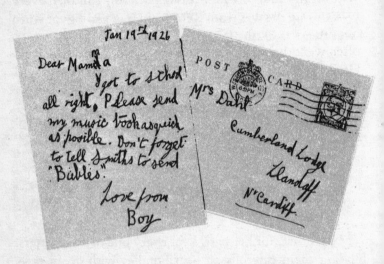

Letter-writing was a serious business at St Peter's. It was as much a lesson in spelling and punctuation as anything else because the Headmaster would patrol the classrooms all through the sessions, peering over our shoulders to read what we were writing and to point out our mistakes. But that, I am quite sure, was not the main reason for his interest. He was there to make sure that we said nothing horrid about his school.

There was no way, therefore, that we could ever complain to our parents about anything during term-time. If we thought the food was lousy or if we hated a certain master or if we had been thrashed for something we did not do, we never dared to say so in our letters. In fact, we often went the other way. In order to please that dangerous Headmaster who was leaning over our shoulders and reading what we had written, we would say splendid things about the school and go on about how lovely the masters were.

. A man called Mr Nichell gave us a fine lectine last knight on birds, he told us how owls eat mice they ent the hole mouse shin and all, and then all the shin and bones goes into a sort of little parsel in side him and he puts it on the ground, and those are caled pelets, and he showed us some pictures of some witch he has found, and of lotes of other Birds.

Mind you, the Headmaster was a clever fellow. He did not want our parents to think that those letters of ours were censored in this way, and therefore he never allowed us to correct a spelling mistake in the letter itself. If, for example, I had written . . . *last Tuesday knight we had a lecture* . . ., he would say:

'Don't you know how to spell night?'

'Y-yes, sir, k-n-i-g-h-t.'

'That's the other kind of knight, you idiot!'

'Which kind, sir? I . . . I don't understand.'

'The one in shining armour! The man on horseback! How do you spell Tuesday night?'

'I . . . I . . . I'm not quite sure, sir.'

'It's n-i-g-h-t, boy, n-i-g-h-t. Stay in and write it out for me fifty times this afternoon. No, no! Don't change it in the letter! You don't want to make it any messier than it is! It must go as you wrote it!'

Thus, the unsuspecting parents received in this subtle way the impression that your letter had never been seen or censored or corrected by anyone.

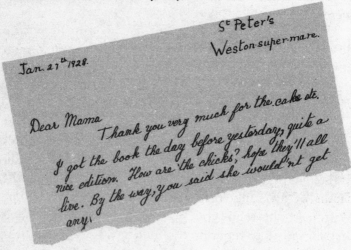

St Peter's
Weston-super-mare.

Jan. 27th 1928.

Dear Mama Thank you very much for the cake etc.
I got the book the day before yesterday, quite a
nice edition. How are 'the chicks'? hope they'll all
live. By the way, you said she would'nt get
any.

The Matron

At St Peter's the ground floor was all classrooms. The first floor was all dormitories. On the dormitory floor the Matron ruled supreme. This was her territory. Hers was the only voice of authority up here, and even the eleven- and twelve-year-old boys were terrified of this female ogre, for she ruled with a rod of steel.

The Matron was a large fair-haired woman with a bosom. Her age was probably no more than twenty-eight but it made no difference whether she was twenty-eight or sixty-eight because to us a grown-up was a grown-up and all grown-ups were dangerous creatures at this school.

Once you had climbed to the top of the stairs and set foot on the dormitory floor, you were in the Matron's power, and the source of this power was the unseen but frightening figure of the Headmaster lurking down in the depths of his study below. At any time she liked, the Matron could send you down in your pyjamas and dressing-gown to report to this merciless giant, and whenever this happened you got caned on the spot. The Matron knew this and she relished the whole business.

She could move along that corridor like lightning, and when you least expected it, her head and her bosom would come popping through the dormitory doorway. 'Who threw that sponge?' the dreaded voice would call out. 'It was *you*, Perkins, was it not? Don't lie to me, Perkins!

Don't argue with me! I know perfectly well it was you! Now you can put your dressing-gown on and go downstairs and report to the Headmaster this instant!'

In slow motion and with immense reluctance, little Perkins, aged eight and a half, would get into his dressing-gown and slippers and disappear down the long corridor that led to the back stairs and the Headmaster's private quarters. And the Matron, as we all knew, would follow after him and stand at the top of the stairs listening with a funny look on her face for the *crack . . . crack . . . crack* of the cane that would soon be coming up from below. To me that noise always sounded as though the Headmaster was firing a pistol at the ceiling of his study.

Looking back on it now, there seems little doubt that the Matron disliked small boys very much indeed. She never smiled at us or said anything nice, and when for example the lint stuck to the cut on your kneecap, you were not allowed to take it off yourself bit by bit so that it didn't hurt. She would always whip it off with a flourish, muttering, 'Don't be such a ridiculous little baby!'

'We've got a new matron. Last term, one night in the washing room, having inspected a boy called Ford she kissed him and —

On one occasion during my first term, I went down to the Matron's room to have some iodine put on a grazed knee and I didn't know you had to knock before you entered. I opened the door and walked right in, and there she was in the centre of the Sick Room floor locked in some kind of an embrace with the Latin master, Mr Victor Corrado. They flew apart as I entered and both their faces went suddenly crimson.

'How *dare* you come in without knocking!' the Matron shouted. 'Here I am trying to get something out of Mr Corrado's eye and in you burst and disturb the whole delicate operation!'

'I'm very sorry, Matron.'

'Go away and come back in five minutes!' she cried, and I shot out of the room like a bullet.

After 'lights out' the Matron would prowl the corridor like a panther trying to catch the sound of a whisper behind a dormitory door, and we soon learnt that her powers of hearing were so phenomenal that it was safer to keep quiet.

Once, after lights out, a brave boy called Wragg tiptoed out of our dormitory and sprinkled castor sugar all over the linoleum floor of the corridor. When Wragg returned and told us that the corridor had been successfully sugared from one end to the other, I began shivering with excitement. I lay there in the dark in my bed waiting and waiting for the Matron to go on the prowl. Nothing happened. Perhaps, I told myself, she is in her room taking another speck of dust out of Mr Victor Corrado's eye.

Suddenly, from far down the corridor came a resounding *crunch*! *Crunch crunch crunch* went the footsteps. It sounded as though a giant was walking on loose gravel.

Then we heard the high-pitched furious voice of the Matron in the distance. 'Who did this?' she was shrieking. 'How *dare* you do this!' She went crunching along the corridor flinging open all the dormitory doors and switching on all the lights. The intensity of her fury was frightening. 'Come along!' she cried out, marching with crunching steps up and down the corridor. 'Own up! I want the name of the filthy little boy who put down the sugar! Own up immediately! Step forward! Confess!'

'Don't own up,' we whispered to Wragg. 'We won't give you away!'

Wragg kept quiet. I didn't blame him for that. Had he owned up, it was certain his fate would have been a terrible and a bloody one.

Soon the Headmaster was summoned from below. The Matron, with steam coming out of her nostrils, cried out to him for help, and now the whole school was herded into the long corridor, where we stood freezing in our pyjamas and bare feet while the culprit or culprits were ordered to step forward.

Nobody stepped forward.

I could see that the Headmaster was getting very angry indeed. His evening had been interrupted. Red splotches were appearing all over his face and flecks of spit were shooting out of his mouth as he talked.

'Very well!' he thundered. 'Every one of you will go at once and get the key to his tuck-box! Hand the keys to Matron, who will keep them for the rest of the term! And all parcels coming from home will be confiscated from now on! I will not tolerate this kind of behaviour!'

We handed in our keys and throughout the remaining six weeks of the term we went very hungry. But all through those six weeks, Arkle continued to feed his frog with slugs through the hole in the lid of his tuck-box. Using an old teapot, he also poured water in through the hole every day to keep the creature moist and happy. I admired Arkle very much for looking after his frog so well. Although he himself was famished, he refused to let his frog go hungry. Ever since then I have tried to be kind to small animals.

Each dormitory had about twenty beds in it. These were smallish narrow beds ranged along the walls on either side. Down the centre of the dormitory stood the basins where you washed your hands and face and did your teeth, always with cold water which stood in large jugs on the floor. Once you had entered the dormitory, you were not allowed to leave it unless you were reporting to the Matron's room with some sickness or injury. Under each bed there was a white chamber-pot, and before getting into bed you were expected to kneel on the floor and empty your bladder into it. All around the dormitory, just before 'lights out', was heard the *tinkle-tinkle* of little boys peeing into their pots. Once you had done this and got into your bed, you were not allowed to get out of it again until next morning. There was, I believe, a lavatory somewhere along the corridor, but only an attack of acute diarrhoea would be accepted as an excuse for visiting it. A journey to the upstairs lavatory automatically classed you as a diarrhoea victim, and a dose of thick white liquid would immediately be forced down your throat by the Matron. This made you constipated for a week.

Thanks for your letter. There are exactly 23 boys with the measles and all the other schools (boys) in the... have got it. Hope Louis hasn't had anything else wrong on...

The first miserable homesick night at St Peter's, when I curled up in bed and the lights were put out, I could think of nothing but our house at home and my mother and my sisters. Where were they? I asked myself. In which direction from where I was lying was Llandaff? I began to work it out and it wasn't difficult to do this because I had the Bristol Channel to help me. If I looked out of the dormitory window I could see the Channel itself, and the big city of Cardiff with Llandaff alongside it lay almost directly across the water but slightly to the north. Therefore, if I turned towards the window I would be facing home. I wriggled round in my bed and faced my home and my family.

From then on, during all the time I was at St Peter's, I never went to sleep with my back to my family. Different beds in different dormitories required the working out of new directions, but the Bristol Channel was always my guide and I was always able to draw an imaginary line from my bed to our house over in Wales. Never once did I go to sleep looking away from my family. It was a great comfort to do this.

chap called Ford has got double Pneumonia on top of measles!!!!!! we're all got to be like mice going up to bed.

Do you know that a

There was a boy in our dormitory during my first term called Tweedie, who one night started snoring soon after he had gone to sleep.

'Who's that talking?' cried the Matron, bursting in. My own bed was close to the door, and I remember looking up at her from my pillow and seeing her standing there silhouetted against the light from the corridor and thinking how truly frightening she looked. I think it was her enormous bosom that scared me most of all. My eyes were riveted to it, and to me it was like a battering-ram or the bows of an icebreaker or maybe a couple of high-explosive bombs.

'Own up!' she cried. 'Who was talking?'

We lay there in silence. Then Tweedie, who was lying fast asleep on his back with his mouth open, gave another snore.

The Matron stared at Tweedie. 'Snoring is a disgusting habit,' she said. 'Only the lower classes do it. We shall have to teach him a lesson.'

She didn't switch on the light, but she advanced into the room and picked up a cake of soap from the nearest basin. The bare electric bulb in the corridor illuminated the whole dormitory in a pale creamy glow.

None of us dared to sit up in bed, but all eyes were on the Matron now, watching to see what she was going to do next. She always had a pair of scissors hanging by a white tape from her waist, and with this she began shaving thin slivers of soap into the palm of one hand. Then she went over to where the wretched Tweedie lay and very carefully she dropped these little soap-flakes into his open mouth. She had a whole handful of them and I thought she was never going to stop.

What on earth is going to happen? I wondered. Would Tweedie choke? Would he strangle? Might his throat get blocked up completely? Was she going to kill him?

The Matron stepped back a couple of paces and folded her arms across, or rather underneath, her massive chest.

Nothing happened. Tweedie kept right on snoring.

Then suddenly he began to gurgle and white bubbles appeared around his lips. The bubbles grew and grew until in the end his whole face seemed to be smothered in a bubbly foaming white soapy froth. It was a horrific sight. Then all at once, Tweedie gave a great cough and a splutter and he sat up very fast and began clawing at his face with his hands. 'Oh!' he stuttered. 'Oh! Oh! Oh! Oh no!

Wh-wh-what's happening? Wh-wh-what's on my face? Somebody help me!'

The Matron threw him a face flannel and said, 'Wipe it off, Tweedie. And don't ever let me hear you snoring again. Hasn't anyone ever taught you not to go to sleep on your back?'

With that she marched out of the dormitory and slammed the door.

very bad, he got better on Friday but has again got very ill. P.S. We have just been informed that poor little Ford died early this morning.

Homesickness

I was homesick during the whole of my first term at St Peter's. Homesickness is a bit like seasickness. You don't know how awful it is till you get it, and when you do, it hits you right in the top of the stomach and you want to die. The only comfort is that both homesickness and seasickness are instantly curable. The first goes away the moment you walk out of the school grounds and the second is forgotten as soon as the ship enters port.

I was so devastatingly homesick during my first two weeks that I set about devising a stunt for getting myself sent back home, even if it were only a few days. My idea was that I should all of a sudden develop an attack of acute appendicitis.

You will probably think it silly that a nine-year-old boy should imagine he could get away with a trick like that, but I had sound reasons for trying it on. Only a month before, my ancient half-sister, who was twelve years older than me, had actually *had* appendicitis, and for several days before her operation I was able to observe her behaviour at close quarters. I noticed that the thing she complained about most was a severe pain down in the lower right side of her tummy. As well as this, she kept being sick and refused to eat and ran a temperature.

You might, by the way, be interested to know that this sister had her appendix removed not in a fine hospital operating-room full of bright lights and gowned nurses but on our own nursery table at home by the local doctor and his anaesthetist. In those days it was fairly common

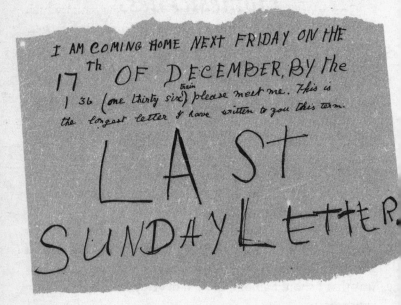

I AM COMING HOME NEXT FRIDAY ON THE 17th OF DECEMBER, BY the 1 36 (one thirty six) train please meet me. This is the longest letter I have written to you this term.

LAST SUNDAY LETTER.

practice for a doctor to arrive at your own house with a bag of instruments, then drape a sterile sheet over the most convenient table and get on with it. On this occasion, I can remember lurking in the corridor outside the nursery while the operation was going on. My other sisters were with me, and we stood there spellbound, listening to the soft medical murmurs coming from behind the locked door and picturing the patient with her stomach sliced open like a lump of beef. We could even smell the sickly fumes of ether filtering through the crack under the door.

The next day, we were allowed to inspect the appendix itself in a glass bottle. It was a longish black wormy-looking thing, and I said, 'Do *I* have one of those inside me, Nanny?'

'Everybody has one,' Nanny answered.

'What's it for?' I asked her.

'God works in his mysterious ways,' she said, which was her stock reply whenever she didn't know the answer.

'What makes it go bad?' I asked her.

'Toothbrush bristles,' she answered, this time with no hesitation at all.

'*Toothbrush* bristles?' I cried. 'How can *toothbrush* bristles make your appendix go bad?'

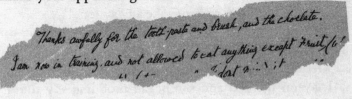

Thanks awfully for the tooth-paste and brush, and the choclate. I am now in training, and not allowed to eat anything except Fruit (so don't ...

Nanny, who in my eyes was filled with more wisdom than Solomon, replied, 'Whenever a bristle comes out of your toothbrush and you swallow it, it sticks in your appendix and turns it rotten. In the war', she went on, 'the German spies used to sneak boxloads of loose-bristled toothbrushes into our shops and millions of our soldiers got appendicitis.'

'Honestly, Nanny?' I cried. 'Is that honestly true?'

'I never lie to you, child,' she answered. 'So let that be a lesson to you never to use an old toothbrush.'

For years after that, I used to get nervous whenever I found a toothbrush bristle on my tongue.

As I went upstairs and knocked on the brown door after breakfast, I didn't even feel frightened of the Matron.

'Come in!' boomed the voice.

I entered the room clutching my stomach on the right-hand side and staggering pathetically.

'What's the matter with you?' the Matron shouted, and the sheer force of her voice caused that massive bosom to quiver like a gigantic blancmange.

'It hurts, Matron,' I moaned. 'Oh, it hurts so much! Just here!'

'You've been over-eating!' she barked. 'What do you expect if you guzzle currant cake all day long!'

'I haven't eaten a thing for days,' I lied. 'I *couldn't* eat, Matron! I simply *couldn't*!'

'Get on the bed and lower your trousers,' she ordered.

I lay on the bed and she began prodding my tummy violently with her fingers. I was watching her carefully, and when she hit what I guessed was the appendix place, I let out a yelp that rattled the window-panes. 'Ow! Ow! Ow!' I cried out. 'Don't, Matron, don't!' Then I slipped in the clincher. 'I've been sick all morning,' I moaned, 'and now there's nothing left to be sick with, but I still feel sick!'

This was the right move. I saw her hesitate. 'Stay where you are,' she said and she walked quickly from the room. She may have been a foul and beastly woman, but she had had a nurse's training and she didn't want a ruptured appendix on her hands.

Within an hour, the doctor arrived and he went through the same prodding and poking and I did my yelping at what I thought were the proper times. Then he put a thermometer in my mouth.

'Hmm,' he said. 'It reads normal. Let me feel your stomach once more.'

'Owch!' I screamed when he touched the vital spot.

The doctor went away with the Matron. The Matron returned half an hour later and said, 'The Headmaster has telephoned your mother and she's coming to fetch you this afternoon.'

I didn't answer her. I just lay there trying to look very ill, but my heart was singing out with all sorts of wonderful songs of praise and joy.

I was taken home across the Bristol Channel on the paddle-steamer and I felt so wonderful at being away from that dreaded school building that I very nearly forgot I was meant to be ill. That afternoon I had a session with Dr Dunbar at his surgery in Cathedral Road, Cardiff, and I tried the same tricks all over again. But Dr Dunbar was far wiser and more skilful than either the Matron or the school doctor. After he had prodded my stomach and I had done my yelping routine, he said to me, 'Now you can get dressed again and seat yourself on that chair.'

He himself sat down behind his desk and fixed me with a penetrating but not unkindly eye. 'You're faking, aren't you?' he said.

'How do you know?' I blurted out.

'Because your stomach is soft and perfectly normal,' he answered. 'If you had had an inflammation down there, the stomach would have been hard and rigid. It's quite easy to tell.'

I kept silent.

'I expect you're homesick,' he said.

I nodded miserably.

'Everyone is at first,' he said. 'You have to stick it out. And don't blame your mother for sending you away to boarding-school. She insisted you were too young to go, but it was I who persuaded her it was the right thing to do. Life is tough, and the sooner you learn how to cope with it the better for you.'

'What will you tell the school?' I asked him, trembling.

'I'll say you had a very severe infection of the stomach which I am curing with pills,' he answered smiling. 'It will mean that you must stay home for three more days. But promise me you won't try anything like this again. Your mother has enough on her hands without having to rush over to fetch you out of school.'

'I promise,' I said. 'I'll never do it again.'

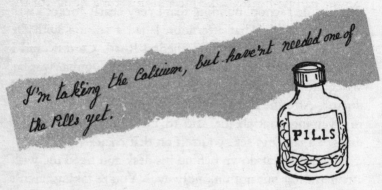

I'm takeing the Calcuim, but have'nt needed one of the Pills yet.

A drive in the motor-car

Somehow or other I got through the first term at St Peter's, and towards the end of December my mother came over on the paddle-boat to take me and my trunk home for the Christmas holidays.

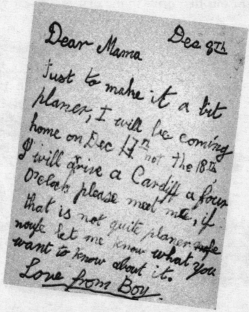

Dear Mama   Dec 8th

Just to make it a bit planer, I will be coming home on Dec 17th not the 18th

I will drive a Cardiff a four O'clock please meet me, if that is not quite planer safe noufe let me know what you want to know about it.

Love from Boy

Oh the bliss and the wonder of being with the family once again after all those weeks of fierce discipline! Unless you have been to boarding-school when you are very young, it is absolutely impossible to appreciate the delights of living at home. It is almost *worth* going away because it's so lovely coming back. I could hardly believe that I didn't have to wash in cold water in the mornings or keep silent in the corridors, or say 'Sir' to every grown-up man I met, or use a chamber-pot in the bedroom, or get flicked with wet towels while naked in the changing-room, or eat porridge for breakfast that seemed to be full of little round lumpy grey sheep's-droppings, or walk all day long in perpetual fear of the long yellow cane that lay on top of the corner-cupboard in the Headmaster's study.

The weather was exceptionally mild that Christmas holiday and one amazing morning our whole family got ready to go for our first drive in the first motor-car we had ever

owned. This new motor-car was an enormous long black French automobile called a De Dion-Bouton which had a canvas roof that folded back. The driver was to be that twelve-years-older-than-me half-sister (now aged twenty-one) who had recently had her appendix removed.

She had received two full half-hour lessons in driving from the man who delivered the car, and in that enlightened year of 1925 this was considered quite sufficient. Nobody had to take a driving-test. You were your own judge of competence, and as soon as you felt you were ready to go, off you jolly well went.

As we all climbed into the car, our excitement was so intense we could hardly bear it.

'How fast will it go?' we cried out. 'Will it do fifty miles an hour?'

'It'll do sixty!' the ancient sister answered. Her tone was so confident and cocky it should have scared us to death, but it didn't.

'Oh, let's make it do sixty!' we shouted. 'Will you promise to take us up to sixty?'

'We shall probably go faster than that,' the sister announced, pulling on her driving-gloves and tying a scarf over her head in the approved driving-fashion of the period.

The canvas hood had been folded back because of the mild weather, converting the car into a magnificent open tourer. Up front, there were three bodies in all, the driver behind the wheel, my half-brother (aged eighteen) and one of my sisters (aged twelve). In the back seat there were four more of us, my mother (aged forty), two small sisters (aged eight and five) and myself (aged nine). Our machine possessed one very special feature which I don't think you see on the cars of today. This was a second windscreen in the back solely to keep the breeze off the faces of the back-seat passengers when the hood was down. It had a long centre section and two little end sections that could be angled backwards to deflect the wind.

We were all quivering with fear and joy as the driver let out the clutch and the great long black automobile leaned forward and stole into motion.

'Are you sure you know how to do it?' we shouted. 'Do you know where the brakes are?'

'Be quiet!' snapped the ancient sister. 'I've got to concentrate!'

Down the drive we went and out into the village of Llandaff itself. Fortunately there were very few vehicles on the roads in those days. Occasionally you met a small truck or a delivery-van and now and again a private car, but the danger of colliding with anything else was fairly remote so long as you kept the car on the road.

The splendid black tourer crept slowly through the village with the driver pressing the rubber bulb of the horn every time we passed a human being, whether it was the butcher-boy on his bicycle or just a pedestrian strolling on the pavement. Soon we were entering a countryside of green fields and high hedges with not a soul in sight.

'You didn't think I could do it, did you?' cried the ancient sister, turning round and grinning at us all.

'Now you keep your eyes on the road,' my mother said nervously.

'Go faster!' we shouted. 'Go on! Make her go faster! Put your foot down! We're only doing *fifteen miles an hour*!'

Spurred on by our shouts and taunts, the ancient sister began to increase the speed. The engine roared and the body vibrated. The driver was clutching the steering-wheel as though it were the hair of a drowning man, and we all watched the speedometer needle creeping up to twenty, then twenty-five, then thirty. We were probably doing about thirty-five miles an hour when we came suddenly to a sharpish bend in the road. The ancient sister, never having been faced with a situation like this before, shouted 'Help!' and slammed on the brakes and swung the wheel wildly round. The rear wheels locked and went into a fierce sideways skid, and then, with a marvellous crunch of mudguards and metal, we went crashing into the hedge. The front passengers all shot through the front windscreen and the back passengers all shot through the back windscreen. Glass (there was no Triplex then) flew in all directions and so did we. My brother and one sister landed on the bonnet of the car, someone else was catapulted out on to the road and at least one small sister landed in the middle of the hawthorn hedge. But miraculously nobody was hurt very much except me. My nose had been cut almost clean off my face as I went through the rear windscreen and now it was hanging on only by a single small thread of skin. My mother disentangled herself from the scrimmage and grabbed a handkerchief from her purse. She clapped the dangling nose back into place fast and held it there.

Not a cottage or a person was in sight, let alone a telephone. Some kind of bird started twittering in a tree farther down the road, otherwise all was silent.

My mother was bending over me in the rear seat and saying, 'Lean back and keep your head still.' To the ancient sister she said, 'Can you get this thing going again?'

The sister pressed the starter and to everyone's surprise, the engine fired.

'Back it out of the hedge,' my mother said. 'And hurry.'

The sister had trouble finding reverse gear. The cogs were grinding against one another with a fearful noise of tearing metal.

'I've never actually driven it backwards,' she admitted at last.

Everyone with the exception of the driver, my mother and me was out of the car and standing on the road. The noise of gear-wheels grinding against each other was terrible. It sounded as though a lawn-mower was being driven over hard rocks. The ancient sister was using bad words and going crimson in the face, but then my brother leaned his head over the driver's door and said, 'Don't you have to put your foot on the clutch?'

The harassed driver depressed the clutch-pedal and the gears meshed and one second later the great black beast leapt backwards out of the hedge and careered across the road into the hedge on the other side.

'Try to keep cool,' my mother said. 'Go forward slowly.'

At last the shattered motor-car was driven out of the second hedge and stood sideways across the road, blocking the highway. A man with a horse and cart now appeared on the scene and the man dismounted from his cart and walked across to our car and leaned over the rear door. He had a big drooping moustache and he wore a small black bowler-hat.

'You're in a fair old mess 'ere, ain't you?' he said to my mother.

'Can you drive a motor-car?' my mother asked him.

'Nope,' he said. 'And you're blockin' up the 'ole road. I've got a thousand fresh-laid heggs in this cart and I want to get 'em to market before noon.'

'Get out of the way,' my mother told him. 'Can't you see there's a child in here who's badly injured?'

'One thousand fresh-laid heggs,' the man repeated, staring straight at my mother's hand and the blood-soaked handkerchief and the blood running down her wrist. 'And if I don't get 'em to market by noon today I won't be able to sell 'em till next week. Then they won't be fresh-laid any more, will they? I'll be stuck with one thousand stale ole heggs that nobody wants.'

'I hope they all go rotten,' my mother said. 'Now back that cart out of our way this instant!' And to the children standing on the road she cried out, 'Jump back into the car! We're going to the doctor!'

'There's glass all over the seats!' they shouted.

'Never mind the glass!' my mother said. 'We've got to get this boy to the doctor fast!'

The passengers crawled back into the car. The man with the horse and cart backed off to a safe distance. The ancient sister managed to straighten the vehicle and get it pointed in the right direction, and then at last the once magnificent automobile tottered down the highway and headed for Dr Dunbar's surgery in Cathedral Road, Cardiff.

'I've never driven in a city,' the ancient and trembling sister announced.

'You are about to do so,' my mother said. 'Keep going.'

Proceeding at no more than four miles an hour all the way, we finally made it to Dr Dunbar's house. I was hustled out of the car and in through the front door with my mother still holding the bloodstained handerchief firmly over my wobbling nose.

'Good heavens!' cried Dr Dunbar. 'It's been cut clean off!'

'It hurts,' I moaned.

'He can't go round without a nose for the rest of his life!' the doctor said to my mother.

'It looks as though he may have to,' my mother said.

'Nonsense!' the doctor told her. 'I shall sew it on again.'

'Can you do that?' My mother asked him.

'I can try,' he answered. 'I shall tape it on tight for now and I'll be up at your house with my assistant within the hour.'

Huge strips of sticking-plaster were strapped across my face to hold the nose in position. Then I was led back into the car and we crawled the two miles home to Llandaff.

About an hour later I found myself lying upon that same nursery table my ancient sister had occupied some months before for her appendix operation. Strong hands held me down while a mask stuffed with cotton-wool was clamped over my face. I saw a hand above me holding a bottle with white liquid in it and the liquid was being poured on to the cotton-wool inside the mask. Once again I smelled the sickly stench of chloroform and ether, and a voice was saying, 'Breathe deeply. Take some nice deep breaths.'

I fought fiercely to get off that table but my shoulders were pinned down by the full weight of a large man. The hand that was holding the bottle above my face kept tilting it farther and farther forward and the white liquid dripped and dripped on to the cotton-wool. Blood-red circles began to appear before my eyes and the circles started to spin round and round until they made a scarlet whirlpool with a deep black hole in the centre, and miles away in the distance a voice was saying, 'That's a good boy. We're nearly there now . . . we're nearly there . . . just close your eyes and go to sleep . . .'

I woke up in my own bed with my anxious mother sitting beside me, holding my hand. 'I didn't think you were ever going to come round,' she said. 'You've been asleep for more than eight hours.'

'Did Dr Dunbar sew my nose on again?' I asked her.

'Yes,' she said.

'Will it stay on?'

'He says it will. How do you feel, my darling?'

'Sick,' I said.

After I had vomited into a small basin, I felt a little better.

'Look under your pillow,' my mother said, smiling.

I turned and lifted a corner of my pillow, and underneath it, on the snow-white sheet, there lay a beautiful golden sovereign with the head of King George V on its uppermost side.

'That's for being brave,' my mother said. 'You did very well. I'm proud of you.'

Captain Hardcastle

We called them masters in those days, not teachers, and at St Peter's the one I feared most of all, apart from the Headmaster, was Captain Hardcastle.

This man was slim and wiry and he played football. On the football field he wore white running shorts and white gymshoes and short white socks. His legs were as hard and thin as ram's legs and the skin around his calves was almost exactly the colour of mutton fat. The hair on his head was not ginger. It was a brilliant dark vermilion, like a ripe orange, and it was plastered back with immense quantities of brilliantine in the same fashion as the Headmaster's. The parting in his hair was a white line straight down the middle of the scalp, so straight it could only have been made with a ruler. On either side of the parting you could see the comb tracks running back through the greasy orange hair like little tramlines.

Captain Hardcastle sported a moustache that was the same colour as his hair, and oh what a moustache it was!

A truly terrifying sight, a thick orange hedge that sprouted and flourished between his nose and his upper lip and ran clear across his face from the middle of one cheek to the middle of the other. But this was not one of those nailbrush moustaches, all short and clipped and bristly. Nor was it long and droopy in the walrus style. Instead, it was curled most splendidly upwards all the way along as though it had had a permanent wave put into it or possibly curling tongs heated in the mornings over a tiny flame of methylated spirits. The only other way he could have achieved this curling effect, we boys decided, was by prolonged upward brushing with a hard toothbrush in front of the looking-glass every morning.

Behind the moustache there lived an inflamed and savage face with a deeply corrugated brow that indicated a very limited intelligence. 'Life is a puzzlement,' the corrugated brow seemed to be saying, 'and the world is a dangerous place. All men are enemies and small boys are insects that will turn and bite you if you don't get them first and squash them hard.'

Captain Hardcastle was never still. His orange head twitched and jerked perpetually from side to side in the most alarming fashion, and each twitch was accompanied by a little grunt that came out of the nostrils. He had been a soldier in the army in the Great War and that, of course, was how he had received his title. But even small insects like us knew that 'Captain' was not a very exalted rank and only a man with little else to boast about would hang on to it in civilian life. It was bad enough to keep calling yourself 'Major' after it was all over, but 'Captain' was the bottoms.

Rumour had it that the constant twitching and jerking and snorting was caused by something called shell-shock, but we were not quite sure what that was. We took it to mean that an explosive object had gone off very close to him with such an enormous bang that it had made him jump high in the air and he hadn't stopped jumping since.

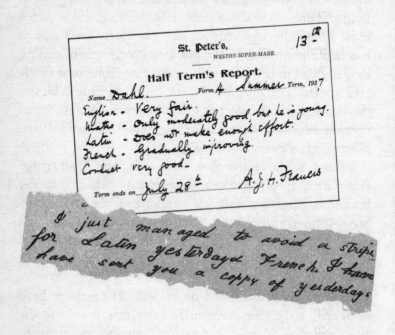

For a reason that I could never properly understand, Captain Hardcastle had it in for me from my very first day at St Peter's. Perhaps it was because he taught Latin and I was no good at it. Perhaps it was because already, at the age of nine, I was very nearly as tall as he was. Or even more likely, it was because I took an instant dislike to his giant orange moustache and he often caught me staring at it with what was probably a little sneer under the nose. I had only to pass within ten feet of him in the corridor and he would glare at me and shout, 'Hold yourself straight, boy! Pull your shoulders back!' or 'Take those hands out of your pockets!' or 'What's so funny, may I ask? What are you smirking at?' or most insulting of all, '*You*, what's-your-name, get on with your work!' I knew, therefore, that it was only a matter of time before the gallant Captain nailed me good and proper.

The crunch came during my second term when I was exactly nine and a half, and it happened during evening Prep. Every weekday evening, the whole school would sit for one hour in the Main Hall, between six and seven o'clock, to do Prep. The master on duty for the week would be in charge of Prep, which meant that he sat high up on a dais at the top end of the Hall and kept order. Some masters read a book while taking Prep and some corrected exercises, but not Captain Hardcastle. He would sit up there on the dais twitching and grunting and never once would he look down at his desk. His small milky-blue eyes would rove the Hall for the full sixty minutes, searching for trouble, and heaven help the boy who caused it.

The rules of Prep were simple but strict. You were forbidden to look up from your work, and you were forbidden to talk. That was all there was to it, but it left you precious little leeway. In extreme circumstances, and I never knew what these were, you could put your hand up and wait until you were asked to speak but you had better be awfully sure that the circumstances were extreme. Only twice during my four years at St Peter's did I see a boy putting up his hand during Prep. The first one went like this:

MASTER. What is it?
BOY. Please sir, may I be excused to go to the lavatory?
MASTER. Certainly not. You should have gone before.

BOY. But sir . . . please sir . . . I didn't want to before . . .
I didn't know . . .

MASTER. Whose fault was that? Get on with your work!

BOY. But sir . . . Oh sir . . . Please sir, let me go!

MASTER. One more word out of you and you'll be in
trouble.

Naturally, the wretched boy dirtied his pants, which
caused a storm later on upstairs with the Matron.

On the second occasion, I remember clearly that it was
a summer term and the boy who put his hand up was called
Braithwaite. I also seem to recollect that the master taking
Prep was our friend Captain Hardcastle, but I wouldn't
swear to it. The dialogue went something like this:

MASTER. Yes, what is it?

BRAITHWAITE. Please sir, a wasp came in through the window and it's stung me on my lip and it's swelling up.

MASTER. A *what*?

BRAITHWAITE. A wasp, sir.

MASTER. Speak up, boy, I can't hear you! A *what* came in
through the window?

BRAITHWAITE. It's hard to speak up, sir, with my lip all
swelling up.

MASTER. With your *what* all swelling up? Are you trying
to be funny?

BRAITHWAITE. No sir, I promise I'm not sir.

MASTER. Talk properly, boy! What's the matter with you?

BRAITHWAITE. I've told you, sir. I've been stung, sir. My
lip is swelling. It's hurting terribly.

MASTER. *Hurting terribly?* What's hurting terribly?

BRAITHWAITE. My lip, sir. It's getting bigger and bigger.

MASTER. What Prep are you doing tonight?

BRAITHWAITE. French verbs, sir. We have to write them out.

MASTER. Do you write with your lip?

BRAITHWAITE. No, sir, I don't sir, but you see . . .

MASTER. All I see is that you are making an infernal noise and disturbing everybody in the room. Now get on with your work.

They were tough, those masters, make no mistake about it, and if you wanted to survive, you had to become pretty tough yourself.

My own turn came, as I said, during my second term and Captain Hardcastle was again taking Prep. You should know that during Prep every boy in the Hall sat at his own small individual wooden desk. These desks had the usual sloping wooden tops with a narrow flat strip at the far end where there was a groove to hold your pen and a small hole in the right-hand side in which the ink-well sat. The pens we used had detachable nibs and it was necessary to dip your nib into the ink-well every six or seven seconds when you were writing. Ball-point pens and felt pens had not then been invented, and fountain-pens were forbidden. The nibs we used were very fragile and most boys kept a supply of new ones in a small box in their trouser pockets.

Prep was in progress. Captain Hardcastle was sitting up on the dais in front of us, stroking his orange moustache, twitching his head and grunting through his nose. His eyes roved the Hall endlessly, searching for mischief. The only noises to be heard were Captain Hardcastle's little snorting grunts and the soft sound of pen-nibs moving over paper. Occasionally there was a *ping* as somebody dipped his nib too violently into his tiny white porcelain ink-well.

Disaster struck when I foolishly stubbed the tip of my

nib into the top of the desk. The nib broke. I knew I hadn't got a spare one in my pocket, but a broken nib was never accepted as an excuse for not finishing Prep. We had been set an essay to write and the subject was 'The Life Story of a Penny' (I still have that essay in my files). I had made a decent start and I was rattling along fine when I broke that nib. There was still another half-hour of Prep to go and I couldn't sit there doing nothing all that time. Nor could I put up my hand and tell Captain Hardcastle I had broken my nib. I simply did not dare. And as a matter of fact, I really *wanted* to finish that essay. I knew exactly what was going to happen to my penny through the next two pages and I couldn't bear to leave it unsaid.

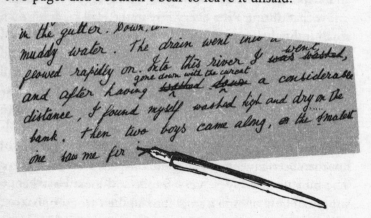

I glanced to my right. The boy next to me was called Dobson. He was the same age as me, nine and a half, and a nice fellow. Even now, sixty years later, I can still remember that Dobson's father was a doctor and that he lived, as I had learnt from the label on Dobson's tuck-box, at The Red House, Uxbridge, Middlesex.

Dobson's desk was almost touching mine. I thought I would risk it. I kept my head lowered but watched Captain

Hardcastle very carefully. When I was fairly sure he was looking the other way, I put a hand in front of my mouth and whispered, 'Dobson . . . Dobson . . . Could you lend me a nib?'

Suddenly there was an explosion up on the dais. Captain Hardcastle had leapt to his feet and was pointing at me and shouting, 'You're talking! I saw you talking! Don't try to deny it! I distinctly saw you talking behind your hand!'

I sat there frozen with terror.

Every boy stopped working and looked up.

Captain Hardcastle's face had gone from red to deep purple and he was twitching violently.

'Do you deny you were talking?' he shouted.

'No, sir, no, b–but . . .'

'And do you deny you were trying to cheat? Do you deny you were asking Dobson for help with your work?'

'N–no, sir, I wasn't. I wasn't cheating.'

'Of course you were cheating! Why else, may I ask, would you be speaking to Dobson? I take it you were not inquiring after his health?'

It is worth reminding the reader once again of my age. I was not a self-possessed lad of fourteen. Nor was I twelve or even ten years old. I was nine and a half, and at that age one is ill equipped to tackle a grown-up man with flaming orange hair and a violent temper. One can do little else but stutter.

'I . . . I have broken my nib, sir,' I whispered. 'I . . . I was asking Dobson if he c–could lend me one, sir.'

'You are lying!' cried Captain Hardcastle, and there was triumph in his voice. 'I always knew you were a liar! *And* a cheat as well!'

'All I w–wanted was a nib, sir.'

'I'd shut up if I were you!' thundered the voice on the

dais. 'You'll only get yourself into deeper trouble! I am giving you a Stripe!'

These were words of doom. A Stripe! *I am giving you a Stripe!* All around, I could feel a kind of sympathy reaching out to me from every boy in the school, but nobody moved or made a sound.

Here I must explain the system of Stars and Stripes that we had at St Peter's. For exceptionally good work, you could be awarded a Quarter-Star, and a red dot was made with crayon beside your name on the notice-board. If you got four Quarter-Stars, a red line was drawn through the four dots indicating that you had completed your Star.

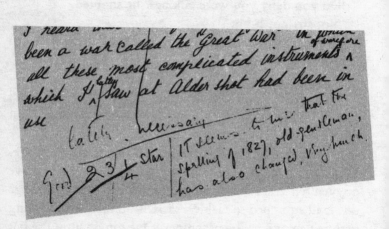

For exceptionally poor work or bad behaviour, you were given a Stripe, and that automatically meant a thrashing from the Headmaster.

Every master had a book of Quarter-Stars and a book of Stripes, and these had to be filled in and signed and torn out exactly like cheques from a cheque book. The Quarter-Stars were pink, the Stripes were a fiendish, blue-green colour. The boy who received a Star or a Stripe would pocket it until the following morning after prayers, when the Headmaster would call upon anyone who had been given one or the other to come forward in front of the whole school and hand it in. Stripes were considered so dreadful that they were not given very often. In any one week it was unusual for more than two or three boys to receive Stripes.

And now Captain Hardcastle was giving one to me. 'Come here,' he ordered.

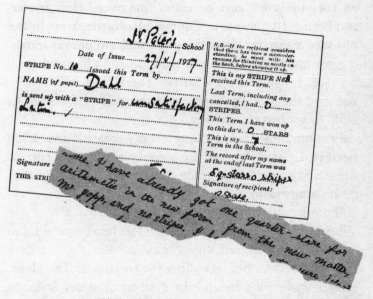

I got up from my desk and walked to the dais. He already had his book of Stripes on the desk and was filling one out. He was using red ink, and along the line where it said *Reason*, he wrote, *Talking in Prep, trying to cheat and lying.* He signed it and tore it out of the book. Then, taking plenty of time, he filled in the counterfoil. He picked up the terrible piece of green-blue paper and waved it in my direction but he didn't look up. I took it out of his hand

and walked back to my desk. The eyes of the whole school followed my progress.

For the remainder of Prep I sat at my desk and did nothing. Having no nib, I was unable to write another word about 'The Life Story of a Penny', but I was made to finish it the next afternoon instead of playing games.

The following morning, as soon as prayers were over, the Headmaster called for Quarter-Stars and Stripes. I was the only boy to go up. The assistant masters were sitting on very upright chairs on either side of the Headmaster, and I caught a glimpse of Captain Hardcastle, arms folded across his chest, head twitching, the milky-blue eyes watching me intently, the look of triumph still glimmering on his face. I handed in my Stripe. The Headmaster took it and read the writing. 'Come and see me in my study', he said, 'as soon as this is over.'

Five minutes later, walking on my toes and trembling terribly, I passed through the green baize door and entered the sacred precincts where the Headmaster lived. I knocked on his study door.

'Enter!'

I turned the knob and went into this large square room with bookshelves and easy chairs and the gigantic desk topped in red leather straddling the far corner. The Head master was sitting behind the desk holding my Stripe in his fingers. 'What have you got to say for yourself?' he asked me, and the white shark's teeth flashed dangerously between his lips.

'I didn't lie, sir,' I said. 'I promise I didn't. And I wasn't trying to cheat.'

'Captain Hardcastle says you were doing both,' the Headmaster said. 'Are you calling Captain Hardcastle a liar?'

'No, sir. Oh no, sir.'

'I wouldn't if I were you.'

'I had broken my nib, sir, and I was asking Dobson if he could lend me another.'

'That is not what Captain Hardcastle says. He says you were asking for help with your essay.'

'Oh no, sir, I wasn't. I was a long way away from Captain Hardcastle and I was only whispering. I don't think he could have heard what I said, sir.'

'So you *are* calling him a liar.'

'Oh no, sir! No, sir! I would never do that!'

It was impossible for me to win against the Headmaster. What I would like to have said was, 'Yes, sir, if you really want to know, sir, I *am* calling Captain Hardcastle a liar because that's what he is!', but it was out of the question. I did, however, have one trump card left to play, or I thought I did.

'You could ask Dobson, sir,' I whispered.

'*Ask Dobson?*' he cried. 'Why should I ask Dobson?'

'He would tell you what I said, sir.'

'Captain Hardcastle is an officer and a gentleman,' the Headmaster said. 'He has told me what happened. I hardly think I want to go round asking some silly little boy if Captain Hardcastle is speaking the truth.'

I kept silent.

'For talking in Prep,' the Headmaster went on, 'for trying to cheat and for lying, I am going to give you six strokes of the cane.'

He rose from his desk and crossed over to the corner-cupboard on the opposite side of the study. He reached up and took from the top of it three very thin yellow canes, each with the bent-over handle at one end. For a few seconds, he held them in his hands, examining them with some care, then he selected one and replaced the other two on top of the cupboard.

'Bend over.'

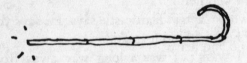

the cane again

I was frightened of that cane. There is no small boy in the world who wouldn't be. It wasn't simply an instrument for beating you. It was a weapon for wounding. It lacerated the skin. It caused severe black and scarlet bruising that took three weeks to disappear, and all the time during those three weeks, you could feel your heart beating along the wounds.

I tried once more, my voice slightly hysterical now. 'I didn't do it, sir! I swear I'm telling the truth!'

'Be quiet and bend over! Over there! And touch your toes!'

Very slowly, I bent over. Then I shut my eyes and braced myself for the first stroke.

Crack! It was like a rifle shot! With a very hard stroke of the cane on one's buttocks, the time-lag before you feel any pain is about four seconds. Thus, the experienced caner will always pause between strokes to allow the agony to reach its peak.

So for a few seconds after the first *crack* I felt virtually nothing. Then suddenly came the frightful searing agonizing unbearable burning across the buttocks, and as it reached its highest and most excruciating point, the second *crack* came down. I clutched hold of my ankles as tight as

I could and I bit into my lower lip. I was determined not to make a sound, for that would only give the executioner greater satisfaction.

Crack! . . . Five seconds pause.

Crack! . . . Another pause.

Crack! . . . And another pause.

I was counting the strokes, and as the sixth one hit me, I knew I was going to survive in silence.

'That will do,' the voice behind me said.

I straightened up and clutched my backside as hard as I possibly could with both hands. This is always the instinctive and automatic reaction. The pain is so frightful you try to grab hold of it and tear it away, and the tighter you squeeze, the more it helps.

I did not look at the Headmaster as I hopped across the thick red carpet towards the door. The door was closed and nobody was about to open it for me, so for a couple of seconds I had to let go of my bottom with one hand to turn the door-knob. Then I was out and hopping around in the hallway of the private sanctum.

Directly across the hall from the Headmaster's study was the assistant masters' Common Room. They were all in there now waiting to spread out to their respective classrooms, but what I couldn't help noticing, even in my agony, was that *this door was open*.

Why was it open?

Had it been left that way on purpose so that they could all hear more clearly the sound of the cane from across the hall?

Of course it had. And I felt quite sure that it was Captain Hardcastle who had opened it. I pictured him standing in there among his colleagues snorting with satisfaction at every stinging stroke.

Small boys can be very comradely when a member of their community has got into trouble, and even more so when they feel an injustice has been done. When I returned to the classroom, I was surrounded on all sides by sympathetic faces and voices, but one particular incident has always stayed with me. A boy of my own age called Highton was so violently incensed by the whole affair that he said to me before lunch that day, '*You* don't have a father. I do. I am going to write to my father and tell him what has happened and he'll do something about it.'

'He couldn't do anything,' I said.

'Oh yes he could,' Highton said. 'And what's more he will. My father won't let them get away with this.'

'Where is he now?'

'He's in Greece,' Highton said. 'In Athens. But that won't make any difference.'

Then and there, little Highton sat down and wrote to the father he admired so much, but of course nothing came of it. It was nevertheless a touching and generous gesture from one small boy to another and I have never forgotten it.

Little Ellis and the boil

During my third term at St Peter's, I got flu and was put to bed in the Sick Room, where the dreaded Matron reigned supreme. In the next bed to mine was a seven-year-old boy called Ellis, whom I liked a lot. Ellis was there because he had an immense and angry-looking boil on the inside of his thigh. I saw it. It was as big as a plum and about the same colour.

One morning, in came the doctor to examine us, and sailing along beside him was the Matron. Her mountainous bosom was enclosed in a starched white envelope, and because of this she somehow reminded me of a painting I had once seen of a four-masted schooner in full canvas running before the wind.

'What's his temperature today?' the doctor asked, pointing at me.

'Just over a hundred, doctor,' the Matron told him.

'He's been up here long enough,' the doctor said. 'Send him back to school tomorrow.' Then he turned to Ellis. 'Take off your pyjama trousers,' he said. He was a very small doctor, with steel-rimmed spectacles and a bald head. He frightened the life out of me.

Ellis removed his pyjama trousers. The doctor bent forward and looked at the boil. 'Hmmm,' he said. 'That's a nasty one, isn't it? We're going to have to do something about that, aren't we, Ellis?'

'What are you going to do?' Ellis asked, trembling.

'Nothing for you to worry about,' the doctor said. 'Just lie back and take no notice of me.'

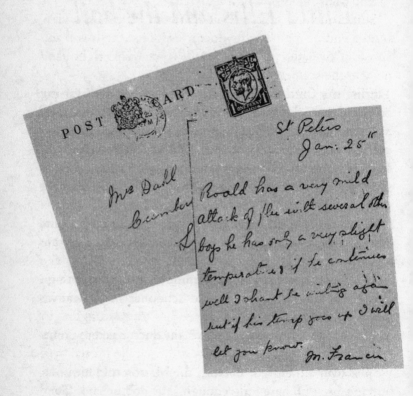

St Peters
Jan: 25th

Mrs Dahl
Cumberland

Roald has a very mild attack of flue with several other boys he has only a very slight temperature if he continues well I shant be writing again but if his temp goes up I will let you know.
M. Francis

Little Ellis lay back with his head on the pillow. The doctor had put his bag on the floor at the end of Ellis's bed, and now he knelt down on the floor and opened the bag. Ellis, even when he lifted his head from the pillow, couldn't see what the doctor was doing there. He was hidden by the end of the bed. But I saw everything. I saw him take out a sort of scalpel which had a long steel handle and a small pointed blade. He crouched below the end of Ellis's bed, holding the scalpel in his right hand.

'Give me a large towel, Matron,' he said.

The Matron handed him a towel.

Still crouching low and hidden from little Ellis's view by the end of the bed, the doctor unfolded the towel and spread it over the palm of his left hand. In his right hand he held the scalpel.

Ellis was frightened and suspicious. He started raising himself up on his elbows to get a better look. 'Lie down, Ellis,' the doctor said, and even as he spoke, he bounced up from the end of the bed like a jack-in-the-box and flung the outspread towel straight into Ellis's face. Almost in the same second, he thrust his right arm forward and plunged the point of the scalpel deep into the centre of the enormous boil. He gave the blade a quick twist and then withdrew it again before the wretched boy had had time to disentangle his head from the towel.

Ellis screamed. He never saw the scalpel going in and he never saw it coming out, but he felt it all right and he screamed like a stuck pig. I can see him now struggling to get the towel off his head, and when he emerged the tears were streaming down his cheeks and his huge brown eyes were staring at the doctor with a look of utter and total outrage.

'Don't make such a fuss about nothing,' the Matron said.

'Put a dressing on it, Matron,' the doctor said, 'with plenty of mag sulph paste.' And he marched out of the room.

I couldn't really blame the doctor. I thought he handled things rather cleverly. Pain was something we were expected to endure. Anaesthetics and pain-killing injections were not much used in those days. Dentists, in particular, never bothered with them. But I doubt very much if you would be entirely happy today if a doctor threw a towel in your face and jumped on you with a knife.

the wart on my thum has come off beautifly, but the one on my knee has'nt even turned into a blister. You meant me to learn singing did'nt you.

Goat's tobacco

When I was about nine, the ancient half-sister got engaged to be married. The man of her choice was a young English doctor and that summer he came with us to Norway.

Manly lover and ancient half-sister (in background)

Romance was floating in the air like moondust and the two lovers, for some reason we younger ones could never understand, did not seem to be very keen on us tagging along with them. They went out in the boat alone. They climbed the rocks alone. They even had breakfast alone. We resented this. As a family we had always done everything together and we didn't see why the ancient half-sister should suddenly decide to do things differently even if she had become engaged. We were inclined to blame the male lover for disrupting the calm of our family life, and it was inevitable that he would have to suffer for it sooner or later.

The male lover was a great pipe-smoker. The disgusting smelly pipe was never out of his mouth except when he was eating or swimming. We even began to wonder whether he removed it when he was kissing his betrothed. He gripped the stem of the pipe in the most manly fashion between his strong white teeth and kept it there while talking to you. This annoyed us. Surely it was more polite to take it out and speak properly.

One day, we all went in our little motor-boat to an island we had never been to before, and for once the ancient half-sister and the manly lover decided to come with us. We chose this particular island because we saw some goats on it. They were climbing about on the rocks and we thought it would be fun to go and visit them. But when we landed, we found that the goats were totally wild and we couldn't get near them. So we gave up trying to make friends with them and simply sat around on the smooth rocks in our bathing costumes, enjoying the lovely sun.

The manly lover was filling his pipe. I happened to be watching him as he very carefully packed the tobacco into the bowl from a yellow oilskin pouch. He had just finished doing this and was about to light up when the ancient half-sister called on him to come swimming. So he put down the pipe and off he went.

I stared at the pipe that was lying there on the rocks. About twelve inches away from it, I saw a little heap of dried goat's droppings, each one small and round like a pale brown berry, and at that point, an interesting idea began to sprout in my mind. I picked up the pipe and knocked all the tobacco out of it. I then took the goat's droppings and teased them with my fingers until they were nicely shredded. Very gently I poured these shredded droppings into the bowl of the pipe, packing them down with my thumb just as the manly lover always did it. When that was done, I placed a thin layer of real tobacco over the top. The entire family was watching me as I did this. Nobody said a word, but I could sense a glow of approval all round. I replaced the pipe on the rock, and all of us sat back to await the return of the victim. The whole lot of us were in this together now, even my mother. I had drawn them into the plot simply by letting them see what I was doing. It was a silent, rather dangerous family conspiracy.

Back came the manly lover, dripping wet from the sea, chest out, strong and virile, healthy and sunburnt. 'Great swim!' he announced to the world. 'Splendid water! Terrific stuff!' He towelled himself vigorously, making the muscles of his biceps ripple, then he sat down on the rocks and reached for his pipe.

Nine pairs of eyes watched him intently. Nobody giggled to give the game away. We were trembling with anticipation, and a good deal of the suspense was caused by the fact that none of us knew just what was going to happen.

The manly lover put the pipe between his strong white teeth and struck a match. He held the flame over the bowl and sucked. The tobacco ignited and glowed, and the lover's head was enveloped in clouds of blue smoke. 'Ah-h-h,' he said, blowing smoke through his nostrils. 'There's nothing like a good pipe after a bracing swim.'

Still we waited. We could hardly bear the suspense. The sister who was seven couldn't bear it at all. 'What *sort* of tobacco do you put in that thing?' she asked with superb innocence.

'Navy Cut,' the male lover answered. 'Player's Navy Cut. It's the best there is. These Norwegians use all sorts of disgusting scented tobaccos, but I wouldn't touch them.'

'I didn't know they had different tastes,' the small sister went on.

'Of course they do,' the manly lover said. 'All tobaccos are different to the discriminating pipe-smoker. Navy Cut is clean and unadulterated. It's a man's smoke.' The man seemed to go out of his way to use long words like discriminating and unadulterated. We hadn't the foggiest what they meant.

The ancient half-sister, fresh from her swim and now clothed in a towel bathrobe, came and sat herself close to her manly lover. Then the two of them started giving each other those silly little glances and soppy smiles that made us all feel sick. They were far too occupied with one another to notice the awful tension that had settled over our group. They didn't even notice that every face in the crowd was turned towards them. They had sunk once again into their lovers' world where little children did not exist.

The sea was calm, the sun was shining and it was a beautiful day.

Then all of a sudden, the manly lover let out a piercing scream and his whole body shot four feet into the air. His pipe flew out of his mouth and went clattering over the rocks, and the second scream he gave was so shrill and loud that all the seagulls on the island rose up in alarm. His features were twisted like those of a person undergoing severe torture, and his skin had turned the colour of snow. He began spluttering and choking and spewing and hawking and acting generally like a man with some serious internal injury. He was completely speechless.

We stared at him, enthralled.

The ancient half-sister, who must have thought she was about to lose her future husband for ever, was pawing at him and thumping him on the back and crying, 'Darling! Darling! What's happening to you? Where does it hurt? Get the boat! Start the engine! We must rush him to a hospital quickly!' She seemed to have forgotten that there wasn't a hospital within fifty miles.

'I've been poisoned!' spluttered the manly lover. 'It's got into my lungs! It's in my chest! My chest is on fire! My stomach's going up in flames!'

'Help me get him into the boat! Quick!' cried the ancient half-sister, gripping him under the armpits. 'Don't just sit there staring! Come and help!'

'No, no, no!' cried the now not-so-manly lover. 'Leave me alone! I need air! Give me air!' He lay back and breathed in deep draughts of splendid Norwegian ocean air, and in another minute or so, he was sitting up again and was on the way to recovery.

'What in the world came over you?' asked the ancient half-sister, clasping his hands tenderly in hers.

'I can't imagine,' he murmured. 'I simply can't imagine.' His face was as still and white as virgin snow and his hands were trembling. 'There must be a reason for it,' he added. 'There's got to be a reason.'

'I know the reason!' shouted the seven-year-old sister, screaming with laughter. 'I know what it was!'

'What was it?' snapped the ancient one. 'What have you been up to? Tell me at once!'

'It's his pipe!' shouted the small sister, still convulsed with laughter.

'What's wrong with my pipe?' said the manly lover.

'You've been smoking goat's tobacco!' cried the small sister.

It took a few moments for the full meaning of these words to dawn upon the two lovers, but when it did, and when the terrible anger began to show itself on the manly lover's face, and when he started to rise slowly and menacingly to his feet, we all sprang up and ran for our lives and jumped off the rocks into the deep water.

Repton and Shell,

1929—36

(age 13—20)

Love from

Roald

Dear Mama

Thanks awfully for the parcel and your letters. We had a great supper last night. We fried the sausages and poured hieny beans over them. then we had force & cream. Those biscuits are awfully good.

Last night we had a heavy snowfall, and there is about ...ol snow on the ground. Tobogganing ...ton

Macdonald & I ...

photography at Repton

On ship to Newfoundland
1933

Getting dressed for
the big school

When I was twelve, my mother said to me, 'I've entered you for Marlborough and Repton. Which would you like to go to?'

Both were famous Public Schools, but that was all I knew about them. 'Repton,' I said. 'I'll go to Repton.' It was an easier word to say than Marlborough.

'Very well,' my mother said. 'You shall go to Repton.'

We were living in Kent then, in a place called Bexley. Repton was up in the Midlands, near Derby, and some 140 miles away to the north. That was of no consequence. There were plenty of trains. Nobody was taken to school by car in those days. We were put on the train.

alfhild, me, Asta, Else
and dogs. Tenby.

I was exactly thirteen in September 1929 when the time came for me to go to Repton. On the day of my departure, I had first of all to get dressed for the part. I had been to

London with my mother the week before to buy the school clothes, and I remember how shocked I was when I saw the outfit I was expected to wear.

'I can't possibly go about in *those*!' I cried. 'Nobody wears things like that!'

'Are you sure you haven't made a mistake?' my mother said to the shop assistant.

'If he's going to Repton, madam, he must wear these clothes,' the assistant said firmly.

And now this amazing fancy-dress was all laid out on my bed waiting to be put on. 'Put it on,' my mother said. 'Hurry up or you'll miss the train.'

'I'll look like a complete idiot,' I said. My mother went out of the room and left me to it. With immense reluctance, I began to dress myself.

First there was a white shirt with a detachable white collar. This collar was unlike any other collar I had seen. It was as stiff as a piece of perspex. At the front, the stiff points of the collar were bent over to make a pair of wings, and the whole thing was so tall that the points of the wings, as I discovered later, rubbed against the underneath of my chin. It was known as a butterfly collar.

To attach the butterfly collar to the shirt you needed a back stud and a front stud. I had never been through this rigmarole before. I must do this properly, I told myself. So first I put the back stud into the back of the collar-band of the shirt. Then I tried to attach the back of the collar to the back stud, but the collar was so stiff I couldn't get the stud through the slit. I decided to soften it with spit. I put the edge of the collar into my mouth and sucked the starch away. It worked. The stud went through the slit and the back of the collar was now attached to the back of the shirt.

I inserted the front stud into one side of the front of the

shirt and slipped the shirt over my head. With the help of a mirror, I now set about pushing the top of the front stud through the first of the two slits in the front of the collar. It wouldn't go. The slit was so small and stiff and starchy that nothing would go through it. I took the shirt off and put both the front slits of the collar into my mouth and chewed them until they were soft. The starch didn't taste of anything. I put the shirt back on again and at last I was able to get the front stud through the collar-slits.

Around the collar but underneath the butterfly wings, I tied a black tie, using an ordinary tie-knot.

Dear mama
Thanks for your letter.
I mean half a dozen Van Heusen Collars. *not* Shirts.
Love from
Roald

Then came the trousers and the braces. The trousers were black with thin pinstriped grey lines running down them. I buttoned the braces on to the trousers, six buttons in all, then I put on the trousers and adjusted the braces to the correct length by sliding two brass clips up and down.

I put on a brand new pair of black shoes and laced them up.

Now for the waistcoat. This was also black and it had twelve buttons down the front and two little waistcoat pockets on either side, one above the other. I put it on and did up the buttons, starting at the top and working down.

I was glad I didn't have to chew each of those button-holes to get the buttons through them.

All this was bad enough for a boy who had never before worn anything more elaborate than a pair of shorts and a blazer. But the jacket put the lid on it. It wasn't actually a jacket, it was a sort of tail-coat, and it was without a doubt the most ridiculous garment I had ever seen. Like the waistcoat, it was jet black and made of a heavy serge-like material. In the front it was cut away so that the two sides met only at one point, about halfway down the waistcoat. Here there was a single button and this had to be done up.

From the button downwards, the lines of the coat separated and curved away behind the legs of the wearer and came together again at the backs of the knees, forming a pair of 'tails'. These tails were separated by a slit and when you walked about they flapped against your legs. I put the thing on and did up the front button. Feeling like an undertaker's apprentice in a funeral parlour, I crept downstairs.

My sisters shrieked with laughter when I appeared. 'He can't go out in *those*!' they cried. 'He'll be arrested by the police!'

'Put your hat on,' my mother said, handing me a stiff wide-brimmed straw-hat with a blue and black band around it. I put it on and did my best to look dignified. The sisters fell all over the room laughing.

the hat-band being something like this: [sketch], the white stripes are realy blue, and the bit filled in is black.

My mother got me out of the house before I lost my nerve completely and together we walked through the village to Bexley station. My mother was going to accompany me to London and see me on to the Derby train, but she had been told that on no account should she travel farther than that. I had only a small suitcase to carry. My trunk had been sent on ahead labelled 'Luggage in Advance'.

'Nobody's taking the slightest notice of you,' my mother said as we walked through Bexley High Street.

And curiously enough nobody was.

'I have learnt one thing about England,' my mother went on. 'It is a country where men love to wear uniforms and eccentric clothes. Two hundred years ago their clothes were even more eccentric then they are today. You can consider yourself lucky you don't have to wear a wig on your head and ruffles on your sleeves.'

'I still feel an ass,' I said.

'Everyone who looks at you', my mother said, 'knows that you are going away to a Public School. All English Public Schools have their own different crazy uniforms. People will be thinking how lucky you are to be going to one of those famous places.'

We took the train from Bexley to Charing Cross and then went by taxi to Euston Station. At Euston, I was put on the train for Derby with a lot of other boys who all wore the same ridiculous clothes as me, and away I went.

Beagling, Repton 1930.

Boazers

At Repton, prefects were never called prefects. They were called Boazers, and they had the power of life and death over us junior boys. They could summon us down in our pyjamas at night-time and thrash us for leaving just one football sock on the floor of the changing-room when it should have been hung up on a peg. A Boazer could thrash us for a hundred and one other piddling little misdemeanours – for burning his toast at tea-time, for failing to dust his study properly, for failing to get his study fire burning in spite of spending half your pocket money on fire-lighters, for being late at roll-call, for talking in evening Prep, for forgetting to change into house-shoes at six o'clock. The list was endless.

'Four with the dressing-gown on or three with it off?' the Boazer would say to you in the changing-room late at night.

Others in the dormitory had told you what to answer to this question. 'Four with it on,' you mumbled, trembling.

This Boazer was famous for the speed of his strokes. Most of them paused between each stroke to prolong the operation, but Williamson, the great footballer, cricketer and athlete, always delivered his strokes in a series of swift back and forth movements without any pause between them at all. Four strokes would rain down upon your bottom so fast that it was all over in four seconds.

A ritual took place in the dormitory after each beating. The victim was required to stand in the middle of the room and lower his pyjama trousers so that the damage could be inspected. Half a dozen experts would crowd round you and express their opinions in highly professional language.

'*What* a super job.'

'He's got *every single* one in the same place!'

'Crikey! Nobody could tell you had more than *one*, except for the mess!'

'Boy, that Williamson's got a *terrific* eye!'

'*Of course* he's got a terrific eye! Why d'you think he's a Cricket Teamer?'

'There's no wet blood though! If you had had just one more he'd have got some blood out!'

'Through a *dressing-gown*, too! It's pretty amazing, isn't it!'

'Most Boazers couldn't get a result like that *without* a dressing-gown!'

'You must have tremendously thin skin! Even Williamson couldn't have done that to *ordinary* skin!'

'Did he use the long one or the short one?'

'Hang *on*! Don't pull them up yet! I've *got* to see this again!'

And I would stand there, slightly bemused by this cool clinical approach. Once, I was still standing in the middle of the dormitory with my pyjama trousers around my knees when Williamson came through the door. 'What on earth do you think you're doing?' he said, knowing very well exactly what I was doing.

'N-nothing,' I stammered. 'N-nothing at all.'

'Pull those pyjamas up and get into bed immediately!' he ordered, but I noticed that as he turned away to go out of the door, he craned his head ever so slightly to one side to catch a glimpse of my bare bottom and his own handiwork. I was certain I detected a little glimmer of pride around the edges of his mouth before he closed the door behind him.

The Headmaster

and again!

The Headmaster, while I was at Repton, struck me as being a rather shoddy bandy-legged little fellow with a big bald head and lots of energy but not much charm. Mind you, I never did know him well because in all those months and years I was at the school, I doubt whether he addressed more than six sentences to me altogether. So perhaps it was wrong of me to form a judgement like that.

What is so interesting about this Headmaster is that he became a famous person later on. At the end of my third year, he was suddenly appointed Bishop of Chester and off he went to live in a palace by the River Dee. I remember at the time trying to puzzle out how on earth a person could suddenly leap from being a schoolmaster to becoming a Bishop all in one jump, but there were bigger puzzles to come.

From Chester, he was soon promoted again to become Bishop of London, and from there, after not all that many years, he bounced up the ladder once more to get the top job of them all, Archbishop of Canterbury! And not long after that it was he himself who had the task of crowning our present Queen in Westminster Abbey with half the world watching him on television. Well, well, well! And this was the man who used to deliver the most vicious beatings to the boys under his care!

By now I am sure you will be wondering why I lay so

much emphasis upon school beatings in these pages. The answer is that I cannot help it. All through my school life I was appalled by the fact that masters and senior boys were allowed literally to wound other boys, and sometimes quite severely. I couldn't get over it. I never have got over it. It would, of course, be unfair to suggest that *all* masters were constantly beating the daylights out of *all* the boys in those days. They weren't. Only a few did so, but that was quite enough to leave a lasting impression of horror upon me. It left another more physical impression upon me as well. Even today, whenever I have to sit for any length of time on a hard bench or chair, I begin to feel my heart beating along the old lines that the cane made on my bottom some fifty-five years ago.

There is nothing wrong with a few quick sharp tickles on the rump. They probably do a naughty boy a lot of good. But this Headmaster we were talking about wasn't just tickling you when he took out his cane to deliver a flogging. He never flogged me, thank goodness, but I was given a vivid description of one of these ceremonies by my best friend at Repton, whose name was Michael. Michael was ordered to take down his trousers and kneel on the Headmaster's sofa with the top half of his body hanging over one end of the sofa. The great man then gave him one terrific crack. After that, there was a pause. The cane was put down and the Headmaster began filling his pipe from a tin of tobacco. He also started to lecture the kneeling boy about sin and wrongdoing. Soon, the cane was picked up again and a second tremendous crack was administered upon the trembling buttocks. Then the pipe-filling business and the lecture went on for maybe another thirty seconds. Then came the third crack of the cane. Then the instrument of torture was put once more upon the table and a box of matches was produced. A match was struck and applied to the pipe. The pipe failed to light properly. A fourth stroke was delivered, with the lecture continuing. This slow and fearsome process went on until ten terrible strokes had been delivered, and all the time, over the pipe-lighting and the match-striking, the lecture on evil and wrongdoing and sinning and misdeeds and malpractice went on without a stop. It even went on as the strokes were being administered. At the end of it all, a basin, a sponge and a small clean towel were produced by the Headmaster, and the victim was told to wash away the blood before pulling up his trousers.

Do you wonder then that this man's behaviour used to puzzle me tremendously? He was an ordinary clergyman at that time as well as being Headmaster, and I would sit in the dim light of the school chapel and listen to him preaching about the Lamb of God and about Mercy and Forgiveness and all the rest of it and my young mind would become totally confused. I knew very well that only the night before this preacher had shown neither Forgiveness nor Mercy in flogging some small boy who had broken the rules.

So what was it all about? I used to ask myself.

Did they preach one thing and practise another, these men of God?

And if someone had told me at the time that this flogging clergyman was one day to become the Archbishop of Canterbury, I would never have believed it.

It was all this, I think, that made me begin to have doubts about religion and even about God. If this person, I kept telling myself, was one of God's chosen salesmen on earth, then there must be something very wrong about the whole business.

Chocolates

Every now and again, a plain grey cardboard box was dished out to each boy in our House, and this, believe it or not, was a present from the great chocolate manufacturers, Cadbury. Inside the box there were twelve bars of chocolate, all of different shapes, all with different fillings and all with numbers from one to twelve stamped on the chocolate underneath. Eleven of these bars were new inventions from the factory. The twelfth was the 'control' bar, one that we all knew well, usually a Cadbury's Coffee Cream bar. Also in the box was a sheet of paper with the numbers one to twelve on it as well as two blank columns, one for giving marks to each chocolate from nought to ten, and the other for comments.

All we were required to do in return for this splendid gift was to taste very carefully each bar of chocolate, give it marks and make an intelligent comment on why we liked it or disliked it.

It was a clever stunt. Cadbury's were using some of the greatest chocolate-bar experts in the world to test out their new inventions. We were of a sensible age, between thirteen and eighteen, and we knew intimately every chocolate bar in existence, from the Milk Flake to the Lemon Marshmallow. Quite obviously our opinions on anything new would be valuable. All of us entered into this game with great gusto, sitting in our studies and nibbling each bar with the air of connoisseurs, giving our marks and making our comments. 'Too subtle for the common palate,' was one note that I remember writing down.

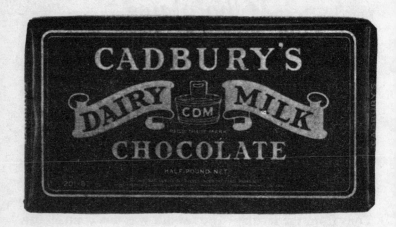

For me, the importance of all this was that I began to realize that the large chocolate companies actually did possess inventing rooms and they took their inventing very seriously. I used to picture a long white room like a laboratory with pots of chocolate and fudge and all sorts of other delicious fillings bubbling away on the stoves, while men and women in white coats moved between the bubbling pots, tasting and mixing and concocting their wonderful new inventions. I used to imagine myself working in one of these labs and suddenly I would come up with something so absolutely unbearably delicious that I would grab it in my hand and go rushing out of the lab and along the corridor and right into the office of the great Mr Cadbury himself. 'I've got it, sir!' I would shout, putting the chocolate in front of him. 'It's fantastic! It's fabulous! It's marvellous! It's irresistible!'

Slowly, the great man would pick up my newly invented chocolate and he would take a small bite. He would roll it round his mouth. Then all at once, he would leap up from his chair, crying, 'You've got it! You've done it! It's a miracle!' He would slap me on the back and shout, 'We'll sell it by the million! We'll sweep the world with this one! How on earth did you do it? Your salary is doubled!'

It was lovely dreaming those dreams, and I have no doubt at all that, thirty-five years later, when I was looking for a plot for my second book for children, I remembered those little cardboard boxes and the newly-invented chocolates inside them, and I began to write a book called *Charlie and the Chocolate Factory*.

Saturday, first I broke it in half, and only half came out, then the other bit came out, it was my dog tooth, and it was a very bad one, I am glad it came out. Will you please send me a *few sweets* because we had none last week, I am sorry my writing is so untidy, but I have not much time on week days.

Corkers

There were about thirty or more masters at Repton and most of them were amazingly dull and totally colourless and completely uninterested in boys. But Corkers, an eccentric old bachelor, was neither dull nor colourless. Corkers was a charmer, a vast ungainly man with drooping bloodhound cheeks and filthy clothes. He wore creaseless flannel trousers and a brown tweed jacket with patches all over it and bits of dried food on the lapels. He was meant to teach us mathematics, but in truth he taught us nothing at all and that was the way he meant it to be. His lessons consisted of an endless series of distractions all invented by him so that the subject of mathematics would never have to be discussed. He would come lumbering into the classroom and sit down at his desk and glare at the class. We would wait expectantly, wondering what was coming next.

'Let's have a look at the crossword puzzle in today's *Times*,' he would say, fishing a crumpled newspaper out of his jacket pocket. 'That'll be a lot more fun than fiddling around with figures. I hate figures. Figures are probably the dreariest things on this earth.'

'Then why do you teach mathematics, sir?' somebody asked him.

'I don't,' he said, smiling slyly. 'I only *pretend* to teach it.'

Corkers would proceed to draw the framework of the

crossword on the blackboard and we would all spend the rest of the lesson trying to solve it while he read out the clues. We enjoyed that.

The only time I can remember him vaguely touching upon mathematics was when he whisked a square of tissue-paper out of his pocket and waved it around. 'Look at this,' he said. 'This tissue-paper is one-hundredth of an inch thick. I fold it once, making it double. I fold it again, making it four thicknesses. Now then, I will give a large bar of Cadbury's Fruit and Nut Milk Chocolate to any boy who can tell me, to the nearest twelve inches, how thick it will be if I fold it fifty times.'

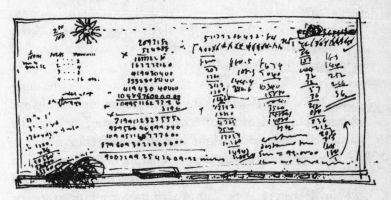

We all stuck up our hands and started guessing. 'Twenty-four inches, sir' . . . 'Three feet, sir' . . . 'Five yards, sir' . . . 'Three inches, sir.'

'You're not very clever, are you,' Corkers said. 'The answer is the distance from the earth to the sun. That's how thick it would be.' We were enthralled by this piece of intelligence and asked him to prove it on the blackboard, which he did.

Another time, he brought a two-foot-long grass-snake into class and insisted that every boy should handle it in order to cure us for ever, as he said, of a fear of snakes. This caused quite a commotion.

I cannot remember all the other thousands of splendid things that old Corkers cooked up to keep his class happy, but there was one that I shall never forget which was repeated at intervals of about three weeks throughout each term. He would be talking to us about this or that when suddenly he would stop in mid-sentence and a look of intense pain would cloud his ancient countenance. Then his head would come up and his great nose would begin to sniff the air and he would cry aloud, 'By God! This is too much! This is going too far! This is intolerable!'

Thanks awfully for the Tablets. I took some a few times and the indigestion has stopped now, they are jolly good

We knew exactly what was coming next, but we always played along with him. 'What's the matter, sir? What's happened? Are you all right, sir? Are you feeling ill?'

Up went the great nose once again, and the head would move slowly from side to side and the nose would sniff the air delicately as though searching for a leak of gas or the smell of something burning. 'This is not to be tolerated!' he would cry. 'This is *unbearable*!'

'But what's the *matter*, sir?'

'I'll tell you what's the matter,' Corkers would shout. 'Somebody's *farted*!'

'Oh no, sir!' . . . 'Not me, sir!' . . . 'Nor me, sir!' . . . 'It's none of us, sir!'

At this point, he would rise majestically to his feet and call out at the top of his voice, '*Use door as fan! Open all windows!*'

This was the signal for frantic activity and everyone in the class would leap to his feet. It was a well-rehearsed operation and each of us knew exactly what he had to do. Four boys would man the door and begin swinging it back and forth at great speed. The rest would start clambering about on the gigantic windows which occupied one whole wall of the room, flinging the lower ones open, using a long pole with a hook on the end to open the top ones, and leaning out to gulp the fresh air in mock distress. While this was going on, Corkers himself would march serenely out of the room, muttering, 'It's the cabbage that does it! All they give you is disgusting cabbage and Brussels sprouts and you go off like fire-crackers!' And that was the last we saw of Corkers for the day.

School dinners!

Fagging

I spent two long years as a Fag at Repton, which meant I was the servant of the studyholder in whose study I had my little desk. If the studyholder happened to be a House Boazer, so much the worse for me because Boazers were a dangerous breed. During my second term, I was unfortunate enough to be put into the study of the Head of the House, a supercilious and obnoxious seventeen-year-old called Carleton. Carleton always looked at you right down

I don't think that I've told you what we do every day sort of thing: the first bell goes at quarter past seven, and the fag who is on water in each bedder, gets up and fills the cans with hot water, and loses the windows. then if he want to get to each bed again, the second cell goes at half past seven, and every one must be down for prayers by quarter to eight. then we ? to an hour ? ? m ? H.

the length of his nose, and even if you were as tall as him, which I happened to be, he would tilt his head back and still manage to look at you down the length of his nose. Carleton had three Fags in his study and all of us were terrified of him, especially on Sunday mornings, because Sunday was study-cleaning time. All the Fags in all the studies had to take off their jackets, roll up their sleeves, fetch buckets and floor-cloths and get down to cleaning out their studyholder's study. And when I say cleaning out, I mean practically sterilizing the place. We scrubbed the floor and washed the windows and polished the grate and dusted the ledges and wiped the picture-frames and carefully tidied away all the hockey-sticks and cricket-bats and umbrellas.

All that Sunday morning we had been slogging away cleaning Carleton's study, and then, just before lunch Carleton himself strode into the room and said, 'You've had long enough.'

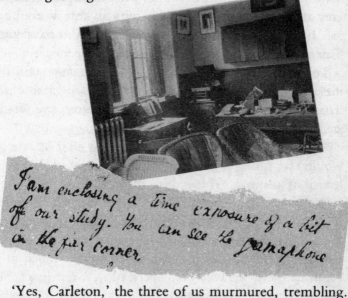

I am enclosing a time exposure of a bit of our study. You can see the Semaphone in the far corner.

'Yes, Carleton,' the three of us murmured, trembling. We stood back, breathless from our exertions, compelled as always to wait and watch the dreadful Carleton while he performed the ritual of inspection. First of all, he would go to the drawer of his desk and take out a pure-white cotton glove which he slid with much ceremony on to his right hand. Then, taking as much care and time as a surgeon in an operating theatre, he would move slowly round the study, running his white-gloved fingers along all the ledges, along the tops of the picture-frames, over the surfaces of the desks, and even over the bars of the fire-grate. Every few seconds, he would hold those white fingers up close to his face, searching for traces of dust, and we three Fags would stand there watching him, hardly daring to breathe, waiting for the dreaded moment when the great man would stop and shout, 'Ha! What's this I see?' A look of triumph would light up his face as he held up a white finger which had on it the tiniest smudge of grey dust, and he would stare at us with his slightly popping pale blue eyes and say, 'You haven't cleaned it have you? You haven't bothered to clean my study properly.'

To the three of us Fags who had been slaving away for the whole of the morning, these words were simply not true. 'We've cleaned every bit of it, Carleton,' we would answer. 'Every little bit.'

'In that case why has my finger got dust on it?' Carleton would say, tilting his head back and gazing at us down the length of his nose. 'This *is* dust, isn't it?'

We would step forward and peer at the white-gloved forefinger and at the tiny smidgin of dust that lay on it, and we would remain silent. I longed to point out to him that it was an actual impossibility to clean a much-used room to the point where no speck of dust remained, but that would have been suicide.

'Do any of you dispute the fact that this is dust?' Carleton would say, still holding up his finger. 'If I am wrong, do tell me.'

'It isn't *much* dust, Carleton.'

'I didn't ask you whether it was *much* dust or *not much* dust,' Carleton would say. 'I simply asked you whether or not it was dust. Might it, for example, be iron filings or face powder instead?'

'No, Carleton.'
'Or crushed diamonds, maybe?'
'No, Carleton.'
'Then what is it?'
'It's . . . it's dust, Carleton.'
'Thank you,' Carleton would say. 'At last you have admitted that you failed to clean my study properly. I shall therefore see all three of you in the changing-room tonight after prayers.'

You seem to have been doing a lot of painting; but when you paint the loo don't paint the seat, leaving it wet and sticky, or some unfortunate person who has not noticed it, will adhere to it, and unless he chooses' to go about with the seat sticking behind him always, he will be doomed to stay where he is

The rules and rituals of fagging at Repton were so complicated that I could fill a whole book with them. A House Boazer, for example, could make any Fag in the House do his bidding. He could stand anywhere he wanted to in the building, in the corridor, in the changing-room, in the yard, and yell 'Fa-a-ag!' at the top of his voice and every Fag in the place would have to drop what he was doing and run flat out to the source of the noise. There was always a mad stampede when the call of 'Fa-a-ag!' echoed through the House because the last boy to arrive would invariably be chosen for whatever menial or unpleasant task the Boazer had in mind.

During my first term, I was in the changing-room one day just before lunch scraping the mud from the soles of my studyholder's football boots when I heard the famous shout of 'Fa-a-ag!' far away at the other end of the House.

I dropped everything and ran. But I got there last, and the Boazer who had done the shouting, a massive athlete called Wilberforce, said, 'Dahl, come here.'

The other Fags melted away with the speed of light and I crept forward to receive my orders. 'Go and heat my seat in the bogs,' Wilberforce said. 'I want it *warm*.'

I hadn't the faintest idea what any of this meant, but I already knew better than to ask questions of a Boazer. I hurried away and found a fellow Fag who told me the meaning of this curious order. It meant that the Boazer wished to use the lavatory but that he wanted the seat warmed for him before he sat down. The six House lavatories, none with doors, were situated in an unheated outhouse and on a cold day in winter you could get frostbite out there if you stayed too long. This particular day was icy-cold, and I went out through the snow into the outhouse and entered number one lavatory, which I knew was reserved for Boazers only. I wiped the frost off the seat with my handkerchief, then I lowered my trousers and sat

down. I was there a full fifteen minutes in the freezing cold before Wilberforce arrived on the scene.

'Have you got the ice off it?' he asked.

'Yes, Wilberforce.'

'Is it *warm*?'

'It's as warm as I can get it, Wilberforce,' I said.

'We shall soon find out,' he said. 'You can get off now.'

I got off the lavatory seat and pulled up my trousers. Wilberforce lowered his own trousers and sat down. 'Very good,' he said. 'Very good indeed.' He was like a winetaster sampling an old claret. 'I shall put you on my list,' he added.

I stood there doing up my fly-buttons and not knowing what on earth he meant.

'Some Fags have cold bottoms,' he said, 'and some have hot ones. I only use hot-bottomed Fags to heat my bog-seat. I won't forget you.'

He didn't. From then on, all through that winter, I became Wilberforce's favourite bog-seat warmer, and I used always to keep a paperback book in the pocket of my tail-coat to while away the long bog-warming sessions. I must have read the entire works of Dickens sitting on that Boazer's bog during my first winter at Repton.

Games and photography

It was always a surprise to me that I was good at games. It was an even greater surprise that I was exceptionally good at two of them. One of these was called fives, the other was squash-racquets.

Fives, which many of you will know nothing about, was taken seriously at Repton and we had a dozen massive glass-roofed fives courts kept always in perfect condition. We played the game of *Eton*-fives, which is always played by four people, two on each side, and basically it consists of hitting a small, hard, white, leather-covered ball with your gloved hands. The Americans have something like it which they call handball, but Eton-fives is far more complicated because the court has all manner of ledges and buttresses built into it which help to make it a subtle and crafty game.

Fives is possibly the fastest ball-game on earth, far faster than squash, and the little ball ricochets around the court at such a speed that sometimes you can hardly see it. You need a swift eye, strong wrists and a very quick pair of hands to play fives well, and it was a game I took to right from the beginning. You may find it hard to believe, but I became so good at it that I won both the junior and the senior school fives in the same year when I was fifteen. Soon I bore the splendid title 'Captain of Fives', and I would travel with my team to other schools like Shrewsbury and

Uppingham to play matches. I loved it. It was a game without physical contact, and the quickness of the eye and the dancing of the feet were all that mattered.

A Captain of any game at Repton was an important person. He was the one who selected the members of the team for matches. He and only he could award 'colours' to others. He would award school 'colours' by walking up to the chosen boy after a match and shaking him by the hand and saying, 'Graggers on your teamer!' These were magic words. They entitled the new teamer to all manner of privileges including a different-coloured hat-band on his straw-hat and fancy braid around the edges of his blazer and different-coloured games clothes, and all sorts of other advertisements that made the teamer gloriously conspicuous among his fellows.

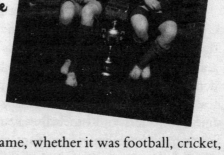

Fives Team
Priory House

A Captain of any game, whether it was football, cricket, fives or squash, had many other duties. It was he who pinned the notice on the school notice-board on match days announcing the team. It was he who arranged fixtures by letter with other schools. It was he and only he who had it in his power to invite this master or that to play against him and his team on certain afternoons. All these responsibilities were given to me when I became Captain of Fives. Then came the snag. It was more or less taken for granted that a Captain would be made a Boazer in recognition of his talents – if not a School Boazer then certainly a House Boazer. But the authorities did not like me. I was not to be trusted. I did not like rules. I was unpredictable. I was therefore not Boazer material. There was no way they would agree to make me a House Boazer, let alone a School Boazer. Some people are born to wield power and to exercise authority. I was not one of them. I was in full agreement with my Housemaster when he explained this to me. I would have made a rotten Boazer. I would have let down the whole principle of Boazerdom by refusing to beat the Fags. I was probably the only Captain of any game who has never become a Boazer at Repton. I was certainly the only unBoazered Double Captain, because I was also Captain of squash-racquets. And to pile glory upon glory, I was in the school football team as well.

A boy who is good at games is usually treated with great civility by the masters at an English Public School. In much the same way, the ancient Greeks revered their athletes and made statues of them in marble. Athletes were the demigods, the chosen few. They could perform glamorous feats beyond the reach of ordinary mortals. Even today, fine footballers and baseball players and runners and all other great sportsmen are much admired by the general public and advertisers use them to sell breakfast cereals.

This never happened to me, and if you really want to know, I'm awfully glad it didn't.

But because I loved playing games, life for me at Repton was not totally without pleasure. Games-playing at school is always fun if you happen to be good at it, and it is hell if you are not. I was one of the lucky ones, and all those afternoons on the playing-fields and in the fives courts and in the squash courts made the otherwise grey and melancholy days pass a lot more quickly.

There was one other thing that gave me great pleasure at this school and that was photography. I was the only boy who practised it seriously, and it was not quite so simple a business fifty years ago as it is today. I made myself a little dark-room in a corner of the music building, and in there I loaded my glass plates and developed my negatives and enlarged them.

Our Arts Master was a shy retiring man called Arthur Norris who kept himself well apart from the rest of the staff. Arthur Norris and I became close friends and during my last year he organized an exhibition of my photographs. He gave the whole of the Art School over to this project and helped me to get my enlargements framed. The exhibition was rather a success, and masters who had hardly ever spoken to me over the past four years would come up and say things like, 'It's quite extraordinary' . . . 'We didn't know we had an artist in our midst' . . . 'Are they for sale?'

Arthur Norris would give me tea and cakes in his flat and would talk to me about painters like Cézanne and Manet and Matisse, and I have a feeling that it was there, having tea with the gentle soft-spoken Mr Norris in his flat on Sunday afternoons that my great love of painters and their work began.

After leaving school, I continued for a long time with photography and I became quite good at it. Today, given a 35mm camera and a built-in exposure-meter, anyone can be an expert photographer, but it was not so easy fifty years ago. I used glass plates instead of film, and each of these had to be loaded into its separate container in the dark-room before I set out to take pictures. I usually carried with me six loaded plates, which allowed me only six exposures, so that clicking the shutter even once was a serious business that had to be carefully thought out before-hand.

You may not believe it, but when I was eighteen I used to win prizes and medals from the Royal Photographic Society in London, and from other places like the Photographic Society of Holland. I even got a lovely big bronze medal from the Egyptian Photographic Society in Cairo,

and I still have the photograph that won it. It is a picture of one of the so-called Seven Wonders of the World, the Arch of Ctesiphon in Iraq. This is the largest unsupported arch on earth and I took the photograph while I was training out there for the RAF in 1940. I was flying over the desert solo in an old Hawker Hart biplane and I had my camera round my neck. When I spotted the huge arch standing alone in a sea of sand, I dropped one wing and hung in my straps and let go of the stick while I took aim and clicked the shutter. It came out fine.

Goodbye school

During my last year at Repton, my mother said to me, 'Would you like to go to Oxford or Cambridge when you leave school?' In those days it was not difficult to get into either of these great universities so long as you could pay.

'No, thank you,' I said. 'I want to go straight from school to work for a company that will send me to wonderful faraway places like Africa or China.'

You must remember that there was virtually no air travel in the early 1930s. Africa was two weeks away from England by boat and it took you about five weeks to get to China. These were distant and magic lands and nobody went to them just for a holiday. You went there to work. Nowadays you can go anywhere in the world in a few hours and nothing is fabulous any more. But it was a very different matter in 1933.

So during my last term I applied for a job only to those companies that would be sure to send me abroad. They were the Shell Company (Eastern Staff), Imperial Chemicals (Eastern Staff) and a Finnish lumber company whose name I have forgotten.

I was accepted by Imperial Chemicals and by the Finnish lumber company, but for some reason I wanted most of all to get into the Shell Company. When the day came for me to go up to London for this interview, my Housemaster told me it was ridiculous for me even to try. 'The Eastern

Staff of Shell are the *crème de la crème,*' he said. 'There will be at least one hundred applicants and about five vacancies. Nobody has a hope unless he's been Head of the School or Head of the House, and you aren't even a *House* Prefect!'

My Housemaster was right about the applicants. There were one hundred and seven boys waiting to be interviewed when I arrived at the Head Office of the Shell Company in London. And there were seven places to be filled. Please don't ask me how I got one of those places. I don't know myself. But get it I did, and when I told my Housemaster the good news on my return to school, he didn't congratulate me or shake me warmly by the hand. He turned away muttering, 'All I can say is I'm damned glad I don't own any shares in Shell.'

I didn't care any longer what my Housemaster thought. I was all set. I had a career. It was lovely. I was to leave school for ever in July 1933 and join the Shell Company two months later in September when I would be exactly eighteen. I was to be an Eastern Staff Trainee at a salary of five pounds a week.

That summer, for the first time in my life, I did not accompany the family to Norway. I somehow felt the need for a special kind of last fling before I became a businessman. So while still at school during my last term, I signed up to spend August with something called 'The Public Schools' Exploring Society'. The leader of this outfit was a man who had gone with Captain Scott on his last expedition to the South Pole, and he was taking a party of senior schoolboys to explore the interior of Newfoundland during the summer holidays. It sounded like fun.

Without the slightest regret I said goodbye to Repton for ever and rode back to Kent on my motorbike. This splendid machine was a 500 cc Ariel which I had bought the year before for eighteen pounds, and during my last term at Repton I kept it secretly in a garage along the Willington road about two miles away. On Sundays I used to walk to the garage and disguise myself in helmet, goggles, old raincoat and rubber waders and ride all over Derbyshire. It was fun to go roaring through Repton itself with nobody knowing who you were, swishing past the masters walking in the street and circling around the

got the job with Shell!

ALL COMMUNICATIONS TO BE ADDRESSED TO THE COMPANY.

TELEGRAPHIC ADDRESS
"AUREOOL, LONDON."

TELEPHONE No.
AVENUE* 8820.

THE ASIATIC PETROLEUM COMPANY, LIMITED.

ST HELENS COURT,
GREAT ST HELENS,
G.P.O. BOX 502.
LONDON, E.C.3.

ALL CODES USED.   DS

IN REPLY PLEASE REFER TO

G.S.E.   16th July, 1934.

Mr. R. Dahl,
    Repton School,
      Repton,
        Derbyshire.

Dear Sir,

    With reference to our recent interview with you, we have now received a satisfactory report on your medical examination and are prepared to offer you a probationary position on our London Staff at a commencing salary of £130 per annum, with a view to your joining one of our foreign branches some time after you reach the age of 21, if your work and conduct in the London Office prove satisfactory, and you show such development during this probationary period as we expect from candidates whom we regard as suitable to be sent abroad in our foreign service.

    In order that there may be no misunderstanding we place on record what was told you at the interview which we had with you - that in the event of your being required to take up a position on our foreign Staff outside Europe it dangerous supercilious School Boazers out for their Sunday strolls. I tremble to think what would have happened to me had I been caught, but I wasn't caught. So on the last day of term I zoomed joyfully away and left school behind me for ever and ever. I was not quite eighteen.

I had only two days at home before I was off to Newfoundland with the Public Schools' Explorers. Our ship sailed from Liverpool at the beginning of August and took

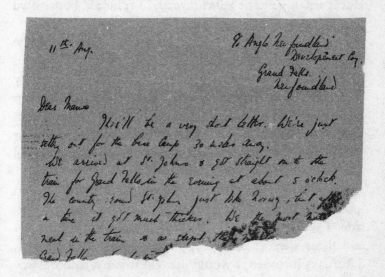

six days to reach St John's. There were about thirty boys of my own age on the expedition as well as four experienced adult leaders. But Newfoundland, as I soon found out, was not much of a country. For three weeks we trudged all over that desolate land with enormous loads on our backs. We carried tents and groundsheets and sleeping-bags and saucepans and food and axes and everything else one needs in the interior of an unmapped, uninhabitable and inhospitable country. My own load, I know, weighed exactly one hundred and fourteen pounds, and someone else always had to help me hoist the rucksack on to my back in the mornings. We lived on pemmican and lentils, and the twelve of us who went separately on what was called the Long March from the north to the south of the island and back again suffered a good deal from lack of food. I can remember very clearly how we experimented with eating boiled lichen and reindeer moss to supplement our diet. But it *was* a genuine adventure and I returned home hard and fit and ready for anything.

There followed two years of intensive training with the Shell Company in England. We were seven trainees in that year's group and each one of us was being carefully prepared to uphold the majesty of the Shell Company in one or another remote tropical country. We spent weeks at the huge Shell Haven Refinery with a special instructor who taught us all about fuel oil and diesel oil and gas oil and lubricating oil and kerosene and gasoline.

After that we spent months at the Head Office in London learning how the great company functioned from the inside. I was still living in Bexley, Kent, with my mother and three sisters, and every morning, six days a week, Saturdays included, I would dress neatly in a sombre grey suit, have breakfast at seven forty-five and then, with a brown trilby on my head and a furled umbrella in my hand, I would board the eight-fifteen train to London together with a swarm of other equally sombre-suited businessmen. I found it easy to fall into their pattern. We were all very serious and dignified gents taking the train to our offices in the City of London where each of us, so we thought, was engaged in high finance and other enormously important matters. Most of my companions wore hard bowler hats, and a few like me wore soft trilbys, but not one of us on that train in the year of 1934 went bareheaded. It wasn't done. And none of us, even on the sunniest days, went without his furled umbrella. The umbrella was our badge of office. We felt naked without it. Also it was a sign of respectability. Road-menders and plumbers never went to work with umbrellas. Business-men did.

the Businessman

I enjoyed it, I really did. I began to realize how simple life could be if one had a regular routine to follow with fixed hours and a fixed salary and very little original thinking to do. The life of a writer is absolute hell compared with the life of a businessman. The writer has to force himself to work. He has to make his own hours and if he doesn't go to his desk at all there is nobody to scold him. If he is a writer of fiction he lives in a world of fear. Each new day demands new ideas and he can never be sure whether he is going to come up with them or not. Two hours of writing fiction leaves this particular writer absolutely drained. For those two hours he has been miles away, he has been somewhere else, in a different place with totally different people, and the effort of swimming back into normal surroundings is very great. It is almost a shock. The writer walks out of his workroom in a daze. He wants a drink. He needs it. It happens to be a fact that nearly every writer of fiction in the world drinks more whisky than is good for him. He does it to give himself faith, hope and courage. A person is a fool to become a writer. His only compensation is absolute freedom. He has no master except his own soul, and that, I am sure, is why he does it.

The Shell Company did us proud. After twelve months at Head Office, we trainees were all sent away to various Shell branches in England to study salesmanship. I went to Somerset and spent several glorious weeks selling kerosene to old ladies in remote villages. My kerosene motor-tanker had a tap at the back and when I rolled into Shepton Mallet or Midsomer Norton or Peasedown St John or Hinton Blewett or Temple Cloud or Chew Magna or Huish Champflower, the old girls and the young maidens would hear the roar of my motor and would come out of their cottages with jugs and buckets to buy a gallon of kerosene for their lamps and their heaters. It is fun for a young man to do that sort of thing. Nobody gets a nervous breakdown or a heart attack from selling kerosene to gentle country folk from the back of a tanker in Somerset on a fine summer's day.

Then suddenly, in 1936, I was summoned back to Head Office in London. One of the Directors wished to see me. 'We are sending you to Egypt,' he said. 'It will be a three-year tour, then six months' leave. Be ready to go in one week's time.'

'Oh, but sir!' I cried out. 'Not *Egypt*! I really don't want to go to *Egypt*!'

The great man reeled back in his chair as though I had slapped him in the face with a plate of poached eggs. 'Egypt', he said slowly, 'is one of our finest and most important areas. We are doing you a *favour* in sending you there instead of to some mosquito-ridden place in the swamps!'

I kept silent.

'May I ask why you do not wish to go to Egypt?' he said.

I knew perfectly well why, but I didn't know how to put it. What I wanted was jungles and lions and elephants and tall coconut palms swaying on silvery beaches, and Egypt had none of that. Egypt was desert country. It was bare and sandy and full of tombs and relics and Egyptians and I didn't fancy it at all.

'What is wrong with Egypt?' the Director asked me again.

'It's . . . it's . . . it's', I stammered, 'it's too *dusty*, sir.'

The man stared at me. 'Too *what*?' he cried.

'Dusty,' I said.

'*Dusty*!' he shouted. 'Too *dusty*! I've never heard such rubbish!'

There was a long silence. I was expecting him to tell me to fetch my hat and coat and leave the building for ever. But he didn't do that. He was an awfully nice man and his name was Mr Godber. He gave a deep sigh and rubbed a hand over his eyes and said, 'Very well then, if that's the way you want it. Redfearn will go to Egypt instead of you and you will have to take the next posting that comes up, dusty or not. Do you understand?'

'Yes, sir, I realize that.'

'If the next vacancy happens to be Siberia,' he said, 'you'll have to take it.'

'I quite understand, sir,' I said. 'And thank you very much.'

Within a week Mr Godber summoned me again to his office. 'You're going to East Africa,' he said.

'Hooray!' I shouted, jumping up and down. 'That's marvellous, sir! That's wonderful! How terrific!'

The great man smiled. 'It's quite dusty there too,' he said.

'Lions!' I cried. 'And elephants and giraffes and coconuts everywhere!'

'Your boat leaves from London Docks in six days,' he said. 'You get off at Mombasa. Your salary will be five hundred pounds per annum and your tour is for three years.'

I was twenty years old. I was off to East Africa where I would walk about in khaki shorts every day and wear a topi on my head! I was ecstatic. I rushed home and told my mother. 'And I'll be gone for three years,' I said.

I was her only son and we were very close. Most mothers, faced with a situation like this, would have shown a certain amount of distress. Three years is a long time and Africa was far away. There would be no visits in between. But my mother did not allow even the tiniest bit of what she must have felt to disturb my joy. 'Oh, well done *you*!' she cried. 'It's wonderful news! And it's just where you wanted to go, isn't it!'

The whole family came down to London Docks to see me off on the boat. It was a tremendous thing in those days for a young man to be going off to Africa to work. The journey alone would take two weeks, sailing through the Bay of Biscay, past Gibraltar, across the Mediterranean, through the Suez Canal and the Red Sea, calling in at Aden and arriving finally at Mombasa. What a prospect that was!

I was off to the land of palm-trees and coconuts and coral reefs and lions and elephants and deadly snakes, and a white hunter who had lived ten years in Mwanza had told me that if a black mamba bit you, you died within the hour writhing in agony and foaming at the mouth. I couldn't wait.

Mama, 1936

Although I didn't know it at the time, I was sailing away for a good deal longer than three years because the Second World War was to come along in the middle of it all. But before that happened, I got my African adventure all right. I got the roasting heat and the crocodiles and the snakes and the long safaris up-country, selling Shell oil to the men who ran the diamond mines and the sisal plantations. I learned about an extraordinary machine called a decorticator (a name I have always loved) which shredded the big leathery sisal leaves into fibre. I learned to speak Swahili and to shake the scorpions out of my mosquito boots in the mornings. I learned what it was like to get malaria and to run a temperature of 105°F for three days, and when the rainy seasons came and the water poured down in solid sheets and flooded the little dirt roads, I learned how to spend nights in the back of a stifling station-wagon with all the windows closed against marauders from the jungle. Above all, I learned how to look after myself in a way that no young person can ever do by staying in civilization.

When the big war broke out in 1939, I was in Dar es Salaam, and from there I went up to Nairobi to join the RAF. Six months later, I was a fighter pilot flying Hurricanes all round the Mediterranean. I flew in the Western Desert of Libya, in Greece, in Palestine, in Syria, in Iraq and in Egypt. I shot down some German planes and I got shot down myself, crashing in a burst of flames and crawling out and getting rescued by brave soldiers crawling on their bellies over the sand. I spent six months in hospital in Alexandria, and when I came out, I flew again.

But all that is another story. It has nothing to do with childhood or school or Gobstoppers or dead mice or Boazers or summer holidays among the islands of Norway. It is a different tale altogether, and if all goes well, I may have a shot at telling it one of these days.

Love from
Boy

Going Solo

For
Sofie Magdalene Dahl
1885–1967

Contents

Haifa, June 1941

A life is made up of a great number of small incidents and a small number of great ones. An autobiography must therefore, unless it is to become tedious, be extremely selective, discarding all the inconsequential incidents in one's life and concentrating upon those that have remained vivid in the memory.

The first part of this book takes up my own personal story precisely where my earlier autobiography, which was called *Boy*, left off. I am away to East Africa on my first job, but because any job, even if it is in Africa, is not continuously enthralling, I have tried to be as selective as possible and have written only about those moments that I consider memorable.

In the second part of the book, which deals with the time I went flying with the RAF in the Second World War, there was no need to select or discard because every moment was, to me at any rate, totally enthralling.

R.D.

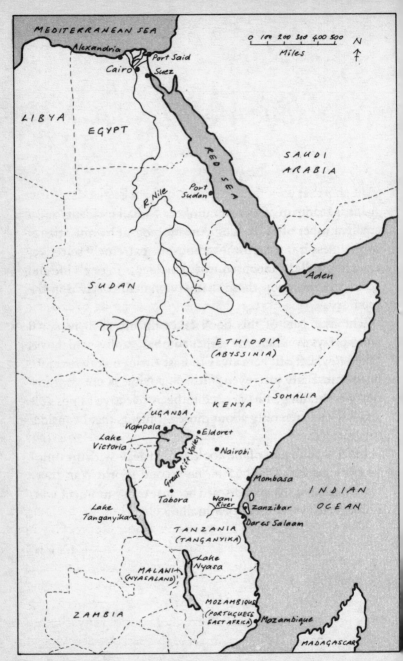

East Africa

The Voyage Out

The ship that was carrying me away from England to Africa in the autumn of 1938 was called the SS *Mantola*. She was an old paint-peeling tub of 9,000 tons with a single tall funnel and a vibrating engine that rattled the tea-cups in their saucers on the dining-room table.

The voyage from the Port of London to Mombasa would take two weeks and on the way we were going to call in at Marseilles, Malta, Port Said, Suez, Port Sudan and Aden. Nowadays you can fly to Mombasa in a few hours and you stop nowhere and nothing is fabulous any more, but in 1938 a journey like that was full of stepping-stones and East Africa was a long way from home, especially if your contract with the Shell Company said that you were to stay out there for three years at a stretch. I was twenty-two when I left. I would be twenty-five before I saw my family again.

What I still remember so clearly about that voyage is the extraordinary behaviour of my fellow passengers. I had never before encountered that peculiar Empire-building breed of Englishman who spends his whole life working in distant corners of British territory. Please do not forget that in the 1930s the British Empire was still very much the British Empire, and the men and women who kept it going were a race of people that most of you have never encountered and now you never will. I consider myself very lucky to have caught a glimpse of this rare species while it

Mrs. S. Dell.
Oakwood.
Oxley.

AIMEZ, PROTÉGE
PIGEON VOYAG
PADUEBOUR DU AYS

MARSEILLE
14
25
1928

A N O
E A

S.S. Mantola
Saturday morning

Dear Mum

We've had a marvellous journey.
Fairly calm in the Bay of Biscay (at least I
wasn't sick) Then as soon as we came
to the Spanish coast the sun came out,
and it has stayed out ever since. We
passed Gibraltar Wednesday morning —

BRITISH INDIA S. N. CO'S S.S. "MANTOLA" 9,065 TONS GROSS

still roamed the forests and foot-hills of the earth, for today it is totally extinct. More English than the English, more Scottish than the Scots, they were the craziest bunch of humans I shall ever meet. For one thing, they spoke a language of their own. If they worked in East Africa, their sentences were sprinkled with Swahili words, and if they lived in India then all manner of dialects were intermingled. As well as this, there was a whole vocabulary of much-used words that seemed to be universal among all these people. An evening drink, for example, was always a sundowner. A drink at any other time was a chota peg. One's wife was the memsahib. To have a look at something was to have a shufti. And from that one, interestingly enough, RAF/ Middle East slang for a reconnaissance plane in the last war was a shufti kite. Something of poor quality was shenzi. Supper was tiffin and so on and so forth. The Empire-builders' jargon would have filled a dictionary. All in all, it was rather wonderful for me, a conventional young lad from the suburbs, to be thrust suddenly into the middle of this pack of sinewy sunburnt gophers and their bright bony little wives, and what I liked best of all about them was their eccentricities.

It would seem that when the British live for years in a foul and sweaty climate among foreign people they maintain their sanity by allowing themselves to go slightly dotty. They cultivate bizarre habits that would never be tolerated back home, whereas in far-away Africa or in Ceylon or in India or in the Federated Malay States they could do as they liked. On the SS *Mantola* just about everybody had his or her own particular maggot in the brain, and for me it was like watching a kind of non-stop pantomime throughout the entire voyage. Let me tell you about two or three of these comedians.

I was sharing my cabin with the manager of a cotton mill in the Punjab called U.N. Savory (I could hardly believe those initials when I first saw them on his trunk) and I had the upper berth. From my pillow I could therefore look out of the port-hole clear across the lifeboat deck and over the wide blue ocean beyond. On our fourth morning at sea I happened to wake up very early. I lay in my bunk gazing idly through the port-hole and listening to the gentle snores of U.N. Savory, who lay immediately below me. Suddenly, the figure of a naked man, naked as a jungle ape, went swooshing past the port-hole and disappeared! He had come and gone in absolute silence and I lay there wondering whether perhaps I had seen a phantom or a vision or even a naked ghost.

A minute or two later the naked figure went by again!

This time I sat up sharply. I wanted to get a better look at this leafless phantom of the sunrise, so I crawled down to the foot of my bunk and stuck my head through the port-hole. The lifeboat deck was deserted. The Mediterranean was calm and milky blue and a brilliant yellow sun was just edging up over the horizon. The deck was so empty and silent that I began to wonder seriously whether I might not after all have seen a genuine apparition, the ghost perhaps of a passenger who had fallen overboard on an earlier voyage and who now spent his eternal life running above the waves and clambering back on to his lost ship.

All of a sudden, from my little spy-hole, I spotted a movement at the far end of the deck. Then a naked body materialized. But this was no ghost. It was all too solid flesh, and the man was moving swiftly over the deck between the lifeboats and the ventilators and making no sound at all as he came galloping towards me. He was short and stocky and slightly pot-bellied in his nakedness, with a big black moustache on his face, and when he was twenty yards away he caught sight of my silly head sticking out of the port-hole and he waved a hairy arm at me and called out, 'Come along, my boy! Come and join me in a canter! Blow some sea air into your lungs! Get yourself in trim! Shake off the flab!'

By his moustache alone I recognized him as Major Griffiths, a man who had told me only the night before at the dinner table how he had spent thirty-six years in India and was returning once again to Allahabad after the usual home leave.

I smiled weakly at the Major as he went prancing by, but I didn't pull back. I wanted to see him again. There was something rather admirable about the way he was galloping round and round the deck with no clothes on at all, something wonderfully innocent and unembarrassed and cheerful and friendly. And here was I, a bundle of youthful self-consciousness, gaping at him through the port-hole and disapproving quite strongly of what he was doing. But I was also envying him. I was actually jealous of his total don't-give-a-damn attitude, and I wished like mad that I myself had the guts to go out there and do the same thing. I wanted to be like him. I longed to be able to fling off my pyjamas and go scampering round the deck in the altogether and to hell with anyone who happened to see me. But not in a million years could I have done it. I waited for him to come round again.

Ah, there he was! I could see him far away down the deck, the gallant galloping Major who didn't give a fig for anybody, and I decided right then that I would say something very casual to him this time to show him I was 'one of the gang' and that I had not even noticed his nakedness.

But hang on a minute! . . . What was this? . . . There was someone with him! . . . There was another fellow scooting along beside him this time! . . . As naked as the Major he was, too! . . . What on earth was going on aboard this ship? . . . Did *all* the male passengers get up at dawn and go tearing round the deck with no clothes on? . . . Was this some Empire-building body-building ritual I didn't know about? . . . The two were coming closer now . . . My God, the second one looked like a woman! . . . It *was* a woman! . . . A naked woman as bare-bosomed as Venus de Milo . . . But there the resemblance ceased for I could see now that this scrawny white-skinned figure was none other than Mrs Major Griffiths herself . . . I froze in my port-hole and my eyes became riveted on this nude female scarecrow galloping ever so proudly alongside her bare-skinned spouse, her elbows bent and her head held high, as much as to say, 'Aren't we a jolly fine couple, the two of us, and isn't he a fine figure of a man, my husband the Major?'

'Come along there!' the Major called out to me. 'If the little memsahib can do it, so can you! Fifty times round the deck is only four miles!'

'Lovely morning,' I murmured as they went galloping by. 'Beautiful day.'

A couple of hours later, I was sitting opposite the Major and his little memsahib at breakfast in the dining-room, and the knowledge that not long ago I had seen that same little memsahib with not a stitch on her made my spine creep. I kept my head down and pretended neither of them were there.

'Ha!' the Major cried suddenly. 'Aren't you the young fellow who had his head sticking through the port-hole this morning?'

'Who, me?' I murmured, keeping my nose in the cornflakes.

'Yes, you!' the Major cried, triumphant. 'I never forget a face!'

'I . . . I was just getting a breath of air,' I mumbled.

'You were getting a darn sight more than that!' the Major cried out, grinning. 'You were getting an eyeful of the memsahib, that's what you were doing!'

The whole of our table of eight people suddenly became silent and looked in my direction. I felt my cheeks beginning to boil.

'I can't say I blame you,' the Major went on, giving his wife an enormous wink. It was his turn to be proud and gallant now. 'In fact, I don't blame you at all. Would *you* blame him?' he asked, addressing the rest of the table. 'After all, we're only young once. And, as the poet says . . .' he paused, giving the dreadful wife another colossal wink . . . 'a thing of beauty is a joy for ever.'

'Oh, do shut up, Bonzo,' the wife said, loving it.

'Back in Allahabad,' the Major said, looking at *me* now, 'I make a point of playing half-a-dozen chukkas every morning before breakfast. Can't do that on board ship, you know. So I have to get my exercise in other ways.'

I sat there wondering how one played this game of chuckers. 'Why can't you do it?' I said, desperate to change the subject.

'Why can't I do what?' the Major said.

'Play chuckers on the ship?' I said.

The Major was one of those men who chewed his porridge. He stared at me with pale-grey glassy eyes, chewing slowly. 'I hope you're not trying to tell me that you have never played polo in your life,' he said.

'Polo,' I said. 'Ah yes, of course, polo. At school we used to play it on bicycles with hockey sticks.'

The Major's stare switched suddenly to a fierce glare and he stopped chewing. He glared at me with such contempt and horror, and his face went so crimson, I thought he might be going to have a seizure.

From then on, neither the Major nor his wife would have anything to do with me. They changed their table in the dining-room and they cut me dead whenever we met on deck. I had been found guilty of a great and unforgivable crime. I had jeered, or so they thought, at the game of polo, the sacred sport of Anglo-Indians and royalty. Only a bounder would do that.

Then there was the elderly Miss Trefusis, who quite often sat at the same dining-room table as me. Miss Trefusis was all bones and grey skin, and when she walked her body was bent forward in a long curve like a boomerang. She told me she owned a small coffee farm in the highlands of Kenya and that she had known Baroness Blixen very well. I myself had read and loved both *Out of Africa* and *Seven Gothic Tales*, and I listened enthralled to everything Miss Trefusis told me about that fine writer who called herself Isak Dinesen.

'She was dotty, of course,' Miss Trefusis said. 'Like all of us who live out there, she went completely dotty in the end.'

'*You* aren't dotty,' I said.

'Oh yes, I am,' she said firmly and very seriously. 'Everyone on this ship is as dotty as a dumpling. *You* don't notice it because you're young. Young people are not watchful. They only look at themselves.'

'I saw Major Griffiths and his wife running round the deck naked the other morning,' I said.

'You call that dotty?' Miss Trefusis said with a snort. 'That's *normal*.'

'*I* didn't think so.'

'You've got a few shocks coming to you, young man, before you're very much older, you mark my words,' she said. 'People go quite barmy when they live too long in Africa. That's where you're off to, isn't it?'

'Yes,' I said.

'You'll go barmy for sure,' she said, 'like the rest of us.'

She was eating an orange at the time and I noticed suddenly that she was not eating it in the normal way. In the first place she had speared it from the fruit bowl with her fork instead of taking it in her fingers. And now, with knife and fork, she was making a series of neat incisions in the skin all around the orange. Then, very delicately, using the points of her knife and fork, she peeled the skin away in eight separate pieces, leaving the bare fruit beautifully exposed. Still using knife and fork, she separated the juicy segments and began to eat them slowly, one by one, with her fork.

'Do you always eat an orange like that?' I said.

'Of course.'

'May I ask why?'

'I never touch anything I eat with my fingers,' she said.

'Good Lord, don't you really?'

'Never. I haven't since I was twenty-two.'

'Is there a reason for that?' I asked her.

'Of course there's a reason. Fingers are filthy.'

'But you wash your hands.'

'I don't *sterilize* them,' Miss Trefusis said. 'Nor do you. They're full of bugs. Disgusting dirty things, fingers. Just think what you do with them!'

I sat there going through the things I did with my fingers.

'It doesn't bear thinking about, does it?' Miss Trefusis said. 'Fingers are just implements. They are the gardening implements of the body, the shovels and the forks. You push them into everything.'

'We seem to survive,' I said.

'Not for long you won't,' she said darkly.

I watched her eating her orange, spearing the little boats one after the other with her fork. I could have told her that the fork wasn't sterilized either, but I kept quiet.

'Toes are even worse,' she said suddenly.

'I beg your pardon?'

'They're the worst of all,' she said.

'What's wrong with toes?'

'They are the nastiest part of the human body!' she announced vehemently.

'Worse than fingers?'

'There's no comparison,' she snapped. 'Fingers are foul and filthy, but *toes*! *Toes* are reptilian and viperish! I don't wish to talk about them!'

I was getting a bit confused. 'But one doesn't eat with one's toes,' I said.

'I never said you did,' Miss Trefusis snapped.

'Then what's so awful about them?' I persisted.

'Uck!' she said. 'They are like little worms sticking out of your feet. I hate them, I hate them! I can't bear to look at them!'

'Then how do you cut your toenails?'

'I don't,' she said. 'My boy does it for me.'

I wondered why she was 'Miss' if she'd been married and had a boy of her own. Perhaps he was illegitimate.

'How old is your son?' I asked, treading carefully.

'No, no, no!' she cried. 'Don't you know *anything*? A

"boy" is one's native servant. Didn't you learn that when you read Isak Dinesen?'

'Ah yes, of course,' I said, remembering.

Absentmindedly I took an orange myself and was about to start peeling it.

'Don't,' Miss Trefusis said, shuddering. 'You'll catch something if you do that. Use your knife and fork. Go on. Try it.'

I tried it. It was rather fun. There was something satisfying about cutting the skin to just the right depth and then peeling away the segments.

'There you are,' she said. 'Well done.'

'Do you employ a lot of "boys" on your coffee farm?' I asked her.

'About fifty,' she said.

'Do they go barefoot?'

'Mine don't,' she said. 'No one works for me without shoes on. It costs me a fortune, but it's worth it.'

I liked Miss Trefusis. She was impatient, intelligent, generous and interesting. I felt she would come to my rescue at any time, whereas Major Griffiths was vapid, vulgar, arrogant and unkind, the sort of man who'd leave you to the crocodiles. He might even push you in. Both of them, of course, were completely dotty. Everyone on the ship was dotty, but none, as it turned out, was quite as dotty as my cabin companion, U.N. Savory.

The first sign of *his* dottiness was revealed to me one evening as our ship was running between Malta and Port Said. It had been a stifling hot afternoon and I was having a brief rest on my upper berth before dressing for dinner.

Dressing? Oh yes, indeed. We all dressed for dinner every single evening on board that ship. The male species of the Empire-builder, whether he is camping in the jungle or is at sea in a rowing-boat, *always* dresses for dinner, and by that I mean white shirt, black tie, dinner-jacket, black trousers and black patent-leather shoes, the full regalia, and to hell with the climate.

I lay still on my bunk with my eyes half open. Below me, U. N. Savory was getting dressed. There wasn't room in the cabin for two of us to change our clothes simultaneously, so we took it in turns to go first. It was his turn to dress first tonight. He had tied his bow-tie and now he was putting on his black dinner-jacket. I was watching him rather dreamily through half-closed eyes, and I saw him reaching into his sponge-bag and take out a small carton. He stationed himself in front of the washbasin mirror, took the lid off the carton and dipped his fingers into it. The fingers came out with a pinch of white powder or crystals, and this stuff he proceeded to sprinkle very carefully over the shoulders of his dinner-jacket. Then he replaced the lid on the carton and put it back in the sponge-bag.

Suddenly I was fully alert. What on earth was the man up to? I didn't want him to know I'd seen, so I closed my eyes and pretended to be asleep. This is a rum business, I thought. Why in the world would U.N. Savory want to sprinkle white stuff on to the shoulders of his dinner-jacket? And what *was* it, anyway? Could it be some subtle perfume or a magic aphrodisiac? I waited until he had left the cabin, then, feeling only slightly guilty, I hopped down from my bunk and opened his sponge-bag. EPSOM SALTS, it said on the little carton! And Epsom salts it was! Now what good could Epsom salts possibly do him sprinkled on his shoulders? I had always thought of him as a queer fish, a man with secrets, though I hadn't discovered what they were. Under his bunk he kept a tin trunk and a black leather case. There was nothing odd about the tin trunk, but the case puzzled me. It was roughly the size of a violin case but the lid didn't bulge as the lid of a violin case does, and it wasn't tapered. It was simply a three-foot-long rectangular leather box with two very strong brass locks on it.

'Do you play the violin?' I had once said to him.

'Don't be daft,' he had answered. 'I don't even play the gramophone.'

Perhaps it contained a sawn-off shotgun then, I told myself. It was about the right size.

I put the carton of Epsom salts back in his sponge-bag, then I took a shower, dressed and went upstairs to have a drink before dinner. There was one stool vacant at the bar so I sat down and ordered a glass of beer. There were eight sinewy sunburnt gophers including U.N. Savory sitting on high stools at the bar. The stools were screwed to the floor. The bar was semi-circular so that everyone could talk across to everyone else. U.N. Savory was sitting about five places away from me. He was drinking a gimlet, which was the Empire-builder's name for a gin with lime juice in it. I sat there listening to the small talk about pig-sticking and polo and how curry will cure constipation. I felt a total outsider. There was nothing I could contribute to the conversation so I stopped listening and concentrated on trying to solve the riddle of the Epsom salts. I glanced at U.N. Savory. From where I sat, I could actually see the tiny white crystals on his shoulders.

Then a funny thing happened.

U.N. Savory suddenly began brushing the Epsom salts off one of his shoulders with his hand. He did it ostentatiously, slapping the shoulder quite hard and saying at the same time in a rather loud voice, 'Ruddy dandruff! I'm fed up with it! Do any of you fellers know a good cure?'

'Try coconut oil,' one said.

'Bay rum and cantharides,' another said.

A tea-planter from Assam called Unsworth said, 'Take my word for it, old man, you've got to stimulate the circulation in the scalp. And the way to do that is to dunk your hair in ice-cold water every morning and keep it there for five minutes. Then dry vigorously. You've got a fine head of hair at the moment, but you'll be as bald as a coot in no time if you don't cure that dandruff. You do as I say, old man.'

U.N. Savory did indeed have a fine head of black hair, so why in the world should he have wanted to pretend he had dandruff when he hadn't?

'Thanks a lot, old man,' U. N. Savory said. 'I'll give it a go. See if it works.'

'It'll work,' Unsworth told him. 'My grandmother cured her dandruff that way.'

'Your *grandmother*?' someone said. 'Did *she* have dandruff?'

'When she combed her hair', Unsworth said, 'it looked like it was snowing.'

For the hundredth time, I told myself that they were all totally and incurably dotty, every one of them, but I was beginning to think now that U.N. Savory might beat them all to it. I sat there staring into my beer and trying to figure out why he should go around trying to kid everyone he had dandruff. Three days later I had the answer.

It was early evening. We were moving slowly through the Suez Canal and it was hotter than ever. It was my turn to dress first for dinner. While I showered and put on my clothes, U.N. Savory lay on his bunk staring into space. 'It's all yours,' I said at last as I opened the door and went out. 'See you upstairs.'

As usual, I seated myself at the bar and began sipping a beer. By gosh, it was hot. The big slowly-revolving fan in the ceiling seemed to be blowing *steam* out of its blades. Sweat trickled down my neck and under my stiff butterfly collar. I could feel the starch in the collar going soggy around the back. The sinewy sunburnt ones around me didn't seem to notice the heat. I decided to go out on deck and smoke a pipe before dinner. It would be cooler there. I

Suez Canal, near Ismailia

felt for my pipe. Damnation, I had left it behind. I stood up and made my way downstairs to the cabin and opened the door. There was a strange man sitting in shirtsleeves on U.N. Savory's bunk and as I stepped inside, the man gave a queer little yelp and jumped to his feet as though a cracker had gone off in the seat of his pants.

The stranger was totally bald and that is why it took me a second or two to realize that he was in fact none other than U.N. Savory himself. It is extraordinary how hair on the head or the lack of it will completely change a person's appearance. U.N. Savory looked like a different man. To start with, he looked fifteen years older, and in some subtle way he seemed also to have diminished, grown much shorter and smaller. As I said, he was almost totally bald, and the dome of his head was as pink and shiny as a ripe peach. He was standing up now and holding in his two hands the wig he had been about to put on as I walked in. 'You had no right to come back!' he shouted. 'You said you'd finished!' Little sparks of fury were flashing in his eyes.

'I'm . . . I'm most awfully sorry,' I stammered. 'I forgot my pipe.'

He stood there glaring at me with that dark malevolent glint in his eye and I could see little droplets of perspiration oozing out of the pores on his bald head. I felt very bad. I didn't know what to say next. 'Just let me get my pipe and I'll clear out,' I mumbled.

'Oh no you don't!' he shouted. 'You've seen it now and you're not leaving this room until you've made me a promise! You've got to promise me you won't tell a soul! Promise me that!'

Behind him I could see that curious black leather 'violin case' lying open on his bunk, and in it, nestling alongside each other like three large black hairy hedgehogs, lay three more wigs.

'There's nothing wrong with being bald,' I said.

'I didn't ask for your opinion,' he shouted. He was still very angry. 'I just want your promise.'

'I won't tell anyone,' I said. 'I give you my word.'

'And you'd better keep it,' he said.

I reached out and took hold of the pipe that was lying on my bunk. Then I began rummaging round in various places for my tobacco pouch. U.N. Savory sat down on the lower bunk. 'I suppose you think I'm crazy,' he said. Suddenly all the bark had gone out of his voice.

I said nothing. I could think of nothing to say.

'You do, don't you?' he said. 'You think I'm crazy.'

'Not at all,' I answered. 'A man can do as he likes.'

'I'll bet you think it's just vanity,' he said. 'But it's not vanity. It's nothing to do with vanity.'

'It's OK,' I said. 'Really it is.'

'It's business,' he said. 'I do it purely for business reasons. I work in Amritsar, in the Punjab. That is the homeland of the Sikhs. To a Sikh, hair is a sort of religion. A Sikh never cuts his hair. He either rolls it up on the top of his head or in a turban. A Sikh doesn't respect a bald man.'

'In that case I think it's very clever of you to wear a wig,' I said. I had to live in this cabin with U.N. Savory for several days yet and I didn't want a row. 'It's quite brilliant,' I added.

'Do you honestly think so?' he said, melting.

'It's a stroke of genius.'

'I go to a lot of trouble to convince all those Sikh wallahs it's my own hair,' he went on.

'You mean the dandruff bit?'

'You saw it, then?'

'Of course I saw it. It was brilliant.'

'It's just *one* of my little ruses,' he said. He was getting just a trifle smug now. 'No one's going to suspect me of wearing a wig if I've got dandruff, are they?'

'Certainly not. It's quite brilliant. But why bother doing it here? There aren't any Sikhs on this ship.'

'You never know,' he said darkly. 'You never can tell who might be lurking around the corner.'

The man was as potty as a pilchard.

'I see you have more than one,' I said, pointing to the black leather case.

'One's no good,' he said, 'not if you're going to do it properly like me. I always carry four, and they're all slightly different. You are forgetting that hair *grows*, old man, aren't you? Each one of these is longer than the other. I put on a longer one every week.'

'What happens after you've worn the longest one and you can't go any further?' I asked.

'Ah,' he said. 'That's the clincher.'

'I don't quite follow you.'

'I simply say, "Does anyone know of a good barber round here?" And the next day I start all over again with the shortest one.'

'But you said Sikhs didn't approve of cutting hair.'

'I only do that with Europeans,' he said.

I stared at him. The man was stark raving barmy. I felt I would go barmy myself if I went on talking to him much longer. I edged towards the door. 'I think you're amazing,' I said. 'You're quite brilliant. And don't worry about a thing. My lips are sealed.'

'Thanks old man,' U.N. Savory said. 'Good lad.'

I flew out of the cabin and shut the door.

And that is the story of U.N. Savory.

You don't believe it?

Listen, I could hardly believe it myself as I staggered upstairs to the bar.

I kept my promise though. I told no one. Today it no longer matters. The man was at least thirty years older than me, so by now his soul is at rest and his wigs are probably being used by his nephews and nieces for playing charades.

SS *Mantola*
4 October 1938

Dear Mama,

We're now in the Red Sea, and it is *hot*. The wind is behind us and going at exactly the same speed as the boat so there is not a breath of air on board. Three times they have turned the ship round against the wind to get some air into the cabins and into the engine room. Fans merely blow hot air into your face.

The deck is strewn with a lot of limp wet things for all the world like a lot of wet towels steaming over the kitchen boiler. They just smoke cigarettes & shout, 'Boy – another iced lager.'

I don't feel the heat much – probably because I'm thin. In fact as soon as I've finished this letter I'm going off to have a vigorous game of deck tennis with another thin man – a government vet called Hammond. We play with our shirts off, throwing the coit as hard as we can – & when we have to stop for fear of drowning in our own sweat we just jump into the swimming bath.

Dar es Salaam

The temperature in the shade was around 120°F on board the SS *Mantola* as she crept southwards down the Red Sea towards Port Sudan. The breeze was behind us and it blew at exactly the same speed as the ship. There was, therefore, no movement of air at all on board. Three times during the first day they turned the ship around and sailed against the wind to blow some air through the port-holes and over the decks. This made little difference and even the sinewy sunburnt gophers and their tough bony little wives became silent and exhausted. Like me, they sprawled in deck-chairs under the awning, gasping for breath while the sweat ran down their faces and necks and arms and dripped from their elbows on to the wooden deck. It was even too hot to read.

During the second day in the Red Sea, the *Mantola* passed very close to an Italian ship which, like us, was going south. She wasn't more than 200 yards away from us and her decks were crowded with women! There must have been several thousand of them all over the ship and not a man in sight. I couldn't believe my eyes.

'What's going on?' I asked one of the ship's officers, who was standing near me on the rail. 'Why all the girls?'

'They're for the Italian soldiers,' he said.

'What Italian soldiers?'

'The ones in Abyssinia,' he said. 'Mussolini is trying to

conquer Abyssinia and he's got a hundred thousand troops in there. Now they are shipping out Italian girls to keep the soldiers happy.'

'You're pulling my leg.'

'They're going out in boatloads,' the officer said. 'One girl for every soldier in the ranks, two for each Colonel and three for a General.'

'Be serious,' I said.

'They really *are* for the soldiers,' he said. 'It is such a rotten pointless war and the soldiers all hate it and they are fed up with massacring the wretched Abyssinians. So Mussolini is sending out thousands of girls to boost their morale.'

I waved to the girls on the other ship and about 2,000 of

Crossing The Equator. Me being ducked.

them waved back at me. They seemed very cheerful. I wondered how long they would be feeling that way.

At last the *Mantola* reached Mombasa, and there I was met by a man from the Shell Company who told me I was to proceed at once down the coast to Dar es Salaam, in Tanganyika (now Tanzania). 'It will take you a day and a night to get there,' he said, 'and you travel on a little coastal vessel called the *Dumra*. Here's your ticket.'

I transferred to the *Dumra* and it sailed the same day. That evening we called in at Zanzibar where the air was filled with the amazing spicy-sweet scent of cloves, and I stood by the rail gazing at the old Arab town and thinking what a lucky young fellow I was to be seeing all these marvellous places free of charge and with a good job at the end of it all. We left Zanzibar at midnight and I went to bed in my tiny cabin knowing that tomorrow would be journey's end.

When I woke up the next morning the ship's engines had stopped. I jumped out of my bunk and peered through the port-hole. This was my first glimpse of Dar es Salaam and I have never forgotten it. We were anchored out in the middle of a vast rippling blue-black lagoon and all around the rim of the lagoon there were pale-yellow sandy beaches, almost white, and breakers were running up on to the sand, and coconut palms with their little green leafy hats were growing on the beaches, and there were casuarina trees, immensely tall and breathtakingly beautiful with their delicate grey-green foliage. And then behind the casuarinas was what seemed to me like a jungle, a great tangle of tremendous dark-green trees that were full of shadows and almost certainly teeming, so I told myself, with rhinos and lions and all manner of vicious beasts. Over to one side lay the tiny town of Dar es Salaam, the houses white and yellow and pink, and among the houses I could see a narrow church steeple and a domed mosque and along the waterfront there was a line of acacia trees splashed with scarlet flowers. A fleet of canoes was rowing out to take us ashore and the black-skinned rowers were chanting weird songs in time with their rowing.

Dar-es-Salaam Harbour

The whole of that amazing tropical scene through the port-hole has been photographed on my mind ever since. To me it was all wonderful, beautiful and exciting. And so it remained for the rest of my time in Tanganyika. I loved it all. There were no furled umbrellas, no bowler hats, no sombre grey suits and I never once had to get on a train or a bus.

Only three young Englishmen ran the Shell Company in the whole of that vast territory, and I was the youngest and the junior. When we were not 'on the road', we lived in the splendid large Shell Company house perched on the top of

the cliffs outside Dar es Salaam, and we were treated like
princes. Our domestic staff consisted of a male native cook
affectionately called Piggy because the Swahili for cook is
mpishi. There was a shamba-boy or gardener called Salimu.

Shell House, Dar-es-Salaam

and a personal 'boy' for each of us. Your boy was really a kind of valet and jack of all trades. He was expert at sewing and mending and washing and ironing and polishing and making sure there weren't scorpions in your mosquito boots before you put them on, and he became your friend. He looked after nobody else but you and there was nothing he did not know about your life and your habits. In return, you looked after him and his wives (never less than two) and his children who lived in their own quarters at the back of the house.

My boy was called Mdisho. He was a Mwanumwezi tribesman, which meant a lot out there because the Mwanumwezi was the only tribe who had ever defeated the gigantic Masai in battle. Mdisho was tall and graceful and soft-spoken, and his loyalty to me, his young white English master, was absolute. I hope, and I believe, that I was equally loyal to him.

The first thing you had to do when you came to work in Dar es Salaam was to learn Swahili, otherwise you could not communicate either with your own boy or with any other native of the country because none of them spoke a word of English. In those benighted days of Empire it was considered impertinent for a black man to understand English, let alone to speak it. The result was that none of them made any effort to learn our language, so we had to learn theirs instead. Swahili is a relatively simple language, and with the help of a Swahili–English dictionary and a grammar book, plus some hard work in the evenings, you could become pretty fluent in a couple of months. Then you took an exam and if you passed it, the Shell Company gave you a bonus of a hundred pounds, which was a lot of money in those days when a case of whisky cost only twelve pounds.

. ., *v.* lazimu.

Conceal, *v.* ncha, setiri.
Concubine, *s.*, suria, *plur.* ma-.
be Condemned, *v.* (*by a judge*)
  pasishwa hatia.
Condition, *s.* hali, (*necessary re-
  quirement*) kanuni.
Conduct, *s.* mwenendo, matendo,
  (*good conduct*) adili.
Conduct, *v.* peleka, leta, fikisha.
Confess, *v.* ungama.
Confidence, *s.* matumaini.
become Confident, *v.* tumaini.
come Confused, *v.* (*of persons*)
  (*of things*) chafuka.

ongea.
Convert, *s.* mwongofu.
Convert, *v.* ongoa, geuza.
be Converted, *v.* ongoka, geuka.
Cook, *v.* pika.
Cook, *s.* mpishi.
Cooked rice, *s.* wali.
Cooking-place, *s.* jiko.
Cooking-pot, *s.* (*earthenware*) chu
  ngu, mkungu, (*metal*) sufuria.
Cooking-stones, *s.* (*to rest a pot
  on*) mafya.
Cool, *a.* -a baridi.
Cool   ) poza.

my Swahili dictionary

Sometimes I would have to go on safari upcountry and
Mdisho always came with me. We would take the Shell
station-wagon and be gone for a month, driving all over
Tanganyika on dirt roads that were covered with millions
of tiny close-together ruts. Driving over those ruts in a
station-wagon felt as though you were riding on top of a
gigantic vibrator. We would drive far west to the edge of
Lake Tanganyika in central Africa and on down south to the
borders of Nyasaland, and after that we would head east
towards Mozambique, and the purpose of these trips was to
visit our Shell customers. These customers ran diamond
mines and gold mines and sisal plantations and cotton
plantations and goodness knows what else besides, and my
job was to keep their machinery supplied with the proper
grades of lubricating oil and fuel oil. Not a great deal of
intelligence or imagination was required, but by gum you
needed to be fit and tough.

I loved that life. We saw giraffe standing unafraid right
beside the road nibbling the tops of the trees. We saw plenty
of elephant and hippo and zebra and antelope and very
occasionally a pride of lions. The only creatures I was
frightened of were the snakes. We used often to see a big one
gliding across the dirt road ahead of the car, and the golden

rule was never to accelerate and try to run it over, especially if the roof of the car was open, as ours often was. If you hit a snake at speed, the front wheel can flip it up into the air and there is a danger of it landing in your lap. I can think of nothing worse than that.

The really bad snake in Tanganyika is the black mamba. It is the only one that has no fear of man and will deliberately attack him on sight. If it bites you, you are a gonner.

One morning I was shaving myself in the bathroom of our Dar es Salaam house, and as I lathered my face I was absent-mindedly gazing out of the window into the garden. I was watching Salimu, our shamba-boy, as he slowly and methodically raked the gravel on the front drive. Then I saw the snake. It was six feet long and thick as my arm and quite black. It was a mamba all right and there was no doubt that it had seen Salimu and was gliding fast over the gravel straight towards him.

I flung myself toward the open window and yelled in Swahili, 'Salimu! Salimu! Angalia nyoka kubwa! Nyuma wewe! Upesi upesi!', in other words, 'Salimu! Salimu! Beware huge snake! Behind you! Quickly quickly!'

The mamba was moving over the gravel at the speed of a running man and when Salimu turned and saw it, it could not have been more than fifteen paces away from him. There was nothing more I could do. There was not much Salimu could do either. He knew it was useless to run because a mamba at full speed could travel as fast as a galloping horse. And he certainly knew it was a mamba. Every native in Tanganyika knew what a mamba looked like and what to expect from it. It would reach him in another five seconds. I leant out of the window and held my breath. Salimu swung round and faced the snake. I saw him go into a crouch. He crouched very low with one leg behind the other like a runner about to start a hundred yard sprint, and he was holding the long rake out in front of him. He raised it, but no higher than his shoulder, and he stood there for those long four or five seconds absolutely motionless, watching the great black deadly snake as it glided so quickly over the gravel towards him. Its small triangular snake's head was raised up in the air, and I could hear the soft rustling of the gravel as the body slid over the loose stones. I have the whole nightmarish picture of that scene still before my eyes – the morning sunshine on the garden, the massive baobab tree in the background, Salimu in his old khaki shorts and shirt and bare feet standing brave and absolutely still with the upraised rake in his hands, and to one side the long black snake gliding over the gravel straight towards him with its small poisonous head held high and ready to strike.

Salimu waited. He never moved or made a sound during the time it took the snake to reach him. He waited until the very last moment when the mamba was not more than five feet away and then *wham*! Salimu struck first. He brought the metal prongs of the rake down hard right on to the middle of the mamba's back and he held the rake there with all his weight, leaning forward now and jumping up and down to put more weight on the fork in an effort to pin the snake to the ground. I saw the blood spurt where the prongs had gone right into the snake's body and then I rushed downstairs absolutely naked, grabbing a golf club as I went through the hall, and outside on the drive Salimu was still there pressing with both hands on the rake and the great snake was writhing and twisting and throwing itself about, and I shouted to Salimu in Swahili, 'What shall I do?'

'It is all right now, bwana!' he shouted back. 'I have

broken its back and it cannot travel forward any more! Stand away, bwana! Stand well away and leave it to me!'

Salimu lifted the rake and jumped away and the snake went on writhing and twisting but it was quite unable to travel in any direction. The boy went forward and hit it accurately and very hard on the head with the metal end of the rake and suddenly the snake stopped moving. Salimu let out a great sigh and passed a hand over his forehead. Then he looked at me and smiled.

'Asanti, bwana,' he said, 'asanti sana,' which simply means, 'Thank you, bwana. Thank you very much.'

It isn't often one gets the chance to save a person's life. It gave me a good feeling for the rest of the day, and from then on, every time I saw Salimu, the good feeling would come back to me.

Dar es Salaam
19 March 1939

Dear Mama,
 If a war breaks out you've jolly well got to go to Tenby otherwise you'll be bombed. Don't forget, you've got to go if war breaks out . . .

Simba

About a month after the black mamba incident, I set out on a safari upcountry in the old Shell station-wagon with Mdisho and our first stop was the small town of Bagomoyo. I mention this only because the name of the Indian trader I had to go and see in Bagomoyo was so wonderful I have never been able to get it out of my mind. He was a tiny little man with an immense low-slung protuberant belly of the kind that women have when they are eight and a half months pregnant, and he carried this great ball in front of him very proudly, as if it were a special medal or a coat of arms. He called himself Mister Shanker-bai Ganderbai, and across the top of his business notepaper was printed in red capital letters the full title he had conferred upon himself, MISTER SHANKERBAI GANDERBAI OF BAGOMOYO, SELLER OF DECORTICATORS. A decorticator is a huge clanking piece of machinery that converts the leaves of the sisal plant into fibres for making rope, and if you wanted to buy one, the man to go and see was Mister Shankerbai Ganderbai of Bagomoyo.

After three more days of dusty travelling and visiting customers, Mdisho and I came to the town of Tabora. Tabora is some 450 miles inland from Dar es Salaam, and in 1939 it was not much of a town, just a scattering of houses and a few streets where the Indian traders had their shops. But because by Tanganyikan standards it was a sizeable place, it was honoured by the presence of a British District Officer.

The District Officers in Tanganyika were a breed I admired. Admittedly they were sunburnt and sinewy, but they were not gophers. They were all university graduates with good degrees, and in their lonely outposts they had to be all things to all men. They were the judges whose decisions settled both tribal and personal disputes. They were the advisers to tribal chiefs. They were often the givers of medicines and the saviours of the sick. They administered their own vast districts by keeping law and order under the most difficult circumstances. And wherever there was a District Officer, the Shell man on safari was welcome to stay the night at his house.

The DO in Tabora was called Robert Sanford, a man in his early thirties who had a wife and three very small children, a boy of six, a girl of four and a baby.

That evening I was sitting on the veranda having a sundowner with Robert Sanford and his wife Mary, while two of the children were playing out on the grass in front of the house under the watchful eye of their black nurse. The heat of the day was becoming less intense as the sun went down, and the first whisky and soda was tasting good.

'So what's been going on in Dar?' Robert Sanford asked me. 'Anything exciting?'

I told him about the black mamba and Salimu. When I had finished, Mary Sanford said, 'That's the one thing I'm always frightened of in this country, those beastly snakes.'

'Damn lucky you happened to see it behind him,' Robert Sanford said. 'He was certain to have been killed.'

'We had a spitting cobra near our back door not long ago,' Mary Sanford said. 'Robert shot it.'

The Sanford house was on a hill outside the town. It was a

white wooden two-storey building with a roof of green tiles. The eaves of the house projected far out beyond the walls to provide extra shade, and this gave the building a sort of Japanese pagoda appearance. The surrounding countryside was to me a very pleasant sight. It was a vast brown plain with many quite large knolls and hummocks dotted all over it, and although the plain itself was mostly burnt-up scrubland, the hills were covered with all sorts of huge jungle trees, and their dense foliage made little emerald-green dots all over the plain. On the burnt-up plain itself there grew nothing but those bare spiky thorn trees that you find all over East Africa, and there were about six huge vultures sitting quite motionless on every thorn tree in sight. The vultures were brown with curved orange beaks and orange feet, and they spent their whole lives sitting and watching and waiting for some animal to die so they could pick its bones.

'Do you like this sort of life?' I said to Robert Sanford.

'I love the freedom,' he said. 'I administer about two thousand square miles of territory and I can go where I want and do more or less exactly as I please. That part of it is marvellous. But I do miss the company of other white men. There aren't many even moderately intelligent Europeans in the town.'

We sat there watching the sun go down behind the flat brown plain that was covered with thorn trees, and we could see the sinister vultures waiting like feathered undertakers for death to come along and give them something to work on.

'Keep the children a bit closer to the house!' Mary Sanford called out to the nurse. 'Bring them closer, please!'

Robert Sanford said, 'My mother sent me out Beethoven's Third Symphony from England last week.

Government House, Dar-es-Salaam

Haircut in
Dar-es-Salaam

Sundowner at Shell House

HMV, two records, four sides in all, Toscanini conducting. I'm using a thorn needle instead of a steel one so as not to wear out the grooves. It seems to work.'

'Don't you find the records warp a lot out here?' I asked.

'I keep them lying flat with a pile of books on top of them,' he said. 'What I'm terrified of is dropping one and breaking it.'

The sun had gone down now and a lovely soft light was spreading over the landscape. I could see a group of zebra grazing among the thorn trees about half a mile away. Robert Sanford was also watching the zebras.

'I keep wondering', he said, 'if it wouldn't be possible to catch a young zebra and break it in for riding, just like a horse. After all, they are only wild horses with stripes on.'

'Has anyone ever tried?' I asked.

'Not that I know,' he said. 'Mary's a good rider. What do you think, darling? How would you like to have a private zebra to ride on?'

'It might be fun,' she said. Even though she had a bit of a jaw, she was a handsome woman. I didn't mind the jaw. The shape of it gave her the look of a fighter.

'Perhaps we could cross one with a horse,' Robert Sanford said, 'and call it a zorse.'

'Or a hebra,' Mary Sanford said.

'Right,' her husband said, smiling.

'Shall we try it?' Mary Sanford said. 'It would be rather splendid to have a baby zorse or hebra. Oh darling, *shall* we try it?'

'The children could ride it,' he said. 'A black zorse with white stripes all over it.'

'Please can we play your Beethoven after supper?' I said.

'Absolutely,' Robert Sanford said. 'I'll put the gramophone out here on the veranda and then those tremendous chords can go booming out through the night over the plain. It's terrific. The only trouble is I have to wind the thing up twice for each side.'

'I'll wind it for you,' I said.

Suddenly, the voice of a man yelling in Swahili exploded into the quiet of the evening. It was my boy, Mdisho. 'Bwana! Bwana! Bwana!' he was yelling from somewhere behind the house. 'Simba, bwana! Simba! Simba!'

Simba is Swahili for lion. All three of us leapt to our feet, and the next moment Mdisho came tearing round the corner of the house yelling at us in Swahili, 'Come quick, bwana! Come quick! Come quick! A huge lion is eating the wife of the cook!'

That sounds pretty funny when you put it on paper back here in England, but to us, standing on a veranda in the middle of East Africa, it was not funny at all.

Robert Sanford flew into the house and came out again in five seconds flat holding a powerful rifle and ramming a cartridge into the breech. 'Get those children indoors!' he shouted to his wife as he ran down off the veranda with me behind him.

Mdisho was dancing about and pointing towards the back of the house and yelling in Swahili, 'The lion has taken the wife of the cook and the lion is eating her and the cook is chasing the lion and trying to save his wife!'

The servants lived in a series of low whitewashed out-buildings at the back of the house, and as we came running round the corner we saw four or five house-boys leaping about and pointing and shrieking, 'Simba! Simba! Simba!' The boys were all clothed in spotless white cotton robes that looked like long night-shirts, and each had a fine scarlet tarboosh on his head. The tarboosh is a sort of top-hat without a brim, and there is often a black tassel on it. The women had come out of their huts as well and were standing in a separate group, silent, immobile and staring.

'Where is it?' Robert Sanford shouted, but he had no need to ask, for we very quickly spotted the massive sandy-coloured lion not more than eighty or ninety yards off and trotting away from the house. He had a fine bushy collar of fur around his neck, and in his jaws he was holding the wife of the cook. The lion had the woman by the waist so that her head and arms hung down on one side and her legs on the other, and I could see that she was wearing a red and white spotted dress. The lion, so startlingly close, was loping away from us in the calmest possible manner with a slow, long-striding, springy lope, and behind the lion, not more than the length of a tennis court behind, ran the cook himself in his white cotton robe and with his red hat on his head, running most bravely and waving his arms like a whirlwind, leaping, clapping his hands, screaming, shouting, shouting, shouting, 'Simba! Simba! Simba! Simba! Let go of my wife! Let go of my wife!'

Oh, it was a scene of great tragedy and comedy both mixed up together, and now Robert Sanford was running full speed after the cook who was running after the lion. He was holding his rifle in both hands and shouting to the cook, 'Pingo! Pingo! Get out of the way, Pingo! Lie down on the ground so I can shoot the simba! You are in my way! You are *in my way*, Pingo!'

But the cook ignored him and kept on running, and the lion ignored everybody, not altering his pace at all but continuing to lope along with slow springy strides and with the head held high and carrying the woman proudly in his jaws, rather like a dog who is trotting off with a good bone.

Both the cook and Robert Sanford were travelling faster

than the lion who really didn't seem to care about his pursuers at all. And as for me, I didn't know what to do to help them so I ran after Robert Sanford. It was an awkward situation because there was no way that Robert Sanford could take a shot at the lion without risking a hit on the cook's wife, let alone on the cook himself who was still right in his line of fire.

The lion was heading for one of those hillocks that was densely covered with jungle trees and we all knew that once he got in there, we would never be able to get at him. The incredibly brave cook was actually catching up on the lion and was now not more than ten yards behind him, and Robert Sanford was thirty or forty yards behind the cook. 'Ayee!' the cook was shouting. 'Simba! Simba! Simba! Let go my wife! I am coming after you, simba!'

Then Robert Sanford stopped and raised his rifle and took aim, and I thought surely he is not risking a shot at a moving lion when it's got a woman in its jaws. There was an almighty *crack* as the big gun went off and I saw a spurt of dust just ahead of the lion. The lion stopped dead and turned his head, still holding the woman in his jaws. He saw the arm-waving shouting cook and he saw Robert Sanford and he saw me and he had certainly heard the rifle shot and seen the spurt of dust. He must have thought an army was coming after him because instantaneously he dropped the cook's wife on to the ground and broke for cover. I have never seen anything accelerate so fast from a standing start. With great leaping bounding strides he was in among the jungle trees on the hillock before Robert Sanford could ram another cartridge into his gun.

The cook reached the wife first, then Robert Sanford, then me. I couldn't believe what I saw. I was certain that the grip of those terrible jaws would have ripped the woman's waist and stomach almost in two, but there she was sitting up on the ground and smiling at the cook, her husband.

'Where are you hurt?' shouted Robert Sanford, rushing up.

The cook's wife looked up at him and kept smiling, and she said in Swahili, 'That old lion he couldn't scare me. I just lay there in his mouth pretending I was dead and he didn't even bite through my clothes.' She stood up and smoothed down her red and white spotted dress which was wet with the lion's saliva, and the cook embraced her and the two of them did a little dance of joy in the twilight out there on the great brown African plain.

Robert Sanford just stood there gaping at the cook's wife. So, for that matter, did I.

'Are you absolutely sure the simba didn't hurt you?' he asked her. 'Did not his teeth go into your body?'

'No, bwana,' the woman said, laughing. 'He carried me as gently as if I had been one of his own cubs. But now I shall have to wash my dress.'

We walked slowly back to the group of astonished onlookers. 'Tonight', Robert Sanford said, addressing them all, 'nobody is to go far from the house, you understand me?'

'Yes, bwana,' they said. 'Yes, yes, we understand you.'

'That old simba is hiding over there in the wood and he may come back,' Robert Sanford said. 'So be very careful. And Pingo, please continue to cook our dinner. I am getting hungry.'

The cook ran into the kitchen, clapping his hands and leaping for joy. We walked over to where Mary Sanford was standing. She had come round to the back of the house soon after us and had witnessed the whole scene. The three of us then returned to the veranda and fresh drinks were poured.

Dar es Salaam
5 June 1939

Dear Mama,

It's pleasant lying back and listening to and at the same time watching the antics of Hitler and Mussolini who are invariably on the ceiling catching flys and mosquitoes. Hitler & Mussolini are 2 lizards which live in our sitting room. They're always here, and apart from being very useful about the house they are exciting to watch. You can see Hitler (who is smaller than Musso and not so fat) fixing his unfortunate victim – often a small moth – with a very hypnotic eye. The moth, terrified, stays stock still, then suddenly, so quickly that you can hardly see the movement at all, he darts his neck forward, shoots out a long tongue, and that's the end of the moth. They're quite small only about 10 inches long, and they've taken on the colour of the walls & ceiling which are yellow & become quite transparent. You can see their appendixes, at least we think we can . . .

'I don't believe anything like this has ever happened before,' Robert Sanford said as he sat down once again in his cane armchair. There was a little round slot in one of the arms of the chair to carry his glass and he put the whisky and soda carefully into it. 'In the first place,' he went on, 'lions do not attack people around here unless you go near their cubs. They can get all the food they want. There's plenty of game on the plain.'

'Perhaps he's got a family in that patch of wood on the hill,' Mary Sanford said.

'That could be,' Robert Sanford said. 'But if he had thought the woman was threatening his family, he would have killed her on the spot. Instead of that, he carries her off as soft and gentle as a good gun-dog with a partridge. If you want my opinion, I do not believe he ever meant to hurt her.'

We sat there sipping our drinks and trying to find some sort of an explanation for the astonishing behaviour of the lion.

'Normally,' Robert Sanford said, 'I would get together a bunch of hunters first thing tomorrow morning and we'd flush out that old lion and kill him. But I don't want to do it. He doesn't deserve it. In fact, I'm *not going* to do it.'

'Good for you, darling,' his wife said.

The story of this strange happening with the lion spread in the end all over East Africa and it became a bit of a legend. And when I got back to Dar es Salaam about two weeks later, there was a letter waiting for me from the *East African Standard* (I think it was called) up in Nairobi asking if I would write my own eye-witness description of the incident. This I did and in time I received a cheque for five pounds from the newspaper for my first published work.

There followed a long correspondence in the columns of the paper from the white hunters and other experts all over Uganda, Kenya and Tanganyika, each offering his or her different and often bizarre explanation. But none of them made any sense. The matter has remained a mystery ever since.

The Green Mamba

Oh, those snakes! How I hated them! They were the only fearful thing about Tanganyika, and a newcomer very quickly learnt to identify most of them and to know which were deadly and which were simply poisonous. The killers, apart from the black mambas, were the green mambas, the cobras and the tiny little puff adders that looked very much like small sticks lying motionless in the middle of a dusty path, and so easy to step on.

One Sunday evening I was invited to go and have a sundowner at the house of an Englishman called Fuller who worked in the Customs office in Dar es Salaam. He lived with his wife and two small children in a plain white wooden house that stood alone some way back from the road in a rough grassy piece of ground with coconut trees scattered about. I was walking across the grass towards the house and was about twenty yards away when I saw a large green snake go gliding straight up the veranda steps of Fuller's house and in through the open front door. The brilliant yellowy-green skin and its great size made me certain it was a green mamba, a creature almost as deadly as the black mamba, and for a few seconds I was so startled and dumbfounded and horrified that I froze to the spot. Then I pulled myself together and ran round to the back of the house shouting, 'Mr Fuller! Mr Fuller!'

Mrs Fuller popped her head out of an upstairs window. 'What on earth's the matter?' she said.

'You've got a large green mamba in your front room!' I shouted. 'I saw it go up the veranda steps and right in through the door!'

'Fred!' Mrs Fuller shouted, turning round. 'Fred! Come here!'

Freddy Fuller's round red face appeared at the window beside his wife. 'What's up?' he asked.

'There's a green mamba in your living-room!' I shouted.

Without hesitation and without wasting time with more questions, he said to me, 'Stay there. I'm going to lower the children down to you one at a time.' He was completely cool and unruffled. He didn't even raise his voice.

A small girl was lowered down to me by her wrists and I was able to catch her easily by the legs. Then came a small boy. Then Freddy Fuller lowered his wife and I caught her by the waist and put her on the ground. Then came Fuller himself. He hung by his hands from the window-sill and when he let go he landed neatly on his two feet.

We stood in a little group on the grass at the back of the house and I told Fuller exactly what I had seen.

The mother was holding the two children by the hand, one on each side of her. They didn't seem to be particularly alarmed.

'What happens now?' I asked.

'Go down to the road, all of you,' Fuller said. 'I'm off to fetch the snake-man.' He trotted away and got into his small ancient black car and drove off. Mrs Fuller and the two small children and I went down to the road and sat in the shade of a large mango tree.

'Who is this snake-man?' I asked Mrs Fuller.

'He is an old Englishman who has been out here for

years,' Mrs Fuller said. 'He actually *likes* snakes. He understands them and never kills them. He catches them and sells them to zoos and laboratories all over the world. Every native for miles around knows about him and whenever one of them sees a snake, he marks its hiding place and runs, often for great distances, to tell the snake-man. Then the snake-man comes along and captures it. The snake-man's strict rule is that he will never buy a captured snake from the natives.'

'Why not?' I asked.

'To discourage them from trying to catch snakes themselves,' Mrs Fuller said. 'In his early days he used to buy caught snakes, but so many natives got bitten trying to catch them, and so many died, that he decided to put a stop to it. Now any native who brings in a caught snake, no matter how rare, gets turned away.'

'That's good,' I said.

'What is the snake-man's name?' I asked.

'Donald Macfarlane,' she said. 'I believe he's Scottish.'

'Is the snake in the house, Mummy?' the small girl asked.

'Yes, darling. But the snake-man is going to get it out.'

'He'll bite Jack,' the girl said.

'Oh, my God!' Mrs Fuller cried, jumping to her feet. 'I forgot about Jack!' She began calling out, 'Jack! Come here, Jack! Jack! . . . Jack! . . . Jack!'

The children jumped up as well and all of them started calling to the dog. But no dog came out of the open front door.

'He's bitten Jack!' the small girl cried out. 'He must have bitten him!' She began to cry and so did her brother who was a year or so younger than she was. Mrs Fuller looked grim.

'Jack's probably hiding upstairs,' she said. 'You know how clever he is.'

Mrs Fuller and I seated ourselves again on the grass, but the children remained standing. In between their tears they went on calling to the dog.

'Would you like me to take you down to the Maddens' house?' their mother asked.

'No!' they cried. 'No, no, no! We want Jack!'

'Here's Daddy!' Mrs Fuller cried, pointing at the tiny black car coming up the road in a swirl of dust. I noticed a long wooden pole sticking out through one of the car windows.

The children ran to meet the car. 'Jack's inside the house and he's been bitten by the snake!' they wailed. 'We know he's been bitten! He doesn't come when we call him!'

Mr Fuller and the snake-man got out of the car. The snake-man was small and very old, probably over seventy. He wore leather boots made of thick cowhide and he had long gauntlet-type gloves on his hands made of the same stuff. The gloves reached above his elbows. In his right hand he carried an extraordinary implement, an eight-foot-long wooden pole with a forked end. The two prongs of the fork were made, so it seemed, of black rubber, about an inch thick and quite flexible, and it was clear that if the fork was pressed against the ground the two prongs would bend outwards, allowing the neck of the fork to go down as close to the ground as necessary. In his left hand he carried an ordinary brown sack.

Donald Macfarlane, the snake-man, may have been old and small but he was an impressive-looking character. His eyes were pale blue, deep-set in a face round and dark and wrinkled as a walnut. Above the blue eyes, the eyebrows were thick and startlingly white but the hair on his head was almost black. In spite of the thick leather boots, he moved like a leopard, with soft slow cat-like strides, and he came straight up to me and said, 'Who are you?'

'He's with Shell,' Fuller said. 'He hasn't been here long.'

'You want to watch?' the snake-man said to me.

'Watch?' I said, wavering. 'Watch? How do you mean watch? I mean where from? Not in the house?'

'You can stand out on the veranda and look through the window,' the snake-man said.

'Come on,' Fuller said. 'We'll both watch.'

'Now don't do anything silly,' Mrs Fuller said.

The two children stood there forlorn and miserable, with tears all over their cheeks.

The snake-man and Fuller and I walked over the grass towards the house, and as we approached the veranda steps the snake-man whispered, 'Tread softly on the wooden boards or he'll pick up the vibration. Wait until I've gone in, then walk up quietly and stand by the window.'

The snake-man went up the steps first and he made absolutely no sound at all with his feet. He moved soft and cat-like on to the veranda and straight through the front door and then he quickly but very quietly closed the door behind him.

I felt better with the door closed. What I mean is I felt better for myself. I certainly didn't feel better for the snake-man. I figured he was committing suicide. I followed Fuller on to the veranda and we both crept over to the window. The window was open, but it had a fine mesh mosquito-netting all over it. That made me feel better still. We peered through the netting.

The living-room was simple and ordinary, coconut

matting on the floor, a red sofa, a coffee-table and a couple of armchairs. The dog was sprawled on the matting under the coffee-table, a large Airedale with curly brown and black hair. He was stone dead.

The snake-man was standing absolutely still just inside the door of the living-room. The brown sack was now slung over his left shoulder and he was grasping the long pole with both hands, holding it out in front of him, parallel to the ground. I couldn't see the snake. I didn't think the snake-man had seen it yet either.

A minute went by . . . two minutes . . . three . . . four . . . five. Nobody moved. There was death in that room. The air was heavy with death and the snake-man stood as motionless as a pillar of stone, with the long rod held out in front of him.

And still he waited. Another minute . . . and another . . . and another.

And now I saw the snake-man beginning to bend his knees. Very slowly he bent his knees until he was almost squatting on the floor, and from that position he tried to peer under the sofa and the armchairs.

And still it didn't look as though he was seeing anything.

Slowly he straightened his legs again, and then his head began to swivel around the room. Over to the right, in the far corner, a staircase led up to the floor above. The snake-man looked at the stairs, and I knew very well what was going through his head. Quite abruptly, he took one step forward and stopped.

Nothing happened.

A moment later I caught sight of the snake. It was lying full-length along the skirting of the right-hand wall, but hidden from the snake-man's view by the back of the sofa. It lay there like a long, beautiful, deadly shaft of green glass, quite motionless, perhaps asleep. It was facing away from us who were at the window, with its small triangular head resting on the matting near the foot of the stairs.

I nudged Fuller and whispered, 'It's over there against the wall.' I pointed and Fuller saw the snake. At once, he started waving both hands, palms outward, back and forth across the window hoping to get the snake-man's attention. The snake-man didn't see him. Very softly, Fuller said, 'Pssst!', and the snake-man looked up sharply. Fuller pointed. The snake-man understood and gave a nod.

Now the snake-man began working his way very very slowly to the back wall of the room so as to get a view of the snake behind the sofa. He never walked on his toes as you or I would have done. His feet remained flat on the ground all the time. The cowhide boots were like moccasins, with neither soles nor heels. Gradually, he worked his way over to the back wall, and from there he was able to see at least the head and two or three feet of the snake itself.

But the snake also saw him. With a movement so fast it was invisible, the snake's head came up about two feet off the floor and the front of the body arched backwards, ready to strike. Almost simultaneously, it bunched its whole body into a series of curves, ready to flash forward.

The snake-man was just a bit too far away from the snake to reach it with the end of his pole. He waited, staring at the snake and the snake stared back at him with two small malevolent black eyes.

Then the snake-man started speaking to the snake. 'Come along, my pretty,' he whispered in a soft wheedling voice. 'There's a good boy. Nobody's going to hurt you. Nobody's going to harm you, my pretty little thing. Just lie still and relax . . .' He took a step forward towards the snake, holding the pole out in front of him.

What the snake did next was so fast that the whole movement couldn't have taken more than a hundredth of a second, like the flick of a camera shutter. There was a green flash as the snake darted forward at least ten feet and struck at the snake-man's leg. Nobody could have got out of the way of that one. I heard the snake's head strike against the thick cowhide boot with a sharp little *crack*, and then at once the head was back in that same deadly backward-curving position, ready to strike again.

'There's a good boy,' the snake-man said softly. 'There's a clever boy. There's a lovely fellow. You mustn't get excited. Keep calm and everything's going to be all right.' As he was speaking, he was slowly lowering the end of the pole until the forked prongs were about twelve inches above the middle of the snake's body. 'There's a lovely fellow,' he whispered. 'There's a good kind little chap. Keep still now, my beauty. Keep still, my pretty. Keep quite still. Daddy's not going to hurt you.'

I could see a thin dark trickle of venom running down the snake-man's right boot where the snake had struck.

The snake, head raised and arcing backwards, was as tense as a tight-wound spring and ready to strike again. 'Keep still, my lovely,' the snake-man whispered. 'Don't move now. Keep still. No one's going to hurt you.'

Then *wham*, the rubber prongs came down right across the snake's body, about midway along its length, and pinned it to the floor. All I could see was a green blur as the snake thrashed around furiously in an effort to free itself. But the snake-man kept up the pressure on the prongs and the snake was trapped.

What happens next? I wondered. There was no way he could catch hold of that madly twisting flailing length of green muscle with his hands, and even if he could have done so, the head would surely have flashed around and bitten him in the face.

Holding the very end of the eight-foot pole, the snake-man began to work his way round the room until he was at the tail end of the snake. Then, in spite of the flailing and the thrashing, he started pushing the prongs forward along the snake's body towards the head. Very very slowly he did it, pushing the rubber prongs forward over the snake's flailing body, keeping the snake pinned down all the time and pushing, pushing, pushing the long wooden rod forward millimetre by millimetre. It was a fascinating and frightening thing to watch, the little man with white eyebrows and black hair carefully manipulating his long implement and sliding the fork ever so slowly along the length of the twisting snake towards the head. The snake's body was thumping against the coconut matting with such a noise that if you had been upstairs you might have thought two big men were wrestling on the floor.

Then at last the prongs were right behind the head itself, pinning it down, and at that point the snake-man reached forward with one gloved hand and grasped the snake very firmly by the neck. He threw away the pole. He took the sack off his shoulder with his free hand. He lifted the great still twisting length of the deadly green snake and pushed the head into the sack. Then he let go the head and bundled the rest of the creature in and closed the sack. The sack started jumping about as though there were fifty angry rats inside it, but the snake-man was now totally relaxed and he held the sack casually in one hand as if it contained no more than a few pounds of potatoes. He stooped and picked up his pole from the floor, then he turned and looked towards the window where we were peering in.

'Pity about the dog,' he said. 'You'd better get it out of the way before the children see it.'

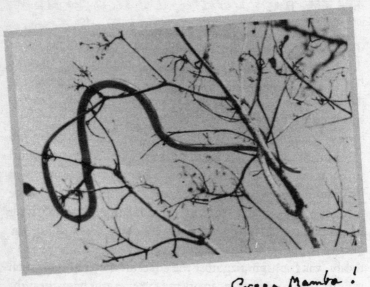

Green Mamba!

The Beginning of the War

Breakfast in Dar es Salaam never varied. It was always a delicious ripe pawpaw picked that morning in the garden by the cook, on to which was squeezed the juice of a whole fresh lime. Just about every white man and woman in Tanganyika had pawpaw and lime juice for breakfast, and I believe those old colonials knew what was good for them. It is the healthiest and most refreshing breakfast I know.

On a morning towards the end of August 1939, I was breakfasting on my pawpaw and thinking a great deal, like everyone else, about the war that we all knew was very soon going to break out with Germany. Mdisho was moving around the room and pretending to be busy.

'Did you know there is going to be a war before very long?' I asked him.

'A war?' he cried, perking up immediately. 'A real war, bwana?'

'An enormous war,' I said.

Mdisho's face was now alight with excitement. He was of the Mwanumwezi tribe and there wasn't a Mwanumwezi anywhere who did not have fighting in his blood. For hundreds of years they had been the greatest warriors in East Africa, conquering all before them, including the Masai, and even now the mere mention of war caused such dreams of glory in Mdisho's mind that he could hardly stand it.

'I still have my father's weapons in my hut!' he cried. 'I shall get the spear out and start sharpening it immediately! Who are we going to fight, bwana?'

'The Germani,' I said.

'Good,' he said. 'There are plenty of Germani around here for us to kill.'

Mdisho was right about there being plenty of them. Only twenty-five years ago, before the First World War, Tanganyika had been German East Africa. But in 1919 after the Armistice, Germany had been forced to hand the territory over to the British, who renamed it Tanganyika. Many Germans had stayed on and the country was still full of them. They owned diamond mines and gold mines. They grew sisal and cotton and tea and ground-nuts. The owner of the soda-water bottling-plant in Dar es Salaam was a German and so was Willy Hink, the watchmaker. In fact the Germans greatly outnumbered all the other Europeans in Tanganyika put together, and when war broke out, as we now knew it must, they could present a dangerous and difficult problem to the authorities.

'When is this enormous war going to begin?' Mdisho asked me.

'They say quite soon,' I told him, 'because over in Europe, which is ten times as far away as from here to Kilimanjaro, the Germans have a leader called Bwana Hitler who wishes to conquer the world. The Germans think this Bwana Hitler is a wonderful fellow. But he is actually a raving mad maniac. As soon as the war begins, the Germani will try to kill us all, and then, of course, we shall have to try to kill them before they can kill us.'

Mdisho, being a true child of his tribe, understood the principle of war very well. 'Why don't we strike first?' he said, excitedly. 'Why don't we take them by surprise, these

Germani out here, bwana? Why don't we kill all of them *before* the war begins? That is always the best way, bwana. My ancestors always used to strike first.'

'I am afraid we have very strict rules about war,' I said. 'With us, nobody is allowed to kill anyone until the whistle blows and the game is officially started.'

'But that is ridiculous, bwana!' he cried. 'In a war there are no rules! Winning is all that counts!'

Mdisho was only nineteen years old. He had been born and brought up 700 miles inland from Dar es Salaam, near a place called Kigoma, on the shores of Lake Tanganyika, and both his parents had died before he was twelve years old. He had then been taken into the household of a kindly District Officer in Kigoma and given the job of assistant shamba-boy or gardener. From there he had graduated into the household as a house-boy and had charmed everybody by his good manners and gentle bearing. When the District Officer had been moved back to the Secretariat in Dar es Salaam, the family had taken Mdisho with them. A year or so later, the DO had been transferred to Egypt and poor Mdisho was suddenly without a job or a home, but he did have in his possession one very valuable document, a splendid reference from his former employer. That was when I was lucky enough to find him and take him on. I made him my personal 'boy' and soon the two of us had formed a friendship that I found rather marvellous.

Mdisho could neither read nor write, and it was impossible for him to imagine that the world extended much beyond the shores of the African continent. But he was undoubtedly intelligent and quick to learn, and I had begun to teach him how to read. Every weekday, as soon as I got home from the office, we would have three-quarters of an hour of reading. He learnt fast, and although we were still on single words, we would soon be progressing to short sentences. I insisted on teaching him how to read and write not only Swahili words but also their English equivalents, so that he would learn a little basic English at the same time. He loved his lessons and it was touching to see him already seated at the table in the dining-room with his exercise book open in front of him when I came home in the evenings.

Mdisho was about six feet tall, superbly built, with a rather scrunched-up flat-nosed face and the most beautiful pure white absolutely even teeth I had ever seen.

'It is most important to obey the rules of war,' I told him. 'No Germani can be killed until war has been properly declared. And even then the enemy must be given the chance to surrender before you kill him.'

'How will we know when war is declared?' Mdisho asked me.

'They will tell us on the wireless from England,' I said. 'We shall all know within a few seconds.'

'And then the fun will begin!' he cried, clapping his hands. 'Oh bwana, I can hardly wait for that time to come!'

'If you want to fight, you must become a soldier first,' I told him. 'You will have to join the Kenya Regiment and become an askari.' An askari was a soldier in the King's African Rifles, the KAR.

'The askaris have guns and I don't know how to use a gun,' he said.

'They will teach you,' I said. 'You might enjoy it.'

'That would be a very serious step for me to take, bwana,' he said. 'I shall have to give it a great deal of thought.'

A few days after that, things started hotting up in Dar es Salaam. War was clearly imminent, and elaborate plans

Dar es Salaam
Sunday, no date

Dear Mama,

Last week I finally succumbed to Malaria and went to
bed on Wednesday night with the most terrific head and a
temp of 103°. Next day it was 104° and on Friday 105°.
They've got some marvellous new stuff called Atebrin
which they straightway inject into your bottom in vast
quantities which suddenly brings the temperature down;
then they give you an injection of 15 or 20 grams of
quinine and by that time you haven't got any bottom left at
all – one side's just Atebrin and the other's quinine.

I suppose that by the time you get this letter war will
either be declared or it'll be off, but at the moment things,
even here, are humming a bit. We're all temporary army
officers, with batons, belts & all sorts of secret
instructions. If we go out of the house we've got to leave
word where we've gone to so that we can be called at a
moments notice. We know exactly where to go if anything
happens but everything's very secret, and as I'm not sure
whether our letters are being censored or not I'm not going
to tell you any more. But if war breaks out it'll be our job
to round up all the Germans here, and after that things
ought to be pretty quiet . . .

were made to round up the hundreds of Germans in Dar es
Salaam and upcountry as soon as war was declared. There
were not a lot of young Englishmen in Dar, perhaps fifteen
or twenty at the most and all of us were ordered to leave our
jobs and to become, by some magic process, temporary
army officers. I was given a red armband and a platoon of
askaris to command, but never having been a soldier in my
life, except at school, I felt rather at a loss with twenty-five

highly trained troops with rifles and one machine-gun in my charge.

I was summoned to the army barracks in Dar es Salaam where a British Captain in the KAR gave me my orders. He was seated at a wooden table with his hat on in a swelteringly hot tin hut, and he had a little clipped brown moustache that kept jumping about when he spoke.

'As soon as war is declared,' he said, 'all male Germans must be rounded up at the point of a gun and put into the prison camp. The prison camp is ready, and the Germans know it is ready, so many of them will try to escape from the country before we can catch them. The nearest neutral

---

Dar es Salaam
Friday 15 Sept

Dear Mama,

  I'm very sorry I haven't written to you for such ages but you can guess that things have been humming a bit here. Now all the Germans in the Territory, and its a pretty big place in which to try to catch them, have been safely put inside an internment camp. And we army officers were the people who had to collect them. The moment that war broke out at about 1.15 p.m. on Sunday the alarm was given on a series of telephones and certain key men dashed round and collected their squads, & proceeded to the police lines to be armed and to receive orders. At the time, I was actually out guarding the road going down the South Coast to Kilwa and Lindi with native troops (Askaris) and a blockade across the road. All I heard was a grim voice down the field telephone which said, 'War has been declared – standby – arrest all Germans attempting to leave or enter the town.' Then the fun started. I better not say any more or the censor might hold up the letter . . .

territory is Portuguese East Africa, and there is only one road running there from Dar es Salaam, the coast road going south. Do you know it?'

I told him I knew it very well.

'Down that road', the Captain said, 'every German in Dar es Salaam will try to run the moment war is declared. It will be your duty to stop them and round them up and bring them back to the prison camp.'

'Who, *me*?' I cried, aghast.

'You and your platoon,' he said. 'We can't spare any more men. We've got the entire country to cover. Make sure you take up a sensible defensive position and deploy your troops under good cover. Some of those Germans may try to shoot their way out.'

'You mean', I said, 'that just me and my platoon are going to try to stop every German in Dar?'

'Those are your orders,' he said.

'But there must be hundreds of them.'

'There are,' he said, smirking a bit.

'What happens if they *do* have guns and put up a fight?' I asked.

'Mow them down,' the Captain said. 'You've got a machine-gun, haven't you? One machine-gun can defeat 500 men with rifles.'

I was getting nervous. I didn't want to be the person who gave the order to mow down 500 civilians out there on the dusty coast road that led to Portuguese East Africa. 'What happens if they've got their women and children with them?' I asked.

'You'll have to use your discretion,' the Captain said, evading the issue.

'But . . . but,' I stammered, 'that road is the most important escape route in the whole country. Don't you think that you or some other regular officer should be doing this job?'

'We've all got our hands full,' the Captain said.

I tried once more. 'I am really not trained for this sort of thing,' I said. 'I'm just a chap who works for Shell.'

'Rubbish!' he barked. 'Off you go now! And don't let us down!'

So off I went.

I found a telephone and called Mdisho at the house to tell him not to expect me back until he saw me.

'I know where you are going, bwana!' he shouted down the phone. 'You are going after the Germani! Am I right?'

'Well,' I said, 'we'll see.'

'Let me come with you, bwana!' he cried. 'Oh, *please* let me come with you!'

'I'm afraid that's not possible this time, Mdisho,' I said. 'You'll just have to stay and look after the house.'

'Be careful, bwana,' he said. 'You *will* be careful they do not kill you.'

I went out into the barrack square where my platoon was waiting for me. The askaris looked very smart in their khaki shorts and shirts, and they were lined up at attention beside two open trucks with their rifles at their sides. As soon as I arrived, the Sergeant saluted me and told the men to get into the trucks. I sat in the cabin of the front truck between the driver and the Sergeant, and we drove through the town towards the coast road that would lead eventually to Mozambique in Portuguese East Africa. In the second truck the askaris had a huge reel of telephone cable which they were going to lay along our route so that I could keep in touch with headquarters and be told the moment war was declared. There were no radios for that sort of thing out there.

'How much cable have you got?' I asked the Sergeant. 'How far along the road can we go?'

'Only about three miles, bwana,' he answered, grinning.

Just outside Dar es Salaam we stopped by a small hut and two signallers jumped out and unlocked the door and connected up our telephone cable to a plug inside. Then we drove on and the signallers fed the telephone cable out on to the grass verge as we went slowly forward. The road ran right along the edge of the Indian Ocean, and the water out there was calm and clear and pale green. I could see the sandy bottom under the water for a long way out and on the little strip of sand between us and the water there grew those everlasting coconut palms waving their tops high up against the hot blue sky. It was a very beautiful sight and a little breeze was blowing from the sea into the cabin of our truck.

After a couple of miles, we came to a place where the road sloped steeply uphill and curved inland and went right through some very thick jungle. 'What about over there in the trees?' I asked the Sergeant.

'It is a good place,' he said, so we stopped where the road entered the jungle and we climbed out of the trucks.

'Leave the trucks outside blocking the road,' I said to the Sergeant, 'and see that each man takes up a concealed position on the edge of the forest. The machine-gun and all the rifles must be able to cover the road just beyond the blockade.'

When all this had been done, I took the Sergeant aside and had a little talk with him in Swahili. 'Look, Sergeant,' I said, 'I am sure you realize that I am not a soldier.'

'I realize that, bwana,' he said politely.

'So if you see me doing something silly, please tell me.'

'Yes, bwana,' he said.

'Are you happy with our positions?' I asked him.

'I think everything is fine, bwana,' he said.

So we hung around through the afternoon waiting for the field telephone to ring. I sat on the ground in a shady place near the phone and smoked my pipe. I remember I was wearing a khaki shirt, khaki shorts, khaki stockings and brown shoes, and I had a khaki topee on my head. That was the regular civilian way of dressing out there and very comfortable it was. But I myself was far from comfortable in my mind. I was twenty-three and I had not yet been trained to kill anyone. I wasn't absolutely sure that I could bring myself to give the order to open fire on a bunch of German civilians in cold blood should the necessity arise. I was feeling altogether very uncomfortable in my skin.

Darkness came and still the telephone did not ring.

There was a 44-gallon drum of drinking water in one of the trucks and everyone helped himself. Then the Sergeant made a fire out of sticks and began cooking supper for his men. He was making rice in an enormous pot, and while the rice was boiling he took from the truck a great stem of bananas and started snapping them off the stem one by one and peeling them and slicing them up and dropping the slices into the pot of rice. When the food was ready, each askari produced his own tin plate and spoon and the Sergeant dished out large portions with a ladle. Up to then I hadn't thought about my own food and I certainly had not brought anything with me. Watching the men eat made me hungry. 'Do you think I could have a little of that, please?' I said to the Sergeant.

'Yes, bwana,' he said. 'Have you got a plate?'

'No,' I said. So he found me a tin plate and a spoon and gave me a huge helping. It was absolutely delicious. The rice was unhusked and brown and the grains did not stick together. The slices of banana were hot and sweet and in some way they oiled the rice, as butter would. It was the best rice dish I had ever tasted and I ate it all and felt good and forgot about the Germans. 'Wonderful,' I said to the Sergeant. 'You are a fine cook.'

'Whenever we are out of the barracks,' he said, 'I must feed my men. It is something you have to learn when you become a Sergeant.'

'It was truly magnificent,' I said. 'You should open a restaurant and become rich.'

All around us in the forest the frogs were croaking incessantly. African frogs have an unusually loud rasping croak and however far away from you they are, the sound always seems to be coming from somewhere near your feet. The croaking of frogs is the night music of the East African coast. The actual croak is made only by the bullfrog and he does it by blowing out his dewlap and letting it go with a *burp*. This is his mating call and when the female hears it she hops smartly over to the side of her prospective mate. But when she arrives a curious thing happens and it is not quite what you are thinking. The bullfrog does not turn and greet the female. Far from it. He ignores her totally and continues to sit there singing his song to the stars while the female waits patiently beside him. She waits and she waits and she waits. The male sings and he sings and he sings, often for several hours, and what has actually happened is this. The bullfrog has fallen so much in love with the sound of his own voice that he has completely forgotten why he started croaking in the first place. *We* know that he started because he was feeling sexy. But now he has become mesmerized by the lovely music he is making so that for him nothing else exists, not even the panting female at his side. There comes a time, though, when she loses all patience and starts nudging him hard with a foreleg, and only then does the bullfrog come out of his trance and turn to embrace her.

Ah well. The bullfrog, I told myself as I sat there in the dark forest, is not after all so very different from a lot of human males that I could think of.

I borrowed an army blanket from the Sergeant and settled down for the night beside the telephone. I thought briefly about snakes and wondered how many there were gliding about on the floor of the forest. Probably thousands. But the askaris were chancing it so why shouldn't I?

The phone did not ring in the night and at dawn the Sergeant built his fire again and cooked us some more rice and bananas. It didn't taste so good early in the morning.

Shortly after eleven o'clock the tinkle of the field telephone made everybody jump. The voice on the other end said to me, 'Great Britain has declared war on Germany. You are now on full alert.' Then he rang off. I told the Sergeant to get all his men into their positions.

For an hour or so nothing happened. The askaris waited behind their guns and I waited out in the open beside the two trucks that were blocking the road.

Then, suddenly, away in the distance I saw a cloud of dust. A little later, I could make out the first car, then close behind it a second and a third and a fourth. All the Germans in Dar must have made arrangements to assemble and travel together in convoy as soon as war was declared, for now I could see a line of cars, each about twenty yards behind the one in front, stretching for half a mile down the road. There were trucks piled high with baggage. There were ordinary saloons with pieces of furniture strapped on their roofs. There were vans and there were station-wagons. I called the

Sergeant out of the forest. 'Here they come,' I said, 'and there's plenty of them. I want you to stay out of sight with the men. I shall remain here and meet the Germans. If I raise two arms above my head, like this, the machine-gun and all the rifles are to fire one burst over the heads of these people. Not *at* them, you understand, but over their heads.'

'Yes, bwana, one burst over their heads.'

'If there is violence towards me and they try to force their way through, then you will be in charge and must do whatever you think right.'

'Yes, bwana,' the Sergeant said, relishing the possibility. He returned to the forest. I stood out on the road waiting for the leader of the convoy to reach me. The lead car was a large Chevrolet station-wagon driven by a man who had two more men beside him in the front seat. The rest of the car was filled with baggage. I put one hand up for him to stop, which he did. I felt like a traffic cop as I strolled over to the driver's window.

'I am afraid you cannot go any further,' I said. 'You and all the others must turn around and go back to Dar es Salaam. One of my trucks will lead you. The other will bring up the rear of the convoy.'

'Vot sort of bull is this?' the man shouted with a heavy German accent. He was middle-aged with a thick neck and he was almost bald. 'Move those trucks off the road! Vi are going through!'

'I'm afraid not,' I said. 'You are now prisoners of war.'

The bald man got slowly out of the car. He was very angry and his movements were full of menace. The two men with him also got out. The bald man turned and signalled with his arm to the fifty odd cars that were lined up behind him, and immediately a man, and sometimes two, got out of each car and came walking towards us. There were women and children in many of the cars as well, but they stayed where they were.

I didn't at all like the way things were shaping up. What *was* I going to do, I asked myself, if they refused to go back and tried to barge their way through? I knew there and then that I could never quite bring myself to give the order for the machine-gun to mow them all down. It would be an appalling massacre. I stood there and said nothing.

In a few minutes a crowd of not less than seventy Germans were standing in a half-circle behind the bald man, who was clearly their leader.

The bald man turned away from me and addressed his countrymen. 'OK,' he said. 'Let's get these two trucks off the road and move on.'

'Hold it!' I said, trying to sound twice my age. 'I have orders to stop you at all costs. If you try to go on, we shall shoot.'

'Who vill shoot?' asked the bald man contemptuously. He drew a revolver from the back pocket of his khaki trousers and I saw that it was one of those long-barrelled Lugers. Immediately, at least half of the seventy or so men standing around him produced identical weapons. The bald man pointed his Luger at my chest.

I had seen this sort of thing done a thousand times in the cinema, but it was a very different thing in real life. I was properly frightened. I did my best not to show it. Then I raised both arms above my head. The bald man smiled. He thought it was a gesture of surrender.

Crack! Crack! Crack! All the guns behind me including the machine-gun opened up and bullets went whistling over our heads. The Germans jumped. They quite literally jumped. Even the bald man jumped. And so did I.

I lowered my hands. 'There is no way you can get through,' I said. 'The first man who tries to go on from here will be shot. If all of you try, then all of you will be shot. Those are my orders. I have enough fire-power in there to stop a regiment.'

There was absolute silence. The bald man lowered his Luger and suddenly his whole attitude changed. He gave me an ugly forced smile and said softly, 'Vy do you not let us through?'

'Because we are at war with Germany,' I said, 'and you are all of German nationality, therefore you are the enemy.'

'Vi are civilians,' he said.

'Maybe you are,' I said. 'But as soon as you get to Portuguese East, you'll find your way back to the Father-land and become soldiers. You are not going through.'

Suddenly he grabbed my arm and put his Luger to my chest. Then he raised his voice and screamed to my invisible troops in Swahili, 'If you try to stop us I am going to shoot your officer!'

What came next happened very suddenly. There was the *crack* of a single rifle shot fired from the wood and the bald man who was holding me took the bullet right through his face. It was a horrible sight. His head seemed to splash open and little soft bits of grey stuff flew out in all directions. There was no blood, just the grey stuff and fragments of bone. One lump of the grey stuff landed on my cheek. More of it went all over my khaki shirt. The Luger dropped on to the road and the bald man fell dead beside it.

All of us were shaken up, but I managed to pull myself together enough to say, 'Come on, let us not have any more killings. Turn your vehicles round and follow our lead truck back to town. You will be well treated and the women and children will be allowed to go home.'

The crowd of men turned and walked sullenly back towards their cars.

'Sergeant!' I shouted and the Sergeant came out of the forest at the double. 'Put the dead man in one of the trucks and take it to the head of the convoy,' I said to him. 'You go with the front truck and lead them all to the prison camp. I shall bring up the rear in the second truck.'

'Very well, bwana,' the Sergeant said.

And that was how we captured the German civilians in Dar es Salaam when the war broke out.

Mdisho of the Mwanumwezi

By the time we had seen the Germans safely into the prison camp and I had made my report, it was nearly midnight. I went off home to get a shower and some sleep. I was tired and dirty and I was feeling very unhappy about the killing of the bald-headed German. The Captain at the barracks had congratulated me and said it was exactly the right thing to do, but that didn't help.

When I got home, I went straight upstairs and took off my clothes, especially the shirt that was splattered with bits of grey stuff and sticky fragments of bone. I took a long shower, then I put on a pair of pyjamas and went downstairs again for a badly needed whisky and soda.

In the living-room I lay back in my armchair sipping the whisky and ruminating upon the strange events of the last thirty-six hours. The whisky felt good and I was slowly beginning to relax as the alcohol got into the bloodstream. Through the wide-open french windows I could hear the Indian Ocean pounding the cliffs below the house, and as always when I sat in that chair, I turned my head a little in order to allow my eyes to rest upon my beautiful silver Arab sword that hung on the wall over the door. I nearly dropped my whisky. The sword was gone. The scabbard was still there but the sword itself was not in it.

I had bought my sword about a year before from the

Captain of an Arab dhow in Dar es Salaam harbour. This Captain had sailed his old dhow clear across from Muscat to Africa on the north-east monsoon and the journey had taken him thirty-four days. I happened to be down in the harbour when she came sailing in and I gladly accepted the invitation of the Customs Officer to accompany him on board. That is where I found the sword and fell in love with it at first sight and bought it from the Captain on the spot for 500 shillings.

The sword was long and curved and the silver scabbard was wonderfully chased with an intricate design showing various phases in the life of the Prophet. The curved blade was over three feet in length and was as sharp as a well-honed chisel. My friends in Dar es Salaam who knew about such things told me it was almost certainly from the middle of the eighteenth century and should properly be in a museum.

I had carried my treasure back to the house and had handed it to Mdisho. 'I want you to hang it on the wall over the door,' I told him. 'And I shall hold you responsible for seeing that the silver scabbard is always polished and the blade is wiped with an oily rag once a week to prevent it from rusting.'

Mdisho took the sword from me and examined it with reverence. Then he drew the blade from the scabbard and tested the edge with his thumb. 'Ayee!' he cried out. 'What a weapon! I could win a war with this in my hand!'

And now I sat in my armchair in the living-room with my whisky, staring appalled at the empty scabbard.

'Mdisho!' I shouted. 'Come here! Where is my sword?' There was no answer. He was probably in bed. I got up and went out to the back of the house where the native quarters were. There was a half-moon in the sky and plenty of stars and I could see Piggy the cook squatting outside his hut with one of his wives.

'Piggy,' I said, 'where is Mdisho?'

Piggy was old and wrinkled, and he was very good at making baked potato with crabmeat inside. He stood up when he saw me and his woman disappeared into the shadows.

'Where is Mdisho?' I said.

'Mdisho went away early in the evening, bwana.'

'Where to?'

'I do not know. But he said he was coming back. Perhaps he has gone to see his father. You were away in the jungle and I expect he thought you would not mind if he went off to pay a call on his father.'

'Where is my sword, Piggy?'

'Your sword, bwana? Is it not hanging over the door?'

'It's gone,' I said. 'I'm afraid someone may have stolen it. The big french windows into the sitting-room were wide open when I came in. That is not right.'

'No bwana, that is not right. I don't understand it at all.'

'Nor do I,' I said. 'Go to bed.'

I went back into the house and flopped down again into the armchair. I felt too tired to move any more. It was a very hot night. I reached up and switched off the reading light, then I closed my eyes and dozed off.

I don't know how long I slept, but when I woke up it was still night and Mdisho was standing just inside the french windows with the light of the half-moon shining down on him from behind. He was breathing fast and there was a wild ecstatic look on his face and he was naked except for a small pair of black cotton shorts. His superb black body was literally dripping with sweat. In his right hand he held the sword.

I sat up abruptly.

'Mdisho, where have you been?' Little flashes of moonlight were glinting on the sword and I noticed that the middle of the blade was darkened with something that looked to me very much like dried blood.

'Mdisho!' I cried. 'For heaven's sake what have you done?'

'Bwana,' he said, 'oh bwana, I have had a most tremendous victory. I think you will be very pleased about it when I tell you.'

'Tell me,' I said. I was getting nervous.

I had never seen Mdisho like this before. The wild look on his face and the heavy breathing and the sweat all over his body made me more nervous than ever. 'Tell me at once,' I said again. 'Explain to me what you have been doing.'

When he started to speak, the words came rushing out in a cascade of crazy excited sentences, and he didn't stop until he had finished his story. I didn't interrupt him, and I will try to give you a fairly literal translation from the Swahili of what he said as he stood there looking so splendid in the open doorway with the half-moon shining on him from behind.

'Bwana,' he said, 'bwana, yesterday down in the market I heard that we had started to fight the Germani and I remembered all that you had said about how they would try to kill us. As soon as I heard the news, I started to run back to the house, and as I ran I shouted to everyone I saw in the streets. I shouted, "We are fighting the Germani! We are fighting the Germani!"

'In my country, as soon as we hear that someone is coming to fight us, the whole tribe must know about it as soon as possible. So I ran home shouting the news to the people as I went, and I was also thinking of what I, Mdisho, could do to help. Suddenly, I remembered the rich Germani that lives over the hills, the sisal planter whom we visited in your car not long ago.

'Then I ran even faster towards home, and when I arrived I ran through the kitchen and shouted at Piggy the cook, "We are fighting the Germani!" I ran into this room and took hold of the sword, this wonderful sword which I have been polishing for you every day.

'Bwana, I was very excited to be at war. You were already out with the askari on the roads, and I knew that I should do something too.

'So I pulled the sword out of its glove and ran outside with it. I ran towards the house of the rich sisal-owning Germani over the hills.

'I did not go by the road because the askaris might have stopped me when they saw me running with the sword in my hand. I ran straight through the forest and when I got to the top of the hills, I looked down the other side and saw the great plantation of sisal belonging to the rich Germani. Away beyond it I could see his house, the big white house we visited together, and I set off again down the other side of the hill into the sisal.

'By then it was getting dark and it was not easy dodging around the tall prickly sisal plants, but I went on running.

'Then I saw the white house in front of me in the moonlight and I ran straight up to the front door and pushed it open. I ran into the first room I saw and it was empty. There was a table with some food on it but the room was empty. Then I ran towards the back of the house and pushed open a door at the end of the passage. That was empty too, but suddenly through the window I saw the big Germani standing in the back garden and he had a fire going and he was throwing pieces of paper on to the fire. He had many sheets of paper on the ground beside him and he kept picking up more and more and throwing them on to the fire. And bwana, there was a huge elephant gun lying on the ground by his feet.

'I pushed open the back door and I ran out and the Germani heard me and jumped round and started to reach for the gun but I gave him no time. I had the sword raised in both my hands and I swung it at his neck as he bent down to pick up the gun.

'Bwana, it is a beautiful sword. With one blow it cut through his neck so deeply that his whole head fell forward and dangled down on to his chest, and as he started to topple over I gave the neck one more quick chop and the head came right away from the body and fell to the ground like a coconut and the most enormous fountains of blood came spurting out of his neck.

'I felt good then, bwana, I really felt awfully good, and I remember wishing I had had you with me to see it all happening. But you were far away on the coast road with your askaris doing the same sort of thing to lots of other Germani, so I hurried home. I came home by the road because it was faster and I didn't care any more about the askaris seeing me. I ran all the way and the sword was in my hand and sometimes I waved it above my head as I ran, but I never stopped. Twice people shouted at me and once two men ran after me, but I was flying like a bird and I was bringing good news back home.

'It is a long distance, bwana, and it took four hours each way. That is why I am so late. I am sorry to be so late.'

Mdisho stopped. He had finished his story. I knew it was true. The German sisal–owner was called Fritz Kleiber and he was a wealthy and extremely unpleasant bachelor. It was rumoured that he treated his workers badly and had been known to beat them with a sjambok, which is a murderous whip made of rhinoceros hide. I wondered why he hadn't been rounded up by our people before Mdisho got to him. They were probably on the way out there now. They were in for a shock.

'And *you*, bwana!' Mdisho cried out. 'How many did *you* get today?'

'How many what?' I said.

'Germani, bwana, Germani! How many did you get with that fine machine-gun you had out on the road?'

I looked at him and smiled. I refused to blame him for what he had done. He was a wild Mwanumwezi tribesman who had been moulded by us Europeans into the shape of a domestic servant, and now he had broken the mould.

'Have you told anyone else what you have done?'

'Not yet, bwana, I came to you first.'

'Now listen carefully,' I said. 'You must tell nobody about this, not your father, not your wives, not your best friend and not Piggy the cook. Do you understand me?'

'But I *must* tell them!' he cried. 'You cannot take that pleasure away from me, bwana!'

'You must *not* tell them, Mdisho,' I said.

'But why not?' he cried. 'Have I done something wrong?'

'Quite the opposite,' I lied.

'Then why must I not tell my people?' he asked again.

I tried to explain to him how the authorities would react if they found him out. It simply wasn't done to go round chopping heads off civilians, even in wartime. It could mean prison, I told him, or even worse than that.

He couldn't believe me. He was absolutely shattered.

'I myself am tremendously proud of you,' I said, trying to make him feel better. 'To me you are a great hero.'

'But *only* to you, bwana?'

'No, Mdisho. I think you would be a hero to most of the British people here if they knew what you had done. But that doesn't help. It is the police who would go after you.'

'The police!' he cried in horror. If there was one thing in Dar es Salaam that every local was terrified of, it was the police. The police constables were all blacks, acting under a couple of white officers at the top, and they were not famous for being gentle with prisoners.

l To r: Mdisho, Piggy, Owino, Mtoto, Shamba B...

'Yes,' I said, 'the police.' I felt pretty sure they would charge Mdisho with murder if they caught him.

'If it is the police, then I will keep quiet, bwana,' he said, and all of a sudden he looked so downcast and disillusioned and defeated that I couldn't bear it. I got up from the chair and crossed the room and took the scabbard of the sword down from the wall. 'I shall be leaving you very soon,' I said. 'I have decided to join the war as a flier of aeroplanes.' The only word for aeroplane in the Swahili language is *ndegi*, which means bird, and it always sounded good and descriptive in a sentence. 'I am going to fly birds,' I said. 'I shall fly English birds against the birds of the Germani.'

'Wonderful!' Mdisho cried, brightening again suddenly at the mention of war. 'I will come with you, bwana.'

'Sadly, that will be impossible,' I said. 'In the beginning I shall be nothing but a very humble bird-soldier of the lowest rank, like your most junior askaris here, and I shall be living in barracks. There would be no question of me being allowed to have somebody to help me. I shall have to do everything for myself, including the washing and ironing of my shirts.'

'That would be absolutely impossible, bwana,' Mdisho said. He was genuinely shocked.

'I shall manage quite well,' I told him.

'But do you *know* how to iron a shirt, bwana?'

'No,' I said. 'You must teach me that secret before I go.'

'Will it be very dangerous, bwana, where you are going, and do those Germani birds have many guns?'

'It might be dangerous,' I said, 'but the first six months will be nothing but fun. It takes six months for them to teach you how to fly a bird.'

'Where will you go?' he asked.

'First to Nairobi,' I answered. 'They will start us on very small birds in Nairobi, and then we will go somewhere else to fly the big ones. We shall be travelling a great deal with very little luggage. That is why I shall have to leave this sword behind. It would be impossible to carry a great big thing like this with me wherever I go. So I am giving it to you.'

'To me!' he cried. 'Oh no, bwana, you mustn't do that! You will need it where you are going!'

'Not in a bird,' I said. 'There is no room to swing a sword when you are sitting in one of those.' I handed him the beautiful curved silver scabbard. 'You have earned it,' I said. 'Now go away and wash the blade very well indeed. Make sure there is no trace of blood left on it anywhere. Then wipe it with oil and return it to its glove. Tomorrow I shall hand you a chit saying that I have given it to you. The chit is important.'

He stood there holding the sword in one hand and the scabbard in the other, staring at them with eyes as bright as two stars.

> But one thing you might do – let me know by telegram if you change your address – that is if it isn't too expensive – and mind you *do* change your address pretty soon. It's absolute madness to stay anywhere in the East of England now. You'll have parachute troops landing on the lawn if you don't look out.

'I am presenting it to you for bravery,' I said. 'But you must not tell that to anybody. Tell them simply that I gave it to you as a going-away present.'

'Yes, bwana,' he said. 'That is what I shall tell them.' He paused for a moment and looked me straight in the eye. 'Tell me truthfully, bwana,' he said, 'are you really and truly glad that I killed the big Germani sisal-grower?'

'*We* killed one today as well,' I said.

'You *did*?' Mdisho cried. 'You killed one, too?'

'We had to do it or he would probably have killed me.'

'Then we are equal, bwana,' he said, smiling with his wonderful white teeth. 'That makes us exactly equal, you and me.'

'Yes,' I said. 'I suppose it does.'

Flying Training

In November 1939, when the war was two months old, I told the Shell Company that I wanted to join up and help in the fight against Bwana Hitler, and they released me with their blessing. In a wonderfully magnanimous gesture, they told me that they would continue to pay my salary into the bank wherever I might happen to be in the world and for as long as the war lasted and I remained alive. I thanked them very much indeed and got into my ancient little Ford Prefect and set off on the 600-mile journey from Dar es Salaam to Nairobi to enlist in the RAF.

When one is quite alone on a lengthy and slightly hazardous journey like this, every sensation of pleasure and fear is enormously intensified, and several incidents from that strange two-day safari up through central Africa in my little black Ford have remained clear in my memory.

A frequent and always wonderful sight was the astonishing number of giraffe that I passed on the first day. They were usually in groups of three or four, often with a baby alongside, and they never ceased to enthral me. They were surprisingly tame. I would see them ahead of me nibbling green leaves from the tops of acacia trees by the side of the road, and whenever I came upon them I would stop the car and get out and walk slowly towards them, shouting inane but cheery greetings up into the sky where their small heads were waving about on their long long necks. I often amazed myself by the way I behaved when I was certain that there were no other human beings within fifty miles. All my inhibitions would disappear and I would shout, 'Hello, giraffes! Hello! Hello! Hello! How are you today?' And the giraffes would incline their heads very slightly and stare down at me with languorous demure expressions, but they never ran away. I found it exhilarating to be able to walk freely among such huge graceful wild creatures and talk to them as I wished.

The road northwards through Tanganyika was narrow and often deeply rutted, and once I saw a very large thick greenish-brown cobra gliding slowly over the ruts in the road about thirty yards ahead of me. It was seven or eight feet long and was holding its flat spoon-shaped head six inches up in the air and well clear of the dusty road. I stopped the car smartly so as not to run it over, and to be truthful I was so frightened I went quickly into reverse and kept backing away until the fearsome thing had disappeared into the undergrowth. I never lost my fear of snakes all the time I was in the tropics. They gave me the shivers.

At the Wami river the natives put my car on a raft and six strong men on the opposite bank started to pull me across the hundred yards or so of water with a rope, chanting as they pulled. The river was running swiftly and in midstream the slim raft upon which my car and I were balanced began to get carried down-river by the current. The six strong men chanted louder and pulled harder and I sat helpless in the car watching the crocodiles swimming around the raft, and the crocodiles stared up at me with their cruel black eyes. I was bobbing about on that river for over an hour, but in the end the six strong men won their battle with the currents and pulled me across. 'That will be three shillings, bwana,' they said, laughing.

terry at Wami River

Only once did I see any elephant. I saw a big tusker and his cow and their one baby moving slowly forward in line astern about fifty yards from the road on the edge of the forest. I stopped the car to watch them but I did not get out. The elephants never saw me and I was able to stay gazing at them for quite a while. A great sense of peace and serenity seemed to surround these massive, slow-moving, gentle beasts. Their skin hung loose over their bodies like suits they had inherited from larger ancestors, with the trousers ridiculously baggy. Like the giraffes they were vegetarians and did not have to hunt or kill in order to survive in the jungle, and no other wild beast would ever dare to threaten them. Only the foul humans in the shape of an occasional big-game hunter or an ivory poacher were to be feared, but this small elephant family did not look as though they had yet met any of these horrors. They seemed to be leading a life of absolute contentment. They are better off than me, I told myself, and a good deal wiser. I myself am at this moment on my way to kill Germans or to be killed by them, but those elephants have no thought of murder in their minds.

At the frontier between Tanganyika and Kenya there was a wooden gate across the road with an old shack alongside it, and in command of this great outpost of Customs and Immigration was an ancient and toothless black man who told me he had been there for thirty-seven years. He gave me a cup of tea and said he was sorry he did not have any sugar to put into it. I asked him if he wished to see my passport but he shook his head and said all passports looked the same to him. In any event, he added, smiling secretly, he could not read without spectacles and he did not possess any.

Outside the Customs shack, a group of enormous Masai tribesmen holding spears were crowding round my car. They stared at me curiously and patted the car with their hands, but we were unable to understand each other's language.

A little later on, I was bumping along on a particularly narrow bit of road through some very thick jungle when all of a sudden the sun went down and in ten minutes darkness descended over the jungle land. My headlamps were very dim. It would have been foolish to push on through the night. So I parked just off the road in a scrubby patch of thorn trees to wait for the dawn, and I sat in the car with the window down and poured myself a tot of whisky with water. I drank it slowly, listening to the jungle noises all around me and I was not afraid. A car is good protection against almost any wild animal. I had with me a sandwich with hard cheese inside it and I ate that with my whisky.

Then I wound up the two windows, leaving just a half-inch gap at the top of each, and got into the back seat and curled up and went to sleep.

I reached Nairobi at about three o'clock the next afternoon and drove straight to the aerodrome where the small RAF headquarters was situated. There I was given a medical examination by an affable English doctor who remarked that six feet six inches was not the ideal height for a flier of aeroplanes.

Flying Training, Nairobi

'Does that mean you can't pass me for flying duties?' I asked him fearfully.

'Funnily enough,' he said, 'there is no mention of a height limit in my instructions, so I can pass you with a clear conscience. Good luck, my boy.'

I was fitted out with a simple uniform which consisted of khaki shorts and shirt and jacket and khaki stockings and black shoes, and I was given the rank of Leading Aircraftman (LAC) which is one below a Corporal. Then I was led over to a Nissen hut where my fellow trainees were already installed. There were sixteen of us altogether learning to fly in this Initial Training School in Nairobi, and I liked every one of my companions. They were all young men like me who had come out from England to work for some large commercial concern, usually either Barclays Bank or Imperial Tobacco, and who had now volunteered for flying duties. We were to spend the next six months training together in very close association, and then we would all be separated and posted off to various operational squadrons. It is a fact, and I verified it carefully later, that out of those sixteen, no fewer than thirteen were killed in the air within the next two years.

In retrospect, one gasps at the waste of life.

At the aerodrome we had three instructors and three planes. The instructors were civil airline pilots borrowed by the RAF from a small domestic company called Wilson Airways. The planes were Tiger Moths. The Tiger Moth is or was a thing of great beauty. Everybody who has ever flown a Tiger Moth has fallen in love with it. It is a totally efficient and very aerobatic little biplane powered by a Gypsy engine, and as my instructor told me, a Gypsy engine has never been known to fail in mid-air. You could throw a Tiger Moth about all over the sky and nothing ever broke. You could glide it upside down hanging in your straps for minutes on end, and although the engine cut out when you did that because the carburettor was also upside down, the motor started again at once when you turned her the right way up again. You could spin her vertically downwards for thousands of feet and then all she needed was a touch on the rudder-bar, a bit of throttle and the stick pushed forward and out she came in a couple of flips. A Tiger Moth had no vices. She never dropped a wing if you lost flying speed coming in to land, and she would suffer innumerable heavy landings from incompetent beginners without turning a hair. There were two cockpits in a Tiger Moth, one for the instructor and one for the pupil, and you could talk to each other while in flight through a rubber mouthpiece. She had no refinements and of course no self-starter, so that the only way to start the engine was to stand in front and swing the propeller by hand. When you did this, you took great care not to lose your balance and fall forward otherwise the prop would chop off your head.

Nairobi
4 December 1939

Dear Mama,

I'm having a lovely time, have never enjoyed myself so much. I've been sworn in to the R.A.F. proper and am definitely in it now until the end of the war. My rank – a Leading Aircraftman, with every opportunity of becoming a pilot officer in a few months if I don't make a B.F. of myself. No boys to do everything for me anymore. Get your own food, wash your own knives and forks, fold up your own clothes, and in short, do everything for yourself. I suppose I'd better not say too much about what we do or when we are going because the letter would probably be torn up by the censor, but we wake at 5.30 a.m., drill before breakfast till 7 a.m., fly and attend lectures till 12.30. 12.30/1.30 lunch – 1.30 to 6.00 p.m. flying and lectures. The flying is grand and our instructors are extremely pleasant and proficient. With any luck I'll be flying solo by the end of this week . . .

There was only one runway on the little Nairobi aerodrome and this gave everyone plenty of practice at cross-wind landings and take-offs. And on most mornings, before flying began, we all had to run out on to the airfield and chase the zebras away.

When flying a military aeroplane, you sit on your parachute, which adds another six inches to your height. When I got into the open cockpit of a Tiger Moth for the first time and sat down on my parachute, my entire head stuck up in the open air. The engine was running and I was getting a rush of wind full in the face from the slipstream.

'You are too tall,' the instructor whose name was Flying Officer Parkinson said. 'Are you sure you want to do this?'

'Yes please,' I said.

'Wait till we rev her up for take-off,' Parkinson said. 'You'll have a job to breathe. And keep those goggles down or you'll be blinded by watering eyes.'

Parkinson was right. On the first flight I was almost asphyxiated by the slipstream and survived only by ducking down into the cockpit for deep breaths every few seconds. After that, I tied a thin cotton scarf around my nose and mouth and this made breathing possible.

I see from my Log Book, which I still have, that I went solo after 7 hours 40 minutes, which was about average. An RAF pilot's Log Book, by the way, is, or certainly was in those days, quite a formidable affair. It was an almost square (8″ × 9″) book, 1″ thick and bound between two very hard covers faced with blue canvas. You never lost your Log Book. It contained a record of every flight you had ever made as well as the plane you were flying, the purpose and destination of the trip and the time you had spent in the air.

After I had gone solo, I was allowed to go up alone for much of the time and it was wonderful. How many young

YEAR 1939		AIRCRAFT		PILOT, OR 1ST PILOT	2ND PILOT, PUPIL OR PASSENGER	DUTY (INCLUDING RESULTS AND REMARKS)
Month	Date	Type	No.			TOTALS BROUGHT FORWARD
Nov.	27	TIGER	K16	Mr MARKHAM	SELF	ORIENTATION FLIGHT.
"	28	TIGER	K16	Mr MARKHAM	SELF	LEVEL FLYING - USE TRIM.
"	28	TIGER	K20	Mr MARKHAM	SELF	AIR T. TURN - TAKE OFFS.
"	29	TIGER	A16	Mr MARKHAM	SELF	TAKE OFFS, TURNS, STALLS.
"	30	TIGER	A16	Mr MARKHAM	SELF	TAKE OFFS, LANDING APPROACHES.
"	30	TIGER	A16	Mr MARKHAM	SELF	TAKE OFFS, STEEP TURN, APPROACHES
DEC	1	TIGER	A16	Mr MARKHAM	SELF	TAKE OFFS, LANDINGS
"	4	TIGER	A16	Mr MARKHAM	SELF	TAKE OFF, LANDINGS
"	4	TIGER	A16	Mr MARKHAM	SELF	LANDINGS
"	5	TIGER	A16	Mr MARKHAM	SELF	LANDINGS
"	6	TIGER	A16	Mr MARKHAM	SELF	LANDINGS
"	7	TIGER	A16	Mr MARKHAM	SELF	LANDINGS
"	8	TIGER	K16	Mr MARKHAM	SELF	LANDINGS
"	8	TIGER	K16	Mr MARKHAM	SELF	LANDINGS
"	9	TIGER	A16	Mr MARKHAM	SELF	LANDINGS
"	11	TIGER	A16	Mr MARKHAM	SELF	LANDINGS
"	12	TIGER	A16	Mr MARKHAM	SELF	LANDINGS
"	12	TIGER	A16	Mr MARKHAM	SELF	LANDINGS
"	13	TIGER	K16	Mr MARKHAM	SELF	LANDINGS
"	13	TIGER	K28	SELF	SELF	LANDINGS (FIRST SOLO)
"	14	TIGER	A16	Mr MARKHAM	SELF	LANDINGS

GRAND TOTAL [Cols. (1) to (10)] 12 Hrs 53 Mins.

TOTALS CARRIED FORWARD

SINGLE-ENGINE AIRCRAFT — DAY / NIGHT — MULTI-ENGINE AIRCRAFT — DAY / NIGHT — PASS. UNDER — INSTR/CLOUD FLYING [Incl. in cols. (1) to (10)]

0.05																	
0.15																	
0.30																	
0.40																	
0.45																	
0.25																	
0.35																	
0.35																	
0.30																	
0.30																	
0.30																	
0.40																	
0.35																	
0.35																	
0.35																	
0.30																	
0.30																	
0.40																	
0.40																	
0.10																	
0.10																	
12.53																	

men, I kept asking myself, were lucky enough to be allowed to go whizzing and soaring through the sky above a country as beautiful as Kenya? Even the aeroplane and the petrol were free! In the Great Rift Valley the big game and smaller game were as plentiful as cows on a dairy farm, and I flew low in my little Tiger Moth to look at them. Oh, the animals I saw every day from that cockpit! I would fly for long periods at a height of no more than sixty or seventy feet, gazing down at huge herds of buffalo and wildebeest which would stampede in all directions as I whizzed over. From an illustrated book I had bought in Nairobi, I learnt to recognize kudu, Thomson's gazelle, eland, impala and many other animals. I saw plenty of giraffe and rhino and elephant and lion, and once I spotted a leopard, sleek as silk, lying along the trunk of a large tree. He was watching some impala grazing below him and deciding which one to have for his dinner. I flew over the pink flamingos on Lake Nakuru and I flew all the way round the snow summit of Mount Kenya in my trusty little Tiger Moth. What a fortunate fellow I am, I kept telling myself. Nobody has ever had such a lovely time as this!

The initial training took eight weeks, and at the end of it we were all fairly competent fliers of light single-engined aircraft. We could loop the loop and fly upside down. We could get ourselves out of a spin. We could do forced landings with the engine cut. We could side-slip and land decently in a strong cross-wind. We could navigate our way solo from Nairobi to Eldoret or Nakuru and back with plenty of cloud about, and we were full of confidence.

As soon as we had passed out of Initial Training School in Nairobi, we were put on a train bound for Kampala, in Uganda. The journey took a day and a night, and the train was so slow that we spent a lot of the time, frisky young

Nairobi
18 December 1939

Dear Mama,
    Well, everything here is also going very smoothly. I did
my first solo flight some days ago and now go up alone for
longish periods every day. I've just learnt to loop the loop
and spin and the next thing we've got to do is flying upside
down, which isn't quite so funny. But it's all marvellous
fun . . .

LAC Ballantyne, me, Fabian Wallis

bloods that we were, climbing up on to the roofs of the
carriages and running the whole length of the train and
back, jumping over the gaps between the carriages.

At Kampala there was an Imperial Airways flying-boat moored on the lake and waiting to take the sixteen of us 2,000 miles north, to Cairo. By now we were half-trained pilots and wherever we went we were treated as moderately valuable properties. We ourselves were bursting with energy and exuberance and perhaps a touch of self-importance as well because now we were intrepid flying men and devils of the sky.

The great flying-boat flew low for the whole of the long journey, and as we passed over the wild and barren lands where Kenya meets the Sudan we saw literally hundreds of elephant. They seemed to move around in herds of about twenty, always with a mighty bull tusker leading the herd and with the cows and their babies in the rear. Never, I kept reminding myself as I peered down through the small round window of the flying-boat, never will I see anything like this again.

Soon we found the upper reaches of the Nile and followed it down to Wadi Halfa, where we landed to refuel. Wadi Halfa then was one corrugated-iron shed with a lot of 44-gallon drums of petrol lying around, and the river was narrow and very fast. We all marvelled at the skill of the pilot as he put the great lumbering flying-machine down on that rushing strip of water.

In Cairo we landed on a very different Nile, wide and sluggish, and we were shuttled ashore and taken to Heliopolis aerodrome and put on board a monstrous and ancient transport plane whose wings were joined together with bits of wire.

'Where are they taking us to?' we asked.

'To Iraq,' they answered, 'and jolly good luck to you all.'

'What do you mean by that?'

'We mean that you are going to Habbaniya in Iraq and

273

Habbaniya
20 February 1940

Dear Mama,

   Here is a not very good photo taken of me in the streets
of Cairo by one of those men who pop up from behind a
public lavatory and snap you and hand you a bit of paper
telling you to call tomorrow for the print . . .

Habbaniya is the most godforsaken hell-hole in the entire world,' they said, smirking. 'It is where you will stay for six months to complete your advanced flying training, after which you will be ready to join a squadron and face the enemy.'

Unless you had been there and seen it with your own eyes you could not believe that a place like Habbaniya existed. It was a vast assemblage of hangars and Nissen huts and brick bungalows set slap in the middle of a boiling desert on the banks of the muddy Euphrates river miles from anywhere.

"Filthy" Leuchars, me – Habbaniya

The nearest place to it was Baghdad, about 100 miles to the north.

This amazing and nonsensical RAF outpost was colossal. It was at least a mile long on each of its four sides, and there were paved streets called Bond Street and Regent Street and Tottenham Court Road. There were hospitals and dental surgeries and canteens and recreation halls and I don't know how many thousands of men lived there. What they did I never discovered. It was beyond me why anyone should want to build a vast RAF town in such an abominable, unhealthy, desolate place as Habbaniya.

> Habbaniya
> 10 July 1940
>
> Dear Mama,
>   We've been here nearly 5 months now, and as we get nearer and nearer to the time when our course is finished and we go elsewhere we get more and more thrilled. It will be curious to see ordinary men and actual women doing ordinary things in ordinary places once more, to call a taxi or use the telephone; to order what you want to eat or to see a train; to go up a flight of stairs or see a row of houses. All these things and many more I shall derive the very greatest pleasure from doing . . .

At Habbaniya we flew from dawn until 11 a.m. After that, as the temperature in the shade moved up towards 115°F, everyone had to stay indoors until it cooled down again. We were flying more powerful planes now, Hawker Harts with Rolls-Royce Merlin engines, and everything became suddenly much more serious. The Harts had machine-guns on their wings and we would practise shooting down the enemy by firing at a canvas drogue towed behind another plane.

My Log Book tells me that we were at Habbaniya from 20 February 1940 to 20 August 1940, for exactly six months, and apart from the flying which was always exhilarating, it was a pretty tedious period of my young life. There were minor excitements now and then to relieve the boredom such as the flooding of the Euphrates when we had to evacuate the entire camp to a windswept plateau for ten days. People got stung by scorpions and went into hospital for a while to recover. The Iraqi tribesmen sometimes took pot shots at us from the surrounding hills. Men occasionally got heatstroke and had to be packed in ice. Everyone suffered from prickly heat and itched all over for much of the time.

But eventually we got our wings and were judged ready to move on and confront the real enemy. About one half of the sixteen of us were given commissions and promoted to the rank of Pilot Officer. The other half were made Sergeant Pilots, though how this rather arbitrary class-conscious division was made I never knew. We were also divided up into fighter pilots or bomber pilots, fliers either of single-engined planes or twins. I became a Pilot Officer and a fighter pilot. Then all sixteen of us said goodbye to one another and were whisked off in many different directions.

I found myself at a large RAF station on the Suez Canal called Ismailia, where they told me that I had been posted to 80 Squadron who were flying Gladiators against the Italians in the Western Desert of Libya. The Gloster Gladiator was an out-of-date fighter biplane with a radial engine. Back in England at that time, all the fighter boys were flying

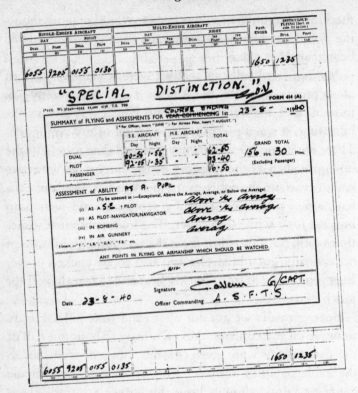

Hurricanes and Spitfires, but they were not sending any of those little beauties out to us in the Middle East quite yet.

The Gladiator was armed with two fixed machine-guns, and these actually fired bullets *through* the revolving propeller. To me, this was about the greatest piece of magic I had ever seen in my life. I simply could not understand how two machine-guns firing thousands of bullets a minute could be synchronized to fire their bullets *through* a propeller revolving at thousands of revs a minute without hitting the propeller blades. I was told it had something to do with a little oil pipe and that the propeller shaft communicated with the machine-guns by sending pulses along the pipe, but more than that I cannot tell you.

At Ismailia, a rather supercilious Flight-Lieutenant pointed to a parked Gladiator on the tarmac and said to me, 'That one's yours. You'll be flying it out to your squadron tomorrow.'

'Who will teach me how to fly it?' I asked, trembling.

'Don't be an ass,' he said. 'How can anyone teach you when there's only one cockpit? Just get in and do a few circuits and bumps and you'll soon get the hang of it. You had better get all the practice you can because the next thing you know you'll be dicing in the air with some clever little Italian who will be trying to shoot you down.'

I remember thinking at the time that this was surely not the right way of doing things. They had spent eight months and a great deal of money training me to fly and suddenly

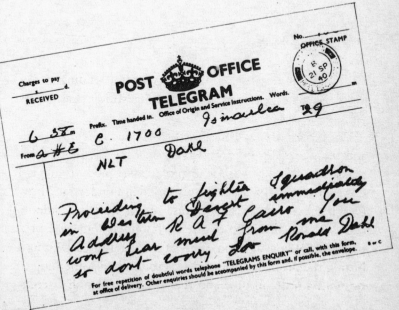

that was the end of it all. Nobody in Ismailia was going to teach me anything about air-to-air combat, and they were certainly not going to take time off to instruct me when I joined a busy operational squadron. There is no question that we were flung in at the deep end, totally unprepared for actual fighting in the air, and this, in my opinion, accounted for the very great losses of young pilots that we suffered out there. I myself survived only by the skin of my teeth.

Survival

Some forty years ago I described in a story called 'A Piece of Cake' what it was like to find myself strapped firmly into the cockpit of my Gladiator with a fractured skull and a bashed-in face and a fuzzy mind while the crashed plane was going up in flames on the sands of the Western Desert. But there is an aspect of that story that I feel ought to be clarified by me and it is this. There seems, on re-reading it, to be an implication that I was shot down by enemy action, and if I remember rightly, this was inserted by the editors of an American magazine called the *Saturday Evening Post* who originally bought and published it. Those were the war years and the more dramatic the story, the better it was. They actually called it 'Shot Down in Libya', so you can see what they were getting at. The fact is that my crash had nothing whatsoever to do with enemy action. I was not shot down either by another plane or from the ground. Here is what happened.

I had climbed into my new Gladiator at an RAF airfield called Abu Suweir on the Suez Canal, and had set off alone to join 80 Squadron in the Western Desert. This was going to be my very first venture into combat territory. The date was 19 September 1940. They told me to fly across the Nile delta and land at a small airfield called Amiriya, near Alexandria, to refuel. Then I should fly on and land again at a bomber airfield in Libya called Fouka for a second refuelling. At Fouka I was to report to the Commanding

The Eastern Mediterranean

Officer who would tell me precisely where 80 Squadron were at that moment, and I would then fly on and join them. A forward airfield in the Western Desert was in those days never much more than a strip of sand surrounded by tents and parked aircraft, and these airfields were being moved very frequently from one site to another, depending on whether the front line of the army was advancing or retreating.

The flight in itself was a fairly daunting one for someone who had virtually no experience of the aircraft he was flying and none at all of flying long distances over Egypt and Libya with no navigational aids to help him. I had no radio. All I had was a map strapped to one knee. It took me one hour exactly to get from Abu Suweir to Amiriya where I landed with some difficulty in a sandstorm. But I got my plane refuelled and set off as quickly as I could for Fouka. I landed at Fouka fifty-five minutes later (all these times are meticulously recorded in my Log Book) and reported to the CO in his tent. He made some calls on his field telephone and then asked me for my map.

'Eighty Squadron are now there,' he said, pointing to a spot in the middle of the desert about thirty miles due south of the small coastal town of Mersah Matrûh.

'Will it be easy to see?' I asked him.

'You can't miss it,' he said. 'You'll see the tents and about fifteen Gladiators parked around the place. You can spot it from miles away.' I thanked him and went off to calculate my course and distance.

The time was 6.15 p.m. when I took off from Fouka for 80 Squadron's landing strip. I estimated my flight time to be fifty minutes at the most. That would give me fifteen or twenty minutes to spare before darkness fell, which should be ample.

I flew straight for the point where the 80 Squadron airfield should have been. It wasn't there. I flew around the area to north, south, east and west, but there was not a sign of an airfield. Below me there was nothing but empty desert, and rather rugged desert at that, full of large stones and boulders and gullies.

At this point, dusk began to fall and I realized that I was in trouble. My fuel was running low and there was no way I could get back to Fouka on what I had left. I couldn't have found it in the dark anyway. The only course open to me now was to make a forced landing in the desert and make it quickly, before it was too dark to see.

I skimmed low over the boulder-strewn desert searching for just one small strip of reasonably flat sand on which to land. I knew the direction of the wind so I knew precisely the direction that my approach should take. But where, oh where was there one little patch of desert that was clear of boulders and gullies and lumps of rock. There simply wasn't one. It was nearly dark now. I *had* to get down somehow or other. I chose a piece of ground that seemed to me to be as boulder-free as any and I made an approach. I came in as slowly as I dared, hanging on the prop, travelling just above my stalling speed of eighty miles an hour. My wheels touched down. I throttled back and prayed for a bit of luck.

I didn't get it. My undercarriage hit a boulder and collapsed completely and the Gladiator buried its nose in the sand at what must have been about seventy-five miles an hour.

My injuries in that bust-up came from my head being thrown forward violently against the reflector-sight when the plane hit the ground (in spite of the fact that I was strapped tightly, as always, into the cockpit), and apart from the skull fracture, the blow pushed my nose in and knocked out a few teeth and blinded me completely for days to come.

It is odd that I can remember very clearly quite a few of the things that followed seconds after the crash. Obviously I was unconscious for some moments, but I must have recovered my senses very quickly because I can remember hearing a mighty *whoosh* as the petrol tank in the port wing exploded, followed almost at once by another mighty *whoosh* as the starboard tank went up in flames. I could see nothing at all, and I felt no pain. All I wanted was to go gently off to sleep and to hell with the flames. But soon a tremendous heat around my legs galvanized my soggy brain into action. With great difficulty I managed to undo first my seat-straps and then the straps of my parachute, and I can even remember the desperate effort it took to push myself upright in the cockpit and roll out head first on to the sand below. Again I wanted to lie down and doze off, but the heat close by was terrific and had I stayed where I was I should simply have been roasted alive. I began very very slowly to drag myself away from the awful hotness. I heard my machine-gun ammunition exploding in the flames and the bullets were pinging about all over the place but that didn't worry me. All I wanted was to get away from the tremendous heat and rest in peace. The world about me was divided sharply down the middle into two halves. Both of these halves were pitch black, but one was scorching-hot and the other was not. I had to keep on dragging myself away from the scorching-hot side and into the cooler one, and this took a long time and enormous effort, but in the end the temperature all around me became bearable. When that happened I collapsed and went to sleep.

It was revealed at an inquiry into my crash held later that

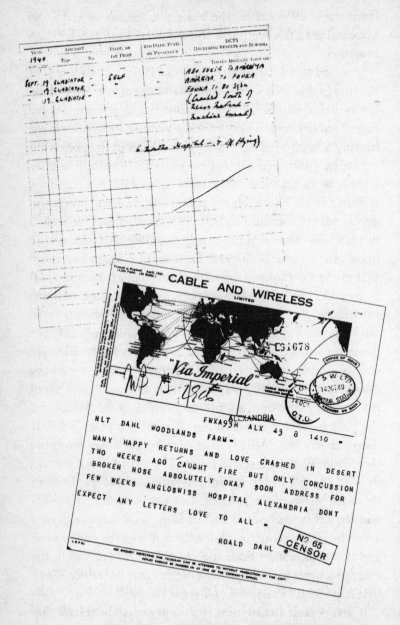

YEAR 1940		AIRCRAFT		PILOT, OR 1ST PILOT	2ND PILOT, PUPIL OR PASSENGER	DUTY (INCLUDING RESULTS AND REMARKS)
		Type	No.			TOTALS BROUGHT FORWARD
SEPT. 19	GLADIATOR		–	SELF	–	ABU SUEIR TO AMIRIYA
ˮ 19	GLADIATOR		–	–	–	AMIRIYA TO FOUKA
ˮ 19	GLADIATOR		–	–	–	FOUKA TO 80 Sqdn
						(Crashed South of Mersa Matruh – machine burned)
						6 months Hospital – (& off flying)

CABLE AND WIRELESS
LIMITED

"Via Imperial"

ALEXANDRIA

FWXA93H ALX 43 8 1410 –

NLT DAHL WOODLANDS FARM =

MANY HAPPY RETURNS AND LOVE CRASHED IN DESERT
TWO WEEKS AGO CAUGHT FIRE BUT ONLY CONCUSSION
BROKEN NOSE ABSOLUTELY OKAY SOON ADDRESS FOR
FEW WEEKS ANGLOSWISS HOSPITAL ALEXANDRIA DONT
EXPECT ANY LETTERS LOVE TO ALL =

ROALD DAHL

Nº 65
CENSOR

NO ENQUIRY RESPECTING THIS TELEGRAM CAN BE ATTENDED TO WITHOUT PRODUCTION OF THIS COPY.
REPLIES SHOULD BE HANDED IN AT ONE OF THE COMPANY'S OFFICES.

the CO at Fouka had given me totally wrong information. Eighty Squadron had never been in the position I was sent to. They were fifty miles to the south, and the place to which I had been sent was actually no-man's-land, which was a strip of sand in the Western Desert about half a mile wide dividing the front lines of the British and Italian armies. I am told that the flames from my burning aircraft lit up the sand dunes for miles around, and of course not only the crash but also the subsequent bonfire were witnessed by the soldiers of both sides. The watchers in the trenches had been observing my antics for some time, and both sides knew that it was an RAF fighter and not an Italian plane that had come down. The remains, if any, were therefore of more interest to our people than to the enemy.

When the flames had died down and the desert was dark, a little patrol of three brave men from the Suffolk Regiment crawled out from the British lines to inspect the wreck. They did not think for one moment that they would find anything but a burnt-out fuselage and a charred skeleton, and they were apparently astounded when they came upon my still-breathing body lying in the sand nearby.

When they turned me over in the dark to get a better look, I must have swum back into consciousness because I can distinctly remember hearing one of them asking me how I felt, but I was unable to reply. Then I heard them whispering together about how they were going to get me back to the lines without a stretcher.

The next thing I can remember a long time later was a man's voice speaking loudly to me and telling me that he knew I was unable to see him or to answer him, but he thought there was a chance I could hear him. He told me he was an English doctor and that I was in an underground first-aid post in Mersah Matrûh. He said they were going to take me to the train by ambulance and send me back to Alexandria.

I heard him talking to me and I understood what he was saying, and I also knew all about Mersah Matrûh and about the train. Mersah was a small town about 250 miles along the Libyan coast west of Alexandria, and our army had a most carefully preserved little railway running across the desert between the two places. This railway was a vital supply line for our forward troops in the Western Desert and the Italians were bombing it all the time but we somehow managed to keep it going. Everyone knew about the single-track railway-line that ran all the way along the coast beside the sparkling white beaches of the southern Mediterranean from Alex to Mersah.

I heard voices around me as they manoeuvred my stretcher into the ambulance, and when the ambulance started to move forward over the very bumpy track, someone above me began screaming. Every time we hit a bump the man above me cried out in agony.

When they were putting me on to the train, I felt a hand on my shoulder and a lovely Cockney voice said, 'Cheer up, matey. You'll soon be back in Alex.'

The next thing I can remember was being taken off the train into the tremendous bustle of Alexandria Station, and I heard a woman's voice saying, 'This one's an officer. He'll go to the Anglo-Swiss.'

Then I was inside the hospital itself and I heard the wheels of my stretcher rumbling softly along endless corridors. 'Put him in here for the moment,' a different woman's voice was saying. 'We want to have a look at him before he goes into the ward.'

Deft fingers began to unroll the bandages around my

head. 'Can you hear me talking to you?' the owner of the fingers was saying. She took one of my hands in hers and said, 'If you can hear what I am saying, just give my hand a squeeze.' I squeezed her hand. 'Good,' she said. 'That's fine. Now we know you're going to be all right.'

Then she said, 'Here he is, doctor. I've taken off the dressings. He is conscious and is responding.'

I felt the close proximity of the doctor's face as he bent over me, and I heard him saying, 'Do you have much pain?'

Now that the bandages had been taken off my head, I found myself able to burble an answer to him. 'No,' I said. 'No pain. But I can't see.'

'Don't worry about that,' the doctor said. 'All you've got to do is to lie very still. Don't move. Do you want to empty your bladder?'

'Yes,' I said.

'We'll help you,' he said, 'but don't move. Don't try to do anything for yourself.'

I believe they inserted a catheter because I felt them doing something down there and it hurt a bit, but then the pressure on my bladder went away.

'Just a dry dressing for the moment, Sister,' the doctor said. 'We'll X-ray him in the morning.'

Then I was in a ward with a lot of other men who talked and joked a good deal among themselves. I lay there dozing and feeling no pain at all, and later on the air-raid sirens started wailing and the ack-ack guns began opening up on all sides and I heard a lot of bombs exploding not very far away. I knew it was night-time now because that was when the Italian bombers came over seven nights a week to raid our navy in Alexandria harbour. I felt very calm and dreamy lying there listening to the terrific commotion of bombs and ack-ack going on outside. It was as though I had ear-phones on and all the noise was coming to me over the wireless from miles and miles away.

I knew when the morning came because the whole ward began to bustle and breakfasts were served all round. Obviously I couldn't eat because my whole head was sheathed in bandages with only small holes left for breathing. I didn't want to eat anyway. I was always sleepy. One of my arms was strapped to a board because tubes were going into the arm, but the other, the right arm, was free and once I explored the bandages on my head with my fingers. Then the Sister was saying to me, 'We are moving your bed into another room where it is quieter and you can be by yourself.'

So they wheeled me out of the ward into a single room, and over the next one or two or three days, I don't know how many, I submitted in a semi-daze to various procedures such as X-rays and being taken several times to the operating theatre. One of my more vivid recollections is of a conversation that went on in the theatre itself between a doctor and me. I knew I was in the theatre because they always told me where they were taking me, and this time the doctor said to me, 'Well, young man, we are going to use a super brand-new anaesthetic on you today. It's just come out from England and it is given by injection.' I had had short talks with this particular doctor several times. He was an anaesthetist and had visited me in my room before each operation to put his stethoscope on my chest and back. All my life I have taken an intense and inquisitive interest in every form of medicine, and even in those young days I had begun to ask the doctors a lot of questions. This man, perhaps because I was blind, always took the trouble to treat me as an intelligent listener.

'What is it called?' I asked him.

'Sodium pentathol,' he answered.

'And you have never used it before?'

'I have never used it myself,' he said, 'but it has been a great success back home as a pre-anaesthetic. It is very quick and comfortable.'

I could sense that there were quite a few other people, men and women, padding silently around the operating theatre in their rubber boots and I could hear the tinkling of instruments lifted and put down, and the talk of soft voices. Both my senses of smell and of hearing had become very acute since my blindness, and I had developed an instinctive habit of translating sounds and scents into a coloured mental picture. I was picturing the operating theatre now, so white and sterile with the masked and green-gowned inmates going priestlike about their separate tasks, and I wondered where the surgeon was, the great man who was going to do all the cutting and the stitching.

I was about to have a major operation performed on my face, and the man who was doing it had been a famous Harley Street plastic surgeon before the war, but now he was a Surgeon-Commander in the navy. One of the nurses had told me about his Harley Street days that morning. 'You'll be all right with him,' she had said. 'He's a wonder-worker. And it's all free. A job like you're having would be costing you five hundred guineas in civvy street.'

'You mean this is the very first time you've ever used this anaesthetic?' I said to the anaesthetist.

This time he didn't answer me directly. 'You'll love it,' he said. 'You go out like a light. You don't even have any sensation of losing consciousness as you do with all the others. So here we go. You'll just feel a little prick on the back of your hand.'

I felt the needle going into a vein on the top of my left hand and I lay there waiting for the moment when I would 'go out like a light'.

I was quite unafraid. I have never been frightened by surgeons or of being given an anaesthetic, and to this day, after some sixteen major operations on numerous parts of my body, I still have complete faith in all, or let me say *nearly* all, those men of medicine.

I lay there waiting and waiting and absolutely nothing happened. My bandages had been taken off for the operation, but my eyes were still permanently closed by the swellings on my face. One doctor had told me it was quite possible that my eyes had not been damaged at all. I doubted that myself. It seemed to me that I had been permanently blinded, and as I lay there in my quiet black room where all sounds, however tiny, had suddenly become twice as loud, I had plenty of time to think about what total blindness would mean in the future. Curiously enough, it did not frighten me. It did not even depress me. In a world where war was all around me and where I had ridden in dangerous little aeroplanes that roared and zoomed and crashed and caught fire, blindness, not to mention life itself, was no longer too important. Survival was not something one struggled for any more. I was already beginning to realize that the only way to conduct oneself in a situation where bombs rained down and bullets whizzed past, was to accept the dangers and all the consequences as calmly as possible. Fretting and sweating about it all was not going to help.

The doctor had tried to comfort me by saying that when you have contusions and swellings as massive as mine, you have to wait at least until the swellings go down and the incrustations of blood around the eyelids have come away.

'Give yourself a chance,' he had said. 'Wait until those eyelids are able to open again.'

Having at this moment no eyelids to open and shut, I hoped the anaesthetist wouldn't start thinking that his famous new wonder anaesthetic had put me to sleep when it hadn't. I didn't want them to start before I was ready. 'I'm still awake,' I said.

'I know you are,' he said.

'What's going on?' I heard another man's voice asking. 'Isn't it working?' This, I knew, was the surgeon, the great man from Harley Street.

'It doesn't seem to be having any effect at all,' the anaesthetist said.

'Give him some more.'

'I have, I have,' the anaesthetist answered, and I thought I detected a slightly ruffled edge to the man's voice.

'London said it was the greatest discovery since chloroform,' the surgeon was saying. 'I saw the report myself. Matthews wrote it. Ten seconds, it said, and the patient's out. Simply tell him to count to ten and he's out before he gets to eight, that's what the report said.'

'This patient could have counted to a hundred,' the anaesthetist was saying.

It occurred to me that they were talking to one another as though I wasn't there. I would have been happier if they had kept quiet.

'Well, we can't wait all day,' the surgeon was saying. It was *his* turn to get irritable now. But I did not want my surgeon to be irritable when he was about to perform a delicate operation on my face. He had come into my room the day before and after examining me carefully, he had said, 'We can't have you going about like that for the rest of your life, can we?'

That worried me. It would have worried anyone. 'Like what?' I had asked him.

'I am going to give you a lovely new nose,' he had said, patting me on the shoulder. 'You want to have something nice to look at when you open your eyes again, don't you. Did you ever see Rudolph Valentino in the cinema?'

'Yes,' I said.

'I shall model your nose on his,' the surgeon said. 'What do you think of Rudolph Valentino, Sister?'

'He's smashing,' the Sister said.

And now, in the operating theatre, that same surgeon was saying to the anaesthetist, 'I'd forget that pentathol stuff if I were you. We really can't wait any longer. I've got four more on my list this morning.'

'Right!' snapped the anaesthetist. 'Bring me the nitrous oxide.'

I felt the rubber mask being put over my nose and mouth, and soon the blood-red circles began going round and round faster and faster like a series of gigantic scarlet flywheels and then there was an explosion and I knew nothing more.

When I regained consciousness I was back in my room. I lay there for an uncounted number of weeks but you must not think that I was totally without company during that time. Every morning throughout those black and sightless days a nurse, always the same one, would come into my room and bathe my eyes with something soft and wet. She was very gentle and very careful and she never hurt me. For at least an hour she would sit on my bed working skilfully on my swollen sealed-up eyes, and she would talk to me while she worked. She told me that the Anglo-Swiss used to be a large civilian hospital and that when war broke out the navy took over the whole place. All the doctors and all the nurses in the hospital were navy people, she said.

'Are you in the navy?' I asked her.

'Yes,' she said. 'I am a naval officer.'

'Why am *I* here if it's all navy?'

'We're taking in the RAF and the army as well now,' she said. 'That's where most of the casualties are coming from.'

Her name, she told me, was Mary Welland, and her home was in Plymouth. Her father was a Commander on a cruiser operating somewhere in the north Atlantic, and her mother worked with the Red Cross in Plymouth. She said with a smile in her voice that it was very bad form for a nurse to sit on a patient's bed, but what she was doing to my eyes was very delicate work that could only be done if she were sitting close to me. She had a lovely soft voice, and I began to picture to myself the face that went with the voice, the delicate features, the green-blue eyes, the golden-brown hair and the pale skin. Sometimes, as she worked very close to my eyes, I would feel her warm and faintly marmalade breath on my cheek and in no time at all I began to fall very quickly and quite dizzily in love with Mary Welland's invisible image. Every morning, I waited impatiently for the door to open and for the tinkling sound of the trolley as she wheeled it into my room.

Her features, I decided, were very much like those of Myrna Loy. Myrna Loy was a Hollywood cinema actress I had seen many times on the silver screen, and up until then she had been my idea of the perfect beauty. But now I took Miss Loy's face and made it even more beautiful and gave it to Mary Welland. The only concrete thing I had to go by was the voice, and so far as I was concerned, Mary Welland's dulcet tones were infinitely preferable to Myrna Loy's harsh American twang.

For about an hour every day I experienced ecstasy as Miss Myrna Mary Loy Welland sat on my bed and did things to my face and eyes with her delicate fingers. And then suddenly, I don't know how many days later, came the moment that I can never forget.

Mary Welland was working away on my right eye with one of her soft moist pads when all at once the eyelid began to open. At first it opened only an infinitesimal crack, but even so, a shaft of brilliant light pierced the darkness in my head and I saw before me very close . . . I saw three separate things . . . and all of them were glistening with scarlet and gold!

'I can see!' I cried. 'I can see something!'

'You can?' she said excitedly. 'Are you sure?'

'Yes! I can see something very close to me! I can see three separate things right in front of me! And nurse . . . they are all shining with red and gold! What are they, nurse? What am I seeing?'

'Try to keep calm,' she said. 'Stop jumping up and down. It's not good for you.'

'But nurse, I really can see something! Don't you believe me?'

'Is this what you are seeing?' she asked me, and now part of a hand and a pointing finger came into my line of sight. 'Is it this? Is it these?' she said, and her finger pointed at the three beautiful things of many colours that lay there shimmering against a background of purest white.

'Yes!' I cried. 'It's those! There are three of them! I can see them all! And I can see your finger!'

When many days of blackness and doubt are pierced suddenly by shining images of red and gold, the pleasure that floods into your mind is overwhelming. I lay propped up on my pillows gazing through the tiny crack in one eye at these amazing sights and wondering whether I wasn't perhaps catching a glimpse of paradise. 'What am I looking at?' I asked her.

'You are looking at a bit of my white uniform,' Mary Welland said. 'It's the bit that goes across my front, and the coloured things you can see in the middle of it make up the emblem of the Royal Naval Nursing Service. It is pinned to the left side of my bosom and it is worn by all nurses in the Royal Navy.'

Alexandria
20 November 1940

Dear Mama,

I sent you a telegram yesterday saying that I'd got up for 2 hours & had a bath – so you'll see I'm making good progress. I arrived here about 8½ weeks ago, and was lying on my back for 7 weeks doing nothing, then sat up gradually, and now I am walking about a bit. When I came in I was a bit of a mess. My eyes didn't open (although I was always quite concious). They thought I had a fractured base (skull), but I think the Xray showed I didn't. My nose was bashed in, but they've got the most marvellous Harley Street specialists out here who've joined up for the war as Majors, and the ear nose & throat man pulled my nose out of the back of my head, and shaped it and now it looks just as before except that its a little bent about. That was of course under a general anesthetic.

My eyes still ache if I read or write much, but they say that they think they'll get back to normal again, and that I'll be fit for flying in about 3 months. In between I still have about 6 or more weeks sick leave here in Alex when I get out, doing nothing in a marvellous sunny climate, just like an English Summer, except that the sun shines every day.

I suppose you want to know how I crashed. Well, I'm not allowed to give you any details of what I was doing or how it happened. But it occurred in the night not very far from the Italian front lines. The plane was on fire and after it hit the ground I was just sufficiently concious to crawl out in time, having undone my straps, and roll on the ground to put out the fire on my overalls which were alight. I wasn't burnt much, but was bleeding rather badly from the head. Anyway I lay there and waited for the ammunition which was left in my guns to go off. One after the other, well over 1000 rounds exploded and the bullets whistled about seeming to hit everything but me.

I've never fainted yet, and I think it was this tendency to remain concious which saved me from being roasted.

Anyway luckily one of our forward patrols saw the blaze, and after some time arrived and picked me up & after much ado I arrived at Mersa Matruh, (you'll see it on the map – on the coast, East of Libya). There I heard a doctor say, 'Oh, he's an Italian is he' (my white flying overalls weren't very recognizable). I told him not to be a B.F., and he gave me some morphia. In about 24 hours time I arrived where I am now, living in great luxury with lots of very nice English nursing sisters to look after me . . .

P.S. The air raids here don't worry us. The Italians are very bad bombaimers.

'But they are so *beautiful*!' I cried, staring at the emblem. There were three separate parts to it, all of them heavily embossed in raised embroidery. On top there was a golden crown with scarlet in the centre and small bits of green near its base. In the middle, below the crown, there was a gold anchor with a scarlet rope twined around it. And below the anchor there was a golden circle with a big red cross in the middle. These images and their brilliant colours have been engraved on my memory ever since.

'Keep still,' Mary Welland said. 'I think we can open this eyelid a bit more.'

I kept still and waited, and a few minutes later she succeeded in getting the eyelid wide open and I saw the whole room through that one eye. In the forefront of everything I saw Nursing Officer Welland herself sitting very close and smiling at me. 'Hello,' she said. 'Welcome back to the world.'

She was a lovely looking girl, much nicer than Myrna Loy and far more real. 'You are even more beautiful than I imagined,' I said.

'Well, thank you,' she said.

The next day she got the other eye open as well and I lay there feeling as though I was about to start my whole life over again.

Mary Welland was certainly lovely. She was gentle and kind. She remained my friend all the time I was in hospital. But there is a world of difference between falling in love with a voice and remaining in love with a person you can see. From the moment I opened my eyes, Mary became a human instead of a dream and my passion evaporated.

All the time I was in hospital, my one obsession was to get back to operational flying. The doctors told me there was virtually no hope of that. They said that even if I managed to get back perfect vision, I would still have the head injuries to contend with. Severe head injuries are not easily overcome, they said, and I had better resign myself to being shipped home eventually as a non-combatant. I admit now, although I didn't tell them at the time, that for several weeks after I had regained my sight I suffered from the most appalling headaches, but even these began gradually to grow less and less severe.

Alexandria
6 December 1940

Dear Mama,

I haven't written to you since my one and only letter some weeks ago, chiefly because the doctors said that it wasn't good for me. As a matter of fact I've been progressing very slowly. As I told you in my telegram I did start getting up, but they soon popped me back to bed again because I got such terrific headaches. A week ago I was moved back into this private room, and I have just completed a whole long 7 days lying flat on my back in semi darkness doing absolutely nothing – not even allowed to lift a finger to wash myself. Well, that's over, and I'm sitting up today, (its 8 o'clock in the evening actually) and writing this and incidentally feeling fine. Tomorrow I think they are going to give me intravenal saline and pituatory injections & make me drink gallons of water – its another stunt to get rid of the headaches. You needn't be alarmed – there's nothing very wrong with me, I've merely had an extremely serious concussion. They say I certainly won't fly for about 6 months, and last week were going to invalid me home on the next convoy. But somehow I didn't want to – once invalided home, I knew I'd never get on to flying again, and who wants to be invalided home anyway. When I go I want to go normally . . .

After four months in hospital I was allowed out of bed, and I used to stand for hours in my dressing-gown looking out of my window at the view. The only view I had was the courtyard of the hospital, and that wasn't much to look at, but directly across the courtyard I could see through a huge window into a long wide corridor. One morning I saw a medical orderly coming down this corridor carrying a very large tray with a white cloth over it. Walking in the opposite direction towards the orderly, was a middle-aged woman, probably somebody from the hospital clerical staff. When the orderly came level with the woman, he suddenly whipped away the cloth from the tray and pushed the tray towards the woman's face. On the tray there lay the entire quite naked amputated leg of a soldier. I saw the poor woman reel backwards. I saw the foul orderly roar with laughter and replace the cloth and walk on. I saw the woman stagger to the window-sill and lean forward with her head in her hands, then she pulled herself together and went on her way. I have never forgotten that little illustration of man's repulsive behaviour towards woman.

I was finally discharged from hospital in February 1941, five months after I was admitted. I was given four weeks' convalescence which I spent in Alexandria living in total luxury in the magnificent house of a charming and very wealthy English family called Peel. Dorothy Peel was a regular hospital visitor at the Anglo-Swiss, and when she heard that I was soon to be allowed out, she said, 'Come and stay with us.' So I did, and I was a lucky fellow to have found such a splendid place among such kind people in which to gather myself together for the next round.

After four weeks with the Peels, I reported to the RAF medical examiners in Cairo, and it was a great day for me when I was once again passed fully fit for flying duties.

But where were my old squadron now?

Eighty Squadron, as it turned out, were no longer in the Western Desert. They were far across the water in Greece,

Convalescing, Peel's garden, Alexandria

where for some weeks they had been flying valiantly against the Italian invaders. But now the German armies and air forces had joined the Italians in Greece and were rapidly over-running the little country. It was obvious to everybody, even then, that the tiny token British Expeditionary Force and the handful of RAF planes in Greece were not going to be able to last long against the German juggernaut.

Where did they want me to go? I asked.

To Greece, of course, they said. They told me that 80 Squadron were no longer flying Gladiators. They were now equipped with Mark 1 Hurricanes. I must learn very quickly to fly a Hurricane and then I must take it to Greece and rejoin the squadron.

When I got this news I was in Ismailia, a large RAF aerodrome on the Suez Canal. A Flight-Lieutenant pointed to a Hurricane standing on the tarmac and said, 'You can have a couple of days to learn how to fly it, then you take it to Greece.'

'Fly that to Greece?' I said.

'Of course.'

'Where do I stop to refuel?'

'You don't,' he said. 'You go non-stop.'

'How long will it take?'

'About four and a half hours,' he said.

Even I knew that a Hurricane had fuel for only one and a half hours' flying, and I pointed this out to the Flight-Lieutenant. 'Don't worry about that,' he said. 'We're fitting extra fuel tanks under the wings.'

'Do they work?'

'Sometimes they work,' he said, smirking. 'You press a little button and if you're lucky a pump pumps petrol from the wing-tanks into the main tank.'

'What happens if the pump doesn't work?'

'You bale out into the Med and swim,' he said.

'No,' I said. 'Be serious. Who picks me up?'

'Nobody,' he said. 'It's a chance you have to take.'

This, I told myself, is a waste of manpower and machinery. I had no experience at all in flying against the enemy. I had never been in an operational squadron. And now they wanted me to jump into a plane I had never flown before and fly it to Greece to fight against a highly efficient air force that outnumbered us by a hundred to one.

I was petrified as I strapped myself into the Hurricane for the first time. It was the first monoplane I had ever flown. It was without a doubt the first *modern* plane I had ever flown. It was many times more powerful and speedy and tricky than anything I had ever seen. I had never flown a plane with a retractable undercarriage before. I had never flown a plane with wing-flaps which had to be used to slow down your landing speed. I had never flown a plane with a variable pitch propeller or one that had eight machine-guns in its wings. I had never flown anything like it. Somehow I managed to get the thing off the ground and back down again without smashing it up, but for me it was like riding a bucking horse. I was just beginning to learn where most of the knobs were located and what they were used for when my two days were up and I had to leave for Greece.

Ismailia
12 April 1941

Dear Mama,

A very short note to say that I'm going north across the sea almost at once to join my squadron. I telegraphed this to you today & told you where to send my letters. You may not hear much from me for quite a long while so don't worry . . .

Baling out into the Mediterranean didn't worry me nearly as much as the thought of spending four and a half hours squashed into that tiny metal cockpit. I was six feet six inches tall, and when I sat in a Hurricane I had the posture of an unborn baby in the womb, with my knees almost touching my chin. I was able to put up with that for short flights, but four and a half hours clear across the sea from Egypt to Greece was something else again. I wasn't quite sure I could do it.

I took off the next day from the bleak and sandy airfield of Abu Suweir, and after a couple of hours I was over Crete and beginning to get severe cramp in both legs. My main fuel tank was nearly empty so I pressed the little button that worked the pump to the extra tanks. The pump worked. The main tank filled up again exactly as it was meant to and on I went.

After four hours and forty minutes in the air, I landed at last on Elevsis aerodrome, near Athens, but by then I was so knotted up with terrible excruciating cramp in the legs I had to be lifted out of the cockpit by two strong men. But I had come home to my squadron at last.

First Encounter with a Bandit

So this was Greece. And what a different place from the hot and sandy Egypt I had left behind me some five hours before. Over here it was springtime and the sky a milky-blue and the air just pleasantly warm. A gentle breeze was blowing in from the sea beyond Piraeus and when I turned my head and looked inland I saw only a couple of miles away a range of massive craggy mountains as bare as bones. The aerodrome I had landed on was no more than a grassy field and wild flowers were blossoming blue and yellow and red in their millions all around me.

The two airmen who had helped to lift my cramped body out of the cockpit of the Hurricane had been most sympathetic. I leant against the wing of the plane and waited for the cramp to go out of my legs.

'A bit scrunched up in there, were you?' one of the airmen said.

'A bit,' I said. 'Yes.'

'You oughtn't to be flyin' fighters a chap of your height,' he said. 'What you want is a ruddy great bomber where you can stretch your legs out.'

'Yes,' I said. 'You're right.'

This airman was a Corporal. He had taken my parachute out of the cockpit and now he brought it over and placed it on the ground beside me. He stayed with me and it was clear that he wanted to do some more talking. 'I don't see the point of it,' he went on. 'You bring a brand-new kite, an *absolutely spanking brand-new kite* straight from the factory and you bring it all the way from ruddy Egypt to this godforsaken place and what's goin' to 'appen to it?'

'What?' I said.

'It's come even *further* than from Egypt!' he cried. 'It's come all the way from *England*, that's where it's come from! It's come all the way from England to Egypt and then all the way across the Med to this soddin' country and all for what? What's goin' to 'appen to it?'

'What *is* going to happen to it?' I asked him. I was a bit taken aback by this sudden outburst.

'I'll tell you what's goin' to 'appen to it,' the Corporal said, working himself up. 'Crash bang wallop! Shot down in flames! Explodin' in the air! Ground-strafed by the One-O-Nines right 'ere where we're standin' this very moment! Why, this kite won't last one week in this place! None of 'em do!'

'Don't say that,' I told him.

'I 'as to say it,' he said, 'because it's the truth.'

'But why such prophecies of doom?' I asked him. 'Who is going to do this to us?'

'The Krauts, of course!' he cried. 'Krauts is *pourin'* in 'ere like ruddy ants! They've got *one thousand planes* just the other side of those mountains there and what've *we* got?'

'All right then,' I said. 'What *have* we got?' I was interested to find out.

'It's pitiful what we've got,' the Corporal said.

'Tell me,' I said.

'What we've got is exactly what you can see on this ruddy field!' he said. '*Fourteen 'urricanes*! No it isn't. It's gone up to fifteen now you've brought this one out!'

I refused to believe him. Surely it wasn't possible that

fifteen Hurricanes were all we had left in the whole of Greece.

'Are you absolutely sure of this?' I asked him, aghast.

'Am I lyin'?' he said, turning to the second airman. 'Please tell this officer whether I am lyin' or whether it's the truth.'

'It's the gospel truth,' the second airman said.

'What about bombers?' I said.

'There's about four clapped-out Blenheims over there at Menidi,' the Corporal said, 'and that's the lot. *Four Blenheims and fifteen 'urricanes* is the entire ruddy RAF in the 'ole of Greece.'

'Good Lord,' I said.

'Give it another week,' he went on, 'and every one of us'll be pushed into the sea and swimmin' for 'ome!'

'I hope you're wrong.'

'There's five 'undred Kraut fighters and five 'undred Kraut bombers just around the corner,' he went on, 'and what've we got to put up against them? We've got a miserable fifteen 'urricanes and I'm mighty glad I'm not the one that's flyin' 'em! If you'd 'ad any sense at all, matey, you'd've stayed right where you were back in old Egypt.'

I could see he was nervous and I couldn't blame him. The ground-crew in a squadron, the fitters and riggers, were virtually non-combatants. They were never meant to be in the front line and because of that they were unarmed and had never been taught how to fight or defend themselves. In a situation like this, it was easier to be a pilot than one of the ground-crew. The chances of survival might be a good deal slimmer for the pilot, but he had a splendid weapon to fight with.

The Corporal, as I could tell by the grease on his hands, was a fitter. His job was to look after the big Rolls-Royce

Merlin engines in the Hurricanes and there was little doubt that he loved them dearly. 'This is a brand-new kite,' he said, laying a greasy hand on the metal wing and stroking it gently. 'It's took somebody *thousands of hours* to build it. And now those silly sods behind their desks back in Cairo 'ave sent it out 'ere where it ain't goin' to last two minutes.'

'Where's the Ops Room?' I asked him.

He pointed to a small wooden hut on the other side of the landing field. Alongside the hut there was a cluster of about thirty tents. I slung my parachute over my shoulder and started to make my way across the field to the hut.

Elevsis

To some extent I was aware of the military mess I had flown in to. I knew that a small British Expeditionary Force, backed up by an equally small air force, had been sent to Greece from Egypt a few months earlier to hold back the

Italian invaders, and so long as it was only the Italians they were up against, they had been able to cope. But once the Germans decided to take over, the situation immediately became hopeless. The problem confronting the British now was how to extricate their army from Greece before all the troops were either killed or captured. It was Dunkirk all over again. But it was not receiving the publicity that Dunkirk had received because it was a military bloomer that was best covered up. I guessed that everything the Corporal had just told me was more or less true, but curiously enough none of it worried me in the slightest. I was young enough and starry-eyed enough to look upon this Grecian escapade as nothing more than a grand adventure. The thought that I might never get out of the country alive didn't occur to me. It should have done, and looking back on it now I am surprised that it didn't. Had I paused for a moment and calculated the odds against survival, I would have found that they were about fifty to one and that's enough to give anyone the shakes.

I pushed open the door of the Ops Room hut and went in. There were three men in there, the Squadron-Leader himself and a Flight-Lieutenant and a wireless-operator Sergeant with ear-phones on. I had never met any of them before. Officially, I had been a member of 80 Squadron for more than six months, but up until now I had not succeeded in getting anywhere near it. The last time I had tried, I had finished up on a bonfire in the Western Desert. The Squadron-Leader had a black moustache and a Distinguished Flying Cross ribbon on his chest. He also had a frowning worried look on his face. 'Oh, hello,' he said. 'We've been expecting you for some time.'

'I'm sorry I'm late,' I said.

'Six months late,' he said. 'You can find yourself a bunk

in one of the tents. You'll start flying tomorrow like the rest of them.'

I could see that the man was preoccupied and wished to get rid of me, but I hesitated. It was quite a shock to be dismissed as casually as this. It had been a truly great struggle for me to get back on my feet and join the squadron at last, and I had expected at least a brief 'I'm glad you made it,' or 'I hope you're feeling better.' But this, as I suddenly realized, was a different ball game altogether. This was a place where pilots were disappearing like flies. What difference did an extra one make when you only had fourteen? None whatsoever. What the Squadron-Leader wanted was *a hundred* extra planes and pilots, not one.

I went out of the Ops Rooms hut still carrying my parachute over my shoulder. In the other hand I carried a brown paper-bag that contained all the belongings I had been able to bring with me, a toothbrush, a half-finished tube of toothpaste, a razor, a tube of shaving soap, a spare khaki shirt, a blue cardigan, a pair of pyjamas, my Log Book and my beloved camera. Ever since I was fourteen I had been an enthusiastic photographer, starting in 1930 with an old double-extension plate camera and doing my own developing and enlarging. Now I had a Zeiss Super Ikonta with an f 6.3 Tessar lens.

Out in the Middle East, both in Egypt and in Greece, unless it was winter we dressed in nothing but a khaki shirt and khaki shorts and stockings, and even when we flew we seldom bothered to put on a sweater. The paper-bag I was now carrying, as well as the Log Book and the camera, had been tucked under my legs on the flight over and there had been no room for anything else.

I was to share a tent with another pilot and when I ducked my head low and went in, my companion was sitting on his camp-bed and threading a piece of string into one of his shoes because the shoe-lace had broken. He had a long but friendly face and he introduced himself as David Coke, pronounced Cook. I learnt much later that David Coke came from a very noble family, and today, had he not been killed in his Hurricane later on, he would have been none other than the Earl of Leicester owning one of the most enormous and beautiful stately homes in England, although anyone acting less like a future Earl I have never met. He was warm-hearted and brave and generous, and over the next few weeks we were to become close friends. I sat down on my own camp-bed and began to ask him a few questions.

'Are things out here really as dicey as I've been told?' I asked him.

David Coke and pet

'It's absolutely hopeless,' he said, 'but we're plugging on. The German fighters will be within range of us any moment now, and then we'll be outnumbered by about fifty to one. If they don't get us in the air, they'll wipe us out on the ground.'

'Look,' I said, 'I have never been in action in my life. I haven't the foggiest idea what to do if I meet one of them.'

David Coke stared at me as though he were seeing a ghost. He could hardly have looked more startled if I had suddenly announced that I had never been up in an aeroplane before. 'You don't mean to say', he gasped, 'that you've come out to this place of all places with absolutely no experience whatsoever!'

'I'm afraid so,' I said. 'But I expect they'll put me to fly with one of the old hands who'll show me the ropes.'

'You're going to be unlucky,' he said. 'Out here we go up in ones. It hasn't occurred to them that it's better to fly in pairs. I'm afraid you'll be all on your own right from the start. But seriously, have you never even been in a squadron before in your life?'

'Never,' I said.

'Does the CO know this?' he asked me.

'I don't expect he's stopped to think about it,' I said. 'He simply told me I'd start flying tomorrow like all the others.'

'But where on earth have you come from then?' he asked. 'They'd never send a totally inexperienced pilot to a place like this.'

I told him briefly what had been happening to me over the last six months.

'Oh Christ!' he said. 'What a place to start! How many hours do you have on Hurricanes?'

'About seven,' I said.

'Oh, my God!' he cried. 'That means you hardly know how to fly the thing!'

'I don't really,' I said. 'I can do take-offs and landings but I've never exactly tried throwing it around in the air.'

He sat there still not quite able to believe what I was saying.

'Have you been here long?' I asked him.

'Not very,' he said. 'I was in the Battle of Britain before I came here. That was bad enough, but it was peanuts compared to this crazy place. We have no radar here at all and precious little RT. You can only talk to the ground when you are sitting right on top of the aerodrome. And you can't talk to each other at all when you're in the air. There is virtually no communication. The Greeks are our radar. We have a Greek peasant sitting on the top of every mountain for miles around, and when he spots a bunch of German planes he calls up the Ops Room here on a field telephone. That's our radar.'

'Does it work?'

'Now and again it does,' he said. 'But most of our spotters don't know a Messerschmitt from a baby-carriage.' He had managed to thread the string through all the eyes in his shoe and now he started to put the shoe back on his foot.

'Have the Germans really got a thousand planes in Greece?' I asked him.

'It seems likely,' he said. 'Yes, I think they have. You see, Greece is only a beginning for them. After they've taken Greece, they intend to push on south and take Crete as well. I'm sure of that.'

We sat on our camp-beds thinking about the future. I could see that it was going to be a pretty hairy one.

Then David Coke said, 'As you don't seem to know

anything at all, I'd better try to help you. What would you like to know?'

'Well, first of all,' I said, 'what do I do when I meet a One-O-Nine?'

'You try to get on his tail,' he said. 'You try to turn in a tighter circle than him. If you let him get on to your tail, you've had it. A Messerschmitt has cannon in its wings. We've only got bullets, and they aren't even incendiaries. They're just ordinary bullets. The Hun has cannon-shells that explode when they hit you. Our bullets just make little holes in the fuselage. So you've got to hit him smack in the engine to bring him down. He can hit you anywhere at all and the cannon-shell will explode and blow you up.'

I tried to digest what he was saying.

'One other thing,' he said, 'never, absolutely never, take your eyes off your rear-view mirror for more than a few seconds. They come up behind you and they come very fast.'

'I'll try to remember that,' I said. 'What do I do if I meet a bomber? What's the best way to attack him?'

'The bombers you will meet will be mostly Ju 88s,' he said. 'The Ju 88 is a very good aircraft. It is just about as fast as you are and it's got a rear-gunner and a front-gunner. The gunners on a Ju 88 use incendiary tracer bullets and they aim their guns like they're aiming a hosepipe. They can see where their bullets are going all the time and that makes them pretty deadly. So if you are attacking a Ju 88 from astern, make quite sure you get well below him so the rear-gunner can't hit you. But you won't shoot him down that way. You have to go for one of his engines. And when you are doing that, remember to allow plenty of deflection. Aim well in front of him. Get the nose of his engine on the outer ring of your reflector sight.'

I hardly knew what he was talking about, but I nodded and said, 'Right. I'll try to do that.'

'Oh my God,' he said. 'I can't teach you how to shoot down Germans in one easy lesson. I just wish I could take you up with me tomorrow so I could look after you a bit.'

'Can't you?' I said eagerly. 'We could ask the CO.'

'Not a hope,' he said. 'We always go up singly. Except when we do a sweep, then we all go up together in formation.'

He paused and ran his fingers through his pale-brown hair. 'The trouble here', he said, 'is that the CO doesn't talk much to his pilots. He doesn't even fly with them. He must have flown once because he's got a DFC, but I've never seen him get into a Hurricane. In the Battle of Britain the Squadron-Leader always flew with his squadron. And he gave lots of advice and help to his new pilots. In England you always went up in pairs and a new boy always went up with an experienced man. And in the Battle of Britain we had radar and we had RT that jolly well worked. We could talk to the ground and we could talk to each other all the time in the air. But not here. The big thing to remember here is that you are totally on your own. No one is going to help you, not even the CO. In the Battle of Britain', he added, 'the new boys were very carefully looked after.'

'Has flying finished for the day?' I asked him.

'Yes,' he said. 'It'll be getting dark soon. In fact it's about time for supper. I'll take you along.'

The officers' mess was a tent large enough to contain two long trestle tables, one with food on it and the other where we sat down to eat. The food was tinned beef stew and lumps of bread, and there were bottles of Greek retsina wine to go with it. The Greeks have a trick of disguising a poor quality wine by adding pine resin to it, the idea being that the taste of the resin is not quite so appalling as the taste of the wine. We drank retsina because that was all there was. The other pilots in the squadron, all experienced young men who had nearly been killed many times, treated me just as casually as the Squadron-Leader had. Formalities did not exist in this place. Pilots came and pilots went. The others hardly noticed my presence. No real friendships existed. The way David Coke had treated me was exceptional, but then he was an exceptional person. I realized that nobody else was about to take a beginner like me under his wing. Each man was wrapped up in a cocoon of his own problems, and the sheer effort of trying to stay alive and at the same time doing your duty was concentrating the minds of everyone around me. They were all very quiet. There was no larking about. There were just a few muttered remarks about the pilots who had not come back that day. Nothing else.

There was a notice-board nailed to one of the tent poles in the mess and on it was pinned a single typed sheet with the names of the pilots who were to go on patrol the next morning as well as the times of their take-offs. I learnt from David Coke that a patrol meant stooging around directly above the airfield and waiting for the ground controller to call you up and direct you to a precise area where German planes had been spotted by one of the Greek comedians on top of his mountain. The take-off time against my name was 10 a.m.

When I woke up the next morning, all I could think about was my ten o'clock take-off time and the fact that I would almost certainly be meeting the Luftwaffe in some form or another and entirely on my own for the first time. Such thoughts as these tend to loosen the bowels and I asked David Coke where I could find the latrines. He told me roughly where they were and I wandered off to find them.

I had been in some fairly primitive lavatories in East Africa, but the 80 Squadron latrines at Elevsis beat the lot. A wide trench six feet deep and sixteen feet long had been dug in the ground. Down the whole length of this trench a round pole had been suspended about four feet above the ground, and I watched in horror as an airman who had got there before me lowered his trousers and attempted to sit on the pole. The trench was so wide that he could hardly reach the pole with his hands. But when he did, he had to turn around and do a sort of backwards leap in the hope of his bottom landing squarely on the pole. Having managed this, but only just, he had to grip the pole with both hands to keep his balance. He lost his balance and over he went backwards into the awful pit. I pulled him out and he hurried away I know not where to try to wash himself. I refused to risk it. I wandered away and found a place behind an olive tree where the wild flowers grew all around me.

At exactly ten o'clock I was strapped into my Hurricane ready for take-off. Several others had gone off singly before me during the past half-hour and had disappeared into the blue Grecian sky. I took off and climbed to 5,000 feet and started circling above the flying field while somebody in the Ops Room tried to contact me on his amazingly inefficient apparatus. My code-name was Blue Four.

Through a storm of static a far-away voice kept saying in my ear-phones, 'Blue Four, can you hear me? Can you hear me?' And I kept replying, 'Yes, but only just.'

'Await orders,' the faint voice said. 'Listen out.'

I cruised around admiring the blue sea to the south and the great mountains to the north, and I was just beginning to think to myself that this was a very nice way to fight a war when the static erupted again and the voice said, 'Blue Four, are you receiving me?'

'Yes,' I said, 'but speak louder please.'

'Bandits over shipping at Khalkis,' the voice said. 'Vector 035 forty miles angels eight.'

'Received,' I said. 'I'm on my way.'

The translation of this simple message, which even I could understand, told me that if I set a course on my compass of thirty-five degrees and flew for a distance of forty miles, I would then, with a bit of luck, intercept the enemy at 8,000 feet, where he was trying to sink ships off a place called Khalkis, wherever that might be.

I set my course and opened the throttle and hoped I was doing everything right. I checked my ground speed and calculated that it would take me between ten and eleven minutes to travel forty miles to this place called Khalkis. I cleared the top of the mountain range with 500 feet to spare, and as I went over it I saw a single solitary goat, brown and white, wandering on the bare rock. 'Hello goat,' I said aloud into my oxygen mask, 'I'll bet you don't know the Germans are going to have you for supper before you're very much older.'

To which, as I realized as soon as I'd said it, the goat might very well have answered, 'And the same to you, my boy. You're no better off than I am.'

Then I saw below me in the distance a kind of waterway or fjord and a little cluster of houses on the shore. Khalkis, I thought. It must be Khalkis. There was one large cargo ship in the waterway and as I was looking at it I saw an enormous fountain of spray erupting high in the air close to the ship. I had never seen a bomb exploding in the water before, but I had seen plenty of photographs of it happening. I looked up into the sky above the ship, but I could see nothing there. I kept staring. I figured that if a bomb had been dropped, someone must be up there dropping it. Two more mighty cascades of water leapt up around the ship. Then suddenly I spotted the bombers. I saw the small black dots wheeling and circling in the sky high above the ship. It gave me quite a shock. It was my first-ever sight of the enemy from my own plane. Quickly I turned the brass ring of my firing-button from 'safe' to 'fire'. I switched on my reflector-sight and a pale red circle of light with two crossbars appeared suspended in the air in front of my face. I headed straight for the little dots.

Half a minute later, the dots had resolved themselves into black twin-engine bombers. They were Ju 88s. I counted six of them. I glanced above and around them but I could see no fighters protecting them. I remember being absolutely cool and unafraid. My one wish was to do my job properly and not to make a hash of it.

There are three men in a Ju 88, which gives it three pairs of eyes. So six Ju 88s have no less than eighteen pairs of eyes scanning the sky. Had I been more experienced, I would have realized this much earlier on and before going any closer I would have swung round so that the sun was behind me. I would also have climbed very fast to get well above them before attacking. I did neither of these things. I simply went straight for them at the same height as they were and with the strong Grecian sun right in my own eyes.

They spotted me while I was still half a mile away and suddenly all six bombers banked away steeply and dived straight for a great mass of mountains behind Khalkis.

I had been warned never to push my throttle 'through the gate' except in a real emergency. Going 'through the gate' meant that the big Rolls-Royce engine would produce absolute maximum revs, and three minutes was the limit of time it could tolerate such stress. OK, I thought, this is an emergency. I rammed the throttle right 'through the gate'. The engine roared and the Hurricane leapt forward. I began to catch up fast on the bombers. They had now gone into a line-abreast formation which, as I was soon to discover, allowed all six of their rear-gunners to fire at me simultaneously.

The mountains behind Khalkis are wild and black and very rugged and the Germans went right in among them flying well below the summits. I followed, and sometimes we flew so close to the cliffs I could see the startled vultures taking off as we roared past. I was still gaining on them, and when I was about 200 yards behind them, all six rear-gunners in the Ju 88s began shooting at me. As David Coke had warned, they were using tracer and out of each one of the six rear turrets came a brilliant shaft of orange-red flame. Six different shafts of bright orange-red came arcing towards me from six different turrets. They were like very thin streams of coloured water from six different hosepipes. I found them fascinating to watch. The deadly orange-red streams seemed to start out quite slowly from the turrets and I could see them bending in the air as they came towards me and then suddenly they were flashing past my cockpit like fireworks.

I was just beginning to realize that I had got myself into the worst possible position for an attacking fighter to be in when suddenly the passage between the mountains on either side narrowed and the Ju 88s were forced to go into line astern. This meant that only the last one in the line could shoot at me. That was better. Now there was only a single stream of orange-red bullets coming towards me. David Coke had said, 'Go for one of his engines.' I went a little closer and by jiggling my plane this way and that I managed to get the starboard engine of the bomber into my reflector-sight. I aimed a bit ahead of the engine and pressed the button. The Hurricane gave a small shudder as the eight Brownings in the wings all opened up together, and a second later I saw a huge piece of his metal engine-cowling the size of a dinner-tray go flying up into the air. Good heavens, I thought, I've hit him! I've actually hit him! Then black smoke came pouring out of his engine and very slowly, almost in slow motion, the bomber winged over to starboard and began to lose height. I throttled back. He was well below me now. I could see him clearly by squinting down out of my cockpit. He wasn't diving and he wasn't spinning either. He was turning slowly over and over like a leaf, the black smoke pouring out from the starboard engine. Then I saw one . . . two . . . three people jump out of the fuselage and go tumbling earthwards with legs and arms outstretched in grotesque attitudes, and a moment later one . . . two . . . three parachutes billowed open and began floating gently down between the cliffs towards the narrow valley below.

I watched spellbound. I couldn't believe that I had actually shot down a German bomber. But I was immensely relieved to see the parachutes.

I opened the throttle again and began to climb up above the mountains. The five remaining Ju 88s had disappeared. I looked around me and all I could see were craggy peaks in every direction. I set a course due south and fifteen minutes later I was landing at Elevsis. I parked my Hurricane and clambered out. I had been away for exactly one hour. It seemed like ten minutes. I walked slowly all the way round my Hurricane looking for damage. Miraculously the fuselage seemed to be completely unscathed. The only mark those six rear-gunners had been able to make on a sitting-duck like me was a single neat round hole in one of the blades of my wooden propeller. I shouldered my parachute and walked across to the Ops Rooms hut. I was feeling pretty good.

As before, the Squadron-Leader was in the hut and so was the wireless-operator Sergeant with the ear-phones on his head. The Squadron-Leader looked up at me and frowned. 'How did you get on?' he asked.

'I got one Ju 88,' I said, trying to keep the pride and satisfaction out of my voice.

'Are you sure?' he asked. 'Did you see it hit the ground?'

'No,' I said. 'But I saw the crew jump out and open their parachutes.'

'OK,' he said. 'That sounds definite enough.'

'I'm afraid there's a bullet hole in my prop,' I said.

'Oh well,' he said. 'You'd better tell the rigger to patch it up as best he can.'

That was the end of our interview. I expected more, a pat on the back or a 'Jolly good show' and a smile, but as I've said before, he had many things on his mind including Pilot Officer Holman who had gone out thirty minutes before me and hadn't come back. He wasn't going to come back.

David Coke had also been flying that morning and I found him sitting on his camp-bed doing nothing. I told him about my trip.

'Never do that again,' he said. 'Never sit on the tails of six Ju 88s and expect to get away with it because next time you won't.'

'What happened to you?' I asked him.

'I got one One-O-Nine,' he said. He said it as calmly as if he were telling me he'd caught a fish in the river across the road. 'It's going to be very dangerous out there from now on,' he added. 'The One-O-Nines and the One-One-O's are swarming like wasps. You'd better be very careful next time.'

'I'll try,' I said. 'I'll do my best.'

The Ammunition Ship

The next morning I was ordered to go on patrol at six o'clock. I took off dead on time and climbed in a tight circle to 5,000 feet over the airfield. The sun had just cleared the horizon and I could see the Parthenon glowing white and wonderful on the famous hill above Athens. My radio crackled almost at once and the voice from the Ops Room gave me precisely the same instructions it had given me the day before. I was to proceed to Khalkis where the enemy was again bombing the shipping. Five Hurricanes had taken off before me that morning and I had watched them all being sent away one by one in different directions. The enemy was all around us now and we were having to spread ourselves extremely thin. Khalkis, it seemed, was reserved for me.

I had learnt the night before from someone in the Ops Room that the big cargo vessel lying off Khalkis was an ammunition ship. It was loaded to the brim with high explosives and the Germans had found out about it. The brave Greeks, who were trying their best to offload the bullets and bombs and whatever other fireworks there were on board, knew that it only needed one direct hit to blow everything sky-high, including the town of Khalkis and most of its inhabitants.

I arrived over Khalkis at 6.15 a.m. The big cargo ship was still there and there was now a lighter alongside it. A derrick was hoisting a large crate up from the ship's forward hold and lowering it into the lighter. I searched the sky for enemy planes but I couldn't see any. A man on the deck of the ship looked up and waved his cap at me. I slid back the roof of my cockpit and waved back at him.

I am writing this forty-five years afterwards, but I still retain an absolutely clear picture of Khalkis and how it looked from a few thousand feet up on a bright-blue early April morning. The little town with its sparkling white houses and red-tiled roofs stood on the edge of the waterway, and behind the town I could see the jagged grey-black mountains where I had chased the Ju 88s the day before. Inland, I could see a wide valley and there were green fields in the valley and among the fields there were splashes of the most brilliant yellow I had ever seen. The whole landscape looked as though it had been painted on to the surface of the earth by Vincent Van Gogh. On all sides and wherever I looked there was this dazzling panorama of beauty, and for a moment or two I was so overwhelmed by it all that I didn't see the big Ju 88 screaming up at me from below until he was almost touching the underbelly of my plane. He was climbing right up at me with the tracer pouring like yellow fire out of his blunt perspex nose and in that thousandth of a second I actually saw the German front-gunner crouching over his gun and gripping it with both hands as he squeezed the trigger. I saw his brown helmet and his pale face with no goggles over the eyes and he was wearing some sort of a black flying-suit. I yanked my stick back so hard the Hurricane shot vertically upwards like a rocket. The violent change of direction blacked me out completely, and when my sight returned my plane was at the top of a vertical climb and standing on its tail with almost no forward movement at all. My engine was spluttering and beginning to vibrate. I've been hit, I thought, I've been hit in the engine. I rammed the stick hard forward and prayed she would respond. By some miracle, the aircraft dropped its nose and the engine began to pick up and within a few seconds the marvellous machine was flying straight and level once again.

But where was the German?

I looked down and spotted him about 1,000 feet below me. His wings were silhouetted against the blue water of the bay, and I could hardly believe it but he was actually ignoring me completely and was beginning to make his bombing run over the ammunition ship! I opened the throttle and dived after him. In eight seconds I was on him, but I was diving so steeply and so fast that when the great grey-green bomber came into my sights, I was only able to get in a very short burst and then I was past him and yanking back hard on the stick to stop myself from diving on into the water.

I had made a mess of it. For the second time running I had gone barging in to the attack without pausing for just a fraction of a second to work out the best way of doing things. I roared upwards again and banked round sharply to have another go at him. He was still heading for the ship. But then something quite startling happened. I saw his nose drop suddenly downwards and he went plunging head first in an absolutely straight vertical line into the blue waters of Khalkis Bay. He hit the water not far from the ship and there was a tremendous white splash and then the waves closed over him and he was gone.

How on earth did I manage that? I wondered. The only explanation I could think of was that a lucky bullet must have hit the pilot so that he slumped over his stick and pushed it forward and down she went. I could see several

Greek seamen on the deck of the ship waving their caps at me and I waved back at them. That is how stupid I was. I quite literally sat there in my cockpit waving away at the Greek seamen below, forgetting that I was in a hostile sky that could be seething with German aircraft. When I stopped waving and looked around me, I saw something that made me jump. There were aeroplanes everywhere. They were diving and climbing and turning and banking wherever I looked, and they all had black and white crosses on their bodies and black swastikas on their tails. I knew right away what they were. They were the dreaded little German Messerschmitt 109 fighters. I had never seen one before but I knew darn well what they looked like. I swear there must have been thirty or forty of them within a few hundred yards of me. It was like having a swarm of wasps around your head and quite honestly I did not know what to do next. It would have been suicide to stay and fight, and in any event my duty was to save my plane at all costs. The Germans had hundreds of fighters. We had only a few left.

I shoved the stick forward and opened the throttle and dived flat out for the ground. I had a feeling that if I could fly very low and very dangerously over the treetops and hedges then the German pilots might not be prepared to take the same risk.

When I levelled out from the dive I was doing about 300 miles an hour and flying some twenty feet above the ground. That is below rooftop level and is a fairly hairy thing to do at such a speed. But I was in a hairy situation. I was flying up the yellow Van Gogh valley now and a swift glance in my rear-view mirror showed a bunch of 109s right on my tail. I went lower. I went so low I actually had to leapfrog over the small olive trees that were scattered around everywhere. Then I took a huge but calculated risk and went lower still, almost brushing the grass in the fields. I knew the Germans couldn't hit me unless they came down to my height, and even if they did, the concentration required to fly a plane very fast at almost ground level was so great they would hardly be able to shoot straight at the same time. You may not believe it but I can remember having literally to lift my plane just a tiny fraction to clear a stone wall, and once there was a herd of brown cows in front of me and I'm not sure I didn't clip some of their horns with my propeller as I skimmed over them.

Suddenly the Messerschmitts had had enough. In the mirror I saw them pull away one after the other, and oh the relief of being able to climb up to a safer height and to go whistling back over the mountains to Elevsis.

The bad news I brought with me to the squadron was that the German fighter planes were now within range of us. In their hundreds they could reach our airfield any time they liked.

The Battle of Athens –
the Twentieth of April

The next three days, 17, 18 and 19 April 1941, are a little
blurred in my memory. The fourth day, 20 April, is not
blurred at all. My Log Book records that from Elevsis
aerodrome

> on 17 April I went up three times
> on 18 April I went up twice
> on 19 April I went up three times
> on 20 April I went up four times.

Each one of those sorties meant running across the
airfield to wherever the Hurricane was parked (often 200
yards away), strapping in, starting up, taking off, flying to a
particular area, engaging the enemy, getting home again,
landing, reporting to the Ops Room and then making sure
the aircraft was refuelled and rearmed immediately so as to
be ready for another take-off.

Twelve separate sorties against the enemy in four days is
a fairly hectic pace by any standards, and each one of us
knew that every time a sortie was made, somebody was
probably going to get killed, either the Hun or the man in
the Hurricane. I used to figure that the betting on every
flight was about even money against my coming back,
but in reality it wasn't even money at all. When
you are outnumbered by at least ten to one on nearly
every occasion, then a bookmaker, had there been one

on the aerodrome, would probably have been willing to lay something like five to one against your return on each trip.

Like all the others, I was always sent up alone. I wished I could sometimes have had a friendly wing-tip alongside me, and more importantly, a second pair of eyes to help me watch the sky behind and above. But we didn't have enough aircraft for luxuries of that sort.

Sometimes I was over Piraeus harbour, chasing the Ju 88s that were bombing the shipping there. Sometimes I was around the Lamia area, trying to deter the Luftwaffe from blasting away at our retreating army, although how anyone could think that a single Hurricane was going to make any difference out there was beyond me. Once or twice, I met the bombers over Athens itself, where they usually came along in groups of twelve at a time. On three occasions my Hurricane was badly shot up, but the riggers in 80 Squadron were magicians at patching up holes in the fuselage or mending a broken spar. We were so frantically busy during these four days that individual victories were hardly noticed or counted. And unlike the fighter aircraft back in Britain, we had no camera-guns to tell us whether we had hit anything or not. We seemed to spend our entire time running out to the aircraft, scrambling, dashing off to some place or other, chasing the Hun, pressing the firing-button, landing back at Elevsis and going up again.

My Log Book records that on 17 April we lost Flight-Sergeant Cottingham and Flight-Sergeant Rivelon and both their aircraft.

On 18 April Pilot Officer Oofy Still went out and did not return. I remember Oofy Still as a smiling young man with freckles and red hair.

That left us with twelve Hurricanes and twelve pilots

with which to cover the whole of Greece from 19 April onwards.

As I have said, 17, 18 and 19 April seem to be all jumbled up together in my memory, and no single incident has remained vividly with me. But 20 April was quite different. I went up four separate times on 20 April, but it was the first of these sorties that I will never forget. It stands out like a sheet of flame in my memory.

On that day, somebody behind a desk in Athens or Cairo had decided that for once our entire force of Hurricanes, all twelve of us, should go up together. The inhabitants of Athens, so it seemed, were getting jumpy and it was assumed that the sight of us all flying overhead would boost their morale. Had I been an inhabitant of Athens at that time, with a German army of over 100,000 advancing swiftly on the city, not to mention a Luftwaffe of about 1,000 planes all within bombing distance, I would have been pretty jumpy myself, and the sight of twelve lonely Hurricanes flying overhead would have done little to boost my morale.

However, on 20 April, on a golden springtime morning at ten o'clock, all twelve of us took off one after the other and got into a tight formation over Elevsis airfield. Then we headed for Athens, which was no more than four minutes' flying time away.

I had never flown a Hurricane in formation before. Even in training I had only done formation flying once in a little Tiger Moth. It is not a particularly tricky business if you have had plenty of practice, but if you are new to the game and if you are required to fly within a few feet of your neighbour's wing-tip, it is a dicey experience. You keep your position by jiggling the throttle back and forth the whole time and by being extremely delicate on the rudder-bar and the stick. It is not so bad when everyone is flying straight and level, but when the entire formation is doing steep turns all the time, it becomes very difficult for a fellow as inexperienced as I was.

Round and round Athens we went, and I was so busy trying to prevent my starboard wing-tip from scraping against the plane next to me that this time I was in no mood to admire the grand view of the Parthenon or any of the other famous relics below me. Our formation was being led by Flight-Lieutenant Pat Pattle. Now Pat Pattle was a legend in the RAF. At least he was a legend around Egypt and the Western Desert and in the mountains of Greece. He was far and away the greatest fighter ace the Middle East was ever to see, with an astronomical number of victories to his credit. It was even said that he had shot down more planes than any of the famous and glamorized Battle of Britain aces, and this was probably true. I myself had never spoken to him and I am sure he hadn't the faintest idea who I was. I wasn't anybody. I was just a new face in a squadron whose pilots took very little notice of each other anyway. But I had observed the famous Flight-Lieutenant Pattle in the mess tent several times. He was a very small man and very soft-spoken, and he possessed the deeply wrinkled doleful face of a cat who knew that all nine of its lives had already been used up.

On that morning of 20 April, Flight-Lieutenant Pattle, the ace of aces, who was leading our formation of twelve Hurricanes over Athens, was evidently assuming that we could all fly as brilliantly as he could, and he led us one hell of a dance around the skies above the city. We were flying at about 9,000 feet and we were doing our very best to show the people of Athens how powerful and noisy and brave we were, when suddenly the whole sky around us seemed to explode with German fighters. They came down on us from high above, not only 109s but also the twin-engined 110s. Watchers on the ground say that there cannot have been fewer than 200 of them around us that morning. We broke formation and now it was every man for himself. What has become known as the Battle of Athens began.

I find it almost impossible to describe vividly what happened during the next half-hour. I don't think any fighter pilot has ever managed to convey what it is like to be up there in a long-lasting dog-fight. You are in a small metal cockpit where just about everything is made of riveted aluminium. There is a plexiglass hood over your head and a sloping bullet-proof windscreen in front of you. Your right hand is on the stick and your right thumb is on the brass firing-button on the top loop of the stick. Your left hand is on the throttle and your two feet are on the rudder-bar. Your body is attached by shoulder-straps and belt to the parachute you are sitting on, and a second pair of shoulder-straps and a belt are holding you rigidly in the cockpit. You can turn your head and you can move your arms and legs, but the rest of your body is strapped so tightly into the tiny cockpit that you cannot move. Between your face and the windscreen, the round orange-red circle of the reflector-sight glows brightly.

Some people do not realize that although a Hurricane had eight guns in its wings, those guns were all immobile. You did not aim the guns, you aimed the plane. The guns themselves were carefully sighted and tested beforehand on the ground so that the bullets from each gun would converge at a point about 150 yards ahead. Thus, using your reflector-sight, you aimed the plane at the target and pressed the button. To aim accurately in this way requires skilful flying, especially as you are usually in a steep turn and going very fast when the moment comes.

Over Athens on that morning, I can remember seeing our tight little formation of Hurricanes all peeling away and disappearing among the swarms of enemy aircraft, and from then on, wherever I looked I saw an endless blur of enemy fighters whizzing towards me from every side. They came from above and they came from behind and they made frontal attacks from dead ahead, and I threw my Hurricane around as best I could and whenever a Hun came into my sights, I pressed the button. It was truly the most breathless and in a way the most exhilarating time I have ever had in my life. I caught glimpses of planes with black smoke pouring from their engines. I saw planes with pieces of metal flying off their fuselages. I saw the bright-red flashes coming from the wings of the Messerschmitts as they fired their guns, and once I saw a man whose Hurricane was in flames climb calmly out on to a wing and jump off. I stayed with them until I had no ammunition left in my guns. I had done a lot of shooting, but whether I had shot anyone down or had even hit any of them I could not say. I did not dare to pause for even a fraction of a second to observe results. The sky was so full of aircraft that half my time was spent in actually avoiding collisions. I am quite sure that the German planes must have often got in each other's way because there were so many of them, and that, together with the fact that there were so few of us, probably saved quite a number of our skins.

When I finally had to break away and dive for home, I knew my Hurricane had been hit. The controls were very soggy and there was no response at all to the rudder. But you can turn a plane after a fashion with the ailerons alone, and that is how I managed to steer the plane back. Thank heavens the undercarriage came down when I engaged the lever, and I landed more or less safely at Elevsis. I taxied to a parking place, switched off the engine and slid back the hood. I sat there for at least one minute, taking deep gasping breaths. I was quite literally overwhelmed by the feeling that I had been into the very bowels of the fiery furnace and had managed to claw my way out. All around me now the sun was shining and wild flowers were blossoming in the grass of the airfield, and I thought how fortunate I was to be seeing the good earth again. Two airmen, a fitter and a rigger, came trotting up to my machine. I watched them as they walked slowly all the way round it. Then the rigger, a balding middle-aged man, looked up at me and said, 'Blimey mate, this kite's got so many 'oles in it, it looks like it's made out of chicken-wire!'

I undid my straps and eased myself upright in the cockpit. 'Do your best with it,' I said. 'I'll be needing it again very soon.'

I remember walking over to the little wooden Operations Room to report my return and as I made my way slowly across the grass of the landing field I suddenly realized that the whole of my body and all my clothes were dripping with sweat. The weather was warm in Greece at that time of year and we wore only khaki shorts and khaki shirt and stockings even when we flew, but now those shorts and shirt and stockings had all changed colour and were quite black with wetness. So was my hair when I removed my helmet. I had never sweated like that before in my life, even after a game of squash or rugger. The water was pouring off me and dripping to the ground. At the door of the Ops Room three or four other pilots were standing around and I noticed that each one of them was as wet as I was. I put a cigarette between my lips and struck a match. Then I found that my hand was shaking so much I couldn't put the flame to the end of the cigarette. The doctor, who was standing nearby, came up and lit it for me. I looked at my hands again. It was ridiculous the way they were shaking. It was embarrassing. I looked at the other pilots. They were all holding cigarettes and their hands were all shaking as much as mine were. But I was feeling pretty good. I had stayed up there for thirty minutes and they hadn't got me.

They got five of our twelve Hurricanes in that battle. One of our pilots baled out and was saved. Four were killed. Among the dead was the great Pat Pattle, all his lucky lives used up at last. And Flight-Lieutenant Timber Woods, the second most experienced pilot in the squadron, was also among those killed. Greek observers on the ground as well as our own people on the airstrip saw the five Hurricanes going down in smoke, but they also saw something else. They saw twenty-two Messerschmitts shot down during that battle, although none of us ever knew who got what.

So we now had seven half-serviceable Hurricanes left in Greece, and with these we were expected to give air cover to the entire British Expeditionary Force which was about to be evacuated along the coast. The whole thing was a ridiculous farce.

I wandered over to my tent. There was a canvas washbasin outside the tent, one of those folding things that stand on three wooden legs, and David Coke was bending over it, sloshing water on his face. He was naked except for a small towel round his waist and his skin was very white.

'So you made it,' he said, not looking up.

'So did you,' I said.

'It was a bloody miracle,' he said. 'I'm shaking all over. What happens next?'

Elevsis

'I think we're going to get killed,' I said.

'So do I,' he said. 'You can have the basin in a moment. I left a bit of water in the jug just in case you happened to come back.'

The Last Day But One

But the twentieth of April was not over yet.

I was standing quite naked beside the three-legged basin outside the tent with David Coke trying to wash off some of the sweat of battle when *boom bang woomph wham rat-tat-tat-tat-tat* a tremendous explosion of noises slammed into us overhead with a rattle of machine-guns and a roar of engines. I jumped and David jumped and looking up we saw a long line of Messerschmitt 109s coming straight at us very fast and low with guns blazing. We threw ourselves flat on the grass and waited for the worst.

I had never been ground-strafed before and I can promise you it is not a nice experience, especially when they catch you out in the open with your pants down. You lie there watching the bullets running through the grass and kicking up chunks of turf all around you and unless there is a deep ditch nearby there is nothing you can do to protect yourself. The 109s were coming at us in line astern, one after the other, skimming just over the tents, and as each one roared past overhead I could feel the wind of its slipstream on my naked back. I remember twisting my head sideways to watch them and I could see the pilots sitting upright in their cockpits, black helmets on and khaki-coloured oxygen masks over their noses and mouths, and one pilot was sporting a bright yellow scarf around his neck tucked neatly into his open shirt. They wore no goggles and once or twice

I caught a glimpse of a pair of German eyes bright with concentration and staring directly ahead.

'We've had it now!' David was shouting. 'They'll get every one of our planes!'

'To hell with the planes!' I shouted back. 'What about us?'

'They're after the Hurricanes,' David shouted. 'They'll pick them off one by one. You watch.'

The Germans knew that the few planes we had left in Greece had just landed after a battle and were now refuelling, which is the classic moment for a ground-strafe. But what they did not know was that our airfield defences consisted of no more than a single Bofors gun tucked away somewhere in the rocks behind our tents. Most front-line aerodromes in those days were heavily protected against low-level attacks and because of this no pilot enjoyed going on a ground-strafe. I did some of it myself later on and I didn't like it one bit. You are flying so fast and so low that if you happen to get hit there is very little you can do to save yourself. The Germans couldn't know we had only one wretched gun to protect the whole aerodrome so they played it safe and made just that one swift pass over our field and then beat it for home.

They had disappeared as suddenly as they had arrived, and when they had gone the silence across our flying field was amazing. I wondered for a moment whether perhaps everyone had been killed except David and me. We stood up and surveyed the scene. Then several voices began shouting for stretchers and over by the Ops Hut I could see someone with blood on his clothes being helped towards the doctor's tent. But the surprise of the moment was that our single Bofors gun had actually managed to hit one of the Messerschmitts. We could see him across the aerodrome

about forty feet up with black smoke and orange flames
pouring from his engine. He was gliding in silently for an
attempted landing, and David and I stood watching him as
he made a steep turn in towards the field.

'That poor sod will be roasted alive if he doesn't hurry,'
David said.

Me 109 crashed, Elevsis

The plane hit the ground on its belly with a fearful
scrunch of tearing metal and it slid on for about thirty yards
before stopping. I saw several of our people running out to
help the pilot and someone had a red fire-extinguisher in his
hand and then they were out of sight in the black smoke and
trying to get the German out of the plane. When we saw
them again they were hauling him by his arms away from
the fire and then a pick-up truck drove out and they put him
in the back.

But what of our own planes? We could see them in the distance scattered around the perimeter of the airfield at their dispersal points and not one of them was burning.

'They were in such a bloody hurry I think they've missed them altogether,' David said.

'I think so, too,' I said.

Then the Duty Officer was running between the tents and shouting, 'All pilots to their aircraft! All aircraft to scramble at once! Hurry up there! Get a move on!' He ran past David and me shouting, 'Get your clothes on, you two! Get out there at the double and get your planes in the air!'

It was common practice for a second wave of ground-strafers to come in and attack soon after the first, and the CO rightly wanted our planes in the air before they arrived. David and I flung on shirts and shorts and shoes and dashed towards our Hurricanes, and as I ran I was wondering whether my own plane was even capable of taking off again so soon after the last battle. Less than one hour had gone by since I had landed. When I reached the Hurricane, there were three airmen fussing around the fuselage, including our Flight-Sergeant rigger.

'Have you repaired the rudder?' I shouted at him.

'We've put a new wire in,' the Flight-Sergeant said. 'It was cut clean through.'

'Is she refuelled and rearmed?'

'All ready for you,' the Flight-Sergeant said.

I gave the plane a quick once over. It was remarkable what they had managed to do in so little time. Bullet holes had been stopped up and torn metal had been flattened out and cracks had been filled and there were little patches of red canvas over all eight of the gun ports on the leading edges of the wings, showing that the guns had been serviced and rearmed. I climbed into the cockpit and the Flight-Sergeant came up on to the wing to help me strap in. 'You want to be careful out there now,' he said. 'They're swarming like gnats all over the sky.'

'You'd better be careful yourself,' I said. 'I'd rather be in the air than down here next time they come in.'

He gave me a friendly pat on the back and then slid the hood closed over my head.

It was astonishing that the ground-strafers had not hit a single one of our Hurricanes, and all seven of us got safely up into the air and circled the flying field for about an hour. We were hoping now that they would come back again then we could swoop on them from above and the whole thing would have been a piece of cake. They did not return and down we went once more and landed.

But the twentieth of April was still not over.

I went up twice more during that afternoon, both times to tangle with the clouds of Ju 88s that were bombing the shipping over Piraeus, and by the time evening came I was a very tired young man.

That night we were told (and by we I mean the seven remaining pilots in the squadron) that at first light the next morning we were to take off and fly to a very secret small landing field about thirty miles along the coast. It was clear that if we stayed another day at Elevsis we would be wiped out, planes and all. We crowded around a table in the mess tent and by the light of a paraffin lamp someone, I think it was the squadron Adjutant, tried to show us where this secret landing field was. 'It's right on the edge of the coast,' he said, 'beside a little village called Megara. You can't miss it. It's the only flat bit of land around.'

'Are we going to operate from there?' someone asked.

'God knows,' the Adjutant said.

'But what do we do after we've landed?' we asked him. 'Will there be *anybody* there except us?'

'Just get the hell out of here at dawn tomorrow and go there,' the wretched man said.

'But what's the point of it all?' someone said. 'Right at this moment we have seven quite decent Hurricanes and if we hang around with them here in this crazy country they are certain to be destroyed on the ground or shot down in the air in the next couple of days. So why don't we fly them all to Crete tomorrow morning and save them for better things? We'd be there in an hour and a half. And from Crete we could fly them to Egypt. I'll bet they could use seven extra Hurricanes in the Western Desert.'

'Just do as you're told,' the Adjutant said. 'Our job is to keep these seven planes going so that we can give air cover to the army which is about to be evacuated off the coast by the navy.'

'With seven machines!' a young pilot said. 'And flying out of a little field along the coast with no fitters and no riggers and no refuelling wagons! It's ridiculous!'

The Adjutant looked at the young pilot and said simply, 'It's not my idea. I'm only passing on orders.'

David Coke said, 'Will anyone be at this place Megara when we arrive at dawn tomorrow?'

'I don't think so,' the Adjutant said.

'So what are we supposed to do? Just sit around on the grass?'

'Look,' the poor Adjutant said, 'if I knew any more, I'd tell you.' He was about forty, a volunteer, too old for flying, and he had been a seller of agricultural implements before the war. He was a good man, but he was as much in the dark as we were. 'They're going to come over here and shoot this place to pieces tomorrow,' he went on. 'All of us, ground-crews included, are pulling out tonight. By the time you get up tomorrow morning the place will be empty. So make sure you all get away the moment there's enough daylight for a take-off. Don't hang about.'

'Where are you all going to?' somebody asked him. 'Are you joining us at our secret little landing ground?'

'No,' he said, 'we're not. We're going farther along the coast. I don't even know myself where it is.'

'Is it another secret landing field?'

'I think it is,' the Adjutant said.

'Then why don't we fly there direct tomorrow?' someone asked him. 'What's the point of going to this deserted Megara place?'

'*I don't know!*' the Adjutant shouted, exasperated.

'Where's the CO?' somebody asked.

'*That's enough!*' the Adjutant shouted. 'Go to bed all of you and get some sleep!'

One of us had an alarm clock and the next morning he woke us all up at 4.30 a.m. When I stepped out of our tent, Elevsis aerodrome lay silent and deserted in the pale half-light of the dawn. All tents except for those being used by the pilots had been struck and taken away. Only the old corrugated-iron hangar and the Ops Room hut and a few other wooden huts remained. The seven of us assembled in a little group, rubbing our hands together in the chill morning air. 'Isn't there a hot drink anywhere?' someone said.

There wasn't anything.

'We'd better get going,' David Coke said.

It was about 5 a.m. when we walked across the deserted and silent landing field to our planes. I think all of us felt very lonely at that moment. An aircraft is never unattended when you go out to it. There is always a fitter or a rigger to pull the chocks away from the wheels after you have started the engine. And if the engine won't start or if the batteries are low, someone brings along the trolley and plugs it in to give your batteries a boost. But there was nobody around. Not a soul. The top rim of the sun was just coming up above the hills beyond Athens and little sparks of sunlight were glinting on the dew in the grass.

I climbed into my Hurricane and hooked up all the straps. I switched on, set the mixture to 'rich' and pressed the starter button. The airscrew began to turn slowly and then the big Merlin engine gave a couple of coughs and started up. I looked around for the other six. They had all managed to get started and were taxiing out for take-off.

The seven of us assembled at about 1,000 feet over the aerodrome and then we flew off along the coast to look for our secret landing strip. Soon we were circling the little

My Hurricane at Megara

village of Megara, and we saw a green field alongside the village and there was a man on an ancient steam-roller rolling out a kind of makeshift landing strip across the field. He looked up as we flew over and then he drove his steam-roller to one side and we landed our planes on the bumpy field and taxied in among some olive trees for cover. The cover was not very good, so we broke branches off the olive trees and draped them over the wings of our planes, hoping to make them less conspicuous from the air. Even so, I figured that the first German to fly over would be sure to see us and then it would be curtains.

The time was 5.15 a.m. There was not a soul on the field except for the man sitting on his steam-roller. We wondered what we ought to do next. If our planes were going to be strafed, then the further away from them we were the better, just so long as we kept them in view. There was a stony ridge about 200 feet high between us and the sea and we decided that this might be as safe a vantage point as any. So up we went and when we got to the top we sat down on the big smooth white boulders and lit cigarettes. Immediately below us and to one side lay the olive grove with the seven Hurricanes half-hidden but still pretty conspicuous among the trees. To the other side lay the blue Gulf of Athens, and I could have thrown a stone into the water it was so close.

A large oil tanker was lying about 500 yards off the shore.

'I wouldn't want to be on that tanker,' somebody said.

Somebody else said, 'Why doesn't the silly sod get the hell out of here? Hasn't he heard about the Germans?'

In a way it was very pleasant to be sitting high up on that rocky ridge early on a bright blue Grecian morning in April. We were young and quite fearless. We were undaunted by the thought that there were only seven of us with seven Hurricanes on a bare field and fifty miles to the north about one half of the entire German Air Force was trying to hunt us down. From where we sat we had a fine view of the Bay of Athens and the blue-green sea and the crazy oil tanker lying at anchor.

Breakfast-time came but there was no breakfast. Then we heard the roar of aircraft engines close by and a group of some thirty 109s came whistling very low over the village of Megara, not half a mile away from us. They flew on, heading straight for Elevsis, the place we had left at the crack of dawn. We had got out just in time.

Only a few minutes later, a bunch of Stuka dive-bombers flew directly over our heads at about 3,000 feet, going straight towards the tanker, and above them a host of protective fighters were swarming like locusts.

'Get down!' somebody shouted. 'Hide under the rocks and keep still! Don't let them see us!'

But surely, I thought, they would see our planes in the olive grove? They were by no means completely hidden.

The Stukas came over in line astern and when the leader was directly above the oil tanker he dropped his nose and went into a screaming vertical dive. We lay among the boulders on top of the ridge watching the first Stuka. Faster and faster it went and we could hear the engine note changing from a roar to a scream as the plane dived absolutely vertically down upon the tanker. To me it looked as though the pilot was aiming to dive his plane straight into the funnel of the ship, but he pulled out just in time and then I saw the bomb coming out of the belly of the plane. It was a big black lump of metal and it fell quite slowly right on to the tanker's forward deck. The Stuka was well away and skimming over the sea as the bomb exploded, and when the great flash came, the whole ship seemed to lift about ten feet out of the water, and already a second Stuka was screaming down followed by a third and a fourth and a fifth.

Only five Stukas dived on to that tanker. The remainder stayed up high and watched because the ship was already blazing from end to end. We were very close to the whole thing, not more than 500 yards away, and when the tanks blew open, the oil spread out over the surface of the water and turned the ocean into a fiery lake. We could see half a dozen of the crew climbing on to the rails and jumping over the side and we heard their screams as they were roasted alive in the flames.

Up above us the Stukas which hadn't dived turned round and headed for home and the escorting fighters went with them. Soon they were all out of sight and the only sounds we heard were the hissing noises of water meeting fire all along the sides of the stricken tanker.

We had seen plenty of bombings in our time, but we had never seen men jumping into a burning sea to be roasted and boiled alive like that. It shook us all.

'It doesn't seem as though anybody has any brains around here,' somebody said. 'Why didn't the Greeks tell that tanker Captain to get the hell out?'

'Why doesn't someone tell us what to do next?' somebody else said.

'Because they don't know,' another voice said.

'Seriously,' I said, 'why don't we all just take off and fly to Crete? We've got full tanks.'

'That's a bloody good idea,' David Coke said. 'Then we can refuel and fly to Egypt. They've hardly got any Hurricanes at all in the Desert. These seven would be worth their weight in gold.'

'You know what I think,' a young man called Dowding said, 'I think someone wants to be able to say that the brave

RAF in Greece fought gallantly to the last pilot and the last plane.'

I figured that Dowding was probably right. It was either that, or our superiors were so muddle-headed and incompetent that they simply didn't know what to do with us. I kept thinking about what the Corporal had said to me only a week before when I had first landed in Greece. 'This is a brand new kite,' he had said, 'and it's cost somebody *thousands* of hours to build it. And now those silly sods behind their desks in Cairo 'ave sent it out 'ere where it ain't goin' to last two minutes!' It had lasted more than that, but I couldn't see how it was going to last much longer.

We sat up on our rocky ridge beside the deep blue sea and occasionally we glanced at the burning tanker. No one had got out of her alive, but there were a number of charred corpses floating in the water. Either the current or the tide was bringing the corpses slowly towards the shore and every half hour or so I looked over my shoulder to see how close they were getting. There were about nine of them and by eleven o'clock they were only fifty yards from the rocks below us.

Somewhere around midday a large black motor-car came creeping on to our landing field. All of us became suddenly very alert. The car crept slowly over the field as though searching for something, then it turned and headed for the olive grove below us where our planes were parked. We could make out a driver at the wheel and a shadowy figure sitting in the back seat, but we couldn't see who they were or what they were wearing.

'They might be Germans with submachine-guns,' somebody said. We realized we were totally unarmed. None of us carried even a revolver.

'What make of car is it?' David asked.

We could none of us recognize the make. Someone thought it might be a Mercedes-Benz. All eyes were watching the big black motor-car.

It pulled up beside the olive grove. We sat in a close group up on our rocky ridge, alert and apprehensive. The back door opened and out stepped a formidable figure in RAF uniform. We were close enough to see him quite clearly. He had a pale orange-coloured moustache and a thick body. 'My God, it's the Air Commodore!' Dowding said, and it was. This man, who had his headquarters in Athens, had been, and indeed still was, in command of all the RAF in Greece. A few weeks ago he had directed the activities of three fighter squadrons and several bomber squadrons, but now we were all he had left. I was surprised he had managed to find out where we were.

'Where the hell is everybody?' the Air Commodore shouted.

'We're up here, sir!' we called back.

He looked up and saw us. 'Come down at once!' he shouted.

We clambered down and straggled up to him. He was standing beside the motor-car and his fierce pale-blue eyes travelled slowly over our little group. He reached into the car and brought out a thick parcel wrapped in white paper and sealed with red sealing-wax. The parcel was about the size of an average Bible, but it was floppy and bent slightly as he held it in his hands.

'This package', he said, 'must be delivered back to Elevsis at once. It is of vital importance. It must not be lost and it must not fall into enemy hands. I want a volunteer to fly there with it immediately.'

Nobody leapt forward, but that wasn't because we were afraid of returning to Elevsis. None of us was afraid of anything. We were just fed up with being pushed around.

Finally I said, 'I'll take it.' I am a compulsive volunteer. I'll say yes to anything.

'Good man,' said the Air Commodore. 'When you land, there'll be somebody waiting for you. His name is Carter. Ask him his name before you give him the package. Is that clear?'

Someone said, 'They've just been ground-strafing Elevsis again, sir. We saw them go by. One-O-Nines. Masses of them.'

'I know that,' snapped the Air Commodore. 'It makes no difference. Now you,' he said, staring at me with his fierce pale-blue eyes, 'you're to deliver this package to Carter right away and don't fail me.'

'I understand, sir,' I said.

'Carter will be the only person on the place,' the Air Commodore said. 'That is if the Germans haven't got there already. If you see any German planes on the aerodrome, for God's sake don't land. Get away at once.'

'Yes, sir,' I said. 'Where shall I go?'

'Back here. Fly straight back here. What's your name?'

'Pilot Officer Dahl, sir.'

'Very well, Dahl,' he said, weighing the package up and down in one hand. 'This is on no account to fall into enemy hands. Guard it with your life. Do I make myself clear?'

'Yes, sir,' I said, feeling important.

'Fly very low all the way,' the Air Commodore said, 'then they won't spot you. Land quickly, find Carter, give this to him and get the hell out.' He handed me the package. I wanted very much to know what was in it but I didn't dare ask.

'If you are shot down on the way, make sure you burn it,'

the Air Commodore said. 'You've got a match on you, I hope?'

I stared at him. If this was the kind of genius that had been directing our operations, no wonder we were in a mess.

'Burn it,' I said. 'Very well, sir.'

Good old David Coke said, 'If he's shot down, sir, I imagine it'll burn with him.'

'Exactly,' the Air Commodore said. 'Now then, when you arrive back here, don't land. Just circle the field.' He turned to the others and said, 'The rest of you will be waiting in your cockpits, and as soon as you see him overhead, you are to taxi out and take off. You', he said, pointing at me, 'will join up with them and all of you will fly on to Argos.'

'Where's that, sir?'

'It's another fifty miles along the coast,' the Air Commodore said. 'You'll see it on your maps.'

'What happens at Argos, sir?'

'At Argos', the Air Commodore said, 'everything has been properly organized to receive you. Your ground crews are there already. So is your Squadron-Leader.'

'Is there an aerodrome at Argos, sir?' somebody asked.

'It's a landing strip,' the Air Commodore said. 'It's about a mile from the sea and our navy is standing offshore waiting to take off the troops. Your task will be to give air cover to the navy.'

'There are only seven of us, sir,' someone said.

'You'll be doing a vital job,' the Air Commodore announced, his moustache bristling. 'You will be responsible for the protection of half the Mediterranean fleet.'

God help them, I thought.

The Air Commodore pointed a finger at me. 'You,' he

said, 'get cracking! Deliver that parcel and get back here as fast as you can!'

'Yes, sir,' I said. I went over to my Hurricane and got in and did up my straps. I put the mysterious package on my lap. On the floor of the cockpit under my legs I had the paper-bag with my belongings, as well as my Log Book. My camera, I remember clearly, was hanging by its strap from my neck. I taxied out and took off. I flew very low and fast, and in eight minutes I had reached Elevsis airfield. I circled the field once, looking for Germans or their planes. The place seemed totally deserted. I glanced at the windsock and banked straight in to land against the wind.

Just as I came to the end of my landing run, I heard the air-raid sirens wailing somewhere in the distance. I jumped out of my plane with my precious package and lay down in the ditch that surrounded the field. A great swarm of Stuka dive-bombers came over with their escort of fighters above them, and I watched them as they flew on to Piraeus harbour. At Piraeus they began dive-bombing the ships.

I got back into my Hurricane and taxied up to the Operations Hut. The small buildings were splattered with bullet marks and the glass in all the windows was shattered. Several of the huts were smouldering.

I got out of my plane and walked towards the wreckage of huts. There was not a soul in sight. The entire aerodrome was deserted. In the distance I could hear the Stukas diving on to the shipping in Piraeus harbour and I could hear the bombs exploding.

'Is there anybody here?' I called out.

I felt very lonely. It was like being the only man on the moon. I stood between the Ops Hut and another small wooden hut alongside. The small hut had grey-blue smoke coming out of its shattered windows. I held the famous package tightly in my right hand.

'Hello?' I called out. 'Is there anybody here?'

Again the silence. Then a figure shimmered into sight beside one of the huts. He was a small middle-aged man wearing a pale-grey suit and he had a trilby hat on his head. He looked absurd standing there in his immaculate clothes amidst all that wreckage.

'I believe that parcel is for me,' he said.

'What is your name?' I asked him.

'Carter,' he said.

'Take it,' I said. 'By the way, what's in it?'

'Thank you for coming,' he said, smiling slightly.

I took an instant liking to Mr Carter. I knew very well he was going to stay behind when the Germans took over. He was going underground. And then he would probably be caught and tortured and shot through the head.

'Will you be all right?' I said to him. I had to raise my voice to make it heard over the crash of bombs falling on Piraeus harbour.

He reached out and shook my hand. 'Please leave at once,' he said. 'Your machine is rather conspicuous out there.'

I returned to the Hurricane and started the engine. From my cockpit I glanced back to where Mr Carter had been standing. I wanted to wave him goodbye, but he had disappeared. I opened the throttle and took off straight from where I was parked. I flew back fast and low to the field at Megara where the other six were waiting for me on the ground with their engines running. When they saw me overhead, they took off one by one and we all joined up in loose formation and flew on to look for this place that was called Argos.

The Air Commodore had said it was a landing strip. It was in fact the narrowest, bumpiest, shortest little strip of grass any of us had ever been asked to land a plane upon. But we had to get down, so down we went.

It was now about noon. The Argos landing strip was surrounded by those ever-present olive trees and in among the trees we could see that a whole lot of tents had been put up. Nothing stands out from the air more than a bunch of tents, even when they are tucked away among the olive trees. Oh brother, I thought. How long will it take them to find us here? A few hours at the most. No one should have put up any tents. The ground-crews should have slept under the trees. So should we. Our Squadron-Leader had his own tent and we found him sitting in it behind a trestle table. 'Here we are,' we said.

'Good,' he said. 'You'll be doing a patrol over the fleet this evening.'

We stood there looking at the Squadron-Leader as he sat behind his trestle table that had no papers on it.

There is something wrong about this, I told myself. There is no way in the world the Germans are going to allow us to operate our seven aircraft from this place. Our superiors were evidently expecting the worst because deep slit-trenches had been dug amongst the olive trees. But you cannot hide aeroplanes in slit-trenches and you cannot hide tents anywhere, especially tents that are a brilliant shining white.

'How long will it take them to find us here, sir?' I remember asking.

The Squadron-Leader passed a hand over his eyes, then rubbed his eye-sockets with his knuckles. 'Who knows?' he said.

'They'll wipe us out by tomorrow,' I said, greatly daring.

'We can't run away and leave the army with no air cover,' the Squadron-Leader said. 'We must do our best.'

We all trooped out of the tent feeling not very happy about anything.

The Argos Fiasco

When we left the Squadron-Leader's tent, David and I wandered off together to have a look around the camp. What we were really searching for was something to eat. We had been up since four-thirty that morning and it was now about two in the afternoon. None of us pilots had had anything at all to eat or drink since the night before. We were famished and very thirsty.

There must have been twenty-five tents scattered around that olive grove, but David and I soon located the mess tent. In the rush to move out of Elevsis during the night, it seemed that somebody had forgotten to bring the food. The local Greeks very quickly got wise to this state of affairs and they were now streaming into the camp bearing vast quantities of black olives and bottles of retsina wine. David and I bought a bucket of olives and two bottles of wine and found a shady patch of grass under a tree where we could sit down to eat and drink. We chose a spot right between our two Hurricanes so that we could keep an eye on them all the time. The number of Greek villagers mooching around was amazing. We must have been the first operational military airfield in history that was open to the public.

So we sat there, the two of us, in the shade of an olive tree on a lovely warm April afternoon, eating the small black juicy olives and drinking the retsina out of the bottles. From where we sat we could see the whole of Argos Bay, but there was no sign of an evacuation fleet nor of the Royal Navy. There was just one fairly large cargo vessel lying out in the bay and there was a plume of grey smoke rising from her forward hold. We were told that she was yet another fully-laden ammunition ship and that the Germans had been over and bombed her that morning. There was now a fire below decks and everyone was waiting for the enormous explosion.

'Well, here we are,' David said, 'sitting in the sun and drinking pine juice and what a terrific cock-up it all is.'

I said, 'The Germans know very well that there are seven Hurricanes left in Greece. They intend to find us and they intend to wipe us out. Then they will have the sky all to themselves.'

'Exactly,' David said. 'And they're going to find us very quickly.'

'When they do, this camp will be an inferno,' I said.

'I shall be in the nearest slit-trench,' David said.

It was curiously peaceful sitting there chewing the delicious slightly bitter black olives and spitting out the stones and taking gulps of retsina in between. I kept looking at the ammunition ship out in the bay and waiting for her to blow up.

'I don't see any army getting into any ships,' David said. 'Who are we going to patrol over this evening?'

'Tell me seriously,' I said, 'do you think we'll come out of here alive?'

'No,' David said. 'I think we'll be dead within twenty-four hours. We'll either cop it in the air or they'll get us right here on the ground. They've got enough planes to totally *annihilate* us.'

We were still sitting in the same place at 4.30 p.m. when

there was a sudden roar overhead and a single Messer-schmitt 110 swept in low over our camp. The One-One-O, as we called it, was a fast twin-engined fighter with a crew of two and with a longer range than the single-engined 109. We stood up to watch him as he banked round over the water of the bay and came back again straight towards us, still flying low. He showed utter contempt for our defences because he knew we had none, and as he flashed over the second time, we could see both the pilot and the rear-gunner peering down at us with their cockpit hoods wide open. A fighter pilot never expects to come face to face with an enemy flier. To him the *machine* is the enemy. But now it was only the humans that I saw. All of a sudden those two Germans were so close they made my skin prickle. I saw their pale faces turned towards me, each face framed in a black helmet with the goggles pushed up high over the forehead, and for one thousandth of a second I fancied that my eyes looked into the eyes of the pilot.

That pilot made three workmanlike passes over our camp, then he flew off to the north.

'That's it!' David Coke said. 'That's done it!'

Men were standing up all over the camp. They were discussing the consequences of the 110's visit. It hadn't taken the Germans long to find us.

David and I knew exactly what the sequence of events would be from now on. 'We can work it out,' I said. 'It'll take him roughly half an hour to get back to his base and report our precise whereabouts. It'll take his squadron another half hour to get ready for take-off. Then another half hour for the whole lot of them to arrive back here and knock the daylights out of us. We can expect to be ground-strafed by a squadron of One-One-Os in an hour and a half's time, at six o'clock this evening.'

'We could jump them,' David said. 'If the seven of us are all airborne and waiting for them directly overhead at six o'clock we could jump them beautifully.'

The Adjutant came up to us. 'CO's orders,' he said. 'All seven of you to patrol over the fleet for as long as you can this evening. Take-off is at six o'clock sharp.'

'*Six o'clock!*' David cried. 'But that's just when they'll be coming over.'

'Who will be coming over?' the Adjutant asked.

'A squadron of One-One-Os,' David said. 'We've worked it all out. They'll be coming over to strafe us at six o'clock.'

'You seem to have better information than your commanding officer,' the Adjutant said.

We tried to explain exactly how we thought things were going to happen, but it was no good. 'Just stick to your orders,' the Adjutant said. 'Our job is to give cover to the ships evacuating our army.'

'What ships?' David said. 'And what army?'

I was only a very junior Pilot Officer, but I was damned if I was going to leave it like that. 'Look,' I said, 'will you please try to get permission for us to take off at say half-past five or even a quarter to six instead of six o'clock. It might make all the difference.'

'I can try,' the Adjutant said and he went away. He was not a bad fellow.

He returned five minutes later and shook his head. 'It's still six o'clock,' he said.

'And precisely where *are* all these ships that we are meant to be protecting?' I asked.

'Between you and me,' the Adjutant said, 'they don't actually seem to know. You'd better just fly out to sea and try to find them.'

When he had gone, I said, 'I know darn well what I'm going to do. At five fifty-five I'm going to be sitting in my cockpit at the end of the landing strip with my engine running, waiting for the signal. Then I'll be off like a dingbat.'

'I'll be right behind you,' David said. 'I think we'll be lucky if we get away before they arrive.'

At five minutes to six I was in position at the end of the strip with my engine running, ready for take-off. David was to one side, all set to follow me. The Ops Officer stood on the ground nearby looking at his watch. The five other pilots were beginning to taxi their planes out of the olive trees.

At six o'clock, the Ops Officer raised his arm and I opened the throttle. In ten seconds I was airborne and heading for the sea. I glanced round and saw David not far behind me. He caught up with me and settled in just behind my starboard wing. After a minute or so, I looked round, expecting to see the other five Hurricanes coming up to join us. They weren't there. I saw David looking over his shoulder. Then he looked across at me and shook his head. We couldn't speak to each other because our radios didn't work. But we had to obey orders so we continued flying out over the sea. We gave the smoking ammunition ship a wide berth in case it blew up beneath us and we flew on, searching for the Royal Navy.

We stayed up there for over an hour but during all that time we saw not a single ship. We learnt later that the main evacuation was taking place from the beaches of Kalamata, many miles further to the west, where our navy was getting a terrible bombing from the Ju 88s and the Stukas. But nobody had told us. We were on our way back and were just coming into the Bay of Argos again when I spotted something. It was a plane, a smallish twin-engined plane flying towards Argos and hugging the mountains of the coast.

Ha! I thought. A German shufti kite reconnoitring the area. It had to be a German. There were no other aircraft in Greece now except for our Hurricanes, and it wasn't one of those. I'll have him, I told myself. I switched my firing-button from 'safe' to 'on' and flicked on my reflector-sight. Then I opened the throttle and dived flat out for the smallish twin-engined plane. The next thing I saw was David's Hurricane rushing right up alongside me, dangerously close, and he was waggling his wings at me furiously and waving a hand from the cockpit and shaking his helmeted head from side to side. He kept pointing at the plane I was about to attack. I looked at it again. Oh, my God, it had RAF markings on its body! In five more seconds I'd have shot it down! But what on earth was a little unarmed non-combatant plane doing over here in the battle zone? I could see now that it was a de Havilland Rapide, a passenger aircraft that could carry about a dozen people. We let it go and headed back towards our landing field.

We were still several miles away when we saw the smoke. Some of it was black and some was grey and it lay like a thick blanket over the landing strip and the olive grove. I trembled to think what we would discover down there when we landed, if indeed it were possible to land through all that smoke.

We circled round and round the blanket of smoke, hoping it would clear away. There was no wind at all. I could just make out the big rock that marked the beginning of the landing strip but the rest was hidden. My fuel gauge was registering nil so it was now or never. It was the same with David. He went in first and I lost sight of him in the smoke. I waited for sixty seconds, then went in after him. It was no joke trying to land a Hurricane on a small narrow strip of grass through thick smoke, but with the big rock to guide me I managed to touch down in more or less the right place. After that, as the plane ran over the ground at eighty miles an hour, then seventy, then sixty, I shut my eyes and prayed that I wouldn't crash into David or into anything else ahead.

I didn't. I came to a stop and climbed out of the plane right away. 'David!' I called. 'Are you all right?' I couldn't see five yards in front of me.

'I'm here!' he called back. 'I'm getting out!'

Together we groped our way back into camp. There was a certain amount of chaos around the place, but to our astonishment the ground was not littered with bloody corpses. In fact there were remarkably few casualties. What

Argos

A Hurricane, Argos

had happened was this. I had taken off at precisely six o'clock. David had followed me at one minute past six. Then three others had managed to get away, making it five altogether. But as the sixth Hurricane was gathering speed for lift-off, a swarm of Messerschmitts had come swooping in over the olive trees. The pilot who was taking off was shot down and killed. The seventh pilot had leapt out of his plane and dived into a slit-trench. So had everybody else in the camp. And there they all had crouched while the Messerschmitts swooped back and forth methodically shooting up everything they could see, the planes, the tents, the refuelling tanker, the ammunition store, the buckets of olives and the bottles of retsina.

All this was more than forty years ago, but even at that distance there seems little doubt that all seven of us should have been sent up well before six o'clock and ordered to patrol, not over a non-existent evacuation fleet, but over the landing ground itself. Then there would have been a grand battle. We might, of course, have lost more planes that way, but we would certainly have been waiting for them and we could have jumped them out of the sun with plenty of height advantage. We might even have got the lot of them. On the other hand, it is easy to be critical of one's commanders after the event and it is a game that all junior ranks enjoy playing. It is wrong to indulge in it too much.

David and I picked our way into the smoking camp. Somebody, I think it was the Adjutant, was shouting, 'All pilots this way! Hurry up! Hurry up!'

We went towards the voice and we found the Adjutant and we also found grouped around him quite an assortment of pilots who seemed to have trickled into the camp from heaven knows where. There were the six of us who were the survivors of our own squadron, but there were at least eight or ten other faces I had never seen before. An open truck was pulling through the smoke. It stopped alongside us, and then the Adjutant proceeded to read out the names of what turned out to be the five most senior pilots in the group. David and I, of course, were not among them.

'You five', the Adjutant said, 'will fly the five remaining Hurricanes to Crete immediately. All the other pilots, *and only pilots*, are to get into this truck. There is a small aircraft waiting in a field near here to fly you out of the country at once. You are to take nothing with you except your Log Books.'

We raced away to fetch our Log Books from our tents. I looked for my precious camera. It was gone. It had almost certainly been taken by one of the many Greeks wandering round the camp while I was up in the air. I couldn't really blame him, whoever he was. Now he would be able to sell

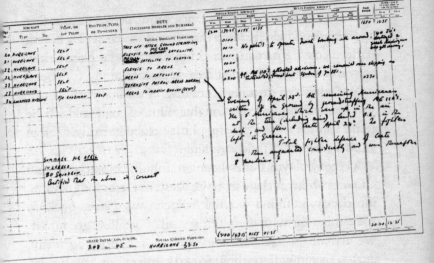

the good Zeiss product back to the Germans when they arrived. But I found two exposed rolls of film and stuffed them into my trouser pocket. I grabbed my Log Book and ran outside with the other pilots and clambered into the truck. We were then driven out of the camp along a rutted dirt road to a smallish field. On the field stood the little de Havilland Rapide that I had nearly shot down thirty minutes before. We piled into the aircraft. I could see now why the Adjutant had forbidden us to bring anything with us other than our Log Books. The field wasn't more than 200 yards long and as the pilot opened his throttles and began his take-off, we none of us thought he was going to make it. Every extra pound of weight in that aeroplane would have narrowed his chances. We bounced over a stone wall at the far end of the field and watched breathlessly as the plane staggered into the air. We just made it. Everyone cheered.

I had a window-seat and David was beside me. Only twenty minutes ago we had been in among the smoking olive trees and the burnt-out tents. Now we were 1,000 feet up over the Mediterranean and flying towards the North African coast. The sun was going down and the sea below us was turning from pale green to dark blue.

'We'll have to do a night landing,' I said.

'That will be nothing for this pilot,' David said. 'If he could take off from a piddling little field like that with all of us on board, he can do anything.'

We landed two hours later on a moonlit patch of sand known as Martin Bagush in the Western Desert of Libya. In the dark we found a truck which was going back to Alexandria through the night and all of us pilots got into it. We arrived in Alexandria early the next morning filthy, unshaven and with nothing to carry except our Log Books. We had no Egyptian money. I led the lot of them, nine young pilots in all, through the streets of Alexandria to the marvellous mansion that was owned by Major Bobby Peel and his wife. They were the wealthy English couple who had put me up during my convalescence a few weeks before. I rang the doorbell. The Sudanese butler answered it. He stared in alarm at the bedraggled group of young men standing on the doorstep.

'Hello Saleh,' I said. 'Are Major and Mrs Peel in?'

He went on staring. 'Oh sir!' he cried. 'It's you! Yes sir, Major and Mrs Peel are having breakfast.'

I walked into the house and called out to my friends in the dining-room. The Peels were wonderful. The whole house was put at our disposal. There were bathrooms on all four floors and we swarmed into them. Razors and shaving soap and towels appeared from nowhere. All of us bathed and shaved and then sat down around the huge dining-table to a sumptuous breakfast and told the Peels about Greece.

'I don't think anyone else is going to get out,' Bobby Peel

said. He was a middle-aged man too old for service, but he had a high-powered job somewhere in military head-quarters. 'The navy is trying to rescue as many of our troops as they can,' he said, 'but they are having a bad time of it. They have no air cover at all.'

'You can say that again,' David Coke said.

'The whole thing was a cock-up,' someone said.

'I think it was,' Bobby Peel said. 'We should never have gone into Greece at all.'

Alexandria
15 May 1941

Dear Mama,
Well, I don't know what news I can give you. We really had the hell of a time in Greece. It wasn't much fun taking on half the German Airforce with literally a handfull of fighters. My machine was shot up quite a bit but I always managed to get back. The difficulty was to choose a time to land when the German fighters weren't ground straffing our aerodrome. Later on we hopped from place to place trying to cover the evacuation – hiding our planes in olive groves and covering them with olive branches in a fairly fruitless endeavour to prevent them being spotted by one or other of the swarms of aircraft overhead. Anyway I don't think anything as bad as that will happen again . . .

The Grecian episode was a very small part of the war that was raging all over the world, but so far as the Middle East was concerned, it was an important one. The troops and planes that were lost in that abortive campaign had all been drawn from our already overstretched forces in the Western Desert, and as a result those forces were now diminished to such an extent that for the next two years our desert army suffered defeat after defeat and Rommel was at one time actually threatening to capture Egypt and the whole of the Middle East. It took two years to rebuild the Desert Army to a point where the Battle of Alamein could be won and the Middle East secured for the rest of the war.

The handful of pilots who survived the Grecian campaign were tremendously lucky. The odds were strongly against any of us coming out alive. The five who flew our remaining Hurricanes to Crete were to fight valiantly on the island when the Germans attacked a short time later with a massive airborne invasion. I know that one of them at least, Bill Vale from 80 Squadron, survived and escaped when the island was captured, and lived to fight again, but I do not know what happened to the others.

Palestine and Syria

After they had taken Greece in May 1941, the Germans mounted a massive airborne invasion of Crete. They captured Crete and they also took the island of Rhodes, and after that, flushed with success, they turned their eyes towards the softest spots in all of the Middle East – Syria and the Lebanon. These spots were soft because they were controlled totally by a large and very efficient pro-German Vichy French army.

Most people know about the very great trouble the Vichy French fleet gave to Britain in 1941 after France had fallen. Our navy actually had to put the French warships out of action by bombarding them at Oran to make sure they didn't fall into German hands. Most people know about that. But not many know about the chaos the Vichy French caused at the same time in Syria and the Lebanon. They were fanatically anti-British and pro-German, and if the Germans with their help had managed to get a foothold in Syria at that particular moment, they could have marched down into Egypt by the back door. The Vichy French had therefore to be dislodged from Syria as soon as possible.

The Syrian Campaign, as it was called, started up almost immediately after Greece, and a very considerable army composed of British and Australian troops was sent up through Palestine to fight the disgusting pro-Nazi Frenchmen. This small war was a bloody affair in which thousands of lives were lost, and I for one have never forgiven the Vichy French for the unnecessary slaughter they caused.

Air cover for our army and navy in this campaign was to be provided by the remnants of good old 80 Squadron, and about a dozen new Hurricanes were speedily brought out from England to replace the ones lost in Greece. I began to see now why it had been important to get us pilots out of the Grecian mess alive, even without our planes. It takes longer to train a pilot than it does to build an aeroplane. Mind you, it would have made even more sense to have saved some of those Grecian Hurricanes as well as the pilots, but that didn't happen.

Eighty Squadron were to assemble at Haifa in northern Palestine in the last week of May 1941. Each pilot was told to collect his new Hurricane at Abu Suweir on the Suez Canal and fly it to Haifa aerodrome. I asked Middle East Fighter Command if someone else could fly my plane to Haifa for me because I wanted to drive myself up there in my own motor-car. I had become the very proud possessor of a nine-year-old 1932 Morris Oxford saloon, a machine whose body had been sprayed with a noxious brown paint the colour of canine faeces, and whose maximum speed on a straight and level track was thirty-five miles per hour. With some reluctance Fighter Command granted my request.

There was a ferry across the Suez Canal at Ismailia. It was simply a wooden float that was pulled from one bank to the other by wires, and I drove the car on to it and was taken to the Sinai bank. But before I was allowed to start the long and lonely journey across the Sinai Desert, I had to show the officials that I had with me five gallons of spare petrol and a five-gallon can of drinking water. Then off I went.

I loved that journey. I loved it, I think, because I had never before in my life been totally without sight of another human being for a full day and a night. Few people have. There was a single narrow strip of hard road running through the soft sands of the desert all the way from the Canal up to Beersheba on the Palestine border. The total distance across the desert was about 200 miles and there was not a village or a hut or a shack or any sign of human life over the entire distance. As I went chugging along through this sterile and treeless wasteland, I began to wonder how many hours or days I would have to wait for another traveller to turn up if my old car should break down.

I was soon to find out. I had been going for some five hours when my radiator began to boil over in the fierce afternoon heat. I stopped and opened the bonnet and waited for everything to cool down. After an hour or so I was able to remove the radiator cap and pour in some more water, but I realized that it would be pointless to drive on again in the full heat of the sun because the engine would simply boil over once more. I must wait, I told myself, until the sun had gone down. But there again I knew I must not drive at night because my headlights did not work and I was certainly not going to run the risk of sliding off the narrow hard strip in the dark and getting bogged down in soft sand. It was a bit of a dilemma and the only way out of it that I could see would be to wait until dawn and make a dash for Beersheba before the sun began to roast my engine again.

I had brought a large water-melon with me as emergency rations, and now I cut a chunk out of it and flipped away the black seeds with the point of my knife and ate the lovely cool pink flesh standing beside the car in the sun. There was no shade anywhere except inside the car, but in there it was like an oven. I longed for a parasol or anything else that would give me a little shade, but I had nothing. I was wearing khaki shorts and a khaki shirt and I had a blue RAF cap on my head. I found a rag and soaked it in the tepid drinking water and draped it over my head and put the cap over it. That helped. I walked slowly up and down the boiling hot strip of road and kept gazing in absolute wonder at the amazing landscape that surrounded me. There was the blazing sun, the vast hot sky, and beneath it all on every side a great pale sea of yellow sand that was not quite of this world. There were mountains now in the distance on the right-hand side of the road, pale Tanagra-coloured mountains faintly glazed with blue that rose up suddenly out of the desert and faded away in a haze of heat against the sky. The stillness was overpowering. There was no sound at all, no voice of bird or insect anywhere, and it gave me a queer godlike feeling to be standing there alone in such a splendid hot inhuman landscape – as though I were on another planet, on Jupiter or Mars, or in some place more desolate still, where never would the grass grow green nor a rose bloom red.

I kept pacing slowly up and down the road, waiting for the sun to go down and for the cool night to come along. Then suddenly, in the sand just a foot or so off the road, I saw a giant scorpion. Jet black she was and fully six inches long, and clinging to her back, like passengers on the top of an open bus, were her babies. I bent a little closer to count them. One, two, three, four, five . . . there were fourteen of them altogether! At that point she saw me. I am quite sure I was the first human she had ever seen in her life, and she curled her tail up high over her body with the pincers wide open, ready to strike in defence of her family. I stepped back a pace but continued to watch her, fascinated. She scuttled over the sand and disappeared into a hole that was her burrow.

When the sun went down, it became dark almost at once,

and with the night came a blessed and dramatic drop in temperature. I ate another hunk of water-melon, drank some water and then curled up as best I could in the back seat of the car and went to sleep.

I started off again the next morning at first light, and in another couple of hours I had crossed the desert and come to Beersheba. I drove on northwards across Palestine, through Jerusalem and Nazareth, and in the late afternoon I skirted Mount Carmel and dropped down into the town of Haifa. The aerodrome was outside the town on the edge of the sea, and I drove my old car in triumph past the guard at the gates and parked it alongside the officers' mess, which was a small hut made of wood and corrugated iron.

My car, Haifa

We had nine Hurricanes at Haifa and the same number of pilots, and in the days that followed we were kept very busy. Our main job was to protect the navy. Our navy had two large cruisers and several destroyers stationed in Haifa harbour and every day they would sail up the coast past Tyre and Sidon to bombard the Vichy French forces in the mountains around the Damour river. And whenever our ships came out, the Germans came over to bomb them. They came from Rhodes, where they had built up a strong force of Junkers Ju 88s, and just about every day we met those Ju 88s over the fleet. They came over at 8,000 feet and we were usually waiting for them. We would dive in amongst them, shooting at their engines and getting shot at by their front- and rear-gunners, and the sky was filled with bursting shells from the ships below and when one of them exploded close to you it made your plane jump like a stung horse. Sometimes the Vichy French air force joined up with the Germans. They had American Glenn Martins and French Dewoitines and Potez 63s, and we shot some of them down and they killed four of our nine pilots. And then

Crashed Vichy French plane, Haifa

the Germans hit the destroyer *Isis* and we spent the whole day circling above her in relays and fighting off the Ju 88s while a naval tug towed her back to Haifa.

Once we went out to ground-strafe some Vichy French planes on an airfield near Rayak and as we swept in surprise low over the field at midday we saw to our astonishment a bunch of girls in brightly coloured cotton dresses standing out by the planes with glasses in their hands having drinks with the French pilots, and I remember seeing bottles of wine standing on the wing of one of the planes as we went swooshing over. It was a Sunday morning and the Frenchmen were evidently entertaining their girlfriends and showing off their aircraft to them, which was a very French thing to do in the middle of a war at a front-line aerodrome. Every one of us held our fire on that first pass over the flying field and it was wonderfully comical to see the girls all dropping their wine glasses and galloping in their high heels for the door of the nearest building. We went round again, but this time we were no longer a surprise and they were ready for us with their ground defences, and I am afraid that our chivalry resulted in damage to several of our Hurricanes, including my own. But we destroyed five of their planes on the ground.

One morning at Haifa the Squadron-Leader called me aside and told me that a small satellite landing field had been prepared about thirty miles inland behind Mount Carmel from which the Squadron could operate should our aerodrome at Haifa be bombed out. 'I want you to fly over there and have a look at it,' the Squadron-Leader said. 'Don't land unless it seems safe and if you do land I want to know what it's like. It's meant to serve as a small secret hideaway where those Ju 88s could never find us.'

I flew off alone and in ten minutes I spotted a ribbon of

My Hurricane, Haifa

dry earth that had been rolled out in the middle of a large field of sweet-corn. To one side was a plantation of fig trees and I could see several wooden huts among the trees. I made a landing, pulled up and switched off the engine.

Suddenly from out of the fig trees and out of the huts burst a stream of children. They surrounded my Hurricane, jumping about with excitement and shouting and laughing and pointing. There must have been forty or fifty of them altogether. Then out came a tall bearded man who strode among the children and ordered them to stand away from the plane. I climbed out of the cockpit and the man came forward and shook my hand. 'Welcome to our little settlement,' he said, speaking with a strong German accent.

I had seen enough English-speaking Germans in Dar es Salaam to know the accent well, and now, quite naturally, anyone who had anything even remotely Germanic about him set alarm-bells ringing in my head. What is more, this place, according to the Squadron-Leader, was meant to be secret and here I was being met by a welcoming committee of fifty screaming children and a huge man with a black beard who looked like the Prophet Isaiah and spoke like a parody of Hitler. I began to wonder whether I had come to the right spot.

'I didn't think anyone knew about this,' I said to the bearded man.

The man smiled. 'We cut down the corn ourselves and helped to roll out the strip,' he said. 'This is our cornfield.'

'But who are you and who are all these children?' I asked him.

'We are Jewish refugees,' he said. 'The children are all orphans. This is our home.' The man's eyes were startlingly bright. The black pupil in the centre of each of them seemed larger and blacker and brighter than any I had ever seen and the iris surrounding each pupil was brilliant blue.

In their excitement at seeing a real live fighter plane, the children were beginning to press right up against the aircraft, reaching out and making the elevators in the tailplane move up and down. 'No, no!' I cried out. 'Please don't do that! Please keep away! You could damage it!'

The man spoke sharply to the children in German and they all fell back.

'Refugees from where?' I asked him. 'And how did you get here?'

'Would you like a cup of coffee?' he said. 'Let's go into my hut.' He picked out three of the older boys and set them to guard the Hurricane. 'Your plane will be quite safe now,' he said.

I followed him into a small wooden hut standing among

fig trees. There was a dark-haired young woman inside and the man spoke to her in German but he did not introduce me. The woman poured some water from a bucket into a saucepan and lit a paraffin burner and proceeded to heat water for coffee. The man and I sat down on stools at a plain table. There was a loaf of what looked like home-baked bread on the table, and a knife.

'You seem surprised to find us here,' the man said.

'I am,' I said. 'I wasn't expecting to find anyone.'

'We are everywhere,' the man said. 'We are all over the country.'

'Forgive me,' I said, 'but I don't understand. Who do you mean by we?'

'Jewish refugees.'

I really didn't know what he was talking about. I had been living in East Africa for the past two years and in those times the British colonies were parochial and isolated. The local newspaper, which was all we got to read, had not mentioned anything about Hitler's persecution of the Jews in 1938 and 1939. Nor did I have the faintest idea that the greatest mass murder in the history of the world was actually taking place in Germany at that moment.

'Is this your land?' I asked him.

'Not yet,' he said.

'You mean you are hoping to buy it?'

He looked at me in silence for a while. Then he said, 'The land is at present owned by a Palestinian farmer but he has given us permission to live here. He has also allowed us some fields so that we can grow our own food.'

'So where do you go from here?' I asked him. 'You and all your orphans?'

'We don't go anywhere,' he said, smiling through his black beard. 'We stay here.'

'Then you will all become Palestinians,' I said. 'Or perhaps you are that already.'

He smiled again, presumably at the naïvety of my questions.

'No,' the man said, 'I do not think we will become Palestinians.'

'Then what will you do?'

'You are a young man who is flying aeroplanes,' he said, 'and I do not expect you to understand our problems.'

'What problems?' I asked him. The young woman put two mugs of coffee on the table as well as a tin of condensed milk that had two holes punctured in the top. The man dripped some milk from the tin into my mug and stirred it for me with the only spoon. He did the same for his own coffee and then took a sip.

'You have a country to live in and it is called England,' he said. 'Therefore you have no problems.'

'No problems!' I cried. 'England is fighting for her life all by herself against virtually the whole of Europe! We're even fighting the Vichy French and that's why we're in Palestine right now! Oh, we've got problems all right!' I was getting rather worked up. I resented the fact that this man sitting in his fig grove said that I had no problems when I was getting shot at every day. 'I've got problems myself', I said, 'in just trying to stay alive.'

'That is a very small problem,' the man said. 'Ours is much bigger.'

I was flabbergasted by what he was saying. He didn't seem to care one bit about the war we were fighting. He appeared to be totally absorbed in something he called 'his problem' and I couldn't for the life of me make it out. 'Don't you care whether we beat Hitler or not?' I asked him.

'Of course I care. It is essential that Hitler be defeated.

But that is only a matter of months and years. Historically, it will be a very short battle. Also it happens to be England's battle. It is not mine. My battle is one that has been going on since the time of Christ.'

'I am not with you at all,' I said. I was beginning to wonder whether he was some sort of a nut. He seemed to have a war of his own going on which was quite different to ours.

I still have a very clear picture of the inside of that hut and of the bearded man with the bright fiery eyes who kept talking to me in riddles. 'We need a homeland,' the man was saying. 'We need a country of our own. Even the Zulus have Zululand. But we have nothing.'

'You mean the Jews have no country?'

'That's exactly what I mean,' he said. 'It's time we had one.'

'But how in the world are you going to get yourselves a country?' I asked him. 'They are all occupied. Norway belongs to the Norwegians and Nicaragua belongs to the Nicaraguans. It's the same all over.'

'We shall see,' the man said, sipping his coffee. The dark-haired woman was washing up some plates in a basin of water on another small table and she had her back to us.

'You could have Germany,' I said brightly. 'When we have beaten Hitler then perhaps England would give you Germany.'

'We don't want Germany,' the man said.

'Then which country did you have in mind?' I asked him, displaying more ignorance than ever.

'If you want something badly enough,' he said, 'and if you *need* something badly enough, you can always get it.' He stood up and slapped me on the back. 'You have a lot to

Ramat David

learn,' he said. 'But you are a good boy. You are fighting for freedom. So am I.'

He led me out of the hut and through the grove of fig trees that were covered with small unripe fruit, and all the children were still clustered around my Hurricane, gazing at it in absolute wonder. I had bought another Zeiss camera in Cairo to replace the one lost in Greece, and I stopped and took a quick photograph of some of the children around the plane. The bearded man gently made a path through the throng of youngsters, tousling the hair of several of them in an affectionate way as he went by and smiling at them all. Then he shook my hand once again and said, 'Do not think we are not grateful. You are doing a fine job. I wish you luck.'

'You too,' I said and I climbed into the cockpit and started the engine. I flew back to Haifa and reported that the landing strip seemed quite serviceable and that there were lots of children for the pilots to play with should we ever have to go there. Three days later, the Ju 88s began bombing Haifa in earnest so we flew our Hurricanes out to the cornfield and a large tent was put up in the fig grove for us to live in. We were only there for a few days and we got on fine with the children, but the tall bearded man, when confronted with so many of us, seemed to close up completely and became very distant. He never spoke intimately to me again as he had done on our first meeting, nor did he have much to say to anyone else.

The name of that tiny settlement of Jewish orphans was Ramat David. It is written in my Log Book. Whether or not anything exists on the site today I do not know. The only name close to it I can find in my atlas is Ramat Dawid, but that is not the same place. It is too far south.

80 Squadron camp, Ramat David

Ramat David

Home

I had been at Haifa for exactly four weeks, flying intensively every day (my Log Book records that on 15 June I went up five times and was in the air for a total of eight hours and ten minutes), when suddenly I began to get the most blinding headaches. I got them only when I was flying and then only when dog-fighting with the enemy. The pain would hit me when I was doing very steep turns and making sudden changes of direction, when the body was subjected to high gravitational stresses, and the agony when it came was like a knife in the forehead. Several times it caused me to black out for seconds on end. I reported this to the squadron doctor. He examined my medical records and gravely shook his head. My condition he said, was without question due to the severe head injuries I had received when my Gladiator crashed in the Western Desert, and I must on no account fly a fighter plane again. He said that if I did, I might well lose consciousness altogether while up in the air and that would be the end of both me and the plane I was flying.

'What happens now?' I asked the doctor.

'You will be invalided home to Britain,' he said. 'You are no use to us out here any longer.'

I packed my kit-bag and said goodbye to my gallant friend David Coke. He would stay with the squadron after this Syrian Campaign was over. He would continue flying his Hurricane for many months in the Western Desert against the Germans. He would be decorated for bravery. And then at long last, tragically but almost inevitably, he would be shot down and killed.

> Haifa, Palestine
> 28 June 1941
>
> Dear Mama,
>   We've been doing some pretty intensive flying just lately – you may have heard about it a little on the wireless. Sometimes I've been doing as much as 7 hours a day, which is a lot in a fighter. Anyway, my head didn't take it any too well, and for the last 3 days I've been off flying. I may have to have another medical board & see if I'm really fit to fly out here. They may even send me to England, which wouldn't be a bad thing, would it. It's a pity in a way though, because I've just got going. I've got 5 confirmed, four Germans and one French, and quite a few unconfirmed – and lots on the ground from groundstraffing landing grounds. We've lost 4 pilots killed in the Squadron in the last 2 weeks, shot down by the French. Otherwise this country is great fun and definitely flowing with milk and honey . . .

I drove my old Morris Oxford back to Egypt and this time the weather was cooler when I came to the Sinai Desert. I made the crossing in seven hours, with only one stop in order to pour more petrol into the tank. Not long after that I embarked at Suez on the great French transatlantic luxury liner *Ile de France*, which had been converted into a troop-ship. We sailed south to Durban and there I was transferred to another troop-ship whose name I have forgotten. On her, we called in at Cape Town, then we went northwards to Freetown in Sierra Leone. I went ashore at

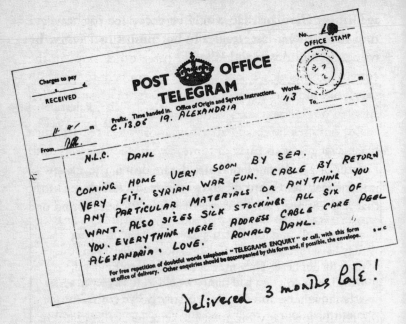

N.L.C. DAHL

COMING HOME VERY SOON BY SEA.
VERY FIT. SYRIAN WAR FUN. CABLE BY RETURN
ANY PARTICULAR MATERIALS OR ANYTHING YOU
WANT. ALSO SIZES SILK STOCKINGS ALL SIX OF
YOU. EVERYTHING HERE ADDRESS CABLE CARE PEEL
ALEXANDRIA. LOVE. RONALD DAHL.

Delivered 3 months late!

Freetown and bought quite literally a sackful of lemons and limes to take home to my family in war-rationed England. I filled another sack with things like tinned marmalade and sugar and chocolate, all of which I knew were virtually unobtainable at home. In a small shop in Freetown I found lengths of superb pre-war French silks and I bought enough of those to make a dress for each of my sisters.

The journey from Freetown to Liverpool was a hazardous affair. Our convoy was continually attacked by packs of U-boats and also by the long-range German Focke-Wulf bombers flying out of western France, and all the servicemen on board were detailed to man machine-guns and Bofors guns which had been scattered in great numbers over the upper decks. We used to bang away at the massive Focke-Wulfs as they swept low overhead, and now and again, when we thought we saw a periscope in the waves we banged away at that, too. Every day for two weeks I thought our ship was going to be finished off either by bombs or by torpedoes. We saw three other ships in the convoy going down and once we stopped to pick up survivors and once we had a near-miss from a bomb which sprayed our entire vessel with water and soaked us all.

But our luck held, and after two more weeks at sea, on a black wet night in early autumn, we nosed our way into Liverpool Docks and tied up. I ran down the gangway immediately and went off to try and find a telephone kiosk that had not been bombed out of action. When I found one at last, I was literally shaking with excitement at the thought of speaking to my mother again after three years. She could not possibly have known that I was on my way home. The censor would not have allowed such things to be written in letters, and I myself had not heard from anyone in the family for many months. No letter from England had found its way up to Haifa. I got the trunk-call operator and asked for our old number in Kent. After a pause, she told me it had been disconnected months ago. I asked her to consult Directory Inquiries. No, she said, there were no Dahls in Bexley or anywhere else in Kent come to that.

The operator sounded like a lovely elderly lady. I told her how I had been abroad for three years and was trying to find my mother. 'She'll have moved,' the operator said. 'She'll probably have been bombed out like all the rest of them and she's had to move somewhere else.' She was too kind to add that the whole family might well have been killed in the bombing, but I knew what she was thinking and she probably guessed that I was thinking it, too.

I waited in the pitch-dark telephone kiosk down in the docks of Liverpool, pressing the receiver hard to my ear and wondering what I was going to say to my mother if I was lucky enough to get through. After a while the operator came back on the line and said, 'I have found one Mrs Dahl. She's a Mrs S. Dahl and she's at a place called Grendon Underwood. Could that be the one?'

'Oh no,' I said, 'I don't think that could be her. But thank you so much for trying.' What I should have said was, 'Try it, we might be lucky,' because that, as it turned out, was my mother's new home. A bomb had landed in their house in Kent while my mother and two of my sisters and their four dogs were sensibly sheltering in the cellar. They had scrambled out the next morning and having seen their house in ruins had simply got into the small family Hillman Minx, the three of them and the four dogs, and had driven through London north into the Buckinghamshire country-side. Then they had cruised slowly through the small villages looking for a house that had a *For Sale* notice by the front gate. In the tiny rural village of Grendon Underwood, ten miles north of Aylesbury, they found a small white cottage with a thatched roof and it had the notice-board they were looking for stuck in the hedge. My mother had no money with which to buy it, but one of the sisters had some savings and she bought the place on the spot and they all moved in. I knew none of this on that dark wet evening in Liverpool docks.

I went back to the ship and collected my kit-bag and my two sacks of lemons and limes and tinned marmalade, and I staggered to the station with this load on my back and found a train for London. I sat all of the next morning by the window of the train gazing in wonder at the green, rain-sodden fields of England. I had forgotten what they looked like. After the dusty plains of East Africa and the sandy deserts of Egypt they looked ridiculously and unnaturally green.

My train did not reach London until nightfall. At Euston Station I shouldered my belongings and trudged through the blacked-out bomb-shattered streets, heading for the West End. When I got to Leicester Square, I somehow managed to find in the darkness a small seedy hotel. I went in and asked the manageress if I could use the telephone. An RAF uniform with wings on the jacket was a great passport to have in England in 1941. The Battle of Britain had been won by the fighters and now the bombers were beginning seriously to attack Germany. The manageress looked at my wings and said that of course I could use her telephone.

With the London telephone directory in my hands, I had a bright idea. I looked up the name of my ancient half-sister who I knew was married to a biochemist called Professor A. A. Miles (the Goat's Tobacco man in *Boy*). They lived in London. I found their number and rang it. The ancient half-sister answered the phone and I told her it was me. When the squeals of surprise had died down, I asked her where my mother and my other sisters were. They were in Buckinghamshire, she told me. She would telephone my mother at once to give her the amazing news.

'Don't do that,' I said. 'Just give me the number. I'll call her myself.'

The half-sister gave me the number and I wrote it down. She also told me she could give me a bed for the night and I wrote down her address in Hampstead. 'Try to get a taxi,' she said. 'If you don't have any money, we can pay for it when you arrive.' I said I would do that.

Then I rang my mother.

'Hello,' I said. 'Is that you, mama?'

She knew my voice at once. There was a brief silence on the line as she struggled to get control of her emotions. I had been away for three years and we had not spoken in that time. In those days you did not telephone to one another from far-away countries as you do today. And three years is a long time to wait for the return of an only son who is flying fighters in places like the Western Desert and Greece. Eight months ago she had seen the village postman standing at the door of the cottage holding a buff-coloured telegram envelope in his hand. Every wife and every mother in the country lived in dread of opening the front door to a postman with a telegram. Many of them refused even to slit the envelope. They could not bear to read the terse War Office message : *We regret to inform you of the death of your husband [or son] killed in action etc. etc.* They would leave the telegram on the dresser until someone else came along to open it for them. My mother had put her telegram aside and had waited for one of her daughters to return from her daily stint of driving a lorry. Then they had both sat down on the sofa and my sister had opened the envelope and unfolded the piece of paper inside. REGRET TO ADVISE YOU, the message read, YOUR SON WOUNDED AND IN HOSPITAL IN ALEXANDRIA. The relief was unbearable.

'I'd like a drink,' my mother had said.

The sister had got out the precious, impossible-to-buy bottle from the cupboard and they had both had a good stiff slug of neat gin there and then.

'Is that really you, Roald?' my mother's voice was saying now very softly on the telephone.

'I'm back,' I said.

'Are you all right?'

'I'm fine,' I said.

There was another pause, and I heard her whispering urgently to one of the sisters who must have been standing beside her.

'When will we see you?' she asked.

'Tomorrow,' I said. 'As soon as I can get a train. I've got some lemons for you, and some limes, and some big tins of marmalade.' I didn't know what else to say.

'Try to get an early train.'

'Yes,' I said. 'I'll get a train as early as I can.'

I thanked the manageress who had been listening from behind her little desk in the hotel lobby, and I went out to try and find a taxi. I was standing just inside the porch of the hotel in Leicester Square in the pitch darkness of the blackout when a group of four or five soldiers peered into the porch. 'It's a bloody officer!' one shouted. 'Let's 'ave 'im!'

The leering slightly drunken faces closed in on me and the fists were coming when one of them called out suddenly, 'Hey stop! 'Ee's RAF! 'Ee's a pilot! 'Ee's got ruddy wings on 'im!' They backed away and disappeared into the darkness.

It shook me a bit to realize that this was a posse of drunken soldiers prowling around the black streets of London searching for an officer to beat up.

No taxi came, so I slung my enormously heavy kit-bags over my shoulders and set out to walk to Hampstead. From Leicester Square that is a long walk even *without* three kit-bags to carry, but I was young and strong and I was on my way home and I felt I could have walked a hundred miles had it been necessary.

It took me an hour and three-quarters to reach the ancient half-sister's house, and there was a happy meeting and I gave presents of lemons and limes and marmalade and then fell gratefully into bed.

Early the next morning, I was driven to Marylebone Station and found a train for Aylesbury. The journey took an hour and fifteen minutes. At Aylesbury I found a bus which, so the driver assured me, would go right through the village of Grendon Underwood. The bus took longer than the train, and all the way I kept asking an old man who sat beside me to be sure to tell me when we were approaching Grendon Underwood.

'We're coming into it now,' he said at last. 'It's not much of a place. Just a few cottages and a pub.'

I caught sight of my mother when the bus was still a hundred yards away. She was standing patiently outside the gate of the cottage waiting for the bus to come along, and for all I knew she had been standing there when the earlier bus had gone by an hour or two before. But what is one hour or even three hours when you have been waiting three years?

I signalled the bus-driver and he stopped the bus for me right outside the cottage, and I flew down the steps of the bus straight into the arms of the waiting mother.

Mama's Cottage

Read more in Puffin

For complete information about books available from Puffin – and Penguin – and how to order them, contact us at the appropriate address below. Please note that for copyright reasons the selection of books varies from country to country.

www.puffin.co.uk

In the United Kingdom: Please write to Dept EP, Penguin Books Ltd, Bath Road, Harmondsworth, West Drayton, Middlesex UB7 ODA

In the United States: Please write to Penguin Putnam Inc., P.O. Box 12289, Dept B, Newark, New Jersey 07101–5289 or call 1–800–788–6262

In Canada: Please write to Penguin Books Canada Ltd, 10 Alcorn Avenue, Suite 300, Toronto, Ontario M4V 3B2

In Australia: Please write to Penguin Books Australia Ltd, P.O. Box 257, Ringwood, Victoria 3134

In New Zealand: Please write to Penguin Books (NZ) Ltd, Private Bag 102902, North Shore Mail Centre, Auckland 10

In India: Please write to Penguin Books India Pvt Ltd, 11 Panscheel Shopping Centre, Panscheel Park, New Delhi 110 017

In the Netherlands: Please write to Penguin Books Netherlands bv, Postbus 3507, NL–1001 AH Amsterdam

In Germany: Please write to Penguin Books Deutschland GmbH, Metzlerstrasse 26, 60594 Frankfurt am Main

In Spain: Please write to Penguin Books S. A., Bravo Murillo 19, 1° B, 28015 Madrid

In Italy: Please write to Penguin Italia s.r.l., Via Felice Casati 20, I–20124 Milano

In France: Please write to Penguin France S. A., 17 rue Lejeune, F–31000 Toulouse

In Japan: Please write to Penguin Books Japan, Ishikiribashi Building, 2–5–4, Suido, Bunkyo-ku, Tokyo 112

In South Africa: Please write to Longman Penguin Southern Africa (Pty) Ltd, Private Bag X08, Bertsham 2013